Stealing Home

Also by Grace Reilly

The Beyond the Play Series

First Down
Breakaway
Stealing Home
Wicked Serve

ABOUT THE AUTHOR

Grace Reilly writes swoony, spicy contemporary romance with
heart – and usually a healthy dose of sports. When she's not dreaming
up stories, she can be found in the kitchen trying out a new recipe,
cuddling her pack of dogs, or watching sports. Originally from New York,
she now lives in Florida, which is troubling given her fear of alligators.

Website: www.gracereillyauthor.com
Instagram: @AuthorGraceReilly
TikTok: @AuthorGraceReilly

Stealing Home

GRACE REILLY

HEADLINE
ETERNAL

First published in 2023 by Moonedge Press, LLC

First published in Great Britain in this paperback edition in 2023
by HEADLINE ETERNAL
HEADLINE PUBLISHING GROUP

6

Cataloguing in Publication Data is available from the British Library

ISBN 978 1 0354 1286 0

Cover Illustration by Gabriela Romero Lacruz and Cover Arrangement by
Sarah Kil Creative

Edited by EJL Editing

Offset in 11.76/15.22pt Fanwood by Jouve (UK), Milton Keynes

Printed and bound in Great Britain by Clays Ltd, Elcograf S.p.A.

Headline's policy is to use papers that are natural, renewable and recyclable
products and made from wood grown in well-managed forests and other
controlled sources. The logging and manufacturing processes are expected
to conform to the environmental regulations of the country of origin.

HEADLINE PUBLISHING GROUP
An Hachette UK Company
Carmelite House
50 Victoria Embankment
London
EC4Y 0DZ

www.headlineeternal.com
www.headline.co.uk
www.hachette.co.uk

To everyone who has wondered:
Your dreams are worth it. Keep going.

AUTHOR'S NOTE

While I have tried to stay truthful to the realities of college baseball and college sports in general throughout this book when possible, there will be inaccuracies within, both intentional and unintentional.

Please visit my website for full content warnings, as some heavy topics are discussed in this book.

1

SEBASTIAN

February 18th

I SWEAR TO GOD, *Mia di Angelo is wearing those jeans to fucking torture me.*

Penelope Ryder's best friend is a lot of things, but right now, 'vixen' is the only descriptor that comes to mind.

She's dancing with Julio, and his hands are low enough on her hips to brush her ass. Her long, dark hair is loose around her bare shoulders. Between the bright green halter top and the black jeans that fit so perfectly, she may as well have painted them on, I can't stop staring. The way she's dancing is mesmerizing—the only issue is that she's doing it with my teammate, not me.

I stare at her toned stomach, listening to her laughter as she grinds against him. My grip tightens around my glass.

Two nights ago, I dipped my tongue into her belly button to make her laugh before I slid to my knees.

Two weeks ago, she dragged me into a classroom on the fifth floor of the library and kissed me until I couldn't breathe.

Two months ago, she smiled at me for the first time. Looked at Penny and my brother, Cooper, then back at me and smiled, and I swear the universe tilted on its axis for half a second. Couldn't breathe, couldn't move, couldn't do a fucking thing but look at that smile and melt. I can see that face in my mind in perfect detail: the slightest little gap between her two front teeth. The black lipstick. The winged eyeliner and earthy brown eyes.

She had given me scowl after scowl, like I was personally responsible for whatever shit was annoying her at that moment, and then suddenly, gifted me a smile.

An angel's smile.

I hear, distantly, Cooper's teammates joking around. His friend Evan Bell asking if they think he could handle Mia.

No.

I know exactly who can handle her, and it's not him. Not Julio, either.

I take a sip of my drink, then clap Evan on the shoulder. "Buddy, respectfully, she'd eat you alive and spit out your jockstrap."

Mickey, another teammate of Cooper's, whistles. "I could fuck with that."

I don't hide my glower all that well. Mickey could win his way into Mia's bed, sure, but he'd have a hell of a time staying there.

I've been with her four times now.

Each time, she tells me it's the last.

But if she's fucking anyone tonight, it's me. I know I should let her turn her attention to Julio or Mickey or anyone else she's interested in. She's made it clear that our connection can't go farther than the physical. I don't know if I'm capable of it, so I ought to be leaving her the hell alone.

Easier said than done.

When Cooper goes to find Penny—something about playing a game of beer pong—I peel away from the wall and cut through the dance floor. "Mind if I take a dance?"

Julio raises an eyebrow, but he doesn't seem too miffed. I haven't told anyone on the team about my back-and-forth with Mia. No one knows, in fact, except me and her.

"It's up to the lady," he says.

Mia stutter-steps through the next beat of music and glares at me. She's wearing some kind of makeup that makes her face shimmer. The glitter even trails down her throat and the swell of her breasts.

Her voice holds a precise amount of venom. A façade. I hope. "Seriously?"

"One dance."

The song fades, and as the notes to the next one start up, I hold out my hand.

"Fine." She makes a show of kissing Julio on the cheek. "You know where to find me."

I pull her close. So we can dance, sure, but to feel her, to experience her warmth. "You couldn't have picked one of the two dozen hockey players in this house to tease me with?"

She spins around, grinding that delicious ass against me. I miss half a step before splaying my hand over her belly, keeping her body close to mine.

"Teasing?" she says, turning so her lips are against my ear.

My grip on her tightens. "Julio's one of my guys."

"Evan, then."

"No." I spin her, and the unexpected, actual dance move

makes her smile. I file that away. She has many expressions, but her smiles are the best. A rarity. "Me."

"Who says I'm still interested?"

I let my breath wash over her ear. Even though it's hot in here, she shivers. "It's pretty fucking obvious, di Angelo."

She twists, looking me in the eye; with her high heels, we're practically the same height. I want to take off those heels, then peel down her jeans real fucking slow. Her eyes are molten, ringed by that trademark eyeliner. "Penny's going to spend the night here."

"Like Cooper would let her out of his sight."

"You can come to the room."

I grin at her. Maybe there's part of her—even if it's buried— that likes my smile.

I shouldn't hope so, but God, I do.

2

MIA

May 6th

I SKID INTO the Bragg Science Center with a minute to spare before my meeting with Professor Santoro. If there's one thing she hates, it's tardiness, so I take the stairs to the fifth floor at a run. I shouldn't have agreed to drinks with Erin, one of the seniors in the physics department, last night—because it wasn't just drinks, of course, we ended up at her place after a few rounds—but I was feeling reckless, and now I'm paying the price.

I nearly heave as I take a breather on the third floor landing. *Definitely* paying the price. My head feels like someone is hitting it with a sledgehammer repeatedly. And the hookup wasn't even worth it. Way too much spit.

I've always been full of bad ideas. Experiments of the explosive variety in the chemistry lab at St. Catherine

Academy. Bonfire parties in the woods at the edge of my hometown in South Jersey. Hookups of all kinds in closets and classrooms and public bathrooms. Lately, I've had plenty of *extra* bad ideas.

It's easier to jump headfirst into hookups and parties with every bit of my spare time than think about *him*, after all.

Sebastian Miller-Callahan. Disgustingly nice. Disgustingly good at making me come. Disgustingly good at baseball, too, and that's something that should have tipped me off—it's never easy with athletes.

Not to mention the fact he's my best friend Penny's boyfriend's *brother*. Nope. Mr. Golden Baseball God is in my life for the long haul, and no number of hookups can change that fact.

Hasn't stopped me from trying for over a month now. Hasn't stopped me from wishing I was a different sort of girl. If I was a nice girl, and deserving of Sebastian, then maybe I wouldn't have fled the day his brother walked in on us about to get down to business.

I smooth my hair as I rush down the hallway. I might be hung over and more heartbroken than I'd ever admit, but there's no way I'm letting that mess up this assignment. Talking my way into Professor Santoro's lab this summer, even though I'm only going into junior year, is something I refuse to take for granted. I worked my ass off in high school to get into McKee and its top five undergraduate astronomy department for this exact moment. A chance to do real research, to start what will hopefully be a long career spent staring at the stars—and to give my application to the astrophysics study abroad program at the University of Geneva a leg up.

I remember the exact moment I fell in love with space. I'd

been aware of it before, of course, but it wasn't until a summer bonfire during a family vacation that I looked up and really *saw* it. My nonno—a dreamer in a family of practical people— brought a telescope to the beach, and while everyone drank wine from paper cups and laughed around the bonfire, I followed him to a quiet spot by the dunes.

"Let's find a planet," he said as he set up the telescope. "Maybe we can see Mars or Jupiter. Summer is a good time for planet hunting."

It felt like magic, peering at the sky through the telescope. We found them, and Saturn too, my eyes wide as I glued my face to the lens.

"One day," he said, hands in the pockets of his linen pants, gazing up with as much reverence as I'd seen when he prayed in church, "maybe they'll find another little girl gazing at the sky through a telescope, wondering about Earth. Maybe you'll be the one to do it, Maria."

He always told me that I could do anything. As I grew up and my interest in space consumed me, he sent me articles from NASA that we'd read together. He encouraged me to sign up for advanced math and science classes and join the robotics club. The morning before he died of a heart attack, he picked me up from school—I'd gotten in trouble with the nuns yet again—and told me that he knew I was destined for something great.

When I get to Professor Santoro's office, I knock on the door, and spend the five seconds waiting for an answer combing through my messy hair. Ugh. Why did I hook up with Erin, again?

Sebastian Miller-Callahan is still in my head, that's why.

That stops now. I have lab work to focus on. A study abroad

program to get into. A future to plan—hello, NASA—that's far away from New Jersey and the di Angelo family, thank you very much.

None of that involves a certain green-eyed baseball player.

I'm the one who walked out on him, anyway.

I bet he hasn't thought about me at all.

"Enter," Professor Santoro calls.

I push open the door gently.

Professor Beatrice Santoro is a major reason I chose McKee University over all the other offers, some with better scholarships, when it came to college acceptances. She's a badass older Italian woman who took one glance at me and understood my background, both the challenges and the love. And now, after two years spent working my ass off in this department to earn credibility, I'm finally in her lab. She rarely lets undergraduate students into her inner sanctum unless they're rising seniors, but I earned this spot. Impeccable lab work and attendance. Fluency in Python and C++. Volunteering at the campus planetarium. Attending every visiting lecture and symposium.

My grandfather had been the only one to tell me he believed in me—until Professor Santoro.

You have a bright future, Mia. A future in the stars, if that's what you want. If you're prepared to work for it.

I've spent two years working to be worthy of those words, and now I'm ready to prove it.

"Mia," she says in a warm voice. "How are you today?"

Professor Santoro's office is a little nook of a room. Books everywhere, framed photographs of space and stars on a gallery wall, her degrees in a row behind her desk. She takes notes by hand, regardless of the computer program she's using, and stacks of those little notebooks line her desk like sentries.

As I sit, she adjusts her thick black glasses, which give her gracefully older face a touch of quirkiness. Her silver-threaded hair hangs loose around her shoulders.

I manage a smile, even though I want to hurl on her desk. "Great. How about you?"

Professor Santoro leans back in her chair, pressing her fingertips together. "I'm well. Very happy to have you as my undergraduate researcher for the summer. I think this assignment will be a good challenge for you, given your interest in exoplanet discovery."

I nearly bounce my leg in excitement, but manage to reel it in. Exoplanets are a relatively recent discovery—they were theoretical, officially speaking, until the 1990s—and now, scientists have discovered thousands. They're simply planets that orbit a star other than our own. Out of the billions out there, one might be capable of sustaining alien life. Professor Santoro has been involved in this research since the beginning, and the thought of working alongside her, even on a small scale, to discover and classify these planets, is enough to make everything else fade away.

"Alice will email you the lab schedule," she says. "You'll have assigned readings for our weekly roundtables, so make sure you come prepared. I want you to work with her to rewrite the program we've been using to measure these planets' atmospheres. I think your eye for code will help us streamline it. I want a mock version up and running for when they release the new James Webb data, so it can be part of the analysis for my current paper."

I nod. "Absolutely."

Her gaze turns shrewd. "How are things, Mia? How is your family?"

"Fine."

"Do they still think you're student teaching?"

My face flushes. I stare at my lap. My family's big idea for a woman's career is temporary—teaching until I have children of my own. My nana did it. My mother and her sister. My older sister Giana is teaching for one more year before squirting out kids with her husband, never mind that growing up, she wanted to become a lawyer. It's what they think I'm studying, and I haven't corrected them. But if I get into the Geneva program, I'll be able to use it as concrete proof that I'm meant to be in this field and explain everything to them. It's not like I want to lie about something this huge, after all.

"It's easier this way. They won't—they won't understand."

"Nevertheless," she says, "they're your family. My parents didn't understand my desire to bury my face in a telescope either, but they came around."

"Your father was a doctor," I say. "My dad installs HVAC systems."

She takes off her glasses, folding them carefully. "I'm hosting a symposium at the end of June. Colleagues from several universities will be coming, and I want you to give a presentation on our research." She holds my gaze. "Do you understand?"

My breath catches in my throat. "Yes."

"Do well, and you won't need a recommendation from me for the Geneva program. Robert Meier will hear you himself. I've already told him he'll be able to see my most promising student when he attends." She stands, signaling my dismissal. I slide my bag over my shoulder. "I hope you will consider inviting some family members to see it."

I can tell it's not much of a suggestion, but I don't touch it. Not now, when the only person I'd want to invite is dead. I nod. "See you on Monday."

She's already turned to the bookshelf, riffling through the tomes. Onto the next problem for the day. "Monday."

3

SEBASTIAN

THIS EARLY IN THE MORNING, the house is quiet.

I rise from my plank, breathing through my nose, and pick up a set of fifteen-pound dumbbells for the next round of exercises. Cooper, by my side, does the same. There's no need to talk, not when we've done this routine together, the exact same way, for years now. Sometimes we play music, but today there's nothing. No distractions except the ones inside my head.

We could have gone to the gym on campus, the nice 24/7 one specific to athletes, thanks to his position on the hockey team and mine on the baseball team, but he's leaving on a post-semester road trip with his girlfriend, Penny, in a few hours, and wanted extra time with the cat currently sitting on the staircase.

She blinks her enormous amber eyes at us, unnervingly intelligent. I'm more of a dog person, but Tangerine has grown on me. Cooper and Penny rescued her last fall, and she's become a permanent fixture in the house since. I still haven't fully forgiven her for leaving a dead mouse in my cleat, but she's cute. I can't tell if being her sole caretaker while they're on the road trip and our little sister, Izzy, is in Manhattan for an internship, will bring us closer together or end with her attacking me in my sleep.

She swishes her tail back and forth, as if she's considering it, while we work through the exercises. After the last one, I set the dumbbells on the floor and swipe my hand through my shaggy hair. Baseball hair, Izzy always teases. It's longer than Cooper's now; after his team went to the Frozen Four—and won—his girlfriend begged him to trim the beard and cut off some of the mop.

He glances at me. "You're quieter than usual."

"I've been up for a while." I stretch; my shoulder protested that last set of reps. During a game a couple days ago, I slammed against the warning track as I chased a deep fly ball. Got the ball. And a bruise. We still lost. Four games in a row now. If we're going to make the playoffs, we need to right the ship—fast.

He makes a sympathetic noise. "I thought that had been getting better."

I shrug as I take a sip of water. "It comes and goes. I didn't manage to fall asleep last night. Got to practice my knife skills, though. And watched a documentary about bread making in France."

He shakes his head. "I was wondering about all the chopped onion in the fridge. Your hobby is weird sometimes, dude."

"They were diced, not chopped. And call it weird all you want, but you eat everything I make."

"Happily. It's fucking delicious." He sets down the dumbbells and stretches. Tangerine pads over on light feet, winding around his bare legs. He picks her up, hugging her to his chest. She purrs contentedly. "That sucks, though. Do you want to talk about it?"

"You all set for the trip? Still visiting James and Bex first, right?"

"Sebastian."

My adoptive brother's deep blue eyes are full of concern. He reaches out to squeeze my shoulder. "Was it..."

A nightmare? One of the persistent, sickening nightmares that years of expensive therapy didn't squash completely? Never mind how hard his parents—my adoptive parents —tried?

I swallow. There's a sudden knot in my throat. "No. Not a nightmare."

Not a maw of crushed metal and broken glass. Not blood on leather seats. Not a scream, cut short thanks to a severed windpipe. I can call up the memory so easily, even a decade removed. You don't look into your mother's lifeless eyes as an eleven-year-old and not remember it like someone cut open your skull and branded the image there.

Cooper's grip on me tightens. He told me once that he can tell when I'm lost in the memory. We were fourteen, sitting under the bleachers during one of our older brother James' many Friday night football games, each with a stolen beer in hand. A rare night in the fall when Cooper didn't have ice time, and I didn't have a training session. It was October, the Long Island air finally turning crisp after a late-season heatwave. Something about the sudden rain triggered it, I think. We were dry, and safe, and the game was still going on, but I froze as I stared at the downpour, and Cooper had to shake me to drag me into the present.

Now, I shrug off his grip. "I just... I couldn't sleep."

His gaze turns shrewd. "Because of her."

I'd never tell Cooper, because he has a strained relationship with his father that's only just getting better—and our own relationship was strained for a time earlier this year, when his piece of shit uncle came crawling back to New York and tried to swindle him out of his trust fund—but when he makes that face, he looks just like Richard Callahan, down to the furrowed brow.

The Callahans all look alike, with their dark hair and deep blue eyes. No one would ever mistake them for anything but family. Richard Callahan, quarterback legend. His son James, two years older than me and Cooper, now finished with his first year in the NFL. Cooper, my best friend and near twin. Our little sister Izzy, a vibrant ball of energy with a wicked volleyball serve and enough swagger to get her in trouble left and right.

I've got my dead mother's blonde hair and my dead father's green eyes, and the last name Callahan now; I've used the name on the back of my baseball jersey ever since I turned twelve. Cooper and his family have been my family for a decade, thanks to a pact Richard and my father, Jacob Miller, made when they were just young men with hopes for futures in the NFL and MLB. Richard and Sandra welcomed me into their family with open arms after my parents' deaths, and I'll never not be grateful.

Given all that, we've been brothers long enough that Cooper knows when I'm holding back. I pet Tangerine between the ears. The silence is confirmation enough: I haven't gotten Mia di Angelo out of my head.

Enjoy watching me leave, Callahan.

Her words taunt me. Over a month later, they still echo in my mind. One minute, I had her in my bed, in my arms, so close to more. The next, she fled—and told me to watch her leave, like I'd never see her again. I *have* seen her since, because she's Penny's best friend and it's impossible to ignore someone going to the same university, but she's acted like every hookup, every conversation, every moment we shared meant nothing.

"Are you ever going to tell me what actually happened?"

"You saw her leave."

He sighs. "I don't understand her. I know Penny loves her, but she can be... difficult."

"She hasn't said anything about me?"

I hate the pathetic note in my words, but I can't stop myself from asking the question. I worry my necklace, the medallion that once belonged to my father, between my thumb and forefinger.

He just shrugs, no doubt thinking about the moment he caught us together. It wasn't like we were in the middle of fucking; we were just making out. Yet the second Mia saw him, any vulnerability I'd won from her melted away. The armor went back up, as solid as steel.

"If she has, she told Penny not to tell me. Probably because she knows I'd tell you."

"Fantastic."

"It's not like you've told me all that much about what went down."

I grimace. "Nope. And I won't."

"You two are ridiculous," Penny says from the top of the

stairs. She shuffles down, her feet bare, wearing a shirt with a dragon on it that I'm sure belongs to my brother. He has enough nerdy fantasy gear to rival a fan convention. Her rust-colored hair, so different from Mia's raven locks, is practically a bird's nest. "For the record, she hasn't told me anything either. She refuses to talk about it."

It's easy to hear the note of concern in her voice. Mia's her best friend, after all. I've kept my own tabs on Mia, and while I know it's not my fucking business, it seems like she's been enjoying a lot of company. That's her right, and sure, I'm doing the same, but after the way we'd been together?

Whenever I think about that moment in my bedroom, I see her smudged lipstick, her bright brown eyes. In between all the kissing, I asked her out to dinner for the second time—for just one dinner, one actual date after months of secretive hookups—and she said yes. Then approximately one minute later, Cooper stumbled in on us, and approximately one minute after that, she hauled her NASA tote bag over her shoulder like a shield and fucking left.

Enjoy watching me leave, Callahan.

Since then, she's acted like she managed to wipe me clean out of her life without a second thought. I haven't been able to bring myself to tell Cooper all the details. I still showed up for the date we planned—I waited over two hours just in case she'd show—but she ghosted me. I don't want to admit that to my own brother. Not when his girlfriend is Mia's best friend.

"You sure you're fine on your own for a while?" he asks. He glances at Penny. "Should we stick around? Come to your games? I know that Mia—"

I shake my head. "No, enjoy the trip. Tell James and Bex I said hi. I'll be fine."

Penny kisses Cooper's cheek. He pulls her closer, rocking her as he rests his chin on her head, an unconscious motion. I swallow my spark of jealousy. When James found Bex, it made sense—he's always been meant for a big love. The soulmate of a wife, kids, the white picket fence, the dog. When Cooper found Penny, it was a surprise to everyone, but it clearly suits him, having one person to focus on, one person to love. I've never seen him happier, which makes it worse, the way I miss being casual players together.

My brothers are both deserving of that love. Yet it sucks to be alone and pining over a girl who, apparently, wants less to do with me than dog shit on the bottom of her shoe.

"We told my dad we'd get breakfast with him before hitting the road," Penny says.

I clear my throat. "Right. I need to head to practice, anyway."

"Text me if you get draft updates while we're away," Cooper says with an easy grin. Since this is his off-season, he's had a ton of time to focus on other things—namely, where he thinks I'm going to end up signing after the MLB draft in July. Whenever I think about it too hard, my stomach ties itself into knots. "Dad mentioned something about the Marlins? Miami would be sick."

I manage to smile back. I haven't had the heart to tell him— any of them, actually—that the looming draft is hanging over me like a rapidly approaching storm. It's ridiculous, because it's what I'm meant to do. My father wanted to create a legacy, so he made sure that I loved the sport from the moment I first picked up a baseball bat. Baseball has always been my life, and once I'm drafted, it'll be my future.

But lately, a tiny part of me, just loud enough that I can't ignore it completely, is wondering if it's the *right* future.

When I turned down the first draft offer the summer after high school, instead committing to McKee, it meant that I wouldn't be eligible for the draft again until I turned twenty-one. It's the way a lot of top baseball players go—see what the offer would be, then stay in college and plan for the next steps when your skills improve, a couple seasons down the line. If the near-daily articles Richard sends me are accurate, I'll go in the first round, likely to the Miami Marlins or the Texas Rangers. There's already talk of the Cincinnati Reds trading for me down the line, so the organization can have a Miller back on the team.

It's what Dad wanted. If I close my eyes and focus, I can still hear the way he spoke about baseball, the beauty of it, the history, the symmetry that has made it so enduring in American culture. He was famously patient, a coiled rod of energy in the batter's box, ready to strike. The National League home run record, set by him in his last season before the accident, remains unbroken.

There are a lot of people out there who expect me to be the one to break it.

It's poetic, his son being drafted a decade after the tragic accident that took one of baseball's best players—ever—from the game, way too soon. Not since Thurman Munson died in that plane crash had there been a bigger tragedy in baseball. *The Sportsman*, the oldest sports magazine in the country, called the other day to ask about me giving an interview, but I haven't replied yet.

However much I care about baseball—however alive I feel when chasing down a fly ball, when hitting a line drive, when sliding into home plate—it isn't just mine. When my future in the MLB begins, the comparisons will just get more and more intense. *The great Jake Miller's son.*

Letting Dad down isn't an option. He wanted one thing for me, and it was this. He died in a horrible, unfair instant, arm flung out as if that could protect my mother from death right alongside him. I might wear 'Callahan' on the back of my jersey right now, but once this is my job, the expectations will be different.

So I just keep that fucking smile plastered to my face.

"Sure," I tell my brother. "Maybe it'll be Miami. Have a good trip. You earned it."

4

MIA

March 13th

I'VE JUST OPENED *Penny's text*—boys are fine, spending the night at Coop's—*when there's a knock at the door.*

I slip out of bed, shivering as my bare feet hit the floor. My head is pounding from the alcohol I threw back at Lark's, something that I'm sure I haven't helped by squinting at my laptop in the dark, letting all that blue light wash over me. But it was between staring at the ceiling and finishing work for my stellar astronomy course, and you don't get into NASA-funded research labs by slacking off.

And fine, maybe I wanted to distract myself from him.

Sebastian Miller-Callahan.

Sebastian, who has been smiling at me ever since the movie theater last fall.

Sebastian, who calls me sweet when I come.

Sebastian, who threw a punch for me.

Who the hell does that?

Callahan boys, apparently. I've heard the stories from Penny about Sebastian's brother, Cooper, who she's pretty much disgustingly in love with. I would hate it, except that I love her and love seeing her happy. She's the kind of girl you want to bring home to your parents. The kind of girl who deserves a loving relationship.

And then there's me.

I shouldn't keep letting Sebastian in. I'm just going to hurt him, one way or another. I tried to earlier, I wore Cooper's teammate's sweater to the hockey game after Seb asked me not to, and he just gave me a once-over and ignored it. Patient as always. And then at the bar, some creep tried to take a video of me and Penny, and he tore me away from the fray before jumping in alongside Cooper.

I pad to the door and ease it open.

"Hey," he breathes. His voice is hoarse—not just from the punch to the throat he took during the fight, but from the game earlier. Only his voice was as loud as Penny's. Penny and I have talked about it before, how we've never seen brothers so close. "Can I come in?"

His eyes are dim and exhausted, his cheek swollen with the makings of a wicked bruise. There's a cut on his forehead, too, half-hidden by his messy hair.

I grab his hand and guide him inside. He sits on the little couch in the common area gingerly. We have a mini fridge, so I grab an ice pack from the freezer and wrap it in a t-shirt before handing it over.

"Sure you don't have a fucking concussion?" I ask, staying by the door.

He turns to me slowly, as if trying to minimize the pain. The movement makes him wince. I shove down the thread of worry working through me. "They checked me out at the urgent care place, I'm fine. Cooper needed stitches."

The worry grows deeper. A rapidly expanding black hole, threatening to suck me in.

He jumped into a fight for me.

That doesn't matter.

I try for a scowl. That's safe. It's the smiles that get me into trouble, not the scowls. "I didn't ask you to be my knight in shining armor."

"I wasn't about to let that asshole smack you around. Or Penny. Or Cooper, for that matter." His voice is sharp. It's a voice that allows no space for argument. I bristle against it, even as part of me—a small, yet annoyingly vocal part of me—likes the tone and what it could promise.

I snort. "Cooper had like thirty more pounds of muscle than that guy. He was nothing. I could've taken him."

"I wasn't about to let that happen."

"I can take care of myself."

"I didn't say you couldn't." He stands, walking over to me, and presses me against the door. I swallow, gazing into those gorgeous green eyes that devour me whenever we're in a room together. It's a secret, our thing, but shit like defending me in a public fight threatens to let that escape. I ought to tell him to go home, and to stop texting. "Just that I'd never let you fight alone."

It can't be more than hookups. Can't be more than these moments, alone at night like we're the only two people alive, my body burning for his. Chemical reactions in our bodies, a web of connections unfurling between us. I reach up, tracing over the bruise, and he hisses, dragging me closer.

Our lips are mere centimeters from each other, and into that space, we lean in. Together. Magnetic.

I bite his lip. He groans, making my stomach swoop. He smiles—then bites my lip back, not to be outdone. His hands grip my hips as easily as they do a baseball bat, and my nails scratch down his back, through the too-thin sweater he's wearing. When we're both gasping, we break apart, only to come even closer; his leg between mine, firm and casually dominant, my hands winding through his hair instead. The blond strands, so different from his adoptive family's, are still cold from the March air outside.

I want to drag him into my bedroom. Penny won't come back tonight, not when she has a boyfriend with stitches to care for. What I'm doing with Sebastian is dangerously close to the same thing, but there are enough differences that I can shove away the thought. Nearly. I ease back, even though I'm trapped between him and the door.

Perhaps steadied is a better word than trapped.

"Mia," he begins.

I don't give him a chance to finish the thought. It's my room or the hallway for him, and the hallway would be safer, but I can't push him out into the cold tonight. Not when he has a bruise on his face because of me. Not when he grabbed me around the waist and told me to stay put like I was breakable. Like I was the kind of girl who needed that knight in shining armor, sword on his shoulder, one of Penny's fantasy heroes made real.

I've never needed it, but some part of me must want it, because I take him to my bedroom, shut the door, and tell him to make me scream.

5

MIA

AS I WALK across campus the next day, a coffee in hand, Giana calls.

Usually, her calls take one of two forms: to complain about our family, or to interrogate me so she can take that information back to our family. Neither sound appealing right now, especially since I'm still standing tall from the conversation with Professor Santoro. My mind is full of ideas for how to contribute to her project. Her research is NASA-affiliated, part of the mission to uncover the billions of exoplanets hiding in the vast darkness of space. The goal is to find another Earth— but every exoplanet reveals something new about the universe.

Since we can't see exoplanets directly with our current technology, we need to hunt for them via other means. Professor Santoro is working on a new way of measuring atmospheric properties to determine details about exoplanets, and if I can rework the code on the program she's been using, we could get much more precise data about confirmed exoplanets.

The thought of all those planets out there, beautiful in alien ways... it's enough to make me stop and stare at the sky, even though it's morning. I school my face into a neutral expression before answering the video call.

At least campus has mostly emptied for the summer, so there's no one around to overhear my conversation. Altocumulus clouds dot the sky, each one as fluffy as a piece of cotton candy. A couple of years ago, scientists discovered WASP-121b, an exoplanet covered in metal clouds that pours liquid gemstones. Rain, just like on Earth, but made completely strange—and 855 light-years away. When I told Penny about that one, she jokingly said it was me as a planet.

"Hey, Mi-Mi," Giana says. Elementary school in New Jersey is still in session, so she must be on her lunch break; I can see the wall behind her, covered in bright posters. Her thick hair is in a ponytail, and little diamonds sparkle in her ears. "How's it going?"

I fight a smile at the sound of my childhood nickname. She's the only one who ever calls me that. In return, I'm the only one who calls her Gi-Gi. "Good."

"It looks nice there."

I keep walking. "It's pretty hot out."

"Right? The kids think it's summer vacation already. They don't want to do any work at all anymore." She takes a sip of water and adds, "Did you start the assignment yet? Mom was asking."

"Um, no." I squint up at the trees. "It's remedial science, so I have to wait for the semester to finish first. Their semester, I mean."

"You should come down for a few days before you start. You didn't even visit for Easter this year."

I hadn't wanted anything to do with Easter. Not the Catholic church service, not Nana's rosemary lamb, or even Mom's pastiera napoletana. Not the egg hunt in the backyard, my little cousins running around with their starched formal outfits and grubby fingers. I spent the day doing schoolwork instead, even though it fell over spring break. I haven't liked holidays since Nonno died.

"I'm picking up extra shifts at the café before it closes."

The Purple Kettle, the on-campus coffee shop that I work at during the semester, closed two days ago for the summer. Another lie to add to the pile. My family thinks I'm sticking around Moorbridge to help high school students who failed their science classes make up the credits, as part of my accelerated teaching degree—but I haven't spent even a second in that department. If I ever teach, it'll be like Professor Santoro. An extension of my research and part of my career, not the whole thing. And certainly not introducing the concept of cloud formation to middle schoolers or whatever the hell my family thinks is the most I can handle.

"Well, if you do get a break, everyone would love to see you. I don't know for certain, but I think Michelle's pregnant again."

I send a prayer to the sky. My brother can be an ass sometimes, but his wife is wonderful. "That's nice."

"Right? I want us to be aunties to a little girl this time. Enough with the boys."

"Anthony wouldn't know what to do with a girl." He has twin sons, and they're both mini tornadoes of chaos. Giana and her husband won't be far behind. I'll bet if Michelle is pregnant, and if it's a girl, Giana won't last until Christmas before trying for a baby of her own.

The thought makes me shudder. Space doesn't terrify me one bit. Pregnancy, though? Being in charge of keeping a baby alive? It's never interested me. In fact, it actively scares me if I think about it too hard. That's another lie I feed my family: *Sure, I can't wait until I get married and have kids.* The one time I told my mother I wasn't sure I wanted to do the whole marriage and babies thing, she blew up at me about my duties as a woman *and* to my family.

"Right?" Giana says. "Anyway, if you can't visit now, at least come for the barbecue in June. Nana will cry if you don't come."

"Nana has never shed a tear in her life." It's one of the many things I respect about her, even though our relationship is difficult at best. At Nonno's funeral, she stood straight-backed in her black veil, her face covered in makeup, her eyes as dry as a riverbed in a heatwave. No tears during the wake, no tears during the funeral. No tears during the private family gathering afterward, as my father and uncles got drunk on grappa and toasted to his life.

I wasn't as strong. I shut myself in my room and cried until I couldn't breathe.

I climb one of McKee's many hills, holding my phone higher so my face is still in the frame. The dorm I'm staying in for the summer is one of the ancient freshmen buildings on the edge of campus, atop one of the steepest hills. Incidentally, it's the same one where I met Penny. I arrived first, and I'd been debating where to put my Andromeda Galaxy poster when she burst in, a whirlwind of ginger hair, all freckles and nervous energy. More books in tow than clothes, and ice skates tossed over her shoulder. She took in my black leather jacket and combat boots, the nervous fuck-this energy I must have been radiating, blinked, and stuck out her hand.

She saw me better than anyone else. Better than my own sister. Still does.

On the phone, my real sister sighs. I can tell I'm about three seconds away from a lecture, so I say, "I'm walking into a meeting. I'll talk to you later."

"Tell me you'll come to the barbecue," she insists. "For me, Mi-Mi, please. Don't worry about our parents or Nana or the cousins."

I swipe the keycard to get into the building and push the heavy door open. It's sweltering in here too. Summer without AC will be murder on my hair.

At least my room is on the first floor. Heat rises, after all.

"Fine," I say. An afternoon surrounded by my very large extended family, the neighborhood friends, everyone from church—I can suck it up. I don't know why or how my parents started this tradition, but it's lasted for over twenty years: the big summer barbecue at the di Angelos. I haven't spent time with my sister since Christmas, and even then, she was with her husband Peter's family for half of it.

"Yay!" Her smile tugs at my heart. "Love you, Mi-Mi."

My breath catches in my throat. "Love you too, Gi-Gi."

I do. I really do. I love my family so much that it hurts to know I'm not the daughter they want. Not who they planned for. I tried to fit myself into that box—with my sexuality, with my passions—and it just didn't work. It was impossible to stay there, squished down, and be able to take a full breath. Nonno was the only one who understood that.

If he was alive, he would be supporting my career

aspirations, and I wouldn't be caught up in this stupid lie. In the past, Giana tried, but ever since she got married, she's acted just like Mom and our aunts.

Despite it all, I still love them and my heritage. And I can be friendly in small doses. Penny has said so herself.

I nearly slip as I walk down the hallway to my room. I glance at the floor, making a face when I see that it's covered in water. Maybe some idiot left the tap running in the bathroom.

At the end of the hallway, I shove my door open; it's sticking to the frame.

My mouth drops open. "Holy shit."

My room is flooded.

Without the door stopping the flow, the water rushes into the hallway, running over my sneakers. I glance up; water weeps from a crack in the ceiling, soaking absolutely everything. The bed. My clothes, still mostly in my opened suitcase on the floor. Shoes bob along in the water.

My gorgeous suede boots, my favorites, are soaked. Ruined.

I take a step forward and promptly trip. I flail, trying to hold on to the bed frame, but instead I land in the cold, disgusting water.

I can't stop myself from letting out a *very* embarrassing scream.

6

SEBASTIAN

"WHAT ABOUT HER? SHE'S HOT."

I scowl at Rafael. He's peering over my shoulder at my phone, the nosy bastard. I didn't ask for his opinion, but sure, the girl in the profile is attractive. She clearly knows she can make guys stop and stare with her smile.

She also happens to be a brunette.

I swipe left.

"Dude," he says. "You've swiped left at least ten times now."

A couple feet away, stretched out in the dugout like it's a comfortable old couch, Hunter raises an eyebrow. He takes off his McKee baseball cap, wiping the sweat from his brow. Even though it's early May, New York's summer humidity has set in. Practice wound down a few minutes ago, but we've lingered to chat about tomorrow's series opener against Bryant University and make plans for later. It's a home game, set for the evening, so we'll be able to go out tonight, have a few beers at Lark's while watching the Mets game, and still handle our pregame routines with ease.

Hunter's game day preparations are meticulous, doused in superstition. I've never cared for that sort of thing—I'd just as likely hit a home run wearing black underwear as I would wearing blue—but I'll never tell him so. Anything to get us hitting again, an issue that's been plaguing us all season. Unless we win a hell of a lot more in the next few weeks, we'll miss out on the playoffs. Our record won't affect my draft capital much, but I need to find a way to bring up my batting average before the official stats go in.

I glance at the next profile. She's blonde. Nice tits. A smile that tilts to one side, a little impish. I swipe right. No surprise, we match.

"Now we're talking," Raf says. He knocks his shoulder against mine. "I'm betting she messages you in three, two..."

The notification pops up. He grins. "So predictable."

I ignore him as I reply to her. Her name is Regina. She's vaguely familiar, but I don't have to wonder about it for long, because she's all too eager to tell me that we sat at the same table in ethics this past semester. She's free in an hour. Staying in one of the dorms for the summer semester.

Too easy.

"Only you would turn avoidance into a way to pick up even more girls than usual," Hunter says. There's a careful note in his voice—a joke before he hits me with something real—and worry on his smooth, light brown face.

I stand. I'm not in the mood. Not to hear about how I've been letting Mia di Angelo stay in my head, rent-free, going on a month and a half now. I've gotten enough of it from Cooper. Hunter has a girlfriend, after all; he's been doing long-distance with his high school sweetheart for as long as I've known him. Rafael's solemn advice was more palatable. He sat me down, wrangled the story from me, and said, with surprising seriousness, "You just need to fuck your way through it."

I wonder who gave Mia that same advice. Certainly not Penny.

Enjoy watching me leave, Callahan.

The only way to make her voice fade, at least for a little while, is to find someone else to distract myself with. It's that or mope. I *really* don't have a leg to stand on when it comes to Mia's own hookups, because I've been trying to find company of my own with all my free time... as long as she's not a brunette.

"He's on a journey," Raf says.

"To fuck every bleach-blonde on McKee's campus?" Hunter counters.

"Well, no," Raf admits. "He should be fucking brunettes too."

I sling my gear bag over my shoulder. "Noted."

"There are other Italian chicks in the world. Less crazy ones, too."

I stop with my foot on the dugout step. "She's not crazy."

"She's something," Hunter mutters.

"Don't," I snap. "Don't call her crazy just because she broke up with me. Don't call anyone crazy, it's fucking rude."

Rafael and Hunter exchange a look. Raf's thick eyebrows get lost in his equally thick hair. "Can you break up with someone if you're not dating? If you, in fact, refuse to label it, then finally say yes to a date when you're asked for the second time, and *then* flee and fucking ghost him?"

Heat colors my cheeks. Put that way, my pursuit of her sounds pathetic. "Stop it."

"I'm just asking the question."

"Stop," I say again, a sharper edge to my voice. My heart pounds with the need to defend her, even with the way things went down. I didn't tell my brother everything, but I had to tell *someone*, and I chose my two best friends outside my family. I regretted it the moment the words left my mouth, especially because I could tell Raf was working on overtime not to say something massively fucking unkind about Mia. Like now. Tact is a foreign concept to him. I never should have mentioned the two hours I waited at Vesuvio's just in case she'd show. "Don't talk about her."

He looks almost sad. "She did a number on you, man. You need to deal with it."

"She's here for the summer, right?" Hunter says. His voice is careful again, as if he's worried I'm about to blow my lid. "You're going to run into her. You need to find a way to move on."

"I'm fine. I am." I take my baseball cap off my head and shove it into my bag, running my hand through my sweaty hair. All I need is a shower, a change of clothes, and a mid-afternoon fuck with Regina from ethics class, and I'll be good to go. Mia is here for the summer, working on her mentor's research project, but I'm sure she'll ignore me if we run into each other at Starbucks or Stop & Shop. I'll catch sight of that gorgeous dark hair and tiny shards of memories will bombard me. The late-night texting. The one time I managed to cook for her—just breakfast but something—and she teased that it was better than an orgasm. The glances we shared when no one was looking, not Cooper or Penny or any of our other friends.

Maybe Rafael is right. I need to fuck a brunette. "I'll see you guys at Lark's later."

"I'll get us a booth," Hunter says. "Julio, Levine, and Big Miggy are coming too. Maybe Hops and Ozzy."

"So, half the team," I say dryly. "We'll need two booths."

"This is the nice time of year," Raf says. "Lark's is quiet."

"Not that we're not fans of your brother's hockey crew," Hunter says with a grin.

That grin is a peace offering. The okay to disappear for the afternoon. I nod, then jog across the diamond to the locker room.

BY THE TIME I reach the tiny corner of campus where this dorm is situated, I'm sweaty again; the drive wasn't long enough for the A/C to kick in. Regina meets me at the door, looking just like my vague memory from ethics class—the lemon blonde hair, the tilted smile—wearing an orange sundress that clings to her body enticingly.

"Sorry that there's no air conditioning in this building," she says, grabbing my hand and dragging me to the stairs.

Her room is on the third floor. The building, which must be mostly empty, echoes with our footsteps. She's wearing flip-flops, the soles smacking against the worn wooden floor, which is wet for some reason. Mia doesn't strike me as a flip-flops kind of girl. I'll bet she wears sandals if it's too hot for close-toed shoes. I do know that she paints her toenails a uniform black.

I give myself a mental shake. Now is definitely not the time to be thinking about Mia di Angelo's toenails. Not when Regina-whatever-her-last-name-is is making bedroom eyes at me. Her eyes are brown, and pretty I guess, but a much lighter shade than Mia's. Mia's remind me of freshly tilled earth. Beautiful in the most natural way.

Before Regina even opens the door to her room, she plays with her dress straps, letting them slip down her toned arms.

"I went to your game the other day," she says, her smile turning sly as she drags her nails down my chest. "Do you have a bruise from that catch?"

I lean in, almost brushing her lips but not quite. "Yes."

"Want me to kiss it better?" She turns her head, her minty breath washing over my ear before she takes the lobe into her mouth. Heat sparks through me at the teasing, the temptation, even if it's with the wrong girl. Her hands find the hem of my shirt, tugging on it, until I get the hint and pull it over my head. "That's not the only part of you I want to kiss, Sebastian."

This is easy—so easy. No thinking required beyond deciding whether I want to let her suck my cock, or if I want to fuck her properly. I made sure I had a condom in my pocket before I got out of the car. I hitch her leg around my waist, groaning as she kisses me. I can't help turning it into a comparison, again. Her kiss is too wet. Her breasts feel nice pressed against me, but are nothing compared to the perkiness of Mia's. She smells wrong, too, citrus instead of jasmine.

She gets the door open, and as soon as we're inside, sinks to her knees, her eyes bright as she flicks her gaze upward. She reaches for my waistband with her long pink nails.

I stare at her, frozen. "Sweetheart—"

Someone screams.

The sound pierces the air, sending me scrambling. I nearly knock Regina over in my haste to get to the door. She calls after me, but I ignore it, thundering down the stairs two at a time. My heart is in my throat, beating in time with my breath.

I know that scream. *Delighted* in that scream. But this isn't a sound of pleasure. This is panic.

And it belongs to Mia.

7

SEBASTIAN

EVEN AS WET as a sewer rat, Mia di Angelo is the most beautiful woman I've ever seen.

My heart rate, which jacked up the moment I heard her scream—that very fucking familiar scream, one that I've heard in my nightmares and my dreams alike—slows as I take in the scene. I grip the doorframe, willing myself to breathe normally.

She's not hurt. Not being axe murdered. Just soaked, standing in nearly a foot of mucky water in this tiny dorm room, surrounded by all the belongings I'd once been familiar with from the suite she shared with Penny. A bead of water runs down her cheek. She wipes at her face furiously, her chest heaving.

Relief runs through me in a torrent. She's scowling. Practically snarling. She looks like an angel, her beautiful dark eyes shining with emotion. She reminds me of Tangerine when Cooper gives her a bath, petulant and displeased with the entire situation, but at least she's physically okay.

I give her a grin, since I figure that's the most likely way to get a reaction from her. "Go for a swim, di Angelo?"

"What the *fuck* are you doing here?"

"I was in the neighborhood."

She gives me a once-over. I tense momentarily, remembering the feeling of her lips on my Celtic knot tattoo—the symbol over my heart that I share with my brothers.

When she speaks, her voice is as dry as a desert breeze. "Shirtless?"

"Let me help you."

"Who were you doing?" she asks, derision in her tone. "The bubbly bitch upstairs with a voice like a dolphin?"

"Oh my God," Regina says, peering through the doorway. She hops from foot to foot as she hands me my shirt. "This is *disgusting*."

Mia crosses her arms over her chest. "So predictable, Callahan."

Was that a flicker of hurt in her expression? I'm probably imagining it. I pull my shirt on and wade through the chilly water. I nearly trip over something but manage to steady myself on the bed frame. A big water droplet hits me in the face. "Let me help you get this stuff out of here."

"Thank God this didn't happen on my floor," Regina says.

"Oh, sure, good for fucking you," Mia snaps.

Regina blinks, but before she can come up with a retort, I say, "Regina, call the housing office and tell them they need to send someone to shut off the water to the building."

"But—"

I squeeze her arm. "It'll be a big help."

She flutters her eyelashes at me. "My phone's upstairs."

I give her my best smile, the one that makes old women giggle and girls my age want to take me to bed. "Please?"

She leans in and kisses me, her hand cupping my jaw. She even nips my lip, the action full of possessiveness. "Only for you, Sebastian."

Before she leaves, she adds, glancing at Mia, "You're *so* sweet to help this poor girl. Don't be too long."

I've seen how Mia looks when she's contemplating murder, and I would say her current expression definitely qualifies. She practically bares her teeth as Regina flounces off. The moment we're alone, however, she bites her thumbnail, worry breaking through her mask.

"Fuck," she says, her voice cracking. "What am I going to do?"

I take in the wet mess of clothes and shoes and other belongings. A beautiful black jacket lined with silk, one I pulled off slowly not too long ago, is no doubt damaged beyond repair. "Like I said, let's get this stuff out of here. I'll grab my gear bag, it's big enough for at least some of the clothes."

"I'm not putting my clothes in your disgusting gym bag."

"No offense, but they're already disgusting." I pick up a lacy bra, letting it dangle from my fingertip. She gives me a stony glare. "Come on, once this is all out of here, we can figure something out."

"I have my car," she says. "I'll put it in there."

"Let's grab the bag anyway." I start down the hallway without glancing back. She might not want anything to do with me right now, but she's smart. She'll take the help I'm offering. "I'm sure they'll have somewhere else for you to stay."

She snorts, but follows along. "Maybe. A lot of the dorms

are being renovated this summer. Guess they should have added this one to the list."

"What about your laptop?"

She peers into her bag. "That was in its case, so it's fine. And my phone seems okay." She inputs the passcode, frowning at the screen.

"That's good."

Her laugh sounds reedy. "Thank God. I don't have the money to replace either of them right now."

I unlock my car and root around in the trunk for my bag. It's filled with the bats I've been using, my glove, and a couple other pieces of gear, but I just dump it all out. "I'm sorry about the clothes and textbooks."

She's biting her thumb again. "Thanks."

It takes a couple trips, but we get all her stuff from the flooded room to the backseat of her car. Some clothes just need to be washed, but she throws out the jacket, plus that pair of suede thigh-high boots I know she adores. The water ruined some of the textbooks beyond repair, which must hurt. The books I need for my history major make a big dent too. I know better than to offer to replace them, though. She'd just chew me out, and now that I'm with her again—however brief—I don't want to waste it.

I can practically hear Cooper's voice. *Whipped for a girl who won't give you the time of day?*

I can't keep the worry at bay as I look at her. She has dark circles underneath her eyes and a pinched edge to her face. She deserves somewhere nice to stay this summer while she's focused on her research, and at least right now, she doesn't have that. I watch her shut the car door, swiping her hand—with that bitten-down thumbnail—through her damp hair.

The absurd urge to invite her to stay at my house rises, but I tamp it down just as quickly. She wouldn't want that help either, and I can't give it, anyway. You don't invite a girl to live with you while you're trying to get over her. That's like deciding to quit smoking and immediately going to buy a new vape.

I keep my gaze on the maintenance truck rolling into the parking lot. The crew will have a hell of a job getting rid of all the water, much less fixing the plumbing and ceilings. We peered into the bathroom next to Mia's room, and sure enough, it had flooded as well.

"Wasn't sure I'd see your underwear again, di Angelo."

"Shut up," she says, but she gives me a tiny smile.

I nearly pump my arm in victory.

"Sebastian," she says, sighing as she leans against her car. "I... I appreciate your help. Thank you."

"Don't mention it. You sure you're good?"

"I guess I'll stop by the housing office. Ask if they have another room I can move to."

I nod, shading my eyes against the afternoon sun. From this angle, the sunlight acts like a halo, accentuating the lighter shades of her hair. It's curling at the ends from the water, calling up a memory. Showering together at my place after one of our rare hookups there. Smelling my shampoo in her hair, watching her redo her makeup in the bathroom. I hugged her from behind, and she giggled—actually giggled—as I kissed her neck.

Fuck it.

I can't have that again, but despite what happened, I'm her friend, and friends help each other. Even if the friend in question is prickly as a cactus and hasn't spoken to you in over a month.

"If they can't get you in somewhere else, come and stay with me."

She blinks. Once. Twice. "No."

"It's just me in the house right now. Me and the cat. You could stay in Izzy's room, there's a private bathroom."

She crosses her arms over her chest, giving me a glimpse of her belly button. "I can't."

"Can't or won't?"

She smirks, masking whatever's going on inside her brilliant head. "You know that wouldn't be a good idea."

"We're friends."

She cocks her head to the side. "Are we?"

Enjoy watching me leave, Callahan.

Whatever connection we might have shared, she doesn't want to explore it anymore. I might hate it, but I can't force her to be with me, even if I feel the urge to take her into my arms and kiss her like a physical ache.

"See you around," she says finally. "Good luck on your game tomorrow."

I watch as she gets into her car and pulls out of the lot. Despite her question—*are we, are we, are we*—I need to bite the inside of my cheek to keep from smiling. She knows I have a game tomorrow. She's paying attention, at least on some level.

Are we?

We better fucking be.

Regina texts me, asking where I went.

Then she sends a picture. That orange sundress is nowhere to be seen.

I get in my car instead.

8

MIA

April 2nd

"DO YOU CARE?"

Sebastian doesn't lift his head from my tits. Even though we finished a couple minutes ago, we're still entwined; his cock halfway inside me, his mouth on my sensitive breasts. I scratch my nails through his hair, whimpering when he sucks on a nipple.

"Care about what?" he says.

I swallow down a rush of embarrassment. It's nothing to be embarrassed about, after all—it's a part of me that I can't change, and don't want to change in the first place. No matter what my family thinks about it.

"That I'm bisexual."

He does look up then. "Why would I care about that?"

I pull away. We're in my room—Penny is with Cooper, again; they went to the Rangers game with his parents—and my body protests leaving the cocoon of warmth, of him. I wrap my arms around my legs, resting my chin on my knees.

I told myself that this wouldn't affect me. It's a fair question to ask the guy I've been sleeping with, exclusively, for months now. "People assume so many negative things about me because of it. My parents—they barely understand. I try not to talk about it with them."

He sits up too, as unselfconscious about his body as always. The silver medallion necklace that he told me belonged to his father glints in the moonlight, accentuated by the dark lines of the tattoo over his heart. "It's part of you. Part of what makes you Mia. I like you, Mia. Every part."

"But people—"

"People are biphobic assholes," he interrupts. He reaches out, brushing his knuckles over my cheek. "I don't care about a bunch of stereotypes that don't mean a thing anyway. All I care about is that you like me."

I choke out a little laugh. "I do like you."

"Then go to dinner with me."

I freeze. The words sink in slowly. He must sense the way my body just seized up, because his hand drops away, putting a little distance between us.

"Vesuvio's," he says. He laughs slightly as he scrubs at the back of his head. His hair has gotten shaggier. Even though he's a baseball player, he reminds me of a surfer. Golden through and through. "We can go out for a proper date, finally."

Vesuvio's is Moorbridge's nicest restaurant. When my parents dropped me off at McKee my first semester, we went to a celebratory dinner there. I figured the next time I'd go, it would be for my graduation dinner. My dad might even have a reservation already. To go there on a date, though? With Sebastian, of all people?

It would be so easy to give in. But to do that would mean putting a label on this thing, and it would lead to expectations that I won't be able to meet.

I swallow, casting around for something else to focus on. Anything but his bottomless green eyes. "I can't."

"Can't?"

"Not... not yet."

He stares. I wonder if maybe he's going to leave, if I drove him away ahead of schedule, but then he shakes his head slightly and says, "Okay. We'll wait a little longer."

He kisses me, and I kiss him back.

And I feel a strange unraveling in my heart.

9

MIA

WHEN EVENING ROLLS AROUND, I end up at Lark's. I have my fake ID in my wallet, but most of the time I don't get carded; this is the sort of place that plays on the fact it's a college bar.

I desperately need a drink. That's the first objective of the evening.

After Sebastian helped me get my things into my car, I drove straight to the housing office and explained the situation. The response was, to put it bluntly, bullshit. Until they shuffle things around, I'm shit out of luck; they recommended staying at a motel, which I can't afford, or crashing with a friend. Then, at the laundromat, half my clothes shrunk in the dryer. I didn't budget for a wardrobe rebuild this summer, but between that and the clothes that were ruined by the flood, I barely have enough underwear to get me through the week.

At least my laptop is intact. I'll need that to work on the code for Professor Santoro unless I want to spend every single moment of my time in the lab itself. And I might've lost my favorite pair of boots, but I still have my dignity.

Tonight, with most of the student population gone for the summer, it's not too crowded. During the semester, a Saturday night would mean a line out the door. Locals in the town of Moorbridge hang out here too, so it's not empty, just quiet. The Mets game plays on one television, the Yankees game on the other. There's a hockey game on the third.

Before Penny started dating Cooper, I didn't give a shit about hockey. Honestly, it still confuses me. Football confuses me too, although my father and brother are huge Eagles fans. Nonno enjoyed baseball, so I watched a fair bit of the Mets when I was younger, and I played softball in middle and high school. I choose a seat at the bar in front of that television and order a beer.

Objective two: find someone who will take me home for the night.

As I drove around earlier, I weighed my options. I could ask my parents to pay for a motel, but that would open the door to conversations I'm not interested in having right now. In terms of "friends," as the McKee University housing office put it, Erin was the first person I thought of, but we're not actually friends. I'm not desperate enough yet to ask Professor Santoro if she has a spare bedroom. I could call Penny and ask if she can check in with her dad, but his girlfriend just moved in, and anyway, she's on a big romantic road trip with her boyfriend. Sebastian is *not* an option, even if he's alone in a nice house with central air conditioning and a cuddly cat that happens to belong to my best friend. I would rather walk barefoot over broken glass than deal with the temptation when I can't fucking have him and don't deserve him in the first place.

That leaves a stranger as my best option.

I might be living in my car temporarily, but I managed to make myself look like a snack in the tiny, moldy laundromat bathroom, so as long as someone reasonably attractive and single walks through the door, I should be good to go. I don't pull out this pink floral sundress that often; it's too bright for my taste, but it'll ensure that everyone who walks through the door notices me. Even if whoever it is sucks in bed, it'll still be a *bed*. That's better than sleeping in my car in the dorm parking lot and hoping that campus security doesn't notice.

"Mets fan?"

A man, probably in his late twenties, slides into the chair next to mine. He gestures to the bartender. "I'll have the same as her, and get her another."

I force myself to smile. He's not unattractive—just ordinary. Beard, brown hair curling over his collar, straight white teeth. The beginnings of a tan on his fair face. If he knows where the clitoris is, I'll take that as a win. "Thanks."

"No problem, darlin'." He angles his body toward mine. He must've come from work; he's wearing a navy suit with a white button-down. I glance at his hand, fingers drumming on the bar top, and nearly do a little dance when I don't find a ring. "Are you here for the game, or the booze?"

I take a long pull of beer. The fizz burns going down. It's not my first choice of drink, but I didn't want to get into the hard alcohol when I'm supposed to be picking someone up. "Can't it be both?"

He clinks his beer against mine. "A woman after my own heart."

"You come from work?"

He nods, setting the beer down after taking a sip. "Finance, in the city. I just had to get out of Manhattan, you know? Don't mind the commute if I have quiet at the end of the day."

Finance. If he's not lying to impress me, and I don't think he is, given the quality of the suit, he must have a nice house. I tuck my hair behind my ear, angling my neck to the side. I chose a necklace long enough that the pendant, a simple gold bar, nestles in the hollow between my breasts, and by the way he glances down, I can tell that he's into it. He scoots closer, heat in his gaze.

I pretend to ponder his words. "I get it. I like the quiet too. I'm a graduate student here at the university."

"What's your field of study? Not that you need to do much beyond flaunting that body." He sets his hand on my thigh.

I nearly choke on my next sip of beer. I turn my surprise into a smile and say, "Chemistry."

I made up my mind to lie before I even arrived, but after that, he definitely doesn't get the truth. Let him think whatever, as long as he's a good enough lay and doesn't hurt me.

I don't think he's that kind of person—just a little forward. Forward isn't a bad thing in this case.

"Chemistry," he repeats. His grip gets a little more deliberate, bunching the fabric of my dress like he wants to push it up to get a glimpse of my panties. "Is it just me, or am I feeling a little chemistry right now?"

Yikes. Yes? No?

Whatever. A bed is a bed.

I duck in close, letting my breath wash over his ear. I don't miss the way he shudders.

"I don't know," I purr. "I'd have to conduct a more thorough experiment."

"There you are, sweetheart," a voice says. "Sorry I'm late."

10

MIA

I JERK BACK—and find myself looking into Sebastian's gem-green eyes.

He glances down, his lip curling with disgust as he takes in the position of the dude's hand. He moves between us, picks up his hand, removes it from my thigh, and pats his arm consolingly. "Thanks for keeping my girl company, man."

I scowl, hoping he hears the venom in every single syllable as I talk. "What the hell do you think you're doing?"

The guy puts up his hands, unsure whether to focus on me or Sebastian. He wets his lips—then throws me an accusing look.

Sebastian has a stony expression on his face, as if he actually just discovered some guy two seconds away from feeling up his girl. I wish I could kick him. From this angle, if I tried, I'd just fall off the bar stool. Indignation rushes through me like wildfire. How *dare* he get in the middle of this.

"I didn't know she belonged to someone. I swear."

Sebastian tilts his head to the side. "Interesting. Does that make women property?"

"What? No, I just—"

"She's her own person." He shrugs, still casual, although something dark simmers in his gaze, like he wishes he could slam the guy's head against the bar top. "So maybe consider that the next time you open your miserable fucking mouth."

"I swear I didn't know. She's the one who came on to me." He gestures to me, any lingering interest in his expression drying up in favor of a snarl. "If I were you, I'd be more worried about your slut of a—"

Sebastian tosses a twenty on the bar top. "Get out."

"I'm not—"

"Goodbye." He jerks his head in the direction of the door. "Go get your pathetic dick sucked somewhere else."

The guy looks around, but everyone is studiously ignoring us. Even the bartender is letting the situation roll, at least for the time being.

"You can't just kick me out," he protests. "This is bullshit."

"Sure I can." Sebastian leans in, close enough I can smell his cologne. He flexes slightly, showing off that tightly corded strength that's easy to forget about, when it comes to him. "You can leave on your own or I can make it hurt first, your pick."

The guy scrambles off the stool and out of the bar.

As soon as he's gone, I whirl on Sebastian. "What the fuck was that?"

"What the fuck was *that*?" He laughs incredulously. "What were you doing, Mia?"

"It's none of your business."

His mouth twists. "I can't believe this was your big solution."

I take a step closer. In these heels, we're nearly the same height, but he still has an inch on me. And enough muscle to throw me around, a fact my body remembers all too eagerly. "What solution, Sebastian? Be specific."

"Let's see," he says, holding out his hand, ticking off the reasons with his fingers as he talks. His voice is quiet enough no one can hear but me, but the force of it comes through loud and clear. "The university emailed two hours ago to say on-campus housing is scrambling to rearrange things after a flood in one of the dorms open for summer students. If you had somewhere to stay, you'd be moving in your things, not here. You're drinking a beer, but you prefer bourbon. You're wearing a pink dress, and you hate pink. You were flirting with a total loser, letting him touch you when you don't like being touched by strangers." He cocks his head to the side. "Want me to keep going?"

I can feel the blush coloring my cheeks, but I keep my head high. "That's not what that was."

"You don't want to crash with me, fine, but call Penny's dad, then. Don't fuck a stranger for the privilege of a bed."

"Maybe I just liked him."

He laughs shortly. "I know what you like, sweetheart, and that's not it."

I cross my arms over my chest. I'm not a crier, but I can feel emotion winding through me, the result of a day full of stress, and need to swallow. "You have *no* idea what I like anymore."

He throws another twenty onto the bar. Another reminder of that special privilege that comes from being a Callahan: wealth. The family is loaded, and Sebastian and his siblings all have trust funds. I, meanwhile, have a careful amount of money stashed away, and I'm planning to touch it as little as possible this summer.

"Come on," he says. "We're going home."

He reaches for my elbow, but I jerk away. "I'm fine. I have somewhere I can go."

"We're friends." Hurt flashes across his face, a bolt of lightning ahead of a summer storm. "Don't lie to me."

Erin. She'll let me spend the night. "I'm not."

"I'm not letting you sleep in your goddamn car."

"Let me? You're not my father." I snort. "You're not my fucking boyfriend, either."

He doesn't rise to the bait. He just shakes his head, calm as always. "We'll talk about this at the house."

"No."

"Outside the bar, then."

I glance around. His baseball buddies sprawl across two of the red leather booths, laughing, beers in hand. They must have come in while I was focusing on my maybe-hookup, and Sebastian saw what was going on. "What, afraid they'll overhear?"

His expression softens slightly. "I won't make your business everyone's business. I wouldn't do that to you."

I let him lead me outside.

He leans against the brick wall outside the bar, concern radiating from him like a beacon. I dig in my purse for my phone. One night with Erin, and then maybe I'll work up the courage to ask Penny if she can talk to her dad. It's not that I don't like her father, he's a nice guy—I just didn't want to impose, to assume to be close enough to Penny to ask for that kind of favor. She's the first true friend I've had in years, and I don't want to do anything to ruin that.

"Come to the house with me," Sebastian says. "No one needs to know unless you want them to. You can sleep in Izzy's pink monstrosity of a bedroom, and I won't bother you, I promise. I have a game tomorrow, so I'll be up and out early."

I became casual friends with Izzy over the past semester, and I've been in her bedroom before. Her bed is ridiculously comfortable, albeit very pink. I barely slept the night before, in that stupid, sticky dorm room, and the thought of conking out amid all those silk throw pillows is more than a little tempting.

If not for the fact that Sebastian's bedroom is next door.

"I can't pay you anything for it," I say.

"I don't want your money."

I shake my head. "And I can't take advantage of you like that."

"Wouldn't be taking advantage." He leans in, and by the way he raises his hand before stuffing it into his pocket, I'd bet that twenty he just left on the bar that part of him wants to pull me into a hug. I'd almost managed to forget about his propensity for physical touch. I ought to scramble away, to safety, but I can't bring myself to move. He's close enough that I can feel his breath on my ear. "But if it makes you feel better, you wouldn't stay for free. I'd need you to tell me something."

I will my voice to become steel. "Tell you what?"

He pulls back far enough that our gazes meet. I wonder if he has this same intensity on his face when he's in the batter's box. The sun has slipped below the horizon, so his face is half-bathed in the streetlamp's light, one eye dark, the other illuminated. He's achingly handsome. Practically golden. My heart thrums from his nearness. My body clenches traitorously, sending heat to places that are all too hard to ignore.

"Why you said you'd go on a date with me, then stood me up."

11

SEBASTIAN

FOUR OR SO HOURS AFTER saying goodnight to Mia, I'm still awake, staring at the ceiling, watching as a spider makes its way across the lightly textured surface. Cooper, if he saw it, wouldn't be able to rest—he'd find a way to trap it and take it outside immediately. I don't mind letting it hang out with me. It makes the night a little less lonely.

I should have known that if I brought Mia home, I wouldn't be able to sleep. Sometimes, it comes easily, but all too often, my mind refuses to relax. I used to think that it was because of the nightmares—dreading them, begging my mind not to succumb to them, only to wake up with a scream in my throat—but now I'm not sure. Maybe it's something chemical.

Regardless, I'm wide awake, with only a spider for company. Tangerine is in Izzy's room; she trotted after Mia the moment she went to bed.

She's down the hall, safe and fast asleep, and that ought to bring me comfort, but my mind hasn't stopped racing since I saw her with that prick at the bar.

Logically, I know she's allowed to do whatever the hell she wants. We aren't dating, and we never actually did.

In that moment?

It took all my restraint not to punch his fucking face in.

The memory of his hand on her thigh, bunching the fabric, taunts me. He acted like he'd earned the right to be possessive over her. Her body language looked forced. She was putting herself into a situation where at worst, she could have ended up hurt, or at best, she would have felt shitty about herself the next day. All because she couldn't swallow her pride and text me about the room.

Was I a passing phase for her, one that she's not interested in repeating? Did it mean anything at all?

I know it did. I know she liked more than just the way I fucked her. At the last moment, something changed, and I have no idea what.

Sleep isn't coming. Not tonight. I slip out of bed and pad to the bathroom. I splash cold water on my face, not that I need the wake-up.

Earlier tonight, when I'd given her my price—because she needed a price, or she wouldn't let herself come home with me, no matter how much sense it made—she smiled. In cataloging her smiles, I'd add it to the 'mask' category. The boldness had surprised her and she tried to play it casual by pretending she was unaffected.

"Still thinking about that day?" she'd said.

"I know you are too."

She didn't try to lie again. Just nodded once, like she

thought what I was asking was fair, and said she'd meet me at the house.

I dry my face on a hand towel, digging my teeth into my lip.

There's a reason why she agreed to the date, then fled like she was on fire. Something deeper than the embarrassment of Cooper bursting into my room and catching the two of us half-clothed. Something that made her toss her hair over her shoulder and say, "Enjoy watching me leave, Callahan," as if she was trying to make an exit from all our lives at once.

When we got to the house, I shut the door behind us and turned to her. She looked around the living room—she hadn't been to the house since that morning, after all—and something flickered on her face as she picked up Tangy, holding her close. Tangerine seemed pleased with the whole situation. Maybe she recognized some of Penny in her friend.

"Tell me," I said. "Please, Mia."

She stroked Tangy between the ears. "You're not very good at bargaining."

"What?"

"I said I would tell you, but not when. Maybe I'll tell you a month from now. Or a year. Or ten."

I took a step closer. "Mia—"

"Not tonight, Sebastian."

Her tired voice, the way she used my first name, not my borrowed last name, made me stop in my tracks. I watched her disappear into my sister's room and didn't try knocking on the door.

I fucked up somehow, that day. I did something that made her think twice about dating me. About even letting me be in her life. As soon as I figure out what, I'm going to apologize for as long as it takes to earn her trust again.

I press the heels of my hands into my eyes until I see stars, then leave the bathroom quietly. There's a light on underneath my sister's door.

Mia doesn't sleep with the light on, so she must be awake.

I could knock. I could beg her to tell me the reason why she fled. But I doubt I'd get the answer tonight, and I don't want to argue.

Usually, when I can't sleep, I cook, but I don't want Mia to hear and come to investigate, so I opt for a nighttime run instead. I'll take a forced nap in the morning before I head to the facility for warmups and the game. As long as I show up on time and perform reasonably well, no one suspects a thing, and that's the way I need to keep going through the rest of the season. Whether I like it or not, by midsummer, I'll be negotiating my first professional contract.

I slip out of the house via the back door, then set a course for the familiar, the narrow sidewalks of Moorbridge's downtown residential neighborhood. I don't listen to music, instead focusing on my breath, the way the soles of my sneakers slap against the pavement. Aside from the occasional streetlamp, there isn't much light. I push myself faster, nearly sprinting through the quiet streets, startling a cat, making something else rustle underneath a shrub.

Overhead, stars. A half-moon.

Mia would know these constellations.

Slap.

She said she'd go to dinner with me.

Slap.

I thought she liked me.

Slap.

I liked her.

Slap.

I could have seen myself *loving* her.

Slap.

She *left*.

I barrel around a tight corner and skid on something—leaves, trash—and end up in the street, on my back. Tears burn my eyes as I pant, staring through the trees for a glimpse of the moon. I stay there until I hear a car coming, then scramble to my feet. I lean against a tree as I catch my breath, my fingers scrabbling on the rough bark, half-hoping I'll have to dig splinters from underneath my fingernails. I press my bruised shoulder against the tree, leaning on it with all my weight, and relish in my hiss of pain.

Maybe I did love her. Not consciously, not completely, not in the way my brothers have given themselves to their partners —but something pretty fucking close. Maybe I mistook the way she touched me, the way she kissed me, for real affection, when it was just another mask.

It's not the same, because nothing will ever be the same as that rainy night; nothing will come close to the horror of being left alone in the world, unexpectedly and completely, but I had her, and she left me.

The other shoe dropped, the way it always does in the end.

Mia might be in my house, sleeping in the next room—but she's not mine. Never was, never will be.

And if I can't find a way to win her friendship, I won't have her in my life at all.

12

MIA

I WAKE UP the next morning with a mouth full of cat fur.

Tangerine, snoring contentedly on my face, doesn't protest when I move her. If she wasn't so cute, I'd suspect she had been attempting murder by suffocation. I pull a piece of orange hair away from my tongue. I need water. Coffee. One of those memory-wiping devices from *Men in Black*.

Why the hell did I agree to spend the night at Sebastian's?

Desperation. Right.

It hurts, being here. There are reminders of the past in every inch of Izzy's room. I got ready for Cooper's birthday party in that bathroom—helped Izzy do Penny's hair—and the way Sebastian looked at me when we met in the kitchen... well, it nearly made me drop the tray of cupcakes I was holding.

It also led to all that dancing with Julio, because I was terrified that people would see us and put two and two together. No one did, and I ended up letting him into my room after the party anyway. My body ached the next morning in the most satisfying way; he fucked me against the door and then again in bed, holding me so close, I felt contained by his strength. Safe. I bit his shoulder, and he just laughed and told me to do it again, harder.

I scrub both hands over my face, willing my mind to erase the memory.

I need to stay in the moment.

Water. Coffee.

First, I should pee and wrangle my hair into shape.

By the time I emerge from the bathroom, which is still filled with Izzy's many beauty products—I guess when you're Izzy Callahan, you can just get new bottles of your expensive skincare products for your summer in Manhattan, no problem —and get dressed, I'm feeling better. Regardless of how it happened, I needed an actual night of sleep, and I managed that, for the most part. Once I have caffeine in hand, I can poke at the code Alice sent me. Maybe I'll get lucky, and the housing department will call me early.

I put my hair into a bun, tuck my laptop underneath my arm, and scoop up Tangy before sneaking into the hallway.

Clear.

I take a deep breath. He's probably eating breakfast.

When I walk downstairs, though, it's obvious that I'm alone. The house is quiet, filled with morning light, and neat as a pin. He even folded the blanket over the back of the couch with precision. I peer through the front curtains, and sure enough, his car is missing from the driveway. He wasn't kidding about having an early start.

In the kitchen, I set Tangerine down. She goes straight to her food bowl and gulps down the breakfast left there.

It's for the best that I'm alone. Maybe I'll be able to move my stuff to a new room before I even need to see him. And then I can work on my secondary summer project: Getting Over Sebastian Miller-Callahan. GOSMC. NASA loves their acronyms. I thought of it last night while I was falling asleep, trying my best to forget he was right next door.

As of now, Project GOSMC is officially underway.

Except... there's a note on the kitchen counter.

Of course he left a note. I can't stop the tiny smile that crosses my face at the sight of that messy handwriting, but by the end of it, I'm scowling again.

> *Hey, diAngelo—*
>
> *I'm at the training facility. There are Nespresso pods in the cabinet above the machine, and the oat milk you like is in the fridge. I made apple-almond oatmeal—also in the fridge. Don't forget the cinnamon.*
>
> *—S*
>
> *P.S. If you want to come to the game, ask for Billy. I'll leave a ticket under 'Captain Kirk.'*
>
> *P.P.S. We are friends.*

I fold the note into a tiny square and set it down carefully. This is good for Project GOSMC. Nothing makes me retreat faster than being told what to do. Outside the bedroom, at least. He might call us friends, but I know better. I could never just be his friend, and he deserves better than me. It's as simple as a math equation or a line of code. With any luck, we'll orbit each other for years to come without ever crossing, for the sake of

Penny and Cooper, and one day I'll see him with another girl, and she'll be perfect for him, and I will *smile* and say they make a lovely couple. She'll become Penny's best friend instead, and when I see pictures of them on whatever the next iteration of Facebook is, I will *keep smiling*.

I really need that cup of coffee.

While the machine warms up, I use the microwave to heat the oatmeal, adding cinnamon on top, and open my laptop.

I need to be working, not thinking. Not... stewing, or whatever my mind wants to do.

Yet after scanning the code for a mindless five seconds, I can't help but take out my phone.

I wince when I see the abandoned text thread I shared with Sebastian. He hasn't texted me recently, but there's a whole string that I left unanswered. I couldn't bring myself to type out a response, not when it meant having to confront how shitty I was to him.

April 4th

> SEBASTIAN
>
> Mia, let's talk about today
>
> Cooper and Penny don't actually care that we're together
>
> Let's talk. Please.

April 9th

> I care about you, Mia. As a friend, if that's all you want anymore
>
> Just talk to me

April 13th

> I'm waiting, if you want to come

> I guess you didn't want to come

April 20th

> Fine, di Angelo. Shut me out, but don't shut out Penny

I swallow, feeling the blush from my cheeks all the way down my neck. It hurt, watching him text me, ignoring each one. But I hadn't wanted to give him an opening. It was for his own benefit, anyway. The sooner he hated me and let me go, the sooner he could work on falling for a girl who actually deserved him.

Except now this... this kindness. He let me into his house, for free—well, minus what I promised I'd tell him, if I ever work up the courage—and made me breakfast. He has every right to hate me, but he called us friends. I scroll to the bottom, past his last text, and reply before I can think better of it.

> Thank you

> For breakfast. For letting me stay over

SEBASTIAN

> Don't mention it, di Angelo

> But I can't make the game later. I have work

> That's okay. Make sure Tangy has water before you leave, okay? There are cat treats in the drawer by the sink, too

My eyes are burning when I reply. Maybe it's the fact I'm alone. Or exhausted by this summer already, only three days in. I don't have work tonight, but I don't want to see him either, not when my body is begging me to ask for things that I don't deserve from him now and never did in the first place. I'll just make a mess of things, again, and hurt him, again.

Let him make oatmeal for someone else. Let him leave tickets at the box office under cute nicknames for some other girl.

> Of course, no problem

SEVERAL HOURS LATER, I've migrated to the couch, bundled up in the blanket, Tangy keeping warm next to my laptop. After I gave in to working at Sebastian's—I considered going out, but the quiet, blessedly cool house was too tempting to resist—I slowly made myself a sort of nest. Laptop charger. Water, heavy on the ice. My blue light-filtering glasses, the legal pad I've been using for notes. *The Mindy Project* plays on the television, muted with subtitles. I asked if anyone needed help with the on-campus planetarium later, so I'm going to run a public show about the solar system. The planetarium is far away from the baseball fields, so there's not even the slightest chance of running into Sebastian.

Working like this is heaven.

My stomach growls, but I ignore it. I should order delivery, since I don't want to raid his refrigerator, but that would be way more effort than puzzling over one more bit of code.

My phone, which is resting atop the coffee table, chimes with an incoming call. Izzy. After breakfast, I texted to let her know I spent the night in her room. I grab the phone, holding it between my shoulder and ear as I scribble out a quick thought.

"Hi, Izzy."

"Mia!" She must be outside; the sounds of cars and a crowd fill my ear. "Are you okay?"

"Um, yeah. I'm fine. I'm sorry I used your room."

"Oh, I don't care about that. One second." She breaks off for a moment, continuing to talk, but I can't catch what she's saying. "Sorry, I'm grabbing some lunch before I have to be back at the office. Weekends don't exist in the wedding planning world. Well, not the office, it's not a corporate thing, but my boss has this nice suite in her apartment that she uses as an office. There's a separate entrance and everything. These buildings on the Upper East Side are so fancy. Anyway, what are you doing? I haven't talked to you in ages. I didn't even get to see you before I left for the summer!"

She finally pauses. I seize the opening, smiling helplessly through it. She's a whirlwind, but an adorable one. "I just didn't want to, um..."

"Be around my brother after you ditched him?"

I wince. "Yes."

"Did you get back together yet?"

"What? No."

The disappointment in her voice comes through clearly. "So, you spent the night at our house, and you didn't even hook up with him?"

"I stayed in your room, Iz. Also, we were never—"

"Oh, I don't care if you fuck in it," she interjects with a sigh. "It's not like I get any action there. Cooper and Sebastian make sure of that."

"That doesn't seem..."

"Oh my God."

"What?"

"Oh, no. Boo. I thought I saw Alexander Skarsgård, but it was just another hot blond guy." She clears her throat. "You know, I think there's one in Moorbridge, too. He plays baseball."

I roll my eyes, even though she can't see me. "Isn't he your brother?"

"When a man's attractive, you notice, Mia."

Fair enough. "He's just... he's too much. He's too fucking *nice*."

She hums. "He tries very hard."

"To do what?"

"To be nice. To be Sebastian."

"What do you mean?"

She thanks someone on her end. "Sandwich acquired. Let me sit down first."

I nearly grind my teeth as I wait on the line for her to find somewhere to sit. I think about asking where she is specifically, but that would derail her, and despite myself, I want to hear what she has to say. Why he tries so hard to be *Sebastian*.

"Okay," she says finally. "This is amazing. Totally worth the wait."

"Izzy," I say. "While I appreciate the play-by-play—"

"I know, I know. It's just, you don't watch your parents die in front of you and not be a little fucked up, right? I don't know for certain, because if he's talking to anyone, it's Cooper, but I think he has nightmares. He's a good guy, but that's because he tries so hard to be positive."

My stomach twists. He went out last night, I'm certain of it.

I heard him in the hallway when I woke up, but I stayed in bed. I nearly texted him, but I thought better of it.

I know the story in broad strokes. His parents died in a car accident when he was eleven. Richard Callahan was his father's best friend, so he and his wife adopted him in the aftermath. I guess since he's so entrenched with the Callahans, I never gave much thought to the family he had before. The mother and father he must have loved and hated losing. I can't imagine losing my own parents, no matter how much we clash.

"That's awful."

Her voice is equally soft. "Yeah. If you're not into him anymore, whatever. But you must have made an impression on him, because he was moping and he never mopes, so just... be his friend, okay? A friend is never a bad thing."

13

SEBASTIAN

THE BEST PART of my pregame routine is batting practice.

For all my talent in left field—and I do love chasing down fly balls and stopping base hits in their tracks—I'm most comfortable in the batter's box. I've always had a good eye for strikes, and when it's just practice, I get plenty of nice pitches to hit. It's what my father was known for, and over the years, every batting coach I've worked with has remarked that our swings are nearly identical. Same leg kick, same sweeping arc.

While Ozzy, a lefty with a fantastic curveball, works something out with our pitching coach, I step out of the batter's box. I tuck my necklace under my collar and adjust my gloves, then tap the end of the bat against my cleats. I'm not superstitious, but I still have a routine.

This game is going to be good. I can feel it. Bryant's pitcher for the evening is at the bottom of their rotation. If I can keep myself focused, I'll do some damage on the bases—and hopefully help us get out of the skid we've been in for a couple weeks now.

I'll likely focus better if Mia doesn't show.

Didn't stop me from leaving a ticket with Billy, the man who manages the box offices for the McKee baseball and softball programs. One ticket for Captain Kirk. Hopefully she thinks it's funny. She loves the stars so much, I figured it was a good bet.

Just as I settle back in the box, Coach Martin beckons me over. He's standing in foul territory, a clipboard underneath his arm. "Callahan, a word."

I give Ozzy a shrug and jog off. Hunter steps into the batter's box instead.

I adjust my baseball cap to block the glare. "Coach?"

I admired Coach Martin from the moment I met him. He's someone who has been around baseball for a long time, and who remains steadfast in his love for it, even as people wonder if America's game is too slow, or too boring, or too time-consuming. When Cooper decided that he was going to play hockey at McKee—or rather, Richard decided for him and gave Cooper the choice between a couple of top hockey schools—the logical choice was to tag along, and lucky for us, McKee's baseball program wasn't too shabby. We were terrible last season and we've been terrible this season too, but that's not for Coach Martin's lack of trying. Sometimes in sports, luck plays a bigger factor than people want to believe. Sometimes, you try your best, but another team bests you.

His hand, a deep, weathered brown, rubs over his goatee as he considers me. "Thought we might start chatting about the draft."

Coach Martin never made it to the majors. He played in the Dodgers minor league system before suffering a career-ending injury and turning his focus to coaching. He knows how grueling that rise to the top can be.

I nod, leaning on my bat. "What about it?"

"That was the plan, heading into today," he says. "Get a sense of where your head is at. But then I got a call this morning, from *The Sportsman*."

Shit. I haven't answered the reporter yet, but I guess she's going ahead with the profile anyway. If she reached out to Coach, Richard and Sandra will be next on the list. They profiled Richard when he retired from the NFL, after all. I remember Sandra running around, totally stressed, as a decorating crew glammed up the entire house for the family photoshoot.

"And?"

"They have the same idea as me, thinking about the draft. It's finally time for Jake Miller's son."

"Yes, sir."

"Do you want me to talk to her?" He regards me with serious eyes. "She said she hadn't heard from you yet."

"She left a message. I just... wasn't sure what to say to her."

He nods. "She'll want you to talk about your father, no doubt."

Over the years, people have tried to pry, but for the most part, Richard and Sandra shielded me from it. Documentary segments. Remembrances by the Reds and by baseball in general. I gave exactly one interview as a teenager; the summer I turned sixteen, the Reds retired my father's number and wanted me at the ceremony. But for the most part, all of this is foreign to me. The thought of a reporter prying in on those memories makes me flinch, and that's without the little scrap of doubt about the future in the back of my mind, stubborn as hell and refusing to fade.

Not that I'd ever give voice to it. I'm a baseball player, end of story.

"I'm sure, sir."

"I don't have to talk to her. It's your call. I'm happy to sing your praises, son, but I understand if you want to lay low. I'm your coach, draft or not, and part of my job is to protect you."

I swallow the lump of emotion in my throat. During these chats, he reminds me of Richard, who is truly like a father to me.

Whenever Richard and I talk about baseball, it brings up pieces of memories, faded now, but with enough color in them to highlight the conversations I used to have with my dad about the same things. He went to as many of my games as he could, even though he was on the road constantly. Professional baseball demands so much of a player. Not just the game itself, but the preparation and the time. It's a marathon from spring training all the way to the postseason, resetting each day for a new game with breaks few and far between.

"Thank you," I manage to say.

Coach squeezes my shoulder with a broad hand and says, "Why don't you get in touch with her and decide. Richard might have some thoughts, too."

I give him a wry smile. "If there's anything Richard always has, it's opinions."

Coach laughs. "You're a good kid, Callahan. Go lead the outfield in some drills before we start whole-team warmups."

I FINALLY GET a chance to check my phone just before the game. After our conversation this morning, I hoped to see some more texts from Mia, but there's nothing. For all I know, when I get back to the house later, she'll be gone, already placed in another dorm.

I hope not. If I'm going to convince her to at least be friends, this is the best bet. Once she's not sleeping next door, who knows if I'll see her until the fall semester.

There is, however, a voicemail from Richard. I know roughly what it says—no doubt the reporter reached out to him for an interview—so I just dial his number instead.

That familiar deep voice fills my ear. "Sebastian?"

Even before he became my father, he was a larger-than-life figure in my mind. When I was little, I loved when the Callahans visited, not only to see James and Cooper, but to see Richard. I remember him and my father on our sprawling back lawn, chucking a football back and forth. James was nine, which meant Cooper and I were seven, and we all took turns playing running back. For that night, being a quarterback sounded cooler than a left fielder. When I told Richard that, he and my father looked at each other and burst into tipsy laughter.

"Hey," I say. "I got your message."

"Game's starting soon, right?"

I glance at the wall clock hanging above the lockers. Most of the guys are in the dugout already, loosening up before first pitch, but I need to finish getting into uniform. "I have a moment."

"Did you connect with the reporter yet?"

"No." I lean my head against my locker with a thud, blinking at the '17' hammered in bronze at the top of the wood panel. "I didn't answer the phone the first time."

"You know you don't have to talk to her."

I nod, then remember he can't see me. "Yes, sir."

"We can always redirect them. I have some influence there. I don't want you doing it if it'll distract you from your game. You know how important it is to give your all until the end of the season."

"I know."

He sighs. "I'd talk to her, get a read on how much she wants to know. What ways she wants to bring your father into this. You're a man now, Sebastian. No one can protect your father's legacy but you. Switch to video chat, I want to see you."

I do, and when his face fills the screen, those blue eyes, so like my siblings', regard me with that familiar seriousness. Even though Richard Callahan has been out of the game for years now, he's physically fit, mentally tough, and capable of withering a man with a mere glance. His retirement has been less of a vacation than a pivot to the media and broadcasting, and I have no doubt he holds sway with *The Sportsman*.

"He'd be proud of you, son. You're getting to the place he always dreamed for you."

I blink. To hear him speak with such frank honesty in this way is rare. Perhaps Cooper changed him more than we realized. "Thank you."

He laughs slightly, running a hand through his still-thick hair, silver now at the temples. "At least you did turn out to be a baseball player. A damn good one, at that, and getting better all the time. Jake would never forgive me if you hadn't."

The edges of the room blur for a half-second as my heart

pounds in my chest, hard and fast. The praise makes me smile, but I can't ignore the little flash of panic it brings, too.

14

MIA

SEBASTIAN DIDN'T SPECIFICALLY SAY that I was welcome to do whatever I wanted in the house.

It's not like he specifically said I *wasn't* welcome, however. And when I spoke to Izzy earlier, she wholeheartedly suggested that I do the following things: use her skincare products, watch whatever I wanted using the shared Callahan streaming accounts, mess around with Cooper and Sebastian's video games, sleep with her brother, use the brownie mix she left in the pantry, use the margarita mix she *also* left in the pantry, read one of the many smutty romance novels that she and Penny have been passing back and forth, have a private sing-along to *Mamma Mia!*—something she's done by herself on more than one occasion, and on an even rarer occasion, with a very drunk James Callahan—or a good cry to *The Notebook*, or, and she mentioned this twice, or perhaps three times, *sleep with her brother*.

I scowl as I poke through the refrigerator. I'd rather get

drunk on margaritas, a silly drink to begin with, and slur my words to ABBA than sleep with Sebastian. I'd even let Izzy record it, if it meant never looking at his stupidly handsome face ever again.

I find a carton of eggs and some bacon. Despite repeated efforts from my mother, Nana, and my many aunts, I've never been good in the kitchen. I don't have enough patience for it—Mom told me that two Christmases ago, when I nearly ruined the sea bass—and most of my efforts end up tasting mediocre at best. Eggs should be easy enough, though. Even I can fry an egg and some bacon.

My stomach growls loudly. I ended up working without stopping right until I had to go to the planetarium, and then the vending machine there didn't have anything but salt-and-vinegar chips, so I just drank from my water bottle and ignored the pang in my belly as I ran the show. It wasn't a bad turnout for a Sunday night, mostly old people looking for something to do.

I also managed to avoid driving by the baseball field. Proud of myself for that one. Hopefully, by the time Sebastian gets back, I'll already be locked in Izzy's room. I might even try one of the romance novels.

I find a pan, temper the blue flame that comes to life when I turn on the burner, and start with the bacon.

If I did read one of those romance novels, and it made me want to *do* something... it'd have to be before he gets to the house. I glance at my phone. I probably have time. I need something to take the edge off. Being in this house, while helpful for my work, has made it difficult to banish him from my mind. The flood ruined my favorite vibrator, unfortunately, but I can make do.

I almost went to the restaurant the night he planned for us to have the date, despite not talking to him for a week before it. I bought a new dress and everything, forest green in a wrap-around style that showed off my figure nicely. I did my makeup and curled my hair. But I couldn't make myself take that step forward. I didn't want to show up, only to realize he wasn't there—and if he was, I didn't know if I actually wanted to go down that road.

What do people even do on dates? What do they talk about? Doesn't the label make everything awkward? A relationship isn't the same thing as conversing around hookups, so how could he have even known he wanted it with me?

I sniff. The air does not smell like delicious bacon.

It's burnt.

Damnit.

"Mia?" Sebastian calls—at the exact moment the fire alarm goes off.

The piercing sound worms its way right into my ear, making me grit my teeth. I lunge forward to turn off the burner, but my hand brushes against the side of the pan. Pain blooms across my knuckles.

Sebastian skids into the kitchen in street clothes, his gear bag thrown over his shoulder. He curses when he sees me, wide-eyed and looking like a fucking fool *again*. I grind my teeth together hard enough I might crack a tooth as he moves the pan to the back of the stove, turns on the fan, and—with a blank, determined sort of expression on his face—pulls me over to the sink.

He turns on the water and gently guides my hand underneath it. I nearly whimper from the sting, but manage to swallow it down.

"Keep that there," he orders. He props open the kitchen door, then grabs a folder from the table and waves it over the fire alarm until it stops. The air is only slightly smoky, but it makes me cough anyway. My heart lurches at the casual command in his voice, a traitorous reaction that has me clenching the countertop with my other hand.

First the flood. Now this. He probably thinks I'm an incompetent idiot. The mere thought is enough to make me want to kick something. I've never been a damsel in distress, but this is the second time in as many days that he swooped in to save me, and we're not even friends.

He turns to me, still wearing that careful expression. I can't tell if it's because of anger or worry. Hopefully anger. Anger is easier to brush off than worry. "Are you okay?"

I scowl. "Fine."

He looks at the burnt bacon. "You incinerated that."

"I got..." I trail off, then brace myself. "I got distracted. Sorry."

He pulls an ice pack from the freezer and wraps it in a dishcloth. "Here. Sit down."

"It's not that bad."

"Don't want it to blister," he says. "Take it."

I study him. Is he thinking about the night after the bar fight, when he came to me with a bruise on his face? That time, I held out the ice pack. When he fucked me after, it was with a slow tenderness that belied anything that came before. The brush of his hands on my skin was so tender, I couldn't imagine him ever throwing a punch, even though I'd seen it earlier that evening. For Penny, and for Cooper, but also for me.

I swallow down the mess of words crowding my throat and take the ice pack. I sit at one of the island stools and watch as he throws out the ruined bacon, washes the pan, then dries it and sets it back on the burner.

"You don't have to do that," I say as he lays out more bacon.

"Don't want you to starve," he says. "You haven't eaten anything since the oatmeal, have you?"

I sit up straighter. "That's none of your business."

"So, I'm right." He takes a beer out of the fridge, uncaps it using the heel of his hand in a gesture so casual, and unfortunately hot, that it has me staring, and downs half of it in one go. "I've seen you when you get into that work mode, you know. Pretty sure I could hit a baseball right at you and you wouldn't notice until it caught you in the stomach."

I roll my eyes but accept the beer he gives me. "You'd never do that."

"No," he agrees. He turns to the stove, tending to the bacon with a much more careful hand than I had. He takes out a bowl, next, and as I watch, he cracks several eggs into it, and beats them with salt, pepper, and paprika. He pulls shredded cheddar cheese and sour cream from the fridge and folds both into the egg mixture. I know I'm staring, but I can't help it; he's working with such a practiced hand, I'm jealous. It reminds me of how Nana flows through the kitchen, as at ease as a sailor on the bow of a ship.

"Why sour cream?" I ask.

"Adds a nice tang," he says. "Keeps them fluffy, too."

"I've never had them this way."

"Izzy can't get enough of them."

"I talked to her earlier." I fiddle with the edge of the dishcloth as he takes out another pan and lights another burner. He flips the bacon, too. The kitchen smells delicious, rather than acrid, and with the night air coming through the back door, there's something cozy about the whole scene. Domestic, almost. "She suggested I drink margaritas and sing along to *Mamma Mia!* like your brother."

He smiles. It's a smile that lights up his already-handsome face, and my breath nearly catches as I look at it.

"That was incredible," he says. "I know you've only met James once, but trust me—he barely drinks, so when he does, it's a party."

I take a sip of my beer. "I decided breakfast for dinner was a more appropriate route."

"You can't give bacon too much heat at once, it'll burn." He sets several perfectly crisp pieces onto a paper-towel lined plate, then pours the eggs into the other pan. There's a fond note in his voice, like he's said this before. I'd bet it was to Izzy.

"Sebastian?"

He glances over his shoulder as he stirs the eggs with a spatula. His hair is still wet from the shower he must have taken after the game.

I wet my lips. "Did you win?"

His expression shutters. "No. Lost in extras."

"I'm sorry."

The frustration disappears from his expression in a blink. He shrugs. "We're in a tough stretch."

A few minutes later, he sets a plate in front of me. A pile of fluffy eggs, speckled with paprika, two pieces of perfectly crisp bacon, and buttered toast, too.

"Let's eat outside," he suggests. "It's a nice night."

I follow him outside, ignoring how my hand aches. Ignoring how much I want to kiss him in thanks, rather than just say it.

There's a fire pit out here, plus chairs grouped around a small table. I settle into one across from him, checking out the sky, but it's cloudy tonight. I can barely see the moon, even though it's going to be full in a couple days. The warm breeze rustles the tops of the trees, and a bird calls out somewhere in the night.

I take a bite of eggs and promptly moan.

There are scrambled eggs—and then there are *scrambled eggs*. Jesus Christ. Sebastian grins at me, clearly pleased. He was right, the sour cream brings them to a whole different dimension. I try not to eat like a barbarian, but I'm so hungry it's difficult. Sebastian, for his part, eats just as fast as me, then goes to grab another beer.

The silence is more comfortable than it has any right to be. I almost relax all the way, relishing in the late-night air and the sharp taste of the beer on my tongue. Sebastian sitting across from me, holding his glass beer bottle by the neck.

It feels... nice. Ordinary, even. As if we texted each other this morning and made these plans, and he's going to kiss me before we head inside.

I give myself a mental shake. I burned that bridge, and Sebastian's inherent kindness is the reason I'm sitting here right now. Nothing else. The sooner I make myself believe it, the faster I can move on, and focus on the right things. The stars and my own future, not the man sitting across from me. Pretty soon, he's going to be playing baseball for a living, and he deserves a partner who is willing for that to be the most important thing in both their lives.

"I don't think we're going to make the playoffs this year," he says.

I wince. "I'm sorry."

"We're not hitting well enough. Our fielding is clean, it's

just that the bats are silent." The grip on his beer tightens. "Including mine."

"There's the draft, right? Pretty soon?"

He nods. "July."

"Maybe you're just stressed about it."

"Maybe. Who fucking knows." He shakes his head slightly. I watch his Adam's apple bob as he swallows. He laughs shortly at some thought of his and sets his beer down. "Mia, what the hell did I do?"

I freeze with my beer halfway to my lips. "What do you mean?"

"You know what I mean. Did I upset you? Did I hurt you? What did I do, to make you decide you wanted nothing to do with me?"

"You didn't do anything."

He leans in, close enough our knees nearly touch. I'm drawn to his eyes again. I can still see the depths in them, even in the near-dark, illuminated only by the soft light from the kitchen. We could be in a void, the two of us. We're the only ones awake in this neighborhood, for sure, past midnight with barely any college kids around for the summer.

"You said you'd tell me."

I shiver as a strong gust of cool nighttime wind washes over us. It ruffles his hair, but he doesn't so much as blink. He might be adopted, but the intensity feels just like Cooper's. There's something electric about the Callahans. I let myself get drawn into Sebastian's orbit, and now I'm doggedly following him, even as I try to escape. If he's the sun, then I'm a comet, burning up from the close contact.

"You didn't hurt me," I say. I scrape my teeth against the inside of my cheek. "I just—can't."

"Bullshit." He puts his hand on my knee—careful, calculated. Even that small amount of contact has my stomach clenching. My knee is cold, and his hand is warm through the leggings. It would be warmer still on my bare skin. If he dragged his hand up several inches, he'd be dangerously close to a part of me that's silently begging for contact. "You cared about me. About us. Tell me what changed."

Nothing changed. I just tore myself away before the inevitable crash. And admitting that would hurt worse than locking myself in Izzy's room for the night.

But he's so close, and I want his warmth. I lean in too, and some part of me sings with satisfaction when I hear his breath hitch.

We could kiss so easily.

Then he pulls away. Gathers himself up. Disappointment hits me like cold water to the face, but I pull back too.

"Goodnight, Mia," he says. There's a softness to his voice, even though he has every right to be angry. This is the Sebastian I couldn't help but develop feelings for, and the Sebastian I need to stay away from. Nice. Understanding. Good. "Keep an eye on your hand."

A million things threaten to escape from my lips, but all I can manage is, "Goodnight, Sebastian."

15

SEBASTIAN

THE NEXT MORNING, I dash out of my room while I'm still putting on my shirt. After I said goodnight to Mia, effectively ruining whatever moment had been brewing, good or bad, with my hand on her thigh, I actually slept... right through my alarm. Which means I'm late to conditioning. I needed to leave ten minutes ago, but I can't find the cat.

I can't have lost the damn cat.

"Tangerine?" I call again. "Where'd you go?"

Mia is awake—I heard her moving around while I dashed from my room to the bathroom and back again—but I don't know whether she invited Tangerine into Izzy's room last night. Probably, but I'm not going to be responsible for losing the cat my brother loves with a passion that's rivaled only by what he feels for his girlfriend. Plus, I like the cat too, however many times she sticks her butt in my face.

I already checked downstairs, including the laundry room, and didn't see her. She's not in Cooper's room, either, which means the only other place in the house she could be is Izzy's room. If she's not there—if last night, while sitting outside with Mia, stewing over the steel fucking barrier between us, I somehow *lost* the cat—I won't be able to forgive myself.

I knock on Izzy's door. "Mia! Is Tangerine in there?"

She says something, but it's muffled. Maybe she's in the bathroom. I try the doorknob; it's unlocked, so I push the door open. "Have you seen the—"

"Get out!" Mia shrieks.

I freeze—because there's a very naked Mia di Angelo standing in my sister's room, towel drying her hair.

The ache that erupts in me nearly makes me see stars. I've gone weeks and weeks without seeing this body, and for a moment, all I can do is stare. The sight of the soft curve of her belly, her wide hips, her gorgeous full tits, the birthmark on her ribcage, makes every single memory come rushing to the forefront of my mind. The way my hands spanned her waist. The little gasps she gave me when I sucked on her pert nipples. The taste of her, rich and edged in salt, and how she loved when I bit her inner thighs. Kissing her while my hands wound through her soft, dark hair until we were both breathless.

I miss her.

My heart thuds, keening, wishing I could hold her close enough to feel her heartbeat right alongside mine. I miss her body, and I miss having the privilege of touching her and tasting her, but I miss *her*—her snark, her intelligence, her fire— most of all.

Even though we didn't hook up until January, the feelings started the moment I saw her at the movie theater last fall. Cooper couldn't resist cutting the line to talk to Penny, and Mia and I shared a look at the sight of our friends flirting. The feelings have only deepened since. Until a couple days ago, I barely saw her for weeks, but that just made them grow on a steady diet of yearning, the roots curling around my heart and digging in.

Reality comes crashing down in an instant. Friends don't look at each other naked. She hasn't magically decided that I'm allowed to see her like this again, which means I'm violating her privacy with every second I stand there, blatantly taking in that beautiful body.

I spin around, swallowing hard.

Friends. I can't convince her—or myself—to be friends if I do shit like this.

"What the hell were you doing?" she demands.

"I'm trying to find Tangy."

"She's not with you?"

I manage to resist glancing over my shoulder. "No. Is she with you?"

"No," she says.

Fuck. I can't help but turn around. Mia has wrapped the towel around her torso. She still looks supremely annoyed, but worried too, as the implication about Tangerine sinks in.

"Let me get dressed," she adds. "I'll help you find her."

"Coop will kill me if I let anything happen to this cat."

She snorts, grabbing a pile of clothes off the bed and retreating into the bathroom. "And Penny will kill me," she calls. "Unless you told Cooper, she doesn't even know I'm here right now."

I check Izzy's room while she gets dressed, but I don't see Tangy amid the throw pillows or the clothes in the closet. She's not underneath the bed, attacking the dust bunnies, either. I rub the back of my neck as I survey the room, eyes peeled for just a hint of that orange fur.

Mia emerges from the bathroom in skinny jeans and a t-shirt that shows off a sliver of her belly. When she passes by, I catch the scent of jasmine, delicate and enticing. She shoves her feet into a pair of leather sandals. "You didn't see her at all today?"

I shake my head, following her downstairs. "I checked downstairs already, too. She hasn't touched her food."

"Fuck." She runs her hand through her hair. "Do you think she got outside last night?"

"Maybe," I admit, even though the thought makes me want to squirm. That'll be a fun call with my brother. *Hey, how's the road trip? By the way, your cat is running around the streets of Moorbridge by herself.*

We poke around the living room, calling for her, and check the closets and laundry room one more time. She's not in the half-bath, or hiding behind the love seat and the window, or buried in the little castle-like bed next to the television that Izzy insisted she needed.

Mia straightens, a grim expression on her face. "We have to check the backyard."

I grab a couple cat treats from the pantry before we step into the backyard. The breeze smells of honeysuckle, and even this early in the morning, the heaviness in the air makes it clear that it's going to be another hot one. We fan out, poking around the bushes, trees, and fire pit. I have my head stuck underneath a chair, getting dirt all over my hands and knees, when Mia speaks.

"Seb," she says. "Over there."

She's pointing at one of the trees, a gnarled old thing with several sweeping branches. Nestled in the crook of one of the branches is Tangy. She stares at us unblinkingly, seemingly annoyed by our presence when *she's* the one who spent the night in a tree.

Relief rushes through me. At least she's here, not squashed by a car on a road somewhere. I brush the dirt away. "How did she get up there?"

"I guess she followed us outside." Mia frowns. "Will she get down on her own? Do you call the fire department for this?"

"I have no idea if that's real or just something the movies made up." I take a couple steps in the direction of the tree, considering it. "She could probably jump, but maybe she'd hurt herself. Wait here, let me see if there's a ladder in the garage."

On the way to the garage, I pull out my phone. I have a string of texts waiting from Hunter—although fortunately none from Coach Martin yet.

> **HUNTER**
>
> Where are you? Conditioning started half an hour ago
>
> Coach is doing that silent annoyed thing
>
> We have a meeting before this afternoon's game FYI
>
> Are you still with Mia?
>
> Morning sex only works if you plan for it

I just ignore him; I got plenty of shit from him and Rafael when I took Mia home from the bar. I wish it *was* morning sex that caused this. Wouldn't that be wonderful.

She looked so goddamn beautiful just now. I could stare at

her for ages, take in every angle, every detail, and never get bored.

In the garage, a cramped little space I've only been in a handful of times, I do find a ladder. I haul it over my shoulder, carrying it back to where Mia stands below the tree, having a staring contest with the cat.

I grin. "Who's winning?"

"Shut it, you'll distract me."

"I found the ladder."

Mia reluctantly tears her gaze away. "Oh, good. You should probably be the one to climb it, she's more familiar with you."

"I think she likes you more than me. She never wants to sleep in my room."

"Maybe she just likes Izzy's room, not me specifically."

I give her a look. "Get on the ladder, di Angelo."

She crosses her arms over her chest, her expression turning stony. "Get up on that rickety old thing and break my arm?"

"I won't let you fall." I brace the ladder. "I'll spot you."

Gingerly, she hauls herself onto the ladder. I hold it as steady as I can on the uneven ground, studiously ignoring how close we are—and how, as she climbs, I have a nice view of her firm ass in those dark wash jeans. She takes a deep breath once she's balancing on the top step. Tangerine shifts, but she's not so far away that Mia can't reach out and scoop her up.

"Mia?"

"Shut up and let me concentrate."

"Just grab her quick."

"Give me a second," she says, sharper now. "I don't like heights."

"Space is up very high, you know."

"That's different." She huffs out a breath, reaching forward and wobbling. "You would never climb on a ladder to get into space."

"Come down. I'll do it."

"No," she says quickly. "I can do it."

"You don't have to be so stubborn—"

"I can do it," she interrupts. She reaches out again. I wrap my arm around her back, securing her in place. She's trembling.

I bite back a curse. Too fucking stubborn. "I wouldn't have made you get on the ladder if you just told me that you didn't feel comfortable."

"It's not about comfort. Come *here*, Tangy."

"If you actually communicated instead of holding everything inside, then—"

"This doesn't have anything to do with that!" She rises onto her toes, snatching Tangy from the tree and hauling her into her arms. She wobbles again, in a much more precarious position than before. "This is just about the damn—"

"Mia, watch—"

She falls right off the ladder.

I wrap my arms around her instinctively as her body hits mine, sending both of us sprawling onto the grass. Tangerine promptly starts yowling. She claws to get out of Mia's arms. Once she's free, she bolts, settling a few feet away. I turn my head to the side, eyeing her as I pant. At least the ladder fell on its side instead of on top of us.

I hug Mia tighter, trying to quell my racing heart. Her hair is in my mouth, and instead of honeysuckle, now I'm smelling jasmine again. "Are you okay?"

"I hate ladders," she says vehemently. She struggles to get out of my grip the same way Tangerine just did with her, panting too as she sits up. She looks down at me, her hair falling into her face, her skin flushed. The thin gold chain around her neck sways.

She's straddling me.

She could lean down and kiss me, just like this.

I sit up on my elbows. She blinks. A beat passes, then another, as we stare at each other.

This is a different sort of staring contest. I don't even dare reach up to brush her hair back, for fear she'll run away and use this moment as another excuse to strengthen the barrier between us. I can feel my body reacting to the comfortable weight of her on top of me.

I've already lost her. I know that. But every single atom in my body is yearning for that kiss, and for everything that could come after.

"Callahan," she starts.

A beeping sound fills the air.

She grimaces, pulling out her phone and answering it. "Hello?"

"You have a ringtone? James is the only other person I know with an actual ringtone."

She just presses her hand over my mouth. "Yes, I'm on my way. My, um, tire was flat. I had to change it."

I lick her hand. She digs her knees into my sides. "Yes, I understand. It won't happen again."

I manage to pull her hand away—she's stronger than she looks—long enough to say, "You're such a dork."

"I'll kick you in the balls," she threatens.

"An actual ringtone," I say. "Do you use a cassette player too?"

"Sebastian." Her voice is sing-song sweet. "I have a big brother and more boy cousins than I can count. Don't test me."

I roll her over, so I'm the one holding her down instead. Her eyes go wide. I take her wrists and pin them to the ground on either side of her head. She bucks, but my weight holds her in place. Now it's my necklace—my father's necklace—swinging between us.

She's so gorgeous my breath catches. I'm always out of breath around her, and this is no different.

"Admit we're friends," I say.

She glares at me. "Let me go. I'm late for work."

"I'm late too." I just settle my weight on top of her more comfortably. She adores it like this, after all, even if she'd never say it aloud again. "But say we're friends, and we'll both be on our way."

She glowers. "What does it matter?"

"It matters. We need to be friends, even if it's just for Cooper and Penny."

Somehow, this is the wrong thing to say. I see the change in her immediately; the way she stiffens, her expression taking on careful blankness. "Let me go."

There's enough poison in her voice that I do.

16

MIA

"LET'S GET HERE ON TIME tomorrow, Mia," Alice says as she passes by my workstation. "We only have so much time to work on this."

I pull my headphones away from my ears as I glance at her. When I work, I try to go into a focus zone, which usually means loud rock music, a phone set to silent, and my long hair in a bun.

She tucks her clipboard underneath her arm as she runs her hand through her perfectly neat, pink-streaked bob. "Earth to Mia." She laughs at her own dumb joke. "Did you hear me?"

"Yes." I grimace, rubbing my forehead. "I'm sorry, it won't happen again. My tire just—"

"I don't care about the reason," she interrupts. "I mean, no offense, but excuses aren't going to cut it around here."

I try my best not to let my irritation show. This morning was a complete mess from start to finish. I can still feel the echo of the way Sebastian held me down, hours later, and whenever

I've lost my focus, that's exactly where it goes. He was half-hard by the time I escaped, and I'd never, ever admit it, but I was so turned on, the drive to campus was a blur.

If he hadn't brought up being friends again, I would have blown him right there in the grass.

"You're right," I say, even though I'm imagining how satisfying it would be to stab her with my pencil. At least she doesn't know the real reason I was late. "Like I said, I'm sorry."

"Just make sure you're here and working when I say you need to be," she says. "Beatrice might love you, but you're still just an undergrad. You report to me, and I need you to make me look good."

She laughs again. I just stare, because I have no idea if she's serious or if she's trying to joke around and doing it badly. I get it, she's a graduate student working on her dissertation, so she has a lot riding on this, but I do too. It's not like this is a joke to me; it's my entire life.

You'd think that as the only two women in the lab besides Professor Santoro herself, she'd want to be supportive, but right now, she's acting like the Space-X wannabe guys in the department. In other words, completely idiotic.

"Right," I say into the awkward silence. "I'm going to get back to work. Let me know if you need anything."

Once she leaves, I let out a breath, redoing my bun.

If this is a taste of this summer, I'm going to need to adjust my expectations. When I'm the graduate student in charge of undergrads, I'm going to be a hell of a lot nicer. We're all colleagues, after all.

I stare at my computer, but I'm all keyed up now. My mind doesn't want to focus. I rub the burn over my knuckles. It's nothing bad, no blistering, but the slight ache reminds me of

Sebastian. Our meal last night was nice, at least until it wasn't. I can still hear his quiet voice, telling me goodnight.

What did he tell me in that voice, once upon a time?

Good girl, Mia Angel.

Project GOSMC has been an utter failure so far.

I don't understand his obsession with wanting to make sure we're friends. Friends is a label too, a promise of something I'm not sure I'm going to be able to keep. Shouldn't he hate me, anyway? I ghosted him. I went back on my word. He has every right to be the one shutting *me* out, and instead, the past few days have been filled with his presence.

My phone lights up by my elbow, and even though I should ignore it, I can't help but pick it up when I notice the name.

> **SEBASTIAN**
>
> Heading to the grocery store after the game
>
> Want anything?
>
> I'll get more of that oat milk you like
>
> I think I'm going to make chicken scarpariello for dinner
>
>> Just some protein bars, thanks. I can pay you back
>
> Those aren't a meal, di Angelo
>
> Do you like my gift?
>
>> ???

Connor, another graduate student in the lab, calls, "Someone just dropped off a package for you, Mia."

> What did you do?

Sebastian chooses that moment to stop responding, so with a sigh, I haul myself up from my worktable. There's a shoebox on an unused desk by the door, cluttered with papers and an old model of the solar system.

Alice raises an eyebrow as she passes by. "It's not the journal proofs Beatrice is waiting on, right?"

There's a note stuck to the top. Sebastian's scrawl. "Nope. It's for me."

"Let me know when those come in," she says, taking a sip from her thermos. She disappears into her office, humming something horribly off-tune. Despite her attitude, I do admire her, but her focus on artistry instead of hard data is annoying. There's a reason why her code is messy—she doesn't pay attention to the right details.

Connor peers at the shoebox, pushing his glasses up his nose. "Who is S?"

"No one." I take the box to my desk. It's obvious that shoes are inside, and judging by the size of the box...

I set the note aside, taking the top off the box. As I expected, a pair of black suede boots, identical to the ones I had to throw away, lay nestled in the tissue paper. I check the size automatically. Eight. They're going to fit perfectly.

I put the lid back on and turn to the note.

Hey, di Angelo —

You can't be a warrior without the proper armor.

—S

P.S. The ticket for Wednesday night's game is under 'Princess Leia.'

P.P.S. We are friends.

I didn't realize he'd paid that much attention to my shoes.

> Really, Sebastian?

> I'm a size 9

His answer comes back swiftly.

> No, you're not

> And you're welcome

> On a scale of one to creepy, this is definitely up there

> Not if you've seen someone in that pair of boots and nothing else, trust me

My fingers hover over the keys, typing and then deleting. Ruminating on *that* memory would *definitely* be a strike against Project GOSMC.

> You're the one who keeps insisting we're friends

> Waving the white flag?

> No. I'm just repeating your assertion. The one you won't let go of, might I add

> Yes, we're friends

I just have a long memory

Don't be late for dinner

Truthfully, my plan had been to work until I felt like passing out, but chicken scarpariello does sound tempting. That's a dish I haven't had in years but remember from the many family dinner parties. The thing I don't want is to leave before everyone else, because I'm the youngest here and have the most to prove. I can't be late again, either.

Starting tomorrow, I'm going to get to the lab even earlier. With any luck, I won't even see Sebastian, which will be a win–win. No hot, athletic distractions, and an extra hour to work before Alice hovers over my shoulder like a pink-feathered bird of prey.

Maybe.

I'll take a maybe :)

17

SEBASTIAN

"OF COURSE, we'll make you aware ahead of time what we choose to publish. We're interested in your story. What you've been up to all this time, living with the Callahans, preparing for your future career."

The reporter, a woman named Zoe Anders, has barely stopped talking throughout the conversation. I thought that a video meeting would be less awkward than a phone call, but I've mostly been silent, nodding my head when necessary and chiming in with one-word answers. It seems like she knows enough about me to write the profile right now, honestly. She has her angle all worked out; she's going to write about how the memory of my father's career has affected my game.

She pauses, finally, giving me a wide smile. "So, what do you think?"

I feel a little nauseous, honestly, but I don't tell her that. I'm exhausted after this afternoon's game—fortunately a win—and this all sounds overwhelming. "Seems... intense."

She laughs shortly. "Sebastian, this is just a small taste of what you'll experience in your career. They're predicting you'll spend maybe two years in the minors before being called up."

I wish I could shut my laptop. When I was a teenager, it was easy not to think about the future, not to give any mind to the scouts in the stands during certain tournaments, or the handshakes from men who looked at me and saw Jake Miller, not his son.

Now, it's almost here, and even if I'm protected by one more year of undergrad, my obligations to whatever club picks me up will start soon. I'll start to *be* someone, a version of Sebastian that has a public persona. There's the version of James I know—my brother, my friend—and the one that's on people's fantasy football teams. Even if I could shut out all the noise, Zoe is right: this is the beginning of more press coverage, more interest, more expectations. If I get to the majors and do badly, I'll disappoint everyone. If I do well, they'll show my stats alongside my father's. If I do exceedingly well, then the attention might be all mine, but that could make me into a national name, a Mike Trout or Aaron Judge, rather than just someone known in baseball circles.

Judging by the gleam in Zoe's eyes, she's trying to get me to that last option as quickly as possible. A story that involves Richard Callahan is one that always gets read, after all.

I don't want to run from it, even if it makes my skin crawl. I don't want to call Richard and ask him to kill the story, because someone else will just write something that doesn't involve me at all, and Richard is right, my father's legacy is mine to protect.

"Perhaps," I admit. "I'm not too concerned about when I get to the majors."

She shifts in her chair. "But your plans haven't changed?"

I wonder what she would say if I told her they had. She'd probably realize, instantly, that she's sitting on a much bigger story than the one she's envisioning now. A son following in his father's footsteps after a tragic loss is good, but renouncing that path and going down a different one?

Not that that's happening, anyway. I'd be a fool to turn away from the only thing I've ever been good at. And I don't *have* another path to consider. Cooking isn't a real path. It's not like I would become the next Gordon Ramsay, and everyone expects great things from me.

"No," I say. "Of course not."

"If this works for your schedule, I can be in Moorbridge for the Binghamton series. I'll conduct other interviews over the phone, but I want to hear from you in person. I'll bring along my team and we'll do a shoot."

I keep the smile on my face, even if internally I'm wilting. "Different from the video segment?"

"We'll do that later, if you can come to our studio a little closer to the draft."

Just fantastic.

"Sounds great," I say.

"Wonderful. I'll have my assistant send over the details to confirm."

When I hang up, I immediately scrub my hands over my face. Interview. Photoshoot. Video segment. Individually, they sound terrible, but together? What a torture fest. I'm not good at talking about myself, anyway. She'd be better off just airing some footage from a game.

At least I have something else to focus on—my chicken scarpariello.

I got my love of baseball from my father, but my love for

cooking came from my mother. I can still remember standing carefully on a step-stool, helping her roll out a pie crust or marinate chicken. She never minded my help, even when I was little. She'd explain how to follow a recipe, and what changes she made to put her unique twist on it. I've always admired how you can tweak a recipe even a little and come up with something new. I'm not an artist, but it feels akin to art. And it's not just art you admire. It's useful art, the kind of art that nourishes the body and the soul all at once.

I kept it up as a teenager, even as my baseball schedule got more intense. I'd help the chef with dinner preparations after school, or help Sandra, if she was cooking instead. Now in college, living off campus, I do most of the cooking during the semester. Izzy burns everything, and Cooper doesn't have interest in anything but eating. When Bex was around, we'd cook together, but we haven't been in the same kitchen since Christmas break.

I give Tangerine, safely curled on the couch, a scratch behind the ears, wash my hands, and take out the ingredients. Chicken scarpariello isn't hard to make, it just requires a little time. The ingredients are simple, too, which I appreciate. A whole chicken, broken into pieces. Sweet Italian sausage, with fennel, of course. Jarred banana peppers, plus the juice, and fresh peppers. White wine, chicken broth, garlic, and rosemary. The result, when you add fried potatoes, is a delicious one-pan meal, with a tangy sauce I could happily drink on its own.

I dare Mia to eat it and still insist we're not friends. I don't break out the good recipes for just anyone.

I thought it would be more palatable to her to pretend it's just for Cooper and Penny, but that didn't help things. Buying her replacement boots probably didn't help either, but I couldn't help myself. She was wearing those boots the first time I saw her. They feel like an extension of her, and I want to see her in them. I hoped she smiled when she read the note, and that she's going to come home in time for dinner.

If not, I'll save her a plate in the fridge, but I want to see her. To talk to her. To remind her that even if she doesn't want to be with me, we have a connection. I'd rather be her friend than have nothing at all. The past few days have been a warm luxury compared to the frozen tundra I've been living in, hoping for a text from her, or for a hint of her smile when we crossed paths, or even a scowl. I'd rather a scowl from her than a smile from anyone else.

She looked cute this morning, pinning me down. Cuter still when I flipped us over. I wish she'd said something about her fear of heights, because I would never have made her get on the ladder, but if there's one thing I know about Mia di Angelo, it's that she'd rather chew off her own arm than admit weakness.

I prep all the ingredients and set out what I need next to the stove. Potatoes first, cubed and browned on the stove so they'll be crispy, and then the chicken and sausage pieces. They'll finish in the oven, but a good sear is important for the taste and the sauce. I turn on some music, too; my favorite classic rock playlist.

I'm humming along to Van Halen when the front door slams.

18

SEBASTIAN

"MIA?"

Mia appears in the doorway, the shoebox tucked underneath her arm, her bag slung over her shoulder. Her hair is in a bun atop her head, tilting to the side like frosting sliding off a too-warm cake. She has a glower on her face, and the tip of her nose is red.

She takes a deep breath, as if trying to calm herself, and says, "I'll be upstairs."

I set down the pair of kitchen tongs I'm holding and take a couple steps in her direction. "You seem upset."

"Just stressed."

"Did something happen?"

She unwinds the bun and shakes out her hair. "I lost a bit of code I was working on. I need to try to reconstruct it now before the graduate student I'm working with notices. She's so... I'm sure I saved it, and the program has auto-backup, so I'm not sure what happened."

"That sucks."

She blows out a breath. "Yeah. I'll be working upstairs."

I gesture to the kitchen table, cleared off because the whirlwinds in my life named Cooper and Izzy aren't home. "Stay down here. I can change the music, or turn it off, if it'll distract you."

"This is what I'd be listening to anyway," she admits, setting her bag on a chair and taking out her laptop. There aren't any stickers on it, in typical Mia fashion. When it comes to work, she's all business, all the time.

I let myself smile at that. "I know, Mia. I've seen you at work before."

"Then why did you offer to turn it off?"

"To be polite to my new roommate."

She roots around in her bag, pulling out a notebook, a stub of a pencil, and a glasses case. "Is that what we are?"

"I figured it was a relatively safe option." I add the peppers to the pan and give it all a shake. "Did they call you?"

"Not today."

"So, we're officially roommates." I turn over the potatoes. "Those glasses are cute on you."

I wasn't kidding; I am fond of the glasses—the circular, wire-framed lenses remind me of a stooped old mathematics professor—but for whatever reason, she's blushing. "They're just for the blue light from the computer. I don't need them to see."

"So, they're your special coding glasses. Like a superhero mask."

"That smells amazing," she says by way of changing the subject, but I catch the hopefully fond roll of her eyes. "I haven't had it in years."

"It's one of my favorites."

She looks over, gifting me a rare smile. "Me too."

She turns to her laptop. Her fingers fly over the keyboard as she types. Her fingernails are black right now, filed down so there's not much of a tip. She leans closer to the screen, frowning in a way that makes her forehead wrinkle cutely. A part of me that has no business being so loud wants to walk over, shove away the laptop and notebook, and lay her out on the table.

I've never been one for dessert before dinner, but now there's only one thing I'm craving.

What a friendly fucking thought to have. It's torture, especially with my cock stirring, but I turn back to the stove. I somehow manage to finish cooking the meal without peering over my shoulder constantly. Her typing is a signal that she's working, and I don't want to distract her.

College has been a way for me to play baseball and fuck around with the most interesting, out-there courses McKee has on offer, but it's different for Mia. This is the foundation of her future, the thing that's going to get her to the top of her field one day. She needs every moment of these four years, meanwhile I'm finished with my history major coursework and have enough credits to graduate after next semester if I wanted.

She's so into it that she doesn't notice when I set down a plate and glass of wine for her. I squeeze her shoulder on the way to my own seat.

She startles, blinking as she pushes the glasses up her nose. "Oh. Thanks."

She shuts her laptop and pushes it to the middle of the table. When she takes a bite, she promptly moans. I hide my grin behind a sip of wine, but her reaction makes butterflies erupt in my stomach. Nothing beats the moment someone tastes my cooking. It's even better than hitting a home run.

"This is delicious." She takes off the glasses, settling back in the chair. "Thank you. You're being... really nice. Which makes me want to stab you with my fork for some reason."

I nearly snort out my wine. "Just eat, di Angelo. Did you even have lunch?"

"I had a protein bar."

"Not a meal."

"It's something."

"It's not real food."

She takes a small, neat bite. "How did you learn to cook this well?"

"My mother, a bit. And Sandra."

"If you weren't a baseball player, you could be a chef." She takes a careful sip of wine. "I could see it. The white jacket thing would look acceptable on you."

If I announced that I wanted to work in a restaurant instead of play baseball, I might give Richard a heart attack. My father would certainly roll over in his grave. Yet part of me, a tiny secret part of me, wishes that I could graduate early and use my inheritance—the money my parents left me, which I'll have access to when I finish college—to travel. Maybe work my way through kitchens, learning different cuisines and deciding whether it could become a career. One conversation with Zoe Anders and I already feel drained. The thought of playing televised games nearly every day of the week for most of the year has started to sound like torture, no matter how much I love the game itself. In a kitchen, I'd be a member of a different kind of team, and no one would compare me to my father every time I seared a steak.

It's easier not to think about it. I can't blow up my life; it's not a real option. It's not something people like me actually *do*. Once the draft happens and I have a sense of where I'll be going after next year, I'll settle down.

I just need to get through the end of the season first.

Mia is still checking me out, so I smirk. "Did you just call me hot?"

"Since when does acceptable equate to hot?"

"You totally just called me hot."

She primly spears a potato and pops it in her mouth. "I did no such thing."

I lean back, glass in hand. I know I need to eat too, but it's more fun to watch her enjoy the meal. I wish it wasn't the first real food she's had since the morning, but I can work on that. "I was hoping you'd come home wearing the boots."

She arches an eyebrow. "How did you find the exact same ones? I got those a few years ago."

"You think I don't pay attention?"

"Not to that."

"Izzy might've helped a little."

"Ah, there we go."

"But for the record, I remembered. I just needed her to source them." I knock my foot into hers underneath the table.

She kicks me in the shin.

I hold back my smile with a sip of wine. "I distinctly remember, for example, you telling me that if I broke the zipper while undressing you, you wouldn't let me eat you out. I took them off like they were made of glass."

She just cuts through a piece of chicken, seemingly unaffected by my words. "You did say that you have a long memory."

"I remember this morning, too."

"Which part? The one where you forgot how knocking works, or the one where you nearly killed me?"

"I am sorry for both."

"So, the boots were an apology."

"No. The boots were a gift."

She shakes her head. "You're so weird."

"So are you." Not my best comeback, but I'm distracted by her pouty lips. Jesus, her mouth is sinful. I take another gulp of wine. Work is always a safe topic, right? "Tell me about what you're working on."

She raises a single eyebrow. "Really?"

"Yeah. You're working with your advisor, right? Professor Santoro?"

She nods. "I'm her undergraduate lab assistant. She doesn't normally take on anyone who isn't heading into senior year, but she let me in a year early, to help boost my chances of getting into a study abroad program next spring at the University of Geneva."

"That would be sick."

She smiles into her wine. "Yeah. It's an intense program, but it would allow me to work at the observatory at the university, which gets data from this amazing telescope that operates in La Silla all the way in Chile. And I'd be able to see so many other research observatories too—they do trips to Sphinx Observatory, which is the tallest observatory in Europe, for example, and the Haute-Provence Observatory in France. It'd help me think about whether I want to get my PhD here or in Europe and build up more connections in the field at the same time. And I'd just be able to see some of the world, period. I've never traveled anywhere before. The sky is beautiful here, but I want to see it from all over the world, you know?"

By the end of her speech, she sounds so excited, her voice is a little high. I don't bother holding back my smile. Her enthusiasm is infectious. If there's anyone who deserves a spot in the program, it's her.

"It would be next spring?"

"Yeah. Spring and summer."

"Cool. And you're studying... what are they called?"

I remember. I remember because I asked her this question while my mouth was on her tits, and she gasped out the word. *Exoplanets*. But I pretend I don't, because I know it will lead to more conversation, and if there's anything I want from this meal, it's to spend time with her. To hear her talk excitedly as she gestures with her hands, and to see passion in her eyes, if not for me, then for something. She's someone who has her future figured out. She has the mind and the passion for what she loves to do.

I have the skills for my sport, and the work ethic, but I don't know where the fire went.

She shakes her head slightly, but doesn't call me out. "Exoplanets. Planets that orbit a star other than ours. One of the most exciting things about the program is that the telescope in La Silla works with something called the CORALIE spectrograph, and together they work at uncovering large exoplanets. So, I'd be continuing to learn about and do work in my area of interest even before I commit to a graduate program."

"That sounds fantastic. Even though I have no idea what a spectrograph is."

She laughs. "It's—are you sure you want to hear about this? I'm not boring you?"

"Nope." I grin at her when her eyes narrow. I know better than to call her adorable right now, but she looks so cute, practically buzzing with nerdy excitement. "I like seeing you get so excited. Tell me everything."

Her face tells me she doesn't quite believe me, but still, she indulges me, and I hang on every word.

19

MIA

I TURN OVER IN BED, the sheets tangling around my legs, so I can stare out the window.

I haven't slept. My body thrums with need. My clit is practically screaming for attention, and still, I ignore it, biting the pillow as I look at the moon.

My body isn't just craving release—it's wanting it from one person in particular.

And he's in his own bed, with only a thin wall between us.

One more night.

It was so hard to tear myself away from Sebastian after dinner. He sat through my whole mini lecture about the work I'm doing, and he seemed interested the whole time, which usually doesn't happen. People are interested at first—they think of aliens and want to know more—and then that wanes as I go into the details. Sebastian asked me thoughtful questions, even though he's not involved in physics or astronomy. He even untangled a problem I'd been pondering with the code just by asking a question that unleashed a new train of thought, which I definitely needed after I lost that stupid bit of work today. I stayed there through dinner and a glass of wine, and debated having a second, but managed to contain myself.

It's the last night, and he doesn't even know it. The university emailed me just before I left the lab with information about a room that I can move into tomorrow. I almost told him during dinner, but I didn't want to see the disappointment on his face.

Now, I can't sleep. I don't even want to try. I'm wide awake, thinking of the rough edges of Sebastian's hands and how good he looked in the kitchen and how badly I wanted to lick his throat. Every time he took a sip of wine, my stomach clenched. I want to touch myself, but I haven't had time to replace Lucinda, my favorite vibrator, after her demise in the flood, and it's nowhere near as satisfying with just my hand.

It would be quiet, however. The only thing worse than rubbing myself off to the thought of Sebastian yet again would be if he overheard it.

It's past midnight. I haven't heard him move in hours.

I inch my hand underneath my sleep shorts.

As I circle my clit with my finger, I breathe in sharply. I bury that sound in the pillow, closing my eyes and focusing on the sensations. Sebastian's hand would be bigger, his fingers rougher. He'd start like this, teasing my clit, nowhere near ready to give in, but reminding me of the end goal. He'd cup my pussy next—I do that, fingers slipping through the wetness— and murmur something dirty against my ear.

Maybe he'd use that special, ridiculous nickname. I'm the furthest thing from an angel, but that never seemed to stop him.

I mouth at the pillow with a pant as my finger brushes my

clit. My body aches, wanting to be filled, to be fucked so deep I feel it in the morning. I make do with my fingers instead, adding one and then the other, crooking them so they hit that spot that makes me tremble. They're not big enough, not even close. I move them in and out, thumb rubbing my clit.

My stomach twists into a knot, aching for release, for that moment of pure clarity as my body spins out in pleasure, but even adding a third finger just makes me whine with frustration. Memories crowd my mind like wishes. I can almost pretend that he's here with me, watching with that quiet, addictive intensity. In my fantasy, I'm teasing him, making him stay put as I touch myself. He's indulging it, letting me put on a show, but if I go too long without letting him take care of me, he'll spank me before *maybe* letting me come.

The first time he did that, I nearly came untouched. It was so surprising, to feel the bloom of pain, to hear his velvet-soft voice as he told me to be a good girl and take it. And after, when my ass was stinging and pleasure burned through me like wildfire, he cradled my jaw and told me to open my mouth, that I had to get his dick nice and wet before he fucked me.

I give my head a shake. I need to stop getting lost in moments of time that I can't get back. I don't like him anymore —I *can't* like him anymore.

If I could just take the edge off...

Yet another moan rips itself from my throat as I plunge my fingers in and out. "Sebastian—"

"Angel?"

I freeze. That wasn't my imagination. I glance at the door, still shut tightly.

"Seb?" My whole body erupts with heat so intense that I wouldn't be surprised if I started glowing. I swallow the sudden lump in my throat as I pull my shorts up, wiping my fingers on my shirt for lack of a better option. "What are you doing?"

"If you needed help, you could've just asked."

Mother of Christ. I take a deep breath, sliding off the bed. "Go to bed."

"Can I open the door?"

I inch closer, until I can rest my head against the door. Somehow, knowing he's on the other side is making me ache even more. Did I wake him? Is his hair all mussed? Is he wearing pajamas? How long has he been there, listening to me? "I... I don't know."

"You sound frustrated. Let me help."

I nearly snap that I *am* frustrated, but manage to rein it in. "That's not a good idea."

"It's past midnight." His voice is even softer than before. "Let me in, Mia."

I can hear the implication in the words. Past midnight means it doesn't count, come morning—something I told him on more than one occasion.

I shouldn't let him in. Nothing whispered in the dark stays there, in the end.

Yet I open the door.

He's shirtless, with a pair of gray sweatpants slung low on his hips. His hair is a messy tangle, falling into his eyes. There's a hint of a smile on his face, but it fades as we look at each other, breathing into the quiet. I hear my heart beating as if it's outside my body.

He's beautiful. I want to touch him so badly, the urge rolls from my fingertips all the way to my toes.

He takes my hand, squeezes it, and then presses a rough kiss to my palm.

"Please," he says.

I can't speak. I don't want to ruin it by saying something sharp and uncalled for. This is a bad idea—but I've always liked bad ideas. This is reckless—but I've never liked being reckless more than when I'm with him.

I nod.

He pulls me to his bedroom. As if worried I'm going to change my mind, he kisses me before we're even over the threshold, his big, warm hands coming up to frame either side of my face. The bruising crush of his lips against mine ignites the rest of my resolve; I'm the one who pushes him to the bed. I climb into his lap, grinding against him. He retaliates by palming my bottom. The squeeze of his hand makes me break off our kiss with a moan, and he huffs out a laugh.

"This doesn't mean anything," I say, breathless because he's skimming his hand up my t-shirt. He cups my breast and squeezes, those rough fingertips I haven't been able to stop thinking about teasing my nipple.

"Sure, Mia Angel. Whatever you say."

The familiar wordplay makes me swallow. *Mia Angel, my angel.* "You're the one who was listening in on me."

"Wasn't exactly hard," he drawls, pinching my ass for good measure. "In fact, I remember you being exactly that loud. Not usually that frustrated, though."

At least it's dark in here. Harder to see my blush. "I was making do with my fingers."

He makes a sympathetic noise as he continues to tease my breasts. "And they were nowhere near enough. I know you need to be filled up."

It's an effort to make my tone dry, not breathless. "Are you actually going to help, or are you just going to sit there stating the obvious?"

His grin is a flash of white in the dark. "Depends. You going to be a good girl and listen to me?"

Those two words are a siren's call, shattering whatever remains of my defenses. In answer, I take his hand and lift his fingers to my mouth. I trace my tongue over his knuckles, then down each finger, then finally take two of them into my mouth, sucking until they're good and wet. Relief floods through me at the expression on his face. He couldn't mask the want if he tried.

He doesn't hate me. He still wants me. I might've ruined any chance at more, but at least I still mean something to him.

"I missed you," he murmurs. "Fucking missed this. Turn around, sweetheart."

He maneuvers us so I'm sitting in his lap with my back to his chest. I tug off my shirt, near-breathless now, and he wraps an arm around my middle, squeezing tight. He hooks my legs over his and spreads them that way, so I'm restrained, kept in place by his body. His other hand strokes over my already-wet panties. He presses a kiss to the side of my head. "How far did you get?"

"Not far enough."

"You missed me too, didn't you? Saying my name in the middle of the night while I'm next door."

My breath sticks in my throat. "Seb."

He just kisses my hair again. "Mia."

His fingers skim the top of my panties. "Go on, tell me."

I try to twist, but he holds me in place. He continues to tease, playing with the scrap of fabric that's covering where I need his touch. I know I'm not getting more until I give him an answer, but I'm not crumbling this easily. I wiggle, so my ass is more firmly against his hardened dick, and relish in his sharp intake of breath. "Miss is a strong word."

He rubs my clit over the panties. My belly clenches. "Come on, angel. Be honest with me."

"Fuck. Fine. I missed you."

He tugs down my panties and cups my cunt. "Was that so hard?"

"I guess not," I grumble.

He huffs out a laugh as he slowly strokes over my folds. For all his teasing, he doesn't wait to push a finger into me. He adds another, scissoring them, as his thumb finds my clit. My head falls against his shoulder as my body presses down, seeking even more contact.

I didn't forget a single detail—not his clean scent, or his soft hair, or his broad chest—but experiencing them again is making me dizzy. He's so strong, his arm is a belt around my middle, keeping me in place effortlessly. He increases the pressure on my clit, wrenching a little sob from my throat. I'm right on the edge, wobbling but not quite falling, and every touch leaves sparks.

"Good," he breathes out. "Come for me, gorgeous girl."

He pushes in a third finger, stretching me enough it's almost a good enough substitute for his cock, and uses his other hand to rub my clit. The effect is no doubt obscene; I'm spread open, moaning as he touches me all over with those long, talented fingers. A distant part of me wonders if tomorrow I'll regret this, but right now? This is everything I've wanted, every moment of every day, since I walked out on him.

"Sebastian," I say without thinking. My voice breaks halfway through, hanging in the warm silence.

He makes a soft noise, not a shush but a soothe, and curls his fingers inside me as he answers, "Mia Angel."

I gasp, my nails digging into his thighs as I come. Stars swim in my eyes, dotting my view of his dark, neat room. He pulls out his fingers slowly, the drag an extra bit of pleasure all on its own, and sets them against my mouth.

I take what he's offering, licking them clean as he strokes his other hand through my hair. His cock is a hot, solid bulge beneath me; I can't decide whether I want it in my mouth or my pussy. I manage to turn around, balancing on his lap as I pull him into a kiss. I run a hand through his hair while the other strokes down the hard planes of his abs, settling at the waistband of his sweatpants.

As much as I love how he fills up my cunt, I want to feel him in my mouth. I want to taste his salt and musk. My mouth is already watering thanks to the promise of it, that familiar tug of want stirring again deep in my core.

He nips my lip. "Better?"

I nod, breathless still, and dive forward to kiss his neck. I bite down gently. "Wanna suck you."

He catches my hand before it can get any further. "Not yet."

I huff. "What?"

"Making you feel good was a favor," he says. "If you want to touch me, I need something from you first."

20

SEBASTIAN

MIA'S SCOWL is always adorable, but this one, with her cheeks flushed and her hair mussed, is the very best iteration. Her lips are so pouty, I'd love to just take her up on her offer to suck me off, but I knocked on her door knowing it would be the last time I danced around us being friends, and I can't back down now. If I hadn't heard my name, I would have ignored it. Tried my best to put it out of my mind and never speak of it to her. But I did hear my name, and the realization that she was thinking about me nearly brought me to my knees right there in the hallway.

She doesn't hate me. She still wants me. I didn't quite know, until I overheard her, how afraid I was that I ruined everything forever. I messed up whatever chance we had at more, but right now, if she admits we're friends, I'll suck up my deeper feelings and be with her however she wants. Friends with benefits with her beats a real relationship with anyone else. Why did I kid myself about that for even a second? The moment I kissed her, the unease in my chest settled.

Mia di Angelo might not want to be my girlfriend, but for these moments? It's a price I'm willing to pay.

She crosses her arms over her chest. It makes me drop my gaze to her perfect tits. Then she clears her throat—so no looking at her breasts right now, got it—and, if it's possible, gets even more beautiful as she purses her lips. "Go on."

"If you're going to touch me, I need you to admit we're at least friends."

"At least?"

I brush her hair over her shoulder, dragging my fingertips over her collarbone. This is risky, but I can't help myself. "I know there's more to the story. But I won't push you on it now."

She reaches for my waistband again, but I intercept her with a tsk. "Come on. You like rules. This is a rule."

She practically grits her teeth. "So, if I admit we're... friends, I can suck you?"

"You can do whatever you want," I say with a grin. "Suck me, ask me to fuck you until you scream, bite me as hard as you want—I know how much you love that. Only second to when I make it hurt a bit, right, sweet girl?"

Her front teeth dig into her lower lip. "You're ridiculous."

I shrug. "Or you can say thank you for the orgasm and go back to Izzy's room."

"You said it was past midnight."

"That might've worked three months ago, but not now. Admit we're friends, Mia. Not because of Cooper and Penny—I shouldn't have said that, yesterday. We're friends because we enjoy spending time together, whether it's like this or like dinner earlier."

"If you're so sure, why do I need to say it?"

"A little direct communication never hurt anyone."

"Never hurt anyone, my ass," she mutters. "Since when doesn't a guy just want a blowjob?"

I wait, with half a mind to hold my breath. If I pushed her too hard and she doesn't say it, or if she just leaves, I won't know what to do with myself. But I can't go on like this now that she's back in my life. If she won't let me take care of her all the way, fine. I'll make do with dinners and encouraging her to talk to me about work and playful stress relief. I'll be her friend plus a little extra forever, if that's all I'm offered, and if there's a sliver of a chance down the line for more, I'll be there for that too.

She blinks. I lean in, brushing my lips over her cheek as I stroke my hand down her spine. I feel, rather than see, her shiver.

"Fine," she says, her voice muffled against my neck. She wraps her arms around me, keeping us close, as if she can only have this conversation without needing to make eye contact. "You're ridiculous, but we're friends."

She slides to her knees in front of me before I can stop her. "Now can I touch you?"

I catch her chin with my fingers and tilt her face up. I press the pad of my thumb against her lower lip, right in the middle. "Thank you."

Her hands run up my legs, pausing right near where I've been craving her touch. I groan, settling myself more comfortably on the edge of the bed.

She shakes her head. "Has anyone ever told you how weird you are?"

I lean down and capture her lips in another kiss. "My

siblings tell me all too often, but I like it better coming from you."

"Of course you do." She strokes her hand over my sweatpants, mimicking the way I teased her earlier. Even the small brush makes my cock throb; it's been torturesome, ignoring how fucking turned on I am. She drags the sweatpants and boxer-briefs down my legs all at once and pulls out my dick, giving it a rough tug that makes me hiss.

"Sorry," she murmurs. She reaches between her legs and gets her hand slick, then uses it to jerk my cock, her thumb pressing against the tip.

My hips nearly come off the bed. She huffs out a laugh. Her eyes gleam in the half-dark. "Someone's eager."

My voice is hoarse when I manage words. "With you in my bed? Who could fucking blame me?"

She just takes the tip into her mouth, sucking gently. Between the sensation of her warm, wet mouth and her hand working over my dick, I'm close to the edge in mere moments. She slowly works me into her mouth even further, an inch at a time, until it's painful not to blow my load. My hand tangles in her hair, tugging hard enough it probably hurts. My body is begging for permission to jerk my hips up, to seize control, but I don't want to hurt her.

I moan, digging my nails into her scalp as she swallows. My breath comes fast and short. I tilt her head back, unable to keep myself from pushing in just a bit deeper. Her eyes meet mine. She manages a nod, looking imperious from the upward tilt of her chin even though I'm the one holding her in place.

The permission loosens something deep in my body. I urge her to pull off, then rise to my feet. From this angle, I tower over her. My body is all muscle, honed to this point from years of baseball training, and I've never been so glad for it when I see the blatant desire on her face at the sight of me. I brush my fingers over her lips, slick with spit and precome, and as if to make up for her ogling, she tries to bite me.

Kneeling, she seems smaller than she actually is, her hair a dark tangle over her bare shoulders. A smirk plays on her lips, no doubt because she knows I'm admiring her just as much.

"So delicate," I murmur, cupping the back of her head.

Just as I expected, her satisfied smirk becomes a scowl. "Fuck off."

I trace over the shell of her ear. "I'm just calling it like I see it, angel."

"I'm not *delicate*. Not your angel, either."

I wrap her silky hair around my hand and tug. "Didn't say a thing about you being mine."

She's still scowling, but she takes my cock back into her mouth like she already misses it, swallowing me deep as she breathes through her nose. I cradle the back of her head with both hands, thrusting experimentally. When it's clear she can handle it, I move with more intensity. I can feel the climax building from my middle all the way to my toes. I groan deeply as I work at a slow, dragging rhythm. How did I live without this? Without *her*?

"You feel so good," I gasp out. I want to say so much more, but I can't hold words in my mind right now. Not while Mia is on her knees for me, working my cock with her skillful mouth.

She hums. The vibrations make my stomach tighten even further. I tremble with the effort to hold back for just a moment longer, but then she digs her nails into my thigh, and it sends me right off the edge in one final push.

"Fuck," I pant. It's too late for me to pull away, to give her the option of anything but drinking my come. I'm holding her so close I can feel the rapid rise and fall of her chest against my legs.

She swallows every drop, then pulls off with a soft, wet pop. She dabs at the corner of her mouth with her thumb, but it's useless. Her chin is a mess of spit. I grab my shirt and wipe her face clean before she can protest.

She scrambles to her feet, breathing just as heavily as me.

"Shit," she murmurs.

For a moment she stares, and I just stare back. I feel exhausted, like she took the edge off whatever was keeping me awake. Even tired, my limbs are loose, my heart lighter than it's been in ages. I can't help smiling, even though I'm sure she's about to turn on her heel and leave the room. I decide to push my luck and drag her into a kiss.

She sighs against my mouth. Curses again. I wait one beat, then two. I taste myself on her lips.

She pulls away—and flops on my bed.

"Mia?"

She tugs the blanket over herself. "Come here, dumbass."

21

MIA

CUDDLING.

Cuddling with Sebastian Miller-Callahan.

I'm such an idiot.

I've been awake for several minutes, and I need to pee, but I'm wrapped against Sebastian so tightly, I couldn't move if I tried. My head is tucked against his chest, his broad arms are wrapped around my back, and one hand is cupping my ass. We're both naked, and I can feel his cock, a little stiff, against my belly. I'm not especially small, but this position makes me feel tiny.

It's heaven.

It's hell.

He heard me, and he came to help, and I let him. Maybe it was the quiet night around us that did it, or the dinner beforehand, although the one glass of wine couldn't have let down my inhibitions all that much. I let him take me to his room. We had sex, and I'd vowed never to experience that with him again. Project GOSMC is crumbling to dust with every moment I spend wrapped up in his ridiculous, lovely, possessive warmth. If it was a NASA mission, they'd declare it a failure and shunt it to the annals of past experiments.

I loved every moment. The way he held me in his lap, his fingers against my teeth. The feel of his cock in my hand, then down my throat. I could barely breathe while he fucked my mouth, and it was exactly how I wanted it. He called me delicate, but he didn't act like he believed it.

I'm sure he doesn't. He just enjoys pushing my buttons. By all rights he should be pissed at me, and instead he got me to admit that we're friends—while in the middle of taking the edge off all the desire I can't shake. And he had the nerve to smile at me like I was a lovely star, not a black hole.

I scowl against his chest.

At least by tonight, I'll have somewhere else to stay. I'll be able to go back to avoiding him, and maybe this time it'll stick. Then autumn will come, I'll endure one semester of seeing him when I'm around Penny, and by the time I'm back from study abroad, he'll have graduated.

Something hooks in my belly and tugs.

I don't want that. I don't want him to be a stranger.

But we all want things we can't have.

Better he learns to hate me now, rather than after I've given him my heart. Any future with him would end like my brother and his wife. My grandparents. My parents. We'd stay together, making each other miserable. I know I'd be too stubborn to compromise my career for his, or to leave if it wasn't working. Sebastian has already proven himself to be an equally stubborn bastard. We'd bite and kick and throw punches until there was nothing left.

I'd ruin him.

The first thing to do is to leave—now. Last night wasn't supposed to happen, and it sure as hell can't happen again.

I wiggle out of his arms.

He wakes as I tug on my shorts.

"Morning," he says with a yawn.

I throw my shirt on, willing my voice to sound flat, even though his own is rough with sleep and sexy as hell. "Hi."

He squints at his phone. "It's barely six."

"I need to get to the lab early."

"Well, let me make you breakfast."

I tuck my hair behind my ears, searching for my phone—but that's still in Izzy's room, along with the rest of my stuff. I need to pack so I'm ready to go later. "I'm good."

"You need to eat."

I dart for the door. "I'll just grab one of those protein bars."

"Not a meal," he says, raising his voice so I still hear him in the hallway.

I grab my bag and start shoving things into it. I'll just toss it in my car and figure out the rest in the evening.

"Mia."

I look up despite myself. "What?"

"What are you doing?"

He's in the doorway again, arms crossed over his chest, wearing underwear and nothing else. His hair sticks up at odd angles, but somehow it doesn't take away from the attraction that spears through my stomach at the sight of him. I wet my lip, distracted by his chest. He's so broad, I could cling to him like a ridiculous little koala.

Instead, I grab a pair of jeans and crush them into a tiny ball at the bottom of my bag. "Getting my stuff together."

"You don't have to go."

"Actually, I do." I straighten, the bag dangling from my hands. "They have a dorm room ready for me."

The ease in his body disappears. He straightens up, his hands falling to his sides. "What?"

"They emailed me yesterday."

"And you didn't tell me?"

"It wasn't like this was supposed to be permanent." I take a deep breath. "Thank you for letting me stay here for a few days. I appreciate it."

"We're friends," he says. "You said so."

"We are. But last night wasn't... friendly."

He swallows, his Adam's apple bobbing. It's easier to focus on those details than the expression on his face.

"I'm sorry," he says. "If I pushed you to do something you didn't want to do. I thought—"

"No," I say, cutting him off. "It wasn't that. I did want it. It's just... you deserve..."

"Don't tell me what I deserve." He takes a step closer. I hold the bag to my chest like a shield. "I know what I deserve, which is what I want. And what I want is for you to be in my life, whatever that looks like. Don't you want me in your life too?"

I swallow. His gaze is an inferno. I'm blistering, but I can't look away.

"Fuck you, Sebastian," I whisper.

He blinks. His eyes shutter, the emotions swirling in their depths dimming. "Tell me, honestly and completely, that you don't want me in your life, and I will leave you alone forever. Forget about being friends. We won't even have to speak."

"I shouldn't have said yes to that date." I turn my head,

seeking a distraction, but there's nothing but Izzy's desk, cluttered now with my computer, legal pad, and stacks of half-annotated articles. I just need to push through. Continue the lie because it's for his own good. "I'm sorry that I made you think I wanted more."

He sighs. "Why do you keep lying to me, Mia? Why do you keep lying to yourself?"

"But I do want to know you." The words burst out of me like a punch. "I want to be in your life, and for you to be in mine."

He lurches forward, pulling me into a kiss. As his lips press against mine, my brain short-circuits, but once it's up and running again, I can't help but kiss him back.

After a long moment, my chest burns for air. I break off, gasping, "But this isn't what you wanted."

"I want to know you, whatever form that takes."

"If we go back to the way things were before—"

"Yes," he murmurs roughly. "Yes, fuck, that's fine. Just stop shutting me out. And stay here. It's better than a dorm, and you can have all the space you need to work."

He kisses me again, his hands cradling my face, effectively cutting off any lingering protests. He's right, this is better than a dorm—and even if it's a bad idea to stay and let myself get attached even further, it's too tempting to pass up. I'll just... figure something out. I'll find a new way to keep Project GOSMC going.

"Fine," I bite out.

He pulls back to smile at me, tugging on my hair.

"I'll pack you lunches for the week," he says. "No protein bars unless they're snacks."

22

MIA

May 13th

I'm sorry, you what?

I know you read it correctly

You're with Sebastian. You're at the house with SEBASTIAN

...How soon are you coming back from the road trip?

You haven't even wanted to talk about him, much less, like, be around him

Dorm flooded, boots ruined

He was, unfortunately, the best option

Let it be known I'm squinting my eyes in your direction

Long distance

Can you feel it?

I'm rolling my eyes

So you totally can

Does Cooper know?

Idk

Be careful

Or, you know, don't

Don't make me regret telling you this

Seb is a good guy

This would be good for you

Nothing's happening

Sure, whatever you say

May 14th

The jacket too, Callahan?

SEBASTIAN

Can't have the boots but not the jacket

Let me pay you for it

Don't you know how gifts work?

May 15th

Good luck on your game

SEBASTIAN

:)

Hopefully won't be back too late

If you are, I'm going to bed

No extra innings, got it

May 17th

Thank you for lunch

It might be saving my life right now

Even if I want to launch it at Alice's face

SEBASTIAN

Bad day?

It's not the work, it's all the shit around it

She mislabeled some data, so it completely
threw my model off

Yet it's somehow my fault

Anyway, thank you. What even is it? It's
delicious

Chana masala

I've made my own naan before, but no time
right now

May 20th

SEBASTIAN

You really played softball?

I was a pitcher

I can't believe you never told me this

I feel like I'm talking to a whole new person

Lol

I never said I was good at it

Come on

I was… decent. I had a nice pitch

You have to show me sometime

May 21st

SEBASTIAN

I'll be back late tonight. Going out with some of the team

I have observatory access tonight anyway

Where will I find you after?

Don't ask questions with an obvious answer

Wasn't sure it was so obvious

I'll wear that set you like

Blue or black lace?

May 22nd

Dr. Ellie Arroway? Seriously?

SEBASTIAN

I know how you admire Jodie Foster

Have you even seen Contact?

Nope

But let's add it to the list

I'm not coming to the game

I'll leave a jersey out just in case

Wait. What list?

A list of movies to watch

Together

Is this code for something?

Unfortunately, I do not speak binary like you do

You're the worst

Don't you know it

We're starting off with a classic

Can't fight it

Fine, what's the classic?

Point Break

Obviously

Damnit

I knew it, you're a sucker for 90s movies like me. Who can resist Patrick Swayze?

It's the surfing and homoeroticism for me

I'm not half bad at surfing, you know

Cooper is terrible at it

Which is a special kind of hilarious

Please tell me you have video

May 23rd

SEBASTIAN

Adding Clueless to the watch list

Why?

We have so many action movies on it already

Why watch a movie without action? If I wanted to watch people talking, I'd just sit in the quad

A woman after my own heart

Still adding it to the list

I'm rolling my eyes at you. Just so you know

Whenever you're ready, I've got the list and a killer popcorn recipe

Since when do you need a recipe for popcorn?

I do things the right way. You ought to know that by now, angel

Nope

Hey, I had to try it out

Good luck on the away game

May 24th

My stupid vibrator died in the flood

And I hate how dramatic that sounded

SEBASTIAN

Is this an invitation?

Perhaps

This is totally a booty call

Ugh

:)

I'll be home in ten. Just leaving the facility

I want your pussy wet already, gorgeous

23

MIA

I SETTLE ONTO THE BENCH, heave a deep sigh, and root in my bag for my lunch. After a long morning spent hunched over my computer, the sunlight and fresh air feels good, even if I didn't manage to snag the nice table by the pond. Before Sebastian, I'd probably have eaten a protein bar at my desk and called it good enough. For the past week and a half, however, he's pressed a carefully packed lunch into my hands before I can escape in the morning. The first day was a turkey sandwich with crisp lettuce and spicy mayo. The second, cold noodles with chicken and sesame sauce. Today's is a Greek salad, dressing encased in a little cup to keep the lettuce from getting soggy, plus toasted pita wedges. He even threw in a brownie, which I'm almost completely certain he made from scratch.

I wouldn't have thought he'd have the time, but he's awake a lot during the night.

Ever since I broke down that boundary and we went back to the way things were before, I've spent the night in his room.

I have all the intentions in the world to sleep in Izzy's room, but then he kisses me, and it's impossible to resist the rough drag of his fingertips on my waist and his smooth lips against mine. Unlike before, however, we're living in the same place, so after we finish, there's nowhere to go. No dorm room, no excuses to run away. I fall asleep in his arms, but more often than not, I wake up a couple hours later, alone except for the cat.

Light usually spills from the kitchen into the darkened living room, but I haven't worked up the nerve to go and sit with him. It's one thing to let him back into my life, and another to let myself be intimate with him again. Acknowledging this issue of his would inevitably lead to another level of intimacy, something deeper than physical desire. I failed on the desire front, but I can keep the feelings at bay.

I pour the dressing over the salad and stab at it with my fork.

He might claim that he's fine with being friends who fuck, but he deserves more than that. A moment of weakness, and it might as well be March again. It's selfish of me, but it feels so fucking good to have him, I just want to cling tighter. We haven't had penetrative sex again, but we've had plenty of fun with all the other stuff. How am I supposed to stay away when being near him makes my belly feel like it's full of fireworks?

Maybe by the time Penny gets back from her road trip, I'll have managed to extricate myself from his orbit. She knows that I'm staying with him, but she doesn't know about the rest.

I shove a bite of salad into my mouth as I check my phone. A text from Giana about our cousin Raquel's new boyfriend. I reply to her, then hover my thumb over Sebastian's contact.

Izzy calls me before I can decide whether to break down and text him.

When I accept the video call, I can't help the smile that crosses my face at the sight of her. She's wearing a yellow sundress with bell sleeves, and somehow, the boldness works for her. A matching headband holds her hair back. Her blue eyes sparkle as she gives me a wave. This is the third time she's called me in as many days. I don't know how she decided that I'm the person she wants to talk to on her lunch break, but I don't mind it.

"Hey," she says. "What are you eating?"

I hold up the salad container. "Courtesy of Sebastian."

She holds up her own salad. "I don't even know why I got this. I'm always excited to be healthy, and then I start eating it and it takes so long, you know? I feel like a rabbit."

I frown down at my salad. "You're right. I'm going to need to take half of this back to my desk."

"Your cave, you mean."

I roll my eyes. "Sure."

"He's still making you lunch," she says. "Interesting."

"I don't even know how he has time for it all." I show her the brownie. "I think he made these from scratch, so your brownie mix is still in the pantry."

"He only breaks out the baked goods for people he likes." She waggles her eyebrows. "Speaking of—"

"Nope," I interject. "We're friends. That's it."

"He sounded suspiciously happy when he called me the other day."

"Which had nothing to do with me." I keep my expression neutral, even if my mind is all too happy to supply me with images of the past few nights. We've fallen into our old routine so quickly, it's hard to remember why I called it off in the first place. One way or another, we end up in bed. Last night, we made out in the shower, and afterward, he feasted on me until I nearly cried. I hated and loved it in equal measure, and I know by his teasing that he could tell.

She gives me a look, but doesn't call me out on my bullshit. "I was thinking of coming to one of the games against Binghamton. Probably the last one, if I can get away. You in?"

"He's been leaving me tickets to the games," I admit. I refrain from mentioning he left the last one under the name of my favorite Jodie Foster character. As far as I know, he's never seen *Contact*, which means he put research into it. He wants us to watch it together, but if we do, we'd actually need to watch it, not use it as an excuse to make out. Jodie deserves better than that.

"Interesting," she says again. She tilts her head to the side. "Have you gone?"

"I am trying to get into a highly competitive study abroad program," I deadpan.

She sighs. "Mia. I admire your focus, but you're not just a space genius."

"It's not like we're dating," I say. "I don't have to go."

"But you want to." When I don't immediately contradict her, she smiles, pleased, as if she just extracted a confession from me. She might be set on a future in event planning, but maybe she should consider law instead. She could be a real-life Elle Woods. "It's okay to admit you want to."

"Whose side are you on?"

"Love."

I roll my eyes.

"You can't work all the time."

The first time we talked, I figured that this was better than confiding in Penny, but now I'm not sure. Izzy's tenaciousness knows no bounds. "I can if I'm serious about preparing for this symposium."

She groans, slumping down in her chair. It looks like she's in her office; framed covers of bridal magazines line the wall behind her. If I had to help someone plan weddings all day, I would lose my shit.

"You're no fun," she says. "No one is going to think you're irrevocably in love if you go to one baseball game and cheer for him. Just don't wear his jersey."

Even if I didn't wear his jersey, my presence would be just like walking into the kitchen at two in the morning. An invasion of a space that I don't belong in, even if it hurts to admit. I can't taunt him—or myself—with things we can't have.

"Maybe," I say, mostly because it's easier to agree with her. I guess I could, technically, pretend that I'm just a fan of McKee's baseball team. She makes everything sound so easy— and for her, most things *are* easy. I'm probably being uncharitable, but since when was something difficult for Izzy Callahan?

"No maybes, only firm commitments," she says with a grin. "I'm going to come to this game with you, Cooper and Penny can come if they're back from their road trip by then, and we'll pregame because I like baseball better when I'm toasted. It's going to be *awesome*."

24

SEBASTIAN

"SO, WHAT'S UP?" Hunter says as he throws the ball in my direction. "You're together now?"

I catch the ball in my glove and fire it back to him. With me in left field, Hunter takes center, and Levine, a senior with nice accuracy, handles right field. We work well as a unit of three, honed over a couple seasons playing together. Communication is important for every position, but the outfield is its own space, and we need to be aware of each other to make plays, back each other up when necessary, and avoid stepping on each other's toes.

My very first game at McKee, I chased a fly ball but forgot to call it, and Hunter and I—both wide-eyed freshmen—went down in a heap. The sting didn't come from the three runs scored or the accidental elbow to the stomach that Hunter gave me, but the exasperated look the pitcher, a senior who was clearly already done with that year's crop of freshmen, gave us.

Haven't made that mistake again, but I still think about it

way too often. I had a dream about it once, but then it morphed into my run-of-the-mill nightmare.

Hunter takes a couple steps back, lengthening the distance between the two of us. Coach Martin decided to use today's double practice to simulate a game first, then wrap things up by analyzing film. We've been tossing the ball back and forth, waiting for the pitcher to warm up so we can start the game.

We talk a lot when we're playing catch, but the further away he gets, the louder our voices will need to be to keep the conversation going. It's one thing to tell Hunter about what's going on with Mia, but I'd rather not broadcast it to the whole team. Plenty of the guys don't know who she is and, honestly, don't care much, but her name will make Rafael, at third base, perk up. Julio, too, from where he's stretched out at first.

I watch as he fields a ground ball, fires it across the diamond to Raf, and then scoops up a nice toss by the pitcher. Coach Martin is seeing if one of the rookie pitchers, back from injury, has his stuff again. If not—well, this might be a rough half inning, once we get going.

I catch the pop up that Hunter lobs my way. The sun is bright in the middle of the sky, but my sunglasses keep away the glare. "It's complicated."

"What is this, Facebook circa 2013?"

I shrug. "It's accurate."

Hunter spits, readjusting his cap. I wait until he's finished before throwing the ball back to him. He catches it neatly, then jogs over to me. His hand settles on my shoulder. "You know you don't have to go along with what she wants."

"It's what I want."

"What you wanted was a nice dinner. Candles and shit."

I pluck the ball from his glove. "Come on. Coach sees us slacking off, he'll give us the look."

Hunter doesn't step back, though. He glances at the diamond, then at me, squinting despite the baseball cap. "How did it even happen?"

"She's been staying with me." I toss the ball into the air and catch it bare-handed, since Hunter refuses to step back for a proper game of catch. "She'll keep staying with me, now. It's a quiet place for her to work."

"It's not your responsibility to give her that."

"I want to."

He shakes his head. "Be careful, man. That's all I'm going to say."

"She's part of my life." I want to smile at my own words, but I manage to rein it in. Weeks of rain and gloom, and now the sun is back in my life. It might not be exactly how I want it, but it's enough. If Hunter doesn't understand, I can't make him. "She'd be in it either way, and I like this better."

"Kirby! Callahan! Stop your chatting!"

I give Hunter a look. "Nice going."

"Understood, Coach!" As he jogs back into position, he snorts. "A quiet place to work, my ass."

I settle my cap on my head, adjust my glove, and smack my fist into the center twice. I'd like to keep thinking about Mia, but the pitcher is ready to go.

It's easy to slip into the rhythm of the game. People have asked me, on occasion, if it gets boring in the outfield, but I never felt that way, even as a little kid. Baseball isn't continuous motion. It involves lying in wait, ready to strike at precisely the right moment—and that anticipation never fails to keep me on my toes.

TWO AND A HALF HOURS LATER, I leave the field with grass stains on my knees, a sunburn on the back of my neck, and a scowl on my face.

A photographer.

At practice.

For *me*.

It's beyond ridiculous, because we were just playing a simulated game, and anyway, it's not like I'm a celebrity. There's no reason to photograph me anywhere, much less at a random midweek practice. He slunk around the fence and took a bunch of photographs, and while at first, we were confused, it quickly became obvious who he was targeting. Coach went out and spoke to him, but he was standing just far enough away from campus property that he couldn't force him to leave.

I refused to look at him, but I felt the gaze of the camera the entire time. It reminded me of the photographers who came to my parents' funeral.

I risk a glance over my shoulder as I reach the dugout. He's gone, off to send the photographs to whatever publication will have them.

Fucking asshole.

"Sebastian," Coach says. My ears prick up at the use of my first name. "Stay back a moment, okay?"

"What's Miller got to mope about?" Ozzy mutters as he passes by. "He knows where he's fucking going."

"Come on, man," Hunter says.

"What?" says Ozzy. "He probably paid the photographer himself."

I glare at him. He just smiles, giving me a cheeky little wave. I barely refrain from rolling my eyes.

It's not that 'Miller' is derogatory, exactly, but the guys know that I go by 'Callahan.' It's like if I insisted on calling Ozzy 'Oswaldo' even though I know he hates his full name. His draft capital isn't nearly as strong as mine, and since the start of the season, that's been bothering him. The MLB draft is more fluid than, say, the NFL's—with James, it was a big fucking deal that he went high in the first round. It's an honor to know that teams think I'm worth a big upfront investment, but the way things go, Ozzy and I might end up in the majors at the same time, a couple years down the line. Everyone, even the most talented college players, spends their fair share of time in the minors. Learning to hit that major league curveball is no joke.

"Why don't you give us his name, so we have the heads up for next time?" he says.

"Perrin," Coach warns. "Keep it up and you'll do laps around the bases."

Ozzy falls silent, but I feel his irritation throughout the post-game debrief. When Coach releases everyone else to the locker room to clean up and take a break before part two of our double practice, I stay in the dugout, staring at the empty field. Hunter stays, too. He gives me a slap on the back with enough force it stings.

"Ouch," I say flatly.

"Ignore him," he says. "He's always been an idiot."

"That had nothing to do with the interview?" Coach Martin asks.

I look over my shoulder at him. "No, sir. That's not happening until we play Binghamton here at home."

"Shit." He rubs his beard as he lets out a sigh. "I'll talk to the school, see what they suggest doing."

Even though Richard is one of the most recognizable men in America, he and Sandra have worked hard to keep that separate from their private lives with us. I didn't realize just how normal everything about my life was—intense training schedule aside—until I came to college. I got rid of all my social media within a month of starting at McKee. Izzy eventually wore me down and made me a public Instagram, which has exactly two pictures on it, both of me in uniform on the field. I never use it, so I have no idea why it has thousands of followers. The thought of being anything like James, who has already had to file a couple of restraining orders to protect him and Bex, is terrifying. I don't want that kind of future.

I'm just a left fielder with a nice swing. I'm not worthy of a feature on an online sports gossip site, or wherever these photographs are going to end up. That photographer only wanted my picture, not Ozzy's, or Hunter's, or anyone else's, because my father was Jacob Miller, and my adoptive father is Richard Callahan.

Richard is going to be pissed when he hears about this.

"Thanks, sir," I tell Coach. "I'm sorry."

"You've got nothing to apologize for." He takes a step closer, squeezing my arm reassuringly. "You understand? They should know better than to try to pull this shit. The athletic department won't let it stand."

"Will it get worse?"

I blurt the words before I can think better of them, my face burning. I stare at the dusty floor of the dugout. It's ridiculous to complain about it. No wonder the whole situation annoyed

Ozzy. Boo for me, so talented and privileged that people are acting like I'm already playing in the majors.

At least I still have one more season of college ball after this. One more season of playing with the teammates I've come to love in a place I feel comfortable. The draft's been screwing with my mind, but my future isn't quite here yet.

"I don't know," Coach Martin says slowly. "That would be a better question for Richard. I do know that talent comes with scrutiny, and you have talent in spades."

"I love baseball, but all the other shit—I can't do it."

"Sure, you can," he says. "You can do anything you set your mind to—that's never going to be the issue for you. I know you, Sebastian. You're someone who sticks around. You keep your head down and grind. Focus on what's important—preparing for the next game."

It should be that easy. Richard certainly makes it seem so, and my brothers and sister, too. When Izzy is in the middle of the volleyball season, she never dwells on the mistakes or missed points.

It used to be easier to tune out the noise. But what about when it's right on the edge of the fence, pointing a camera in your face? What about teammates calling you by the last name you should, by all rights, still be using, even when you've been part of a different family for years? What if when you look in the mirror, you see your father staring back at you?

And what if you're dreaming of something else all the while?

I've wished so many times over the years for more time with my parents. I used to play a game with myself, bargaining for it silently. I'd never talk to Cooper again if it meant another conversation with my father. I'd never accept another hug from

Sandra if it meant breathing in my mother's perfume one more time. I'd grow up with my mother's estranged relatives instead of the Callahans, if only I had five more minutes with my parents first.

Right now, I want more than anything to talk to my dad again.

But since I don't have that option, once Coach sends me and Hunter to the locker room to wash up before the second half of practice, I call Richard.

25

MIA

AFTER DINNER, I have every intention of locking myself in Izzy's room for the evening. Sebastian left a tray of baked ziti in the fridge; I had some standing at the counter, barely waiting for it to cool down before attacking it.

Then I dragged myself upstairs, allowed exactly fifteen minutes for mindless scrolling through Instagram, and sat down with my highlighters and pens. For the past three hours, I've been annotating papers for tomorrow's roundtable with Professor Santoro and the rest of the team. Alice reminded me several times today to make sure I had something useful to contribute. I just told her to focus on her own analysis, which I'm sure didn't win me any points with her.

Yet the moment I notice headlights in the driveway, I set down my highlighter. I didn't lie to Izzy when we last spoke. We're not dating. But that doesn't mean I'm not aware of Sebastian whenever he's nearby. I still have an article and a half to slog through, and maybe if I don't see him right now, I'll manage to keep my hands to myself, but despite those very rational thoughts running through my mind, I find myself hurrying down the stairs.

I get to the last step as he opens the door.

Part of me—a bigger part than I care to think about—wants to jump into his arms. I manage to restrain myself, pulling the sleeves of my sweatshirt over my hands instead. For half a beat, we just smile at each other. I feel, absurdly, like some housewife in an old movie. *Hello, honey.*

"Seb—"

He presses me against the front door, using the force to shut it, and kisses the breath out of me. He tastes of lip balm and sweat. The evening air still clings to his skin, slightly cool and fresh. He works my hair out of its bun, tugging on a fistful as he nips my bottom lip.

Kissing Sebastian makes me *hungry*. Not for food, or for breath, or even just for him. My soul expands, yearning for something on the horizon. Something I can taste in his kiss, feel in his hands, and sense in the air like a mirage.

He makes a low noise as he breaks away; when he leans in again, I yank him close by the collar, licking a line down his throat before finding his lips once more. I only release him when my lungs burn for air, and even then, I reach out, lacing my fingers through his.

I used to hate kissing, but something changed when he pressed his lips to mine for the first time. It was a bitterly cold January day, and my gloves fell in a puddle outside the library, and my phone was full of texts from him, and when he smiled at me in the stacks, I couldn't help it, something inside me snapped, and I dragged him to the nearest private space—an old seminar room hidden on the fifth floor of the library. It was quiet and two degrees too warm, and I felt the hunger in both of us, satiated a little more with each kiss.

Now, he squeezes my fingers as he smirks at me. "Nice to see you too."

I straighten, tossing my hair over my shoulder. The urge to pull him into another kiss is nearly overwhelming, but I stay rooted in place. "I'm sure you're starving."

The look he gives me makes me feel naked, even though I'm in a sweatshirt and leggings. "I could eat."

I manage what I hope is an appropriately stern expression, even as my stomach does a somersault. I don't think he showered before coming home, and the thought of tangling with him while I can taste the salt on his skin makes me shiver. "The pasta you made."

He pretends to think it over. "Nah. I'm starting with dessert."

He scoops me into his arms and starts up the stairs.

"Sebastian!" I twist in his grip, or try to, at least; he's too strong. When I pinch him, he just grins.

"Mia," he repeats, an amused note in his voice. "You can't greet me looking like this and not expect consequences."

He sets me on my feet in front of his bedroom door. I gesture down at myself. "You have eyes, right? Should we go get them checked?"

"You're always beautiful," he says.

A blush erupts on my face, strong enough I have no choice but to hide it with a kiss. He makes an approving noise, backing me into his room as he nips at my lip. His hands tug at my sweatshirt; I pull it over my head and let it fall to the floor. I shove down my leggings as he sheds his own clothes, chucking them in the hamper's direction. I find my way into his arms once more. Heat sparks low in my belly at the brush of his hands on my hips. When we kiss, it's less frenetic than before, more exploratory.

Still, he pushes me onto his bed. I bounce once, sitting up on my elbows to admire him. I wonder if kissing me makes him feel the same things I do. When he looks at me, does he feel that same rich, unending hunger?

By the dark promise in his eyes, I think he does.

"Lie back, sweetheart."

I do as I'm told, swallowing hard as I look at the ceiling. I set this in motion the moment I walked out of Izzy's bedroom. If I was serious about staying away, I would create boundaries.

I need to try better.

Just... not tonight.

He cages me underneath him, kissing me as a hand runs down my side. It settles on my thigh, curling possessively as his thumb rubs at the soft inner skin. I think he says something, but I can't focus on that, not when he's suddenly so close to touching my core.

The anticipation of contact makes my toes curl; I can feel my arousal, which kicked up the moment we kissed, deepening.

He swipes his tongue over mine. I dig my nails into his back, bringing my legs up to hug his hips. He presses another bruising kiss to my lips before starting down my neck and chest. He kisses all the way to my breasts, taking a nipple into his mouth while pinching the other. I arch my back, hoping for more contact, but he just mouths down my stomach instead.

"Sebastian," I can't help but whine. "Don't tease."

"Couldn't hold back even if I wanted," he says against my skin. He spreads my legs and settles between them. I'm trembling now, aching for contact. He presses a chaste kiss to the top of my sex. I tug at his hair sharply, and he just huffs out a laugh. Bastard.

"Easy," he says.

"I'm not a horse."

He laughs harder, which makes me snort. "I'm serious."

He looks up at me. "So am I, Mia Angel."

Damn him. He always knows the right moment to break out that phrase. I dig the heel of my foot into his back for punishment. "I thought you promised no teasing."

"I did, didn't I?" he murmurs.

Then he licks a long stripe down my folds.

I let out a strangled noise, my stomach clenching. I feel his laughter rather than hear it, but it feels too good to retaliate. He knows all the right places to turn me into a trembling mess, even as he avoids my clit. I bite down on my tongue, so I won't do something embarrassing like beg him to suck it. He knows it's what I need, and even if he said no teasing, he's teasing at least a *little*.

Well, screw that. I'm not going to give in.

He fucks me with his tongue as he strokes me with his fingers, deliberately avoiding that little bundle of nerves. I lift my hips, trying to force contact, but he doesn't give in. I'm soaked, but even though my stomach is in knots, I won't come without that little extra push.

"I have a present for you," he says against my inner thigh.

I run my hand through his hair. "Again?"

"I think you'll want this one." He sucks on my sensitive

skin, then bites down. I gasp softly. "Took me a while to find it, but it finally arrived."

"You have to stop buying me presents."

He grins up at me. "Nah, no way. Want it now, or after you come on my face?"

"*Sebastian.*"

"Stay still for me," he says as he slips off the bed.

I nearly whine again at the loss of his warmth. "I hate you."

My heart pounds with the lie. I'm the furthest thing from hate, or dislike, or even indifference. I haven't been indifferent to Sebastian since the moment we met outside the movie theater.

He settles back with a bag in hand. "Such a little liar."

He sounds smug enough that I circle my clit with my finger. "Maybe I'll just get myself off."

He grabs my wrist, holding my hand in place. Even though he raises a single eyebrow—cool, collected—I sense the possessive heat simmering underneath.

He might be trying to push my buttons, but I know his too.

"You wouldn't," he says.

I curve my lips into a pout. "Watch me."

"Tempting thought," he says, "but not today. Open the bag."

I already recognize it—it's the velvet pouch that Lucinda came in. Like the boots and the jacket—and even the lunches— I pause, my heart rate kicking into high gear. I think he'd be a thoughtful person to anyone in his life, but it still took effort to remember what I like. Even though I keep telling him not to buy me gifts, I don't actually want him to stop.

I pull out the toy. It's even the same purple shade that I had before. My cunt clenches at the thought of that friction exactly where I need it. He presses the button for me, and it comes to life in my hand.

"Show me your favorite setting," he says. He reaches down, stroking his cock. I stare unabashedly; he's fully hard, thick and no doubt aching like I am. "Show me, so I know how to take care of you, angel."

26

SEBASTIAN

THE PAST WEEK has been torture.

Perfect, beautiful torture.

And right now? Watching Mia use that pretty purple toy on her sopping wet pussy? That's the biggest agony so far.

She clicks through the settings as she presses the curved end against her clit. Her voice comes out breathy as she talks. I purposefully stayed away from that spot, so she must be feeling extra-sensitive. "I can't believe you found me another Lucinda."

I only semi-successfully hold back my snort. I stroke my hand down her thigh. "She had a name?"

"Obviously," she says. "I'm going to name this one... Cleopatra. Cleo for short."

"Naturally."

Her grin has an edge to it, even as she gasps. "Pay attention."

I dig my blunt nails into her thigh. "Always, angel. I haven't finished my meal yet."

The toy has a rabbit design; a thick, slightly curved part to put inside, plus another part to tease the clit. She circles her hole with the longer end, getting it wet with her own slick. Her breath comes in short bursts as she widens her legs further, putting herself completely on display for me. I grasp my cock again, stroking firmly. My balls are drawn up tight, heavy and aching with the need to come.

I won't be fucking her. I didn't decide that I wouldn't, exactly, but with things the way they are, it makes sense to keep some semblance of a boundary. I was serious when I told her I don't mind just being friends who fuck too if that's all she can give, but until I get my own feelings in check, I need to keep some distance. Even though I want to be inside her desperately, I know it would stir up too many emotions. It's better to stick to teasing and toys than to look into her eyes while I'm buried deep inside her, searching for a hint of true feelings.

Friends I can live with, especially if it involves this: Mia laid out on my bed, fucking herself with her favorite toy, looking like a goddamn masterpiece.

It's enough. It *has* to be enough.

She pushes the longer end in, gasping as she does; I squeeze the base of my cock tightly to avoid blowing my load at the delicious rasp in her voice. I watch hungrily as she fucks herself, the rabbit ears of the toy brushing her clit with every thrust. She's shaking with the effort of keeping her legs apart, so I take pity on her and help, spreading her even wider as I stroke my cock.

"How do you make yourself come?" I ask, my voice low in the room, quiet except for our breathing and the hum of the toy. "Do you keep going until you can't help yourself? What do you imagine, Mia?"

What did you imagine when you pushed me away? I want to ask. I don't. Not now, not in this perfect moment. Not when I've decided that this is more than enough for me. I might be failing at keeping my head down with baseball, but I can white-knuckle through this.

She just moans, her head falling back as she pushes the toy in all the way. I reach out and wrap my hand over hers, keeping the toy inside. She bucks, but I don't give in. She's especially beautiful like this, her breasts swaying gently with each intake of breath, her hips nearly coming off the bed.

"Sebastian," she whines.

"Look at me, gorgeous girl."

Her eyes meet mine. I press the toy in further. "Tell me."

Her lips twist before she bursts out, "You."

"You think of me?" I lean down. The motion changes the angle of the toy, and she lets out a high moan. I brush my lips against her breast. Her hand cups the back of my head, nails digging in. I swirl my tongue around her stiff nipple. "Is it like this?"

She pinches my back. "Usually, you let me come."

I bite down on her nipple—gently—in retaliation. Things are never just sweet with Mia. There's always an edge, and I love jabbing her hard enough that she lets me see it. "Details, angel."

"I fuck myself so hard, I can pretend it's you." She rushes the words, like she's hoping I won't even notice the confession, but she might as well have written them in the air with fire.

My heart thuds as they sink in. The desire to pull out the toy and slide into her velvety core nearly overwhelms me. She'd be so fucking tight, I'd have to work not to come the moment I got inside her. "Fucking hell."

She pinches me again. This time, I drag my lips down her sternum. I dip my tongue into her belly button, and like the first time I did it, all those months ago, she huffs out surprised laughter. I settle between her legs once more, easing out the toy and replacing it with two of my fingers. I crook them. As they brush against her g-spot, she squeezes around my fingers. I bring my tongue to her clit and suck on it hard. Her next cry sounds suspiciously close to a sob.

"Come for me," I whisper against her slick skin. "Let me hear you."

The toy must have put her so far over the edge that she was barely holding on, because the moment after I give the order, she screams, the sound muffled by the crook of her elbow. She squeezes around my fingers so tightly I couldn't pull them out even if I wanted to. I grab the toy and press the rabbit ears to her clit, coaxing her into another wave.

"Babe," she says hoarsely. "I can't—fuck—"

I give her clit another lick before pulling away. "Good fucking girl."

Her foot digs into my side. "Come on me."

I let out a low groan. "Jesus."

Her smile turns feline. "Let me help."

She sits up, taking my cock in hand and giving it a firm pump. My next breath comes out strangled. She runs her nail down the vein running down the length, sending a fiery ache in its wake. I clench my ass to keep from coming, but it's a losing effort. I drag her closer instead, breathing in the smell of her hair, and help her pump my cock. I can't think of a fucking thing but the urge to mark her; to spill my seed on her and see the evidence that I own some part of her, however small. When she squeezes my balls, I come with a choked-off moan, painting her breasts and belly.

She makes a noise that sounds as starved as I feel, and then we're kissing, wrapped up in each other so tightly I'm not sure where I end and she begins. I stroke a rough hand down her back, cupping her ass and squeezing. Her tongue tangles with mine. Despite coming, the ache is still there, deep inside me— an ache to have her just like this, as much as fucking possible. If I try to shove it down, it'll just come back up even stronger, so for a moment, I let myself give in to the fantasy. I work a hand between us, drawing my finger through the mess I made on her skin, and press it against her lips. She sucks my finger into her mouth, humming.

I squeeze my eyes shut briefly, focusing on that delicate jasmine scent of her hair. Mine. My Mia.

"Practice sucked," I admit quietly. "This made things better."

Her brown eyes flick up to mine as my finger slips from her mouth. "Why did it suck?"

I shake my head. "How was your day?"

She frowns. "Not great. Professor Santoro was all stressed out about lining up peer reviews for this paper she's publishing, and my latest model isn't working right, even with the updated data. Alice is up my ass constantly. Why did it suck, Seb?"

I trace my finger down her soft arm. I feel her shiver. I swallow, but the words don't want to come. It should be easy to explain, it's not that big a deal, but somehow—despite being literally naked in bed with her, my come drying on her body—it feels too personal.

"I'm going to grab some pasta." I untangle myself from her,

sliding off the bed. I grab a fresh pair of underwear from my dresser and throw them on, along with a pair of sweatpants.

The frown is still on her face. "If you're getting food, bring me a plate."

I catch her chin in my hand and brush my lips against hers. Once more for good measure. "I'll bring the rest of the tray up."

"Should we watch *Point Break*?" she asks.

That makes me smile despite myself. "Are you game?"

She pretends to think for a moment, tapping her nail against her chin. "Let's see. I think I have room in my life for another acceptably hot blond guy."

"And to be clear, who is the first one?"

"Well, I've had a Hemsworth-sized hole in my heart ever since I watched *Thor*."

"Is it his hammer? You can tell me."

Her lips twitch, but she holds in her laughter. "Honestly, it's probably the fact he gets to kiss Natalie Portman."

"And mess around with Einstein-Rosen bridges."

She puts her hand over her heart. "Sebastian, that was almost sexy."

I roll my eyes. "Beer, bourbon, or wine?"

THOSE ARTICLES WON'T ANNOTATE themselves, but I can't bring myself to feel bad about blowing off work when it means more baked ziti, a cheesy old action movie—my favorite kind—and touches from Sebastian. While he went downstairs to grab the rest of the pasta, plus a glass of bourbon on the rocks for me and a beer for him, I cleaned up in the bathroom, changed into a tank top and pajama shorts, and ran a comb through my hair. I'm usually not big on cuddling, but the past hour, wrapped up in him while we watch the movie, has been nice. Normal. If I don't think about anything beyond this moment, I can pretend that when I look at him, I just see a friend I happen to find attractive.

Sebastian kisses my neck softly. "Someone was photographing me during practice."

I tear my gaze away from his laptop, where Keanu Reeves and Patrick Swayze are parading around in all their 90s glory, and frown. "Wait, what?"

His hand, which is on my bare knee, tightens slightly. "Some creep is probably selling the pictures to a publication as we speak. I spoke to Richard and he's going to try to get anything that crops up taken down, but still. I wonder if he did it freelance, or if someone hired him. And if someone did, why, because it's fucking weird."

I reach over and pause the movie. Whatever I thought he was holding back about earlier, it wasn't this. I figured he just had a tough practice, which must happen sometimes, even when you're locked in. The last time we spoke about baseball, a couple days ago, he was still having trouble at the plate. But this? This is on a whole different level.

Indignation rushes through me at the mere thought of his privacy being violated so callously. "That sounds awful."

"It's stupid, I know there's a lot of interest in me and I should be grateful, but I just... I wish it would stop."

I wriggle around, so I'm facing him instead of sitting back against his chest, and stroke his hair away from his face. "That's not stupid. You have the right to privacy."

"I already agreed to do an interview soon, and that's going to come with an actual photoshoot." He makes a face. I don't blame him; something tells me they'll be a lot more interested in his personal life than his thoughts on baseball. I wouldn't be able to handle that either. "This is making me wish I could cancel the whole thing."

"Can't you?"

"Maybe if I do it, it'll deter other people from doing shit like this."

"Or maybe it'll draw more interest."

"There's going to be interest no matter what," he says. "With the draft, and it being a decade since the accident."

"Oh," I say softly.

His mouth twists. I run my nails over his scalp, hoping to be soothing. I never know what to say in these situations—usually when I open my mouth, I fuck things up somehow. But he's right, if he was eleven when his parents passed, it's been a decade. A decade of a different family, a different life. Even though he was young when it happened, he remembers it all, and I'd bet that's what he's thinking about right now, given the far-off look in his eyes.

"It's okay," he says eventually. "We don't have to—I just —fuck."

"The school knows, right?"

"He wasn't on university property, but my coach said he would tell the athletic department."

"Good."

He grimaces. "It's just stupid. I should be grateful, you know? I'm probably going to go high in the first round. I'm going to be set, if I can navigate the minors and get called up at the right time."

"That doesn't mean you're not allowed to have feelings about it. Even if those feelings aren't what you think they should be."

"Everyone is so excited." He bites his lip. "Why aren't I more excited?"

Before I can respond, he reaches around me and turns the movie on again.

I slide my hand from his hair down to the back of his neck, squeezing lightly. "Seb."

"Let's just watch the movie."

"Are you sure?"

"Please, Mia."

I wet my lips. The urge to push is simmering just underneath the surface, but sometimes a distraction is what someone needs, so I just turn around and settle back into his arms. He wraps an arm around my belly. The weight of it grounds me.

"Thank you," he mumbles.

I hope this is grounding him, too.

A KNEE TO THE STOMACH wakes me.

I gasp, my eyes flying open. As I blink in the blue dark, I remember where I am. Sebastian's bed. *Point Break* and baked ziti. Baseball and photographers. We fell asleep almost the second the credits started to roll, wrapped up in each other.

My belly aches as I take in a breath. Sebastian's arms are still around me, holding tightly, but he's thrashing around. We're dangerously close to the edge of the bed. My heart thuds, panic flooding my half-awake senses. "Seb."

"No," he says, his voice filled with anguish. "No no no—"

"Sebastian," I say, my voice cracking in the middle of the word. I'm frozen; I need to force myself to move so we don't topple to the floor in a heap. I try to wriggle out of his grip, but he's too strong. "Sebastian, wake up."

"Don't," he cries. "Please."

That 'please' tears through me like a bullet. I pull at his arms until his grip breaks. Panting, messy hair falling into my eyes, I press him down against the bed. He nearly bucks me off, but I hang on, digging my nails into his arms. "Sebastian, wake up!"

I thought I'd understood what Izzy meant when she said he

has nightmares. This is on a completely different level, and the adrenaline racing through my body won't calm the fuck down. I can practically feel my heart in my throat as I beg him to wake up. What do you do when someone won't wake from a nightmare? Slap them? Shake them? Keep pleading until they snap out of it? Why the hell don't I know the answer?

"Sebastian," I say again, my voice sharper. There's a blur of orange out of the corner of my eye; Tangerine, streaking off the bed, no doubt scared by the loud noises. "You're having a nightmare. Wake *up*!"

His eyes finally fly open—but they're as wild as an animal's. His body is rigid. I cup his cheek; his skin is clammy.

I whisper his name this time, rubbing my cheek against his.

Relief chases away the adrenaline when I feel his hand cup the back of my head. His fingers stroke through my knotted hair gently.

"Mia," he murmurs. His voice is hoarse. "What..."

"I think you were having a nightmare." I pull back so I can meet his gaze. "I couldn't get you to wake up."

His eyes close briefly. "Fuck. I'm sorry."

"Are you okay?"

"How about you?"

I wince, but I don't want to lie to him. "You, uh, kicked me. But it's okay, it's not—"

He sits up so fast, he nearly knocks me backwards. "What?"

28

SEBASTIAN

I HURT HER.

I fucking *hurt* her.

I sit up in an instant, my heart hammering even harder than before, if possible. I'm all keyed up; the nightmares always leave me with more adrenaline than I can handle. Sometimes I just throw myself onto the floor and do push-ups to force the bloody images from my mind, but that's not an option right now.

"Show me. How badly does it hurt?"

Mia's face looks pale in the dark, her eyes huge and nearly black. Her hair, messier than earlier, hangs around her face; she pushes it behind her ears. "Just my stomach. It's fine."

"Like hell it's fine." I reach out tentatively, brushing my hand over her stomach. Her tank top bunched over her ribs in her sleep, so I stroke her bare skin. She doesn't wince, but knowing her, she could be holding back. "Shit."

"It's fine, Seb."

"Don't lie," I say, a touch too sharply. I swallow. I need to calm the fuck down, but the nightmare is still a rabid beast prowling around my mind. Shattered glass. Blood on leather. My father shouting, throwing his arm over my mother like that would help any more than her seat belt.

The memory played on a loop, morphing with each impact. Richard and Sandra in the front seat instead. James and Cooper. Izzy, her body broken, blood leaking from her mouth.

In the last iteration before Mia shook me awake, I was driving, and Mia was in the passenger seat. I flung my arm out to save her, but I couldn't. One moment she was screaming, and then she was silent.

"I'm fine," she snaps back. "What about you? What happened?"

"I... I have nightmares sometimes." I grimace, jerking my hand through my hair. "I'm so sorry. I didn't mean to hurt you."

"Don't be an idiot, I know that." She scoots closer, taking my hand in hers. She squeezes tightly. "It doesn't even hurt anymore. Do you want to talk about it?"

"This is why I prefer not to sleep." I'm shaking, so I squeeze her back, hoping she doesn't notice. The very last thing I saw before I woke up was her, those golden-brown eyes blank and unseeing, crimson blood smeared on her face. A piece of glass lodged in her throat, cutting straight through the artery. I force myself to study her. She's fine. There's no blood, no broken glass. We're safe in my bedroom, and she's unharmed, aside from my kick.

I need to pull it together.

"Tell me about it," she insists. Her voice is soft again, coaxing me into answering. "Don't keep it inside."

Aside from the therapist I had throughout middle and high

school, and Cooper—although I haven't told him every detail—I haven't spoken about my nightmares. But this is Mia. Not Dr. Barnes or my brother.

Just Mia.

She's safe.

I pull her into a hug so tight I'm worried I'm hurting her again, but before I can force myself to break away, she hugs back, holding me just as tightly. I bury my face in the place where her neck meets her shoulder, taking in a deep, shuddering breath. Tears burn my eyes.

She smells like jasmine.

She's safe.

She's my friend.

She's safe and sound and willing to listen.

"I dream about the accident," I whisper. I went to sleep shirtless; her fingers dig against my bare back. It doesn't hurt, but the pressure keeps me grounded. It's like Cooper's hand on my shoulder, but better. "But it's not just them. It's... it's Richard and Sandra, and my siblings. I even saw you, this time."

She blinks, a stripe of moonlight illuminating part of her face. Her long eyelashes frame her eyes so beautifully. How come I've never noticed her eyelashes? I've looked at her so many times, and I've studied her like she's a painting hanging in the Met, but right now, I might as well be seeing her for the first time. She has a freckle on her earlobe that I never noticed either.

"What happened?" she asks. "I know you were in the car."

"All three of us went out to dinner," I say. "The season had just started, and it was my dad's first night off in two weeks. My mom's birthday was coming up. I remember—fuck, I remember

I didn't want to be there. I thought it was boring, so I was happy that they let me bring a book to the restaurant."

"What was it?"

"What?"

"The book."

"It was a biography for kids about Joe DiMaggio."

"Naturally."

Her slight teasing makes my lips quirk up. "It was pouring that night. We got soaked in the thirty seconds it took to get from the restaurant door to the car. My parents were in a good mood, though. My dad had gotten off to a nice start for the season, and he bought my mother a diamond necklace for her birthday. Gave it to her early since he was supposed to be on the West Coast for a road game on the actual day."

That diamond necklace, absurdly, didn't break in the crash. Glass in my mother's throat, but that necklace stayed intact, shining in the light from the sirens. Sandra has it now, along with the rest of my mother's jewelry. She and Richard handled my parents' estate, and all that stuff is in storage, waiting for me to do something with it.

"That's sweet," she says. Her thumb rubs over my knuckles. "I'm sure she loved it."

"She did. And she loved that we got a whole evening with him. During the season—it's hard, you know? He was around when he could, if there was a day in between series or a day game instead of a night game, but most of the year, it was Mom and me, and lots of phone calls." I swallow, trying to dislodge the lump in my throat. It's hard to imagine that being me one day, so it's easier not to think about it. "It happened so fast. One minute we were driving, and the next, we hit a tree. They said that my father must not have seen the curve in the road, and by the time he tried to course correct, it was too late. The road was wet, and we just spun out."

Her grip on my hand tightens. A silent invitation to continue.

I gather all my courage and say, "He put his arm out, trying to... you know. To save my mother and... and me. But it didn't do any good. They took the impact head-on."

"Oh, Sebastian."

Her voice is so soft, and normally I would love to hear her speak with such tenderness, but right now, it might make me fucking cry. She doesn't say she's sorry, or try to placate me, or any of the things other people have done when they've heard this story. She just keeps looking at me, stroking my knuckles. Letting me set the pace of our conversation. I could stop here, and she'd roll with it.

But I keep going. I've never felt the urge to share all the details of this story with anyone, but it feels important, somehow, that I get to the end. I want her to know it. I trust her with it. With each stroke of her thumb against my skin, my panic fades a little more.

"So sometimes I just... dream of it again. I'm trapped in the backseat, and people I love die in front of me, and there's nothing I can do but watch."

I bite the inside of my cheek, staring at the hazy outline of our evening together: the empty tray that we'd eaten the pasta from, my beer bottle and her bourbon glass. My laptop, decorated with an OBX sticker, on my nightstand next to the Anthony Bourdain memoir I'm reading. After the mess with the photographer earlier, my evening ended up being perfect—because any time spent with Mia is perfect—but that didn't matter once I fell asleep.

"I wish I could have helped them. I just froze. I don't even think I screamed. I froze, and I stared at them, and eventually a passing car called in the accident. I didn't even think to find one of their cell phones."

"You were just a kid," she says. "No one expected you to."

"Still." My voice cracks on the word. "Maybe if I actually *thought*, I could have avoided losing them both."

By the end of the sentence, my voice is loud enough that it echoes in the air.

I've thought about it ever since that moment, but I've never said it aloud.

Most likely, nothing I could've done would have changed the outcome.

But I don't *know*, because I didn't act, and I lost them.

And tonight, in my fucking nightmare, I didn't act, and I lost my family and Mia, one after the other.

She scoots closer, cupping the back of my head. Her fingers curl in my hair. When her lips press against mine, I feel a tear slip down my cheek. I squeeze my eyelids shut. I hold my breath, trying to stifle the sob that wants to work its way out of my throat.

"Breathe," she whispers. "We'll do it together. Hold it and count to five."

It takes a couple tries, but I manage it. Three seconds. Four seconds. Five seconds, then a breath out.

"You're not there," she says. She presses another kiss to my mouth, hard enough that our teeth mash together. The sensation tethers me to her. To reality. "You're here with me."

She tugs on my arm until I fall back into bed with her. I end up with my head pillowed on her stomach, feeling the gentle rise and fall of it as she breathes. She runs her fingers through my hair. More quiet, ordinary comfort. It feels like we're in a little bubble, separate from the rest of the world. It's warm and safe in here, and memories are just memories, no matter how much they try to snap and bite.

Usually, after a nightmare, I stay awake the rest of the night, but my eyelids are heavy, and at least tonight, I don't have to face it alone.

Sleep comes again, and this time, it's deep and dreamless.

29

SEBASTIAN

June 3rd

RICHARD

They're discussing the draft on ESPN's college minute. You're trending at 10th overall.

Wow

That's higher than before, I wonder why

The Reds owner said publicly that he's hoping you'll be on the team eventually.

We spoke to the reporter, too, Zoe Anders. Kept it on you and your potential.

We would love to come up for a game sometime soon.

How are things at the house?

Fine. I'm leaving for a couple games against Albany tomorrow

What about Cooper's cat? Did you find a sitter?

I have a friend staying with me, she's going to take care of her

She?

Just a friend. She's Penny's friend, actually

The draft is almost here. Keep your eyes on the prize, Sebastian.

June 4th

Is Alice behaving herself today?

MIA ANGEL
Barely

I wish I could kick her so bad

I wish I could kick Raf

Right in the balls

He's been singing off-key to Hamilton the entire trip

I thought you loved history

You're the only person I know who reads nonfiction for fun

There's history, and then there's Rafael Dominguez pretending he knows how to rap

This is a 3-game trip, right?

Yeah. Thanks again for watching Tangy

I sent Penny a ton of pics this morning

They should be home pretty soon after you get back from Albany

June 4th – Later

MIA ANGEL

Good luck on today's game

Thanks, angel

Don't make me break out the frowny face

What if I told you I like it

:(

:)

How did you sleep last night?

Albany has a super ugly campus

I miss my kitchen

June 5th

MIA ANGEL

I can't believe you made me dinners, too

The rice bowl was delicious, thank you

I didn't want our future Federation leader to starve

Have you actually ever seen a science fiction movie, or are you just going off of pop culture?

Does Marvel count?

Yes, but it's in a different sub-category

Then yes

I'm making several additions to the movie list

Finally

It's on the notepad on my desk

When are you getting home tomorrow? Too late to watch one?

That's never stopped me

No movies until I greet you properly, though

Define 'properly'

:)

30

SEBASTIAN

"SURE YOU DON'T WANT to come out with us?" Rafael asks from the doorway. "Julio found a decent bar. You could test the waters."

I just pull my t-shirt over my head, stifling a yawn—and a wince. I tweaked my finger while making a sliding catch during the game earlier, and while it's not serious by any means, the trainer still sent me to my room with a huge ice pack and strict instructions to let her know if the bruise feels concerning. "I need to ice my fucking finger."

"Oh, yeah." He taps out a message on his phone and slides it into his pocket. "Forgot about that. Want me to see if any girls are interested in coming up after? A couple chicks at the game were checking you out."

"I'm still with Mia, you know."

He crosses his arms over his chest, drumming his fingers against his arm. "Did I miss something? You dating now?"

"No." I grab the ice pack and set it over my finger. It's

swollen and tender to the touch, but the bruising isn't too bad. "We're just hanging out."

"Who's to say she's not out right now, picking up someone else?"

"She's not." I probably say it too quickly, but I can't tamp down the rush of possessiveness that pours through my veins at the mere thought of her hooking up with someone else. We haven't spoken about it explicitly, but I know that we're exclusive again. We might not be dating, but we're not going to anyone else for sex, either of us.

Rafael snorts. "Okay, man. Do what you want, I guess."

I give him a pointed look. "What I want is to call her, but I need to be alone for that."

He puts his hands up placatingly as he backs away. "Whatever. Enjoy. Text if you end up wanting to join us."

When the door shuts behind him, I flop against the bed. One good thing about most of the guys going out: Hunter, who is bunking with me on this trip, is going too, so I have privacy to call Mia.

I close my eyes, breathing in the bleach smell of the hotel sheets. There was a time when every away trip was exciting. The high school tournaments were fun, and the travel during the playoffs my first year at McKee was a party. Lately, though? It's more of a hassle than anything. I'd rather be at home with Mia than humping all my gear to fucking SUNY Albany. I'm already dreading the grind of the minors, which will involve way more long bus trips and second-rate hotels. The design of the baseball season at any level means that most of your life will be long-distance.

I press the heels of my hands into my eyes. My finger protests as the ice pack plops onto my chest.

I shouldn't call Mia.

This trip is forcing there to be a bit of distance between us, and that's not a bad thing, especially after the nightmare I had the other night. Those first few seconds after I woke up, I thought I was still dreaming. She looked like an angel in the moonlight, her hair spilling over her bare shoulders, delicate perfection in every feature on her face. But it wasn't a dream. She was there and she wanted to help. Maybe it was because of the quiet of the night, which always makes me feel alone— although less alone with her there—or the fact I was so shaken by the images my mind couldn't stop spitting out, but I spilled my guts to her in a way I never have with another person.

Ever since we started hooking up again, I've tried to hold back just enough to prevent a slide into feelings I don't want to have to shut down later, but in that moment? I would have given her anything in the world. I would have gotten on my knees and begged for her love. I've pretended that what we have is enough, but it isn't. It's never been casual for me, not for a moment.

My chest aches. I rub it as I stare at the ceiling. Someone clearly didn't get the memo about leaving stucco ceilings in the past.

I pull up her contact in my phone. My thumb hovers over the call button.

What the hell did I fuck up? What did I do to turn her away after things had been going so well? Why aren't I enough for her, when I know I would treat her better than anyone else in the whole goddamn world?

I stab the button. The phone rings once. Twice. Three times.

"Sebastian?"

Hearing my name from her lips is a balm on my soul. I sit up, putting the ice pack back on my finger. "Hey. You busy?"

"I'm just at the lab."

"Do you get overtime?"

She snorts. I've never been inside the lab where she works, but I can picture her sitting in a desk chair in leggings and an oversized t-shirt, her blue light glasses perched on her nose. Her hair is probably twisted into a messy bun, and I'd be willing to bet that she's wearing the gold hoops she's been favoring lately. I rub Dad's medallion.

"No," she says. "But I was in a meeting for half the afternoon, so I'm trying to make up the time now. How was the game?"

"We won. And I got two hits. A single and a double."

"That's good."

"Yeah. Messed up my finger, but it's not too bad."

"Which one?"

"Just the pinky."

"At least it's not one of the important ones," she says, a teasing note in her voice.

I grin, even though she can't see it. "You're a dirty girl sometimes, di Angelo."

"You like it."

"I do." I settle against the pillows, stretching out my legs. "Although I guess you're too busy for fun right now?"

"What, you miss me that much?"

"Yeah. You're all I've been able to think about since the moment I left the field."

"Oh," she says.

I swallow, pushing past the awkwardness. Maybe this isn't the best way to bring up her unfinished promise to me, but I can't stop thinking about how she helped me in the aftermath of that nightmare.

"I know I've left it alone," I say. "And I can keep being patient if you need that. But you promised me something, and you haven't kept up your end of the bargain."

She's silent for a long moment. I know she didn't hang up on me because I can hear her quiet breathing. Even though she's down in the Hudson Valley and I'm all the way up in Albany, it feels like there's a golden string between us, shining in the dark. I wonder if it only glows for me, or if she can feel it too.

I can't be the only one. Whatever makes her hold back so much, it's not for lack of feeling. If she would just let me in, I'd know how to help her.

"I can't," she says. "Not like this. Not over the phone."

"Whatever it is," I start, "I won't judge you."

Another silence.

"It's not like that," she says eventually.

"Then what's it like?"

"Look outside," she says.

I slide off the bed and walk to the window. Heavy curtains cover it, but I push them aside, peering up at the dark. "What am I looking at?"

"Can you see the moon from where you are?"

It takes me a second, but I find it. "What phase is it in?"

"Waning crescent. See how it's just a sliver? It'll be a new moon again soon."

"It's pretty." I spend enough time awake at night that you'd think I'd notice the moon often, but I can't remember the last time I looked directly at it. When I play night games, the moon and stars are far away, nearly hidden by the stadium floodlights.

"I'm looking at it too." There's a rustling sound on her end of the line. "I miss you."

At her words, my heart starts racing. I press my fingertips to the glass. The sliver of moon shines like a pearl, seemingly small enough to cup in my palm. For a moment, I can almost convince myself that the golden string is tied to the moon, and if I tug on it, she'll be able to feel it. That even if we aren't saying all we mean right now, she'll get the message. "And I miss you."

"Sebastian?"

"Yeah?"

"Will you stay on the line with me until I get back to the house?"

I swallow down everything—the wishes, the dreams, the aching, sticky-hot want—and hope I sound halfway to normal. I can always give more when it comes to her. "Always, angel."

"SEE? SOME OF THESE QUESTIONS are random, but then others are way too personal."

I peer at Sebastian's laptop. On the screen is a list of questions the reporter from *The Sportsman*, Zoe Anders, sent over to "get him thinking" ahead of their interview. It's an odd mix. The first one asks if he's a Reds fan, or if he switched to the Mets or Yankees after years of living on Long Island, but then directly underneath it, she wants to know if he's had any contact with relatives of his father and mother.

The moment I see it, my mind starts mulling over the possibilities. I guess it makes sense that the reporter would wonder about it too, but it's his past. He doesn't have to share it with anyone, especially not a magazine. "You could decline to answer, right?"

He swipes his hand through his hair, then settles his baseball cap back on his head, backwards. "I guess so. The short answer is that no, I haven't."

I look at him sideways. I'm curious too, but that feels like a question I don't have the right to wonder about, considering the fact we're just friends. This is what I wanted, after all, even if it's getting so hard to remember why. "Just tell her you're only going to answer questions that are directly about baseball."

"I guess." He grimaces. "I don't want her to do digging on her own and make up a story, though. My mom's relatives didn't want to adopt me because they hated my dad. It's not that deep."

I can't help myself. "Why?"

"He got her pregnant before they got married. They thought she was settling, that she could have done better." He puts his hand on my knee, squeezing lightly. He laughs shortly. "And then she died, and they *really* thought she could have done better."

"That's awful."

"I don't want anything to do with them anyway." He shuts his laptop firmly and puts it on the coffee table next to mine. "Haven't heard from them in years. I love baseball, but the rest of it is already too much. According to Izzy, those stupid photographs are all over Instagram."

"That is something nice about astrophysics," I say dryly. "No one is going to ask me for an interview."

He winds his arm around my waist and pulls me into his lap. I straddle him, adjusting my skirt so it still covers my butt.

"I have some questions," he murmurs, kissing my neck. His hands stroke down my bare thighs, making me shiver. "They're of a personal nature."

"Oh?"

He pushes up my skirt a couple inches. "Maybe a demonstration would be more effective."

My stomach clenches at the sensation of his fingertips on my sensitive skin. The last time we fucked was over the phone a few days ago; he called me from his hotel room during the Albany trip. I still feel bad about it, but I distracted him rather than give him the truth I owe him, first with the moon and a confession I didn't mind making, and then, when I got back to the house, with some long-distance dirty talk. It was the coward's way out, but I couldn't bring myself to talk about why I ghosted him.

"It would need to be fast. Penny said they'd be back soon."

He bites my jaw lightly before working his way up to a proper kiss. He traces over the lacy edge of my underwear. "I can be quick."

I want to ride him on the couch. I want his hands on my ass, digging in, and to feel just how deep he can get from this angle. I haven't had it that way in months, and I know he's been holding back.

I pull my shirt over my head and let it fall to the floor. I'm wearing his favorite bra of mine, the lime green one with a tiny bow in between the cups. He groans at the sight, burying his face in them. He slips one strap down my arm, then the other.

"It's been so long since you fucked my pussy," I can't help but murmur as he sucks my nipple through the thin fabric.

He muffles a moan against my skin.

I drag my nails down his back. "I'd be so good for you, babe, please."

"I know you would," he rasps. He slips his hand underneath my skirt and spanks me. He doesn't do it hard enough to hurt—although the tease is enough to make me want that. "You make the prettiest goddamn noises when I'm inside you. Angel, I remember them all."

I rock against him. I smile when his breath hitches; I can feel the growing bulge in his pants. I keep rocking gently as I knock the baseball cap off his head, wind my hands through his hair, and tug. "You could use a toy in my ass, too."

"You're gonna kill me."

My smile widens as I kiss him. He's close to giving in. "If it's too much, I can stop."

"Don't you dare."

I pull up his t-shirt, running my fingers over the hard lines of his abs. "Oh yeah? You sure you can handle it, Callahan?"

He throws his t-shirt onto the floor next to mine. His eyes glitter as he unhooks my bra. I let it fall. He rolls one nipple between his thumb and forefinger, lowering his head to capture the other in his mouth. I clench my core from the sensation. My body is yearning for more; my panties are damp already. If I need to finally share the truth that I owe him to get him inside me the way I've been dreaming about, I'll do it. I scratch his scalp, letting my head fall back.

"Always for you, Mia Angel." His voice might be teasing, but his eyes betray a deeper seriousness. "Even if you refuse to just tell—"

The front door opens.

Fuck. Fuck fuck *fuck*.

"Oh, come on," I hear Cooper say. "Not again."

———

PENNY INSPECTS ME up and down as she crosses her arms over her chest. She has a slight sunburn on her face, and her hair, braided back, is frizzy. She's wearing a Grand Canyon t-shirt and I see a tattoo on her wrist, but I don't dare ask about it.

The last time I saw her this indignant was... well, it was when she tried to talk to me after she and Cooper realized that Sebastian and I were more than friends. The moment she got to the hotel in Florida, where the Frozen Four was happening, she called me, and I couldn't bring myself to get into it all. I knew right then that I was going to stand Sebastian up, and the last person I wanted to admit that to was the girlfriend of his brother. No one tells you how much it sucks, sometimes, when your best friend falls in love.

I clear my throat. The moment everyone processed the situation—the situation being me and Sebastian, shirtless, making out on the living room couch like total idiots—and I managed to get my shirt back on, she dragged me upstairs. Penny has seen me shirtless before, thanks to the perils of roommate life, but I could have lived without flashing Cooper.

Now I'm sitting on the end of Izzy's bed, feeling like I just got called to the headmistress's office. And I should know, because I went to Headmistress Donnelly's office way too often in high school. I'm still amazed that I didn't get expelled after the accidental fire in the chemistry lab.

I can feel myself wilting under Penny's gaze the longer she stares at me, so I just start blathering. "You have to tell me all about the road trip. What happened to that poem you wrote for your mom?"

"How long, Mia?"

I try for a smile. "You look good, Pen."

"Mia. How long?"

"The pictures you posted on Instagram are so pretty. You actually got matching tattoos? Was it your idea? I thought you said you were too scared of needles to get one."

"Mia—"

I swallow, pressing forward. "I missed you. I didn't want to bother you while you were getting alone time across the country with your hockey player, but I didn't realize until you were gone just how much we talk. I have a funny story about Tangerine to—"

"Maria Daphne di Angelo!" she exclaims.

I blink. "Um, rude."

"I'm sorry." She unwinds her hair from the braid and shakes it out, taking a deep breath. She flops down next to me. "But you told me I'm allowed to use your full name in emergencies."

"Is this an emergency, Penelope Ann Ryder?"

Her mouth drops open. "Rude!"

"You were rude first."

"I would say this definitely constitutes an emergency," she grumbles. "Are you with Sebastian?"

To be honest, it was so easy to pretend that summer break would last forever, and that I'd never have to talk to anyone about my kind-of-sort-of relationship with Sebastian, that I didn't come up with a plan for this exact moment. I should have, but instead I let myself get caught up in the balance we struck with each other, and now, just like in April, I'm left floundering. And this time, I can't run down the stairs and leave everyone behind. I wouldn't even have anywhere to run *to*, since this is where I live right now.

"Fine, yes," I admit. "We're sleeping together. Happy?"

She blinks. "Well, yes. Ecstatic, actually, but that's beside the point. Why didn't you tell me? When did you start up again?"

"A couple days after I started staying here."

"Oh, wow. So basically the whole time we were away."

"I guess," I say helplessly.

She lurches forward and hugs me. "This is amazing!"

I spit out a bit of her hair and hug her back automatically. Penny is pretty much the only person I never mind hugs from—although I suppose Sebastian is on that list too now. "We're not dating."

"Wait." She pulls back. "But I thought..."

"It's just... it's like before." I grimace. "We're just friends, but with sex."

"Oh," she says with a frown. "Mia... are you sure about that?"

"I'm not forcing him into anything," I say quickly. "It was his idea, actually."

She waves her hand impatiently. "I mean, is it actually what you want?"

I look to the side. The last time I made Izzy's bed, I arranged the pillows in a tower, but it must have been off-balance, because half of them are on the floor now.

When Sebastian had that nightmare before he went to Albany, it was impossible to pretend that it didn't mean anything. There was nothing casual about soothing his panic or holding him in my arms.

I stayed awake long after he fell asleep again, petting his hair, focusing on the way my heart thudded in my chest and imaginary butterflies did swooping dances in my belly. I played a game with myself. Would I rather be in the dorm room I was supposed to have right now? Definitely not. Would I rather be at the University of Geneva? Maybe eventually, but not right then. I was glad I was there for him and that he didn't have to suffer through yet another nightmare alone.

If it happens again, I want to be the one who is there, ready to help.

There's nothing casual about that. Nothing friendly. But helping him through a difficult night isn't the same thing as dating. Feeling something twist in my chest at the sight of him using my stomach for a pillow doesn't mean I should risk everything changing.

And I can't explain all that to Penny, so I just shake my head. "Tell me about the trip."

"I think we should talk about this."

"I don't want to," I snap. I hate the way my tone makes her face fall. "There's nothing to talk about," I add, softer. "We're friends. We're sleeping together. There's nothing wrong with that."

"I didn't say there was. Just that..." She trails off, shaking her head. "Whatever. The road trip was amazing. He's... he's it, Mia. He's it for me."

She holds out her wrist. There's a short phrase inked in black on the inside, but I don't recognize the language. "Is this from *Lord of the Rings*?"

She nods, biting back a smile. "'I love you' in Sindarin. I wanted to do something special with him—something to bind us together before things change. I know we have two more semesters, but still, our lives are going to be a lot different when he's in the NHL."

I swallow. Penny is lucky to be so invested in Cooper's passion. She was a serious athlete herself, so she knows what it takes, and her father is Cooper's coach, so there's no way she's surprised by the level of commitment. I'm sure she's going to have no problem working her life around his career, just like Sebastian's mother did for his father. She's even luckier that

she's a writer. She can bring her future career anywhere. If
Sebastian and I tried to make a relationship work while he was
playing baseball and I was in a graduate program, we'd never
see each other. Forget pining over him during a three-day jaunt
to Albany. I'd be alone and guilty, instead of just alone.

I manage a smile. "It's beautiful, Pen."

"Are you sure that you and Seb—"

I stand, smoothing my skirt. "Let me see if he needs help
with dinner. I think he planned on making something for us."

"You cook with him?" she calls as I hurry downstairs. "I
thought you hated cooking!"

I bite my lip as I resist the urge to reply. When Penny
strong-armed me upstairs for our little chat, Cooper and
Sebastian were in the living room, sitting across from each other
awkwardly. Now, I hear voices coming from the kitchen.

I'm about to tiptoe upstairs when I hear Cooper say my
name.

32

SEBASTIAN

"YOU COULD HAVE GIVEN me a head's up, you know," Cooper says. He moves away from the refrigerator, beer in hand, so I can get out the ingredients I'll need for spaghetti carbonara. It's a little early to start cooking dinner, especially a pasta dish that comes together in less than half an hour, but anything to avoid meeting my brother's eyes. I'm not necessarily embarrassed by what he walked in on—although I do feel bad for Mia—but I didn't plan to broach the subject of getting involved with her again like *this*. "It's not like I *wanted* to see her tits."

I drag my hand over my face. "Don't talk about her tits."

He snorts. "I'm not. I'm not going to say a fucking word, ever, about my girlfriend's best friend's rack. Although I guess now we're even."

"I have tried very hard to erase the image of you and Penny from my mind."

"You do have a bedroom in this house, you know."

"Like that stopped you before." I grab a skillet and slam it on top of the stove. "You got back earlier than we expected."

When it was just the two of us living here, it was easy to forget about normal life. I could pretend that our playing house would go on forever. I've spent the last few days thinking about the moment I woke up from that nightmare. The relief I felt when I saw her in bed with me, safe and beautiful in the moonlight, settled something deep and unendingly restless in my chest. I haven't been able to focus on a fucking thing but that feeling. I missed her when I was on the road trip. Our phone call was nice, but I wish I hadn't needed to leave in the first place, right before normal life came crashing in again in the form of my brother.

He settles atop one of the kitchen stools and leans his elbows on the counter. "So, you were going to lie to me."

I add a couple tablespoons of olive oil and butter to the skillet, turning up the heat. "What? No."

"Because of her?"

"It's just not how I would have wanted you to find out, dumbass."

He takes a sip of beer. "What is this, anyway? Are you together?"

I can't meet his eyes right now. I cut an onion in half and peel away the skin. The back of my neck feels hot. "No."

"So, what was that?" he says. "A bit of casual face-sucking?"

"You did plenty of that before you met Penny."

He puts his hands up. "I'm not judging what you were doing. Just who you were doing it with."

"You know her."

"Yeah, exactly. I know a lot about her. For example, that she walked out on you. But I don't know a thing about that whole fucking situation except for the fact that I've never seen you that upset over a girl, and now what? You're going back for more?"

I focus on dicing the onion. When it's ready to go, I move on to the nice slab of pancetta I picked up at the grocery store today. When I planned this meal earlier, I envisioned cooking it with Mia, then settling down at the table, the four of us, to hear about the road trip. I have a nice bottle of Sancerre chilling in the fridge, plus red velvet cupcakes from the bakery in town. I was prepared to put on a show—just friends, nothing more— like we did for months.

Instead, the whole thing is out in the open, and I still don't know why Mia ghosted me in the first place.

I just hope that she doesn't use this as an excuse to run away again.

"I asked her out," I admit. "The day you walked in on us, I asked her to dinner. I asked her once before, but she wasn't ready. This time she said yes, but the moment she saw you, she backtracked. Fucking left. I texted her about the date anyway, but she stood me up and decided to pretend I didn't exist."

He grimaces. "Because of me?"

"Don't know. Maybe it just got too real. Maybe I did something without realizing it." I hate the bitter note in my voice, but I can't help it. "And right now, we're sleeping together again. Just that. We're friends. It's not a big deal."

"But you still want more."

I put the onions and pancetta into the skillet. They start sizzling immediately in the butter and olive oil mixture. I'm so familiar with this recipe that I could do it blindfolded, but right now I wish I never planned to make it in the first place. "I mean, yeah."

"Seb."

My brother's voice is wheedling, urging me to look at him. I pour half a cup of cream into a prep bowl. I need to separate the egg yolks so I can whisk them with the cream, grate the parmesan cheese, and chop the parsley for garnish. I always add in peas, too, even though the recipe I work from doesn't. A recipe like this is easy to navigate. All recipes are, with patience and a bit of skill. I wish I had more to focus on— anything to avoid this conversation. I should have made dessert myself.

"Sebastian, seriously."

I crack open one of the eggs against the edge of the counter.

"What?"

"She's just stringing you along."

I accidentally puncture the egg yolk. It runs all over my hand, mixing with the whites. I throw it out and rinse off my hands. "It's not like that."

"You need to get out. End it. She's fucking with you because she knows you won't push her away."

"Did I miss the part of this conversation where I asked for your advice?"

"Dude, come on. If she wanted to be with you, she'd be with you."

I manage to separate out the yolk this time around, then make quick work of the other two. I give the mixture in the skillet a too-vigorous stir; a couple pieces of pancetta jump ship. There's a pit in my stomach the size of the moon. "I get it, you're a relationship guy now. Good for fucking you, but not everyone is so lucky."

"You could have that with someone else. Sure, Mia is appealing, I like hanging out with her and she means a lot to

Pen, but there's no way she doesn't know how you feel. She's ignoring it because she likes fucking you. She's acting like a—"

"Don't fucking say it," I snap. "Don't do it, Cooper."

He walks around the counter, jerking his hand through his hair. "I'm trying to help you."

I laugh incredulously. "I know what you're doing. Stop it."

"You're just going to let her play with your heart until she gets bored and moves on?"

I move the skillet away from the heat. "I'd rather have this than nothing."

"You deserve more. You at least deserve the truth about why she fucking ghosted you."

"And she's going to tell me eventually."

He raises an eyebrow as he takes another sip of beer. "Oh, yeah? Did she promise you that before or after she started sucking your cock again?"

I back him against the counter. The beer slips from his hand, crashing against the floor, but neither of us moves to clean it up. Adrenaline rushes through me; my hand clenches into a fist. My bruised finger aches. He stares at me with those stalwart blue eyes, unblinking and unwilling to back down.

The only time we ever fought—a proper fight out on the lawn, with kicks and punches—was back in senior year of high school, when a girl we both had feelings for played us off each other. I thought she liked me, Cooper thought she liked him, and in reality, she was sleeping with us both. Richard let us have it out until we both had bloody noses and were breathing so hard, we couldn't talk, and then he stood us up and corrected our form. We swore we'd never get physical with each other again, but right now I'm tempted to punch him right in the fucking mouth. I grab the front of his shirt, pulling him closer.

"Go on, Sebby," he says, his mouth tilting into a smirk. "Defend the girl you're fine just fucking. Because it's so casual, right?"

I tighten my grip on his shirt, forcing him a little closer. His body is relaxed; I'm the only one here who is close to losing his shit. The pit in my stomach yawns, flashing teeth. I could punch him right in that smug mouth, and he wouldn't do a thing. He'd let me, just to prove a point. I went to bat for Mia in an instant, zero to fucking sixty. No thoughts, no hesitation, just a tidal wave of feeling.

I release him. I take a deep breath. "Fuck you."

I hate the way his mouth twists.

"Watch your back," he says. "Once the feelings are there, they don't go away."

33

MIA

GROWING UP, dinner was non-negotiable.

No matter what was going on, or who was pissed off at who, or if five minutes before my parents were screaming at each other, the moment dinner was ready, everyone sat at the dining room table with their napkins in their laps. Sometimes the energy would radiate through the room like a storm cloud, but without fail, my mother would serve everyone a plate, we'd pray, and eat. If things were particularly bad, we'd eat in silence, but more often than not, we'd all pretend that nothing was wrong.

This meal feels exactly like that. We've barely spoken, and Sebastian and Cooper won't meet each other's eyes.

The moment I heard Cooper say my name, my heart stopped. I couldn't move, even though I knew the polite thing— the decent thing—would have been to flee and pretend I never went downstairs in the first place. Dealing with Penny's questions would have been preferable to listening to Sebastian argue with his brother about me. I didn't see anything, but I heard it all. Cooper and Penny walking in on us I could deal with, but hearing Cooper's true thoughts about me? Or the pain in Sebastian's voice as he defended me?

I feel nauseous.

Cooper's right, I don't deserve that from him. I don't deserve him, period. And I've been too terrified to give in to what Sebastian wants—what I want, in the moments I'm completely honest with myself—that I've been holding him hostage, pretending that friends-with-benefits is an acceptable compromise. It might've been, when this first started, but I know him better now. I've been selfish and unwilling to let him go, and damn Cooper for making that so obvious.

I push the pasta around my bowl. Across from me, Penny frowns.

"Okay, why is everyone acting so weird?" she says. "I think we've all seen boobs before."

"I don't care about that." I try to muster a smile, but it falls flat. "Don't worry about it."

"Did something happen?" she presses. She reaches over and squeezes Cooper's wrist. "Babe?"

"We're fine," Sebastian says quickly. "Tell us about the road trip."

"Yeah," I say. "You spent a while at the Grand Canyon, right? That picture you posted on the rock was so pretty."

"This nice older man who used to come there with his wife took it," Penny says. "Right, Cooper?"

"Yep," he says. "They seemed pretty devoted to each other."

I don't miss the pointed glance he sends my way. I gulp down my wine without tasting it. I know I should ask another question, keep the conversation going, but my mind is blank. I'm all too aware of Sebastian. His foot is brushing against mine underneath the table, and I can practically feel the warmth radiating from his body. I could reach out and lace our fingers together so easily. The spark of electricity that zips down my spine whenever we're in each other's space is impossible to ignore, even with the tension in the room constricting around my heart like a band of iron.

It was so much easier when we were alone. I could pretend that we were dating without *dating*, but that's not how it works. Either you commit to all of it, or not at all.

"It was so sweet," Penny says. "And the Grand Canyon itself is stunning. I know how much you all love the Outer Banks, but it would be a great spot for a family vacation."

"I want to go sometime," Sebastian says. "I'll bet the stars are gorgeous there, right, Mia?"

"Oh, yeah," I say. "The less light pollution, the better. Lowell Observatory is one of the oldest observatories in the country, I've always wanted to tour it."

Cooper leans back in his chair, wrapping an arm around the top of Penny's in the process. He looks at me, and I stare right back, resisting the urge to fidget.

"Just curious," he drawls. "How long were you planning to jerk him around, Mia?"

For a moment, it's completely silent. Penny looks at her boyfriend with confusion in her blue eyes, and next to me, Sebastian's grip on his fork tightens. My mouth goes dry; when I try to swallow, I feel like I'm choking.

"Cooper," Sebastian says eventually, his voice practically crackling with energy. "Stop it."

"Wait, what are you talking about?" Penny says.

Cooper's gaze is piercing, but I hold my chin high. "You knew I was there?"

"Figured you caught the end of it." He takes a deliberate sip of his drink, setting down the glass just hard enough it thuds against the wood. "I'm not going to apologize for protecting my family."

"You don't need to fight my fucking battles for me," Sebastian says.

"You sure about that?" Cooper snorts. "How long were you planning on this lasting? As long as she wanted, right?"

"I told you already to shut the hell up about—"

"He's right." I blink past the sudden burning in my eyes. "Stop, Sebastian, he's right."

I stand in a rush, my chair scraping against the tile floor. I grit my teeth as I push open the screen door. Someone calls after me, and because of the blood rushing in my ears, I can't tell who it is. Penny, probably. If I fuck up things for her and Cooper, I won't be able to forgive myself.

The screen door slams, cutting me off from the rest of them. I hate that I'm running away again, but I need a moment to breathe. To think.

It's dark, the last traces of sunlight lingering on the horizon. A light breeze makes goosebumps erupt on my arms. I cross them tightly and walk to the tree Tangerine got stuck in, leaning my forehead against the rough bark. It smells faintly of rot. I take a deep, shuddering breath. A tear escapes, running down my cheek. That morning feels so long ago. I wanted to kiss him so badly then, but I held back. I should have stuck with it, but instead I gave in to my own desires, and it all came crashing down.

It's over.

It's for the best.

A future with him would break my own future. I made the choice not to compromise that when I was sixteen, after my mother threatened to disown me if I truly decided not to have a marriage and children. I promised myself that if I had to pick between my career and love, I'd always choose my career. A guy like Sebastian—a good guy—deserves more than I can give.

It's a clear night, the stars just starting to wink into existence. They feel farther away than usual. Distant and cold, the way they appear to most people, instead of friendly. The new moon means the sky is darker, too.

It's fitting that I don't have that comfort right now.

I sense Sebastian's presence before I hear him. He wraps an arm around my waist, squeezing. "There you are."

I turn into his arms. I should break away, put some distance between us, but I can't force myself to move. He cups my cheek. His lips brush against mine tenderly.

I don't deserve tender right now. I manage to ease away, but he stays close. The breeze ruffles through his hair. His presence, usually a comfort, feels oppressive. I can't focus on anything but his hand, pressing against the bark next to my head, and the clean citrus of his scent.

I dig my teeth into my bottom lip. Even in the near-dark, I see the green of his eyes. They're a rainforest, lush and layered.

His gaze is too intense. I look at my feet. I didn't even realize that they were bare until now. Didn't feel the grass underneath my feet, slightly cool in the chilled spring evening.

"Talk to me," he murmurs.

I can't help myself; I find his gaze again. I've loved his eyes since the very first moment I saw them, but right now, they're just bringing me pain. Another tear slips down my cheek as my heart cracks, right down the middle. "I can't."

"Sure you can."

I just shake my head, biting my lip so I don't sob. I'd rather sink into the ground than betray a weakness that deep. "Your brother is right."

He scowls; his voice is practically a snarl. "He was being a dick."

"I've been an asshole to you. You're allowed to be upset about that."

"Mia—"

"You've been too fucking nice to me," I snap. I take a deep breath, but it doesn't calm my jackrabbiting heart. "He's right, I have been stringing you along. Not—not to hurt you. But you're allowed to be pissed about it."

"I wanted to do this. If you think you're forcing me into anything, stop."

I shake my head. "You know what Izzy told me when she found out I was living here? You try too hard to be nice. To be you—this version of Sebastian that's endlessly patient and lets his own wants and needs go by the wayside. I've taken advantage of that and I hate it. I fucking hate it."

He runs his hand through his hair, tugging on the ends. "You didn't take advantage of me."

"Admit it."

"It's not true."

"Stop lying to yourself for five seconds!" My voice echoes, too loud, but I can't help myself. I knew from the third hookup the first time around that he wanted more than sex, and I kept pushing it off, and I'm still doing it. He doesn't deserve it. He deserves a girlfriend who can give him everything, now and in the future, and I can't become that girl.

"Fine!" He doesn't yell, exactly, but I hear the pain in his voice, each syllable hammering into my heart. "Yeah, I'm pissed. I've tried to be understanding, and to take what you've given me, but it's not what I fucking want. Happy?"

"Ecstatic," I shoot back.

"But if I'm lying to myself, you are too," he says. "Look me in the eyes and tell me you don't want more, Mia. Go on. Lie to my fucking face if you're so determined to push me away. Why did you stand me up? I know it wasn't because you didn't want more."

It's impossible to lie when I'm gazing into his emerald eyes. I swipe my tongue over my lip, then bite down, wanting the little pinprick of pain. Wishing he was biting it instead. "I did want more."

"Did I do something to fuck it up?" He presses close enough I can feel the warmth of his body. "Did I hurt you?"

I shake my head, not trusting myself to speak for a moment. "No," I whisper. "I was... fuck. I was falling for you."

His shoulders sag. He nearly smiles. My heart leaps traitorously at the sight. "I knew it."

"It was terrifying." I try to swallow, but that just makes me want to sob. "It's still terrifying. I thought maybe if you just moved on, it would be better—for you and for me."

"I don't want to move on." He takes my hand, squeezing my fingers. His touch sends delicious sparks down my spine. I yank my hand away, and he just grabs it again, digging his blunt nails into my palm. "I didn't want to then, and I sure as hell don't want to now. I want you, Mia. Not just to mess around with, or to be your friend. I want everything we can give each other because I'm falling for you too."

"I can't do it." My voice breaks. "I don't know how."

"Try," he murmurs. "I've never tried before either, and I'm scared out of my mind, but I want to try it with you. Only with you. Say you'll try it with me too."

I squeeze his hand back. "What if it doesn't last? What if—"

He starts shaking his head before I finish the sentence. "No what-ifs. Don't think about the future. Think about now."

Something snaps inside me.

More likely than not, this will go up in flames—but I can't walk away from him. Not when my heart feels so full when he's around. Not when I'm aware of his presence from the moment he enters a room. Not when my heart is begging to stay with him, damn the future consequences. Goodbye Project GOSMC.

I nod, wiping at the stubborn tears wanting to escape. He tucks my hair behind my ear, tugging on the lobe gently.

"I really want to kiss you right now," he says.

I balance on my tiptoes. My lips are half an inch from his, so close yet so far. My body thrums with anticipation. "What are you waiting for?"

34

MIA

SEBASTIAN'S LIPS crash against mine with the force of full tide. My fingers bunch in his shirt, pulling it up; he practically rips it off his body. I drag my hands down the hard line of his abs, settling on the waistband of his jeans. He raises an eyebrow in a silent question, and I nod. I want him here, in the grass, with the breeze on our bare skin and the stars winking above.

"Guess we should stay out here for a while longer anyway," he murmurs. I laugh as he tugs off my shirt and bra. "Shit might get awkward otherwise."

"Hopefully we don't flash anyone else tonight."

He snorts as he scoops me into his arms. "I still can't believe that happened."

I crane my neck around. "Where are we going?"

"It's grassier over here." He sets me down, then stretches out alongside me. I breathe in the cool air. It's scented with the wild thicket of honeysuckle by the fence. He spreads his hand over my belly, a warm weight that sends heat to all the right places. "Wanna make sure you're comfortable."

I shiver as he dips his fingertip into my belly button. "How is your pinkie?"

His lips brush over one of my nipples, taut in the cool air. "I think we'll manage."

I arch my back as he sucks on my breast, my skin sparking in his wake. He inches his hand lower, to my skirt. When he lifts his head, his hair falls into his eyes; I push it back, my hand curving over his jaw. He turns his face into it, pressing a quick kiss to my palm. He drags his finger over the skin just above my skirt, making me clench my stomach.

"Hips up for me, angel."

My heart skips a beat as I raise my hips. He pulls down my skirt and panties all at once, groaning when he sees my cunt, already slick. The air on my exposed skin makes me shiver, but his touch is so warm, so perfect, that it's worth it.

"Good girl," he says, a rough edge to his voice. He rubs his knuckles over my folds. "Wish we had a blanket."

I laugh as I reach up and pull him into another kiss. The brush of his fingers against my clit, already swollen and begging for attention, makes me gasp. "We'll just have to have round two in the shower."

"What a drag," he says, grinning against my mouth.

I bite his jaw. "I want you."

"You have me."

"You know what I mean." I tangle my fingers through his hair and tug. "The way we haven't had it since before."

He reaches between us and unbuttons his jeans, kicking them down his legs. "I don't have a condom out here."

I stroke my hand over the sizable bulge in his boxer-briefs.

I'm aching with the bone-deep desire to feel him—not his fingers, or his tongue, but him—deep inside, pressing against places I can't touch myself. I want him to come inside me, claiming me in the most primal way. "I have an IUD. And I tested negative last time I checked."

"I did too." He makes a satisfied noise as I squeeze his cock. "You sure you're good with it?"

My heart swoops in my chest. I don't know the exact moment I started to free-fall, but one way or another, I went over the edge. Another person would gloss over the particulars —and I've experienced that—but Sebastian takes it in his stride. Checking in like this is fucking sexy. It's part of his personality, not an act or something he feels obligated to do. I pull his cock out of his boxer-briefs and give it another firm stroke, swiping my thumb over the head. He's nearly all the way hard, thick and throbbing. I nod, pressing a quick, dry kiss to his cheek.

The edge of his mouth quirks up. "Use your words."

The little push is just enough to make me flush. "I'm good with it. Fuck me, babe, come on."

That must satisfy him, because he pulls off the rest of his clothes and settles over me, caging me in with his strong arms. I stretch, luxuriating in his warmth as he palms my tits, his other hand slipping down to play with my clit again. He tugs at the groomed hair between my legs, making me gasp.

"It's so easy to wind you up," he teases. "I love that about you."

He spares me from thinking of an answer to *that* by kissing me deeply, our tongues tangling together. He nudges my legs further apart, pressing two fingers against my hole as he strokes my clit. I'm slick enough that they go in easily. A moan escapes my throat. He knows my body so well that it doesn't take much to get me dripping, pressing my hips to his, a torrent of begging on the tip of my tongue. It's never been better than with him, and it's never been better than this—right here, under the canopy of stars and the hidden moon, his dick pressing against my thigh as he handles my body like his favored glove. He crooks his fingers, and I gasp, digging my foot into his side. My nails drag down his arm, leaving a long line of red.

It's fully dark now, but light glows from the house, enough that I can see the white of his teeth, the green of his eyes. He keeps rubbing that spot against my core until I'm right on the fucking edge, trembling as I pant. Whatever chill I felt in the air is gone, turned molten. His thumb swipes at my clit as he presses a third finger into my dripping core.

I come so loudly, I slap a hand over my mouth. He shakes with laughter, and in the next second, I dissolve into giggles too. He pulls out his fingers, replacing them with his cock before I have a chance to protest, then pushes in with one long, smooth stroke. He hitches my leg around his hip, deepening the angle.

Our gazes meet. He wets his lip, thrusting experimentally. I squeeze tightly around him, dragging a groan from his throat. He thrusts again, harder this time, and builds up a rhythm. For a moment I can't breathe, can't tease, can't do a thing but take it. He strokes one broad hand through my hair, tangling it around his fist. I smell his cologne, but also the delicious tang of his sweat.

"You're mine," he whispers.

It feels so right, tears well in my eyes again. When one escapes, he licks it away, claiming me in yet another way. It's filthy, and it makes me grin.

"Yours," I whisper back. "Show me, Sebastian."

He shakes his head like he can't believe it. I barely can

either. If I think about it too hard, I start to spiral. The only thing to do is not think at all. To stay in the present, and hope the future is kind. At my urging, he snaps his hips forward, sinking even deeper. I squeeze around him as tightly as I can, making each thrust extra torturous for him.

He drops his head down, letting out a possessive growl as he comes. My heart fucking soars at the sound. He pulls me into his arms, rolling us onto our sides, and buries his head in the crook of my shoulder. The thought of his seed inside me, claiming my body the way he's already claiming my soul, makes me whimper. I want him to paint me inside and out, over and over. I want to leave marks on him too, bites and scratches and enough lipstick kisses that no one will dare look at him twice.

His next words are so quiet, I nearly miss them.

"My angel." He kisses my pulse, squeezing me tight. I squeeze back, tight enough I know he feels it. "My good fucking angel."

35

SEBASTIAN

I HAVEN'T BEEN to New York City since Sandra's Callahan Family Foundation gala a few months ago, so when the car pulls to the curb and I climb out alongside Cooper and Richard, I need to blink as I acclimate to the energy. It smells faintly of garbage, even though it's not that warm out yet, but if I concentrate, I can smell freshly roasted coffee as well. I sidestep a puddle as I take in the tall buildings, hiding a yawn behind my hand. Richard showed up in the SUV at half past six, and now it's eight. I need a coffee if I'm going to manage to keep my eyes open.

"It's just a breakfast meeting. We won't be too long," Richard tells the driver as he glances at his watch. "I'll call for pickup."

"Yes, sir," the driver says. "Have a nice meal, Mr. Callahan."

As we cross the street to the restaurant—the source of the coffee smell, fortunately—Cooper tries to meet my eyes. I ignore him. The past few days have been full of awkward torture, but he hasn't tried to apologize for how he treated Mia, and until he does, I'm not interested in chatting. I didn't expect him to want to come to this meeting, but just before the car left the driveway, he slid into the backseat next to me. We tried to be cordial in front of Richard; he asked Cooper a bunch of questions about the road trip and wanted to know how my Albany trip went, but I doubt he bought it. He's always been able to see through our shit with remarkable accuracy.

As we settle into a booth by the window, I adjust my shirt. I'm wearing slacks and a button-down—Mia and I decided that light blue was formal without trying too hard—and I slicked my hair back with gel. My jaw is smooth, too, thanks to a fresh shave. I tuck my dad's necklace underneath my collar. When Cooper sits next to me, I shift a few inches closer to the window.

He rolls his eyes. "Seriously?"

"I don't recall inviting you."

"It's good for him to hear these conversations," Richard says. He fusses with Cooper's collar. "Was this shirt in the bottom of your closet?"

"He's here for Seb, not me," Cooper says, even though he stays still until Richard, apparently satisfied, leans back.

"Still. You're here, we're sending a united front. You might learn something."

"Not that he would listen," I mutter.

Richard checks his watch with a deliberate air. "We have some time before Andy will be here. What's the matter with the two of you?"

"Nothing," we say at the same time.

"You've been glaring at each other all morning."

The server walks over and says hello. I manage a smile as I order a coffee and an omelet. The moment she leaves, though, I scowl. "It doesn't have anything to do with baseball. Don't worry about it."

"Sebby has a girlfriend," Cooper says. "Just so you know."

Richard raises an eyebrow. "Congratulations, Sebastian. What's the problem?"

"There isn't one," I say before Cooper can reply. "It's— don't worry about it."

"Well, I want to meet this young woman," Richard says. "What's her name?"

"It's Mia, Dad," says Cooper. "You've met her."

Naturally, that doesn't do a thing but confuse Richard. He clasps his hands together, settling them atop the table. "Penny's friend Mia? I don't see the issue. Did they have a falling out?"

"No." I swipe my hand through my hair, grimacing when the gel sticks to my fingers. I feel way too dressed up; the collar is practically choking me.

I'd have preferred to have this meeting—a chat with an agent about my draft prospects—on the baseball field, or at least a regular diner, but Richard wanted to maintain a level of formality. Since this contact is his agent Jessica's colleague, Andy Ross, I couldn't object.

Still, I feel like a show dog, which I suppose is part of the point. NCAA rules dictate that draft-eligible players can't have agents negotiate on their behalf, but it's completely fine to ask them for advice about navigating the draft. The last time we had this kind of meeting, I'd just graduated high school, and we decided that I'd decline MLB's first attempt at drafting me and attend McKee instead, making my next period of eligibility after my junior year.

Now that's here, and I can't settle the jitters in my stomach. I wish I could dig my elbow right into Cooper's ribs for bringing up Mia before the meeting, but that wouldn't fly with Richard. This is, after all, a nice restaurant, with fancily dressed Manhattanites sipping on coffee all around us.

"Everything is good with Penny, right, son?" Richard asks.

"Yeah," Cooper says. "She's great."

"So why—"

I can't help myself. "If you would just apologize for acting like an asshat to Mia, I wouldn't have an issue. You forced her into a corner—"

"That ended with you dating, so you're welcome," he interrupts.

I snort in disbelief. "You don't like her anyway."

"I hated how she was treating you, which is completely different." The server comes back with our coffees. If she notices the tension, she doesn't let on. He waits for her to leave before adding, "But now you're dating, right? No issue."

"If there's no issue, why haven't you apologized?"

"It's not that I haven't—"

"Boys," Richard says warningly.

He stands, a smile on his face as he holds out his hand. "Andy. Nice to meet you in person."

The man who must be Andy gives it a shake. He's tall and broad—an ex-athlete himself, I'd bet anything—and looks like the kind of guy who would be an agent, down to the slick black suit paired with pristine basketball sneakers. There's an AirPod in his ear, but he slips it out as he smiles at us. I don't know much about how agenting works, but I would guess it involves a lot of smooth talking. Cooper and I get out of the booth too, shaking his hand in turn.

"Of course," he says. "I'm thrilled to make time for you. I think I've seen every available piece of film, Sebastian. Your swing is classic. Beautiful. An imprint of your father's."

I swallow down a little spike of anxiety and smile. "Thank you."

"You must be getting excited," he says as he sits next to Richard. "July is going to be here before you know it."

"I'm just focusing on getting through the rest of this season."

"It's been a tough stretch," he says. "There's still a chance you'll make the playoffs, though, right?"

"That's what we're aiming for, always," I say. Privately, I'm not sure we've done enough to earn that spot, but there's still time for the rankings to shake out.

Cooper surprises me by adding, "I think they'll make it. Sebastian is one of the leaders of the team. He knows how to rally."

I wish it was a direct apology, but I hear some of it in his words. My heart clenches. I'm thrilled that Mia finally agreed to give us a shot, but I don't want it to come at the cost of my relationship with my brother and best friend.

"I'm not the biggest hockey expert," Andy says, "but I know talent when I see it in any sport. Congratulations on the Frozen Four win, man."

Cooper dips his chin. "Thank you."

Andy shakes his head, huffing out a little laugh.

"This family," he says. "Manning-level talent and charisma. Richard, you'll have to gather your sons together for endorsements once they're in the pros. Sebastian, too."

I feel Cooper tense next to me. My heart skips a beat. Andy isn't the first person to insinuate that I'm not part of my family because I don't share their blood, and he won't be the last, but that doesn't mean it feels good to hear.

Richard and Sandra tried, from the very beginning, to bring me completely into the Callahan family fold, but it wasn't seamless. I had my own life in Cincinnati, my friends, my baseball team, and of course my mom and dad, and when the accident ripped that away all at once, I felt unmoored.

They were patient; they put me into a new baseball program right away, they made sure I had access to grief counseling, they treated me the same as their other children. Still, I got into way too many fights. My grades were shit, and so was my play on the field. I didn't feel like I belonged until nearly a year in, when the worst of the heartbreak faded. Still, people acted like I was just some kid that Richard and Sandra were babysitting instead of their child, so I changed the name on the back of my uniform to match the rest of my family.

My adoptive parents worked hard from day one to make sure I belonged, and the least I can do is repay them by fulfilling my father's dream for me.

"Sebastian is my son," Richard says. His tone is mild, but I don't miss the way his eyes flash. "I have three sons."

"He wears our name on the back of his jersey," Cooper adds.

"Of course," Andy says, seemingly unfazed by the rebuke. He gives us a grin. "Even better. Think about the advertising potential."

"I've heard plenty about it, over the years," Richard says. He keeps his voice light, but I know him well enough to say with confidence that he won't want me signing with Andy when it comes time to work with an agent. "Sandra and I didn't want to subject the boys to that sort of publicity. But once it's professional, that'll be a different story."

"I know that Jessica's been working on some monster possibilities for James." He thanks the server when she brings him a cup of coffee, taking a quick sip before setting it back down. "Anyway, I brought along some projections, so we can discuss the baseball particulars. I'd say that the current line of thought is accurate. Top ten for sure, but the slot depends upon last minute trades and if some teams decide to chase the high school prospects. Of course, I can't communicate with any clubs on your behalf, but I've been listening to the chatter, and the reception is excellent."

He takes out a tablet and pulls up a spreadsheet. Seeing my slash line—batting average, on-base percentage, and slugging— written out in black and white is strange. I'm aware of the numbers when I play, but they're not the focus. When it comes to scouts for major league clubs, however, it's the language they speak. That's what the Rangers and the Marlins and the Reds are considering, all of them, as they decide how they're going to make a play for me and everyone else that's eligible.

"These are the most recent numbers?" Richard asks. "Sebastian?"

"I think so," I say. I try for a smile, although my face doesn't want to cooperate. "Pretty good, I guess."

"He's being modest," Andy says. He reaches over and claps me on the shoulder. "With these numbers, not to mention your pedigree—seems like all anyone can talk about is how much you remind them of your old man, which is good, you need to milk it—I see no issue with it pushing you up into the top five by draft day. The slot value at the fifth pick, for example, is just over six mil."

"Damn," Cooper says with a whistle. "That's sweet."

Andy keeps going, talking about how much wiggle room I'll want to give teams when they call me. I try to pay attention, but honestly, it's hard to wrap my mind around the specifics. The server stops by with our food, but my omelet doesn't seem appealing anymore. I push the potatoes around my plate, listening to Richard ask Andy questions. My muscles tense.

It's not just nerves. There's something deeper there, scratching beneath the surface. This should be an exciting moment. Who doesn't want to talk about signing a contract worth millions to play a sport for a living?

"Excuse me," I say. "I—I need a moment."

36

SEBASTIAN

I GIVE COOPER A SHOVE. He slides out of the booth so I can escape.

"You okay?" he asks quietly, glancing at Richard.

I nod. "Yeah. I just need a second."

I wind my way through the restaurant, side-stepping our server and a woman with a little dog in her purse. Out on the sidewalk, I lean against the building and take a deep breath.

It's not the talk of the money, or the prospect of the work ahead. I don't know what it is, exactly, but something is making my insides twist like they're caught in a vise. I sink into a crouch, fisting my hands together and pressing them to my mouth. If it was just baseball, just swinging the bat and making plays, it would be so different. But you can't have one without the other, without all this shit about contracts and comparisons and stat lines and endorsements, and sooner or later, I'm going to need to come to terms with that. It's a game, but it's also a business, and once I sign a contract, I'm agreeing to become an employee, not just an athlete.

It's not fear. I shut my eyes, internally checking my gut. I'm not afraid of being unable to perform my future job well; I know I can handle the level of competition. It's this deep, dragging anxiety that won't leave me the fuck alone. A part of me, increasingly loud, that wants to say *no thank you*.

I laugh shortly. What would the Andys of the world say to that? What would Richard say? Or James and Cooper, for that matter? Our respective sports have always bound us together, and if I walked away from that, it would be like Andy insinuated. The two of them, Richard's true sons, and then me.

Mia has a meeting with Alice this morning—right now, exactly, if I remember the time correctly—but I can't help texting her. I type out a mini essay, a rambling run-on of a sentence, then delete it all. I'm not ready for this conversation with anyone, not even her. I delete it all and just ask how she's doing. When it delivers, I stare at my phone, waiting for those three little dots.

"Sebastian?"

I look up at Richard. He's frowning at me as he shields his eyes from the sun, his watch glinting in the light. "Son, what's the matter?"

I shove my phone into my pocket and stand. I brush down my shirt and adjust my collar. "I'm sorry, sir."

His frown deepens as he clasps my shoulder, his hand squeezing tightly. "Sorry for what?"

"Leaving, I guess." I bite my lip. "I know it was rude."

"Do you feel okay?" He presses the back of his hand to my forehead. I blink rapidly; the touch makes my eyes burn. "Are you coming down with something?"

I shake my head, leaning away. "No. It's just... it's a lot."

"Is this about whatever's going on with you and Cooper?"

I feel bad throwing Cooper under the bus, but it's easier to talk about that than the jumbled thoughts running through my mind whenever I think about baseball, so I nod. "It's been this whole thing with Mia."

Richard sighs deeply.

"I suppose I've been lucky with you two," he says. "Same age, and you became friends, not adversaries. I see so much of myself in Cooper, and so much of Jacob in you. Jake and I had our fair share of scuffles, you know."

"Yeah?"

He laughs softly at some far-off memory. "I miss him."

It takes me a moment to reply. "I miss him too."

"Come on," he says. "Let's wrap things up with Andy. Then you and Cooper will sort this out. I want to hear about Mia, too. From what I remember, that girl wears a lot of black."

I smile at the thought of her in one of her trademark dark outfits. "I'm not signing with him."

He snorts as he claps me on the back. "Absolutely not. The guy's a scumbag. He makes some good points about contract structuring, though."

―――

"THIS REALLY ISN'T NECESSARY," Cooper says.

"Yeah," I say. "We're fine."

Richard leans through the open backseat window, fixing each of us with his most serious gaze. Cooper refuses to blink, but I look away. "I'll be outside. Take your time. Roll up the windows, Anderson."

The minute we're alone in the car—locked in to "figure out our shit," as Richard put it when we pulled up to the house—Cooper peers into the front seat, a scowl on his face.

"The car's still running," he says. "Want to make a break for it?"

I flop against the seat with a groan. "That would make things worse."

"We don't *have* to talk."

"No." I rub my temples. Even though I'm a little less pissed at him now, thanks to the conversation with Andy, that doesn't mean I'm thrilled by the prospect of chatting with him about Mia. He didn't have the right to stick his nose in our business, regardless of the result. If he pushed, and Mia had reacted by breaking everything off completely, rather than agreeing to give me a chance—well, we'd have way bigger issues than our dad locking us in a car together to chat.

Cooper glances at his phone. "I could text Penny and see if she'll rescue us. She's not afraid of Dad."

I snort. If there's one person Richard Callahan doesn't intimidate, it's Penny. "No. I don't want this getting back to Mia."

"You scared of her?"

"No, dumbass." I kick him. "I don't want her to feel bad."

He kicks me back. "You really planned a whole date, and she ghosted you? That's the big thing you refused to tell me?"

"It's ancient history now."

"That doesn't mean she didn't hurt you."

I sigh, leaning my head against the seat. Even though the air conditioner is still running, I feel warm, my collar stiff and choking. I undo the top few buttons of my shirt. "I'm not saying that she didn't. Both of you were right, I guess. I was keeping how I felt bottled in rather than rock the boat."

"And you let her drag you along in the process."

I shake my head. "She wasn't doing it to be malicious. I know that. She just has her own shit to deal with."

"You sure?"

"Yeah." I don't know the specifics, but I'm certain that there's something else going on. Something that made her think twice about whether she wanted to get involved with me on a deeper level when she realized that she had feelings for me. It's not like I'm not scared shitless too. I just have to hope that together, we'll be able to make it work. There's no one else I'd want to try it with, after all. "I was trying to be patient, at least until you came along."

"Then I don't regret it."

I roll my eyes. "You could have been nicer about it."

"You deserved more than she was giving."

"And like I said before, it's not your job to defend me. I can handle my own shit."

"I know you can, but you're my brother. You're family. Speaking of, what the hell was wrong with that douche?"

I can't keep myself from laughing. "He's not going to be my agent, that's for sure."

"Good. Because I can accept the Mia thing, but that? No way."

"I like her, Cooper." He meets my eyes. I swallow, pushing past the awkwardness that comes along—always—with honesty. "I like her a hell of a lot. You fell for Penny from the first moment you saw her, right? Something felt different. I think—I think the same thing has been happening with me and Mia. I need you to apologize to her."

After a moment, he nods. "I will. When did you hook up for the first time, anyway?"

"January. Right after winter break." I smile as I remember her scowl, and the way it softened once I got her alone. "But we started talking before then."

"You kept it secret that long?"

"It's how she wanted it."

"So at my birthday party, you were together?"

"In a manner of speaking."

"Huh." He scratches at his beard. "You know what? We should do a double date."

I stare at him in disbelief. "Words I'd never have expected to hear from your mouth."

37

MIA

"SIMPLIFY THE EQUATION HERE," Alice says, pointing to my computer screen. "We don't need to calculate for mass under these conditions."

I nod, grabbing a stack of sticky notes from my desk drawer. "Makes sense."

"I shouldn't have to tell you basic stuff like this," she adds, because of course she needs to get a jab in.

I school my expression into something approaching neutral, even though I want to snap at her, and scribble her feedback onto a sticky note. I slap it on the edge of my computer with way more force than necessary. It wouldn't kill her to stop with the negative comments. Every day it's something else.

Professor Santoro is away at a conference, but before she left, she reviewed the program so far, and Alice and I have spent most of the morning picking our way through her thoughts. It's times like these when I'm the most energized;

when I'm filled with so much love for what I'm doing, the challenges I'm facing, that my heart races as I try to keep up with the thoughts crowding my mind. This feeling, shining with possibility, heady with what feels close to magic, is why I can't give up on this career. Not now, not in the future, not ever. Not even if every other comment that comes out of Alice's mouth is condescending and rude.

She jots down something too. "This is marginally better than the last model you showed me."

Gee, thanks.

"You'll be able to make the changes by the time she gets back, right? She's thinking that we'll be able to—"

My phone starts ringing. I glance at it as she keeps talking. "Sorry. It's my sister. Do you mind if I take this?"

She tucks her pencil behind her ear as she shuts her notebook. "I guess I can give you a minute."

"I have that lunch thing in a bit, too."

She sighs, giving me a look.

"I'll be able to make the changes in time. I promise." I accept the call, pressing the phone to my ear. I settle in my chair, crossing my legs. "Giana?"

"Mi-Mi," she says. "Guess what?"

I frown. I know that tone of voice—it means she has something to share that she's convinced everyone else will love too. "Is everything okay?"

"Oh, yeah. I was talking to my friend April; you know the one who teaches middle school science? She's going to a science pedagogy conference day and thinks she can get you one of the student spots. It's not even that far from Moorbridge, I checked for you. Want me to send her info to you?"

I clean my glasses with the hem of my t-shirt. I called that one right. Crap. "Um—"

"It would be such a good networking opportunity."

"Definitely," I say. "Let me just... sure. Send it to me."

I'll just have to be mysteriously busy on that day, and it'll only be half a lie, because I am busy. Just not with a teaching assignment. Professor Santoro's symposium is inching closer, along with her latest journal deadline. Alice dumps new work in my lap every day. When I'm doing this lab work on top of classes in the fall, I'll barely have time to breathe.

"This is so great," she says. "I am *so* excited about the barbecue, by the way. Mom wants to go all out with the menu. The order she placed at the butcher is probably enough to feed the neighborhood and *then* an army."

"You know how she likes to send people home with leftovers."

"What else is up with you? I've barely heard anything about the high schoolers."

"Oh, it's been good. Just busy. I definitely want to get certified for high school." I hate every word of the lie that comes out of my mouth. I know I need to come clean eventually, but the thought of confessing that to Giana—and the rest of my family—is almost worse than teaching in the first place. "I... I started dating someone, too."

Giana gasps so loudly I have to hold the phone away from my ear. "No way. Who? If they're a girl, don't worry, I've got your back. Nana won't understand, but Mom and Daddy will come around."

I swallow as a rush of emotion goes through me. Mom and Dad found out about my sexuality by accident my senior year of high school, but I told Giana on purpose. I was sixteen, just figuring it out myself, and I didn't have a close enough friend to confide in, so I chose her. I remember three things about that day: the snow on the windowsill, the royal icing smeared on her face because we were in the middle of decorating Christmas cookies, and the way she hugged me, so tightly I nearly suffocated. I was terrified that she wouldn't understand, that I made a miscalculation, but she told me she loved me and promised to keep it a secret until I was ready to share with everyone else.

She kept that promise, and helped Mom and Dad understand—kind of—when they caught me kissing Chloe McDonald behind the bleachers on the softball field after a game. They mostly pretend I never said anything in the first place, but it's better than it could have been, thanks to her. We were closer back then, before she met Peter and gave up law school and started siding with Mom on almost everything.

I shouldn't be lying to her about what I want for my career, but she's not the same Giana who hugged me that day in the kitchen. I can't be sure she wouldn't turn around and tell the rest of our family, bringing a maelstrom of shit into my life.

"Thanks," I say thickly. "His name is Sebastian, though. He's Penny's boyfriend's brother."

"Oh my gosh," she says. "That is the cutest thing I've ever heard. Does he play hockey too?"

"Baseball, actually."

"Daddy will love him. You should bring him to the barbecue."

"Maybe. It's almost the end of the season, he's super busy."

"Do it," she urges. "Bring Penny and Cooper too, goodness knows we'll have more than enough food."

"I guess so." I set my feet back on the floor with a thud. Out of the corner of my eye, I see orange. Penny is at the door, waving wildly. "Penny is here to pick me up for lunch. I'll see you soon."

"I can't wait to hear more about him." Giana sighs happily. "I'm so proud of you, Mi-Mi."

I grab my things, text Alice to let her know I'm running out, and meet Penny at the door. "How did you know which lab to go to?"

"I just picked the nerdiest one." She hugs me. "I may have accidentally interrupted someone working with a scary-looking microscope first. Who were you talking to?"

I bump my shoulder against hers. "Giana."

She leads the way down the staircase. "How is she?"

"She wants me to bring Sebastian to the barbecue."

"Still want me to come?"

I push open the double doors at the bottom of the steps. It's been raining on and off all day. "Yeah. I don't think that I can get out of it at this point. Where do you want to go to lunch?"

"There's this new place near the movie theater that does açai bowls." She sidesteps a puddle. "Do they still think you're going to be a teacher?"

I aim for Cooper's truck, parked haphazardly in the lot ahead. "Yep."

Penny worries her lip. "I thought I was going to die when I told my dad I was failing half my classes, but it ended up being fine."

"There's a distinct difference here," I say. "Your dad is cool."

She snorts out a laugh, skipping ahead to the driver's side of the truck. "Hardly."

"He never threatened to disown you. That qualifies as cool in my book."

Penny waits until we're in the cab of the truck—just in time, because it's spitting rain again—before she replies, "I love you."

"Pen—"

"Just thought you deserved to hear that from someone today." She reaches over and hugs me. I keep still for a moment, but then I wriggle my arms out of her grip and hug her back.

"I'm surprised that Cooper is letting you use his truck."

"Very reluctantly, believe me." She turns it on, peering into the rearview mirror. "It's not the driving, it's the parking. This stupid thing is a tank. And yet watching him do the one-handed wheel thing while he's parallel parking it is so hot, I guess I have to live with it."

I crane my neck around as she backs out of the space. "You're good."

She changes gears and swings out of the lot. "He feels bad for what he said to you, you know. He's going to apologize."

I pull my hair out of its ponytail and run my fingers through it. What he said was shitty, yeah, and I hate how he goaded Sebastian, but I can't blame him. In that moment, he helped clarify everything; I needed to give in or give up. I chose the former, and I have no idea if I'll be able to make it work, but I want to try. One way or another, Sebastian has stolen part of my heart, and I don't want him to give it back.

"It's okay," I say. "He was right."

Penny glances at me. "Sebastian told me pretty much the same thing when I started hooking up with Cooper. Don't fuck with my brother."

I snort at the way she mimics Sebastian's voice. It's not half-bad.

"Callahan protectiveness is unmatched," she adds.

"Fantastic," I say dryly.

She drums her fingers on the steering wheel. "So, how's the sex?"

Heat erupts on my face like a blast from a fireball. "Penny!"

38

MIA

I SLIP MY HAND into Sebastian's, squeezing it as we walk across the parking lot to the bowling alley. When he told me that Cooper wanted us to go on a double date, I figured we'd just hang out at Lark's, or maybe go to the movies. I haven't been bowling in ages, even though the one in town is popular with the McKee crowd, thanks to the beer pitchers and themed nights.

It's ridiculous to be nervous—it's just a couple beers and bowling—but I can't ignore the butterfly explosion in my belly. When I went out in the past, it was always a prelude to a hookup. I've never been on an old-fashioned date, complete with an *activity*.

One thing I've got up my sleeve, though? I rock at bowling. Sebastian might be the athlete in the relationship, but I can hold my own where bowling is concerned. Nonno enjoyed bowling, and he made sure that I knew how to throw a strike. By the way Penny smiles at me as we walk into the building, I know she remembers. Something tells me that this idea was hers, even though Cooper is the one who presented it to Sebastian.

It's not crowded; aside from a group of teenagers at one of the lanes at the far end, we have the place to ourselves. There's a mini arcade next to the bar, the lights flashing, and a mural over the counter that seems to be showing Sasquatch juggling bowling balls, for whatever reason. The smell of popcorn and cheese sauce, the outdated pop playlist blaring through the speakers, and rows of blue and red shoes behind the counter bring back a rush of memories. I had a birthday party at a bowling alley when I was little; I remember the ice cream cake that dripped on the pink dress that Mom insisted I wear.

Sebastian squeezes my hand in return. "Mia, why are you holding on like we're about to go into a haunted house?"

Penny tries and fails to hold back a smile.

I scowl, trying to snatch my hand back. "What?"

He holds on tightly enough I can't break away unless I want to smack into the glass case filled with bowling trophies. "Just teasing. You okay?"

"I've never..." I swallow. "I've never been on a date before."

"I know," he says easily. "Which is why we kept the training wheels on for you, di Angelo. Cooper wanted to throw you into mini golf right away, but I didn't want to scare you off. Us Callahans don't fuck around where mini golf is concerned."

"All games, really," Cooper says. He winds his arm around Penny, tugging on her braid. She pokes him hard in the ribs. "Monopoly is the most cutthroat. Tag always ends in at least one broken window, so we're limited to once a year. Bowling is less intense than pool but more intense than darts."

I raise my eyebrows at Penny. She just shrugs. "I'm waiting for the Monopoly invite, honestly."

"I need the alliance, Red," Cooper says, his voice practically a growl. "James and Bex teaming up completely ruined the strategy."

"You still owe me dinner at Vesuvio's," Sebastian adds, leading the way to the counter. The teenager sitting behind it glances up from his phone, sighs, and ambles in our direction. "But I'll accept this for now."

"If it makes you feel any better," Cooper adds, sounding a little calmer, "I'd never been on a date before Pen."

"I brought you a list of conversation topics," Penny says with a sly smile. "Make sure you ask about his interests."

"I'm going to smack you," I warn.

She just laughs. "You get the shoes. We'll get the beer and nachos."

The moment I'm alone with Sebastian, I feel awkward, which is ridiculous because I've been alone with him so often over the past few weeks. Whenever I think about the label—he's my boyfriend, and I'm his girlfriend—I feel warm enough to start a fire with my bare hands and more than a little turned on, which I think is a good sign, but still, it's different. There's a hint of commitment there, and I've never had that before.

As if he can tell what I'm thinking, he pulls me into a kiss, his palm pressing against my lower back.

"You look gorgeous," he murmurs.

I smooth down my blouse. When Penny and I went to lunch, she convinced me to play hooky after and go to the mall. I splurged on a new top, midnight blue with tank top-style straps and embroidery on the hem. Paired with black jeans and my leather jacket—the new one that he bought me—I knew I looked good when we left the house, but hearing the compliment makes me blush.

I lean in so I can whisper against his ear, "You should see the lingerie."

His hand circles my wrist, thumb stroking softly over my skin. "Any chance I can get a sneak peek?"

That citrus-edged scent of his settles some of the nerves jumping through me. It's a double date with our best friends, after all. I just need to relax and have fun. I kiss him, shivering as he settles his hands low on my hips.

"No chance," I murmur. "But if you're good, I'll put on a show later."

"Let's make things interesting," he says. "Whoever ends up with the most points after we finish gets to be in charge tonight."

"In charge how?"

He strokes one finger up my spine. "If I win, I get a good girl in my bed. But if you win..."

"I get to have my way with you?"

He grins. "Something like that."

He *definitely* doesn't know how good I am at bowling. I almost smirk and give the whole thing away, but I manage to rein it in. "Deal."

"Think you can keep up with me, sweetheart?"

I press another kiss to his lips. He's especially handsome tonight; his t-shirt and jeans are fitted, so they show off his physique, and his jaw is sharp and clean. I watched him shave in the bathroom before we left for the bowling alley, swinging my legs on the counter as I brushed my teeth. I already know what I'll do for him when I win. I have the perfect song to dance to, and a new pair of suede boots to try out. "I'll try my best."

"Hey," the kid behind the counter says. "You gonna rent shoes or what?"

———

HALF AN HOUR LATER, I do a little dance as I step up to the line. "Think I can get six in a row?"

"Hell yeah," Cooper calls. Sebastian punches him in the shoulder. I laugh as I widen my stance. The pins gleam in front of me, perfectly placed and ready to go crashing down yet again. Two nasty-tasting beers in, I'm starting to feel loose—and Sebastian is realizing that I'm absolutely winning our bet.

The first two strikes, he put down to luck. The third, he started to look a little worried. The fourth, he started scowling, and his expression has been stuck that way since. I'm wiping the floor with all three of them. Cooper is decent, but his ball constantly hooks to the left. Penny is terrible, but cares more about the nachos anyway. Sebastian is good at it, but his last two turns, he went into the gutter. With each frame, he's acting more and more like a paranoid pitcher trying to pick off the runner at first instead of focusing on getting the next batter out.

I close my eyes, wind my arm back, and let go. The ball rockets down the alley, completely straight, and crashes into the pins. All ten crash to the floor. I turn, bowing, as Penny whoops. Sebastian groans, tipping his head back.

When I get back to our seats, I lean down far enough that the ends of my hair brush against his face. "Nervous yet? Those gutter balls are costing you, and I'm here with triple points."

He presses a fast kiss to my lips. "Not a chance."

"We could put up the guards," Penny says, stealing another

nacho from the basket. "As someone who has gone into the gutter nearly every frame so far, I am officially advocating for the guardrails."

"Absolutely not," Sebastian says. He sounds so offended that I start giggling. "Give me a ball."

"Try the green one," I say slyly. "I think it's weighted better."

"Sabotage!" Cooper says with delight. "Mia, you're starting to understand how things work."

Penny pushes the nacho basket in my direction. I sit next to her and pick up my beer. It's warm, but I down the rest anyway. "Are these any good?"

"Nope," Penny says. "And yet I can't stop eating them."

I grab a particularly cheesy chip and pop it into my mouth. She's right, it's terrible, but it's the kind of food you want when you're drinking from a beer pitcher. I watch as Sebastian grabs a ball—not the one I suggested, naturally—and sets up.

"Point your feet," I call.

"You point your feet," he grumbles.

I cup my ear. "What was that?"

"Damn," Cooper says. "Mia di Angelo, secret cutthroat bowler."

"I know," Penny says fondly. "Why do you think I turned down every other double date idea?"

"Huh," Cooper says. "I did think it was weird that you didn't want to see the special *How to Lose a Guy in Ten Days* screening at the movie theater."

"There's plenty of time," Penny says. "We're doing this again, right, Mia?"

I watch as Sebastian's ball spirals out of control, landing in the gutter right before the pins. "Oh, definitely."

"What's the bet?" Penny says. "There has to be a bet involved."

I pour myself another beer. "It's a secret."

She gasps. "That means it's naughty. Mia, I'm so proud."

"No wonder Seb's being such a sore loser," Cooper says. He flops over at least three of the tiny plastic seats like a tired puppy. Penny rolls her eyes, but she's smiling.

When Sebastian comes back to the sitting area, Cooper holds out his hand for a high-five. Sebastian gives him the finger instead. I grin into my beer, watching them bicker about technique. It must be weird for them both, not being good at something that involves a degree of athleticism. Sebastian mentioned the other day that even though his sport is baseball, he knows how to shoot a puck properly, and his football throw has a nice spiral.

I wonder what he'd say to football on the lawn with Dad and Anthony. If he comes to the barbecue, he'll be strong-armed into it, that's for sure. And if Dad finds out his brother is the quarterback of his favorite team? He'll spend the whole afternoon talking about James' stats. I might not be able to grab a second with Sebastian to introduce him to Giana or the rest of the family.

It's weird to think about him in my parents' backyard, laughing with my cousins and chatting with my parents. Giana's right, they'll probably love him. But he's easy to love, with that handsome smile and quiet intensity. He's the kind of guy they've always wanted for me, minus the fact he's not Italian. I might actually win a smidge of my mother's approval if I show up with him in tow.

Penny clinks her beer against mine. "This is nice."

"Yeah," I say. I wash down the emotion that's threatening to show on my face with a gulp of my drink. "Good choice, Pen."

"Anything for you," she says. We watch as Sebastian gets Cooper into a headlock. "Should we break them up?"

I lift one shoulder in a shrug. "Eh. Something tells me it's better to just let them go."

At the end of the game, I'm just shy of a perfect score; Sebastian distracted me during the two last frames with kisses. A completely blatant attempt at gaining the upper hand, but it's all too fun to kiss him when he clearly has to keep reminding himself not to get too handsy in front of the old guys playing two lanes over.

I grin at him over my shoulder as I start the next game. "Ready for what I have planned?"

"Wait, wait," Penny says. She waves the empty beer pitcher. "If I'm forced to play another game without the gutter guards, I demand refreshments. Seb, come get another round with me."

Sebastian unwinds himself from me, his eyebrows raised. "You good?"

"I think I'll survive," I say dryly.

Cooper raises his hand in a wave. This is Penny's doing, clearly, but I don't mind if it means clearing the air with her boyfriend. He's my roommate right now, on top of everything else. Over the past few days, he's been *extremely* polite about knocking. I think seeing my boobs scarred him a little, which is hilarious considering the reputation he had before Penny. Not that I'm judging him; Sebastian had a similar reputation, and so did I. There's nothing wrong with wanting casual connections in bed, no matter who you are, but being in a relationship is a lot different.

I guess things change when the right person comes into your life. I'm still scared shitless that it'll all go up in flames, but if I'm trying this relationship thing with anyone, it's Sebastian.

Penny drags him away to the bar. I sit down next to Cooper, stretching my arm over the back of the seat. He scrubs his hand over his neatly trimmed beard as he grimaces.

"Look," he says. "I'm sorry about the way I acted. I was rude to you, and you didn't deserve that. You and Sebastian have your own relationship and I'm not part of it. It's just—I'm always going to protect him. Probably more than he needs, but I can't help it. He's my brother for life."

I duck my head, feeling my face redden. "Thank you, but you were right. I wasn't being fair to him."

"Still. I'm sorry for goading you into something you maybe weren't ready for."

I huff out a laugh. It's still strange to think that Sebastian likes me back; that he's liked me since he saw me outside the movie theater last fall.

I remember that night. It was cold, so I broke out my favorite black scarf. Cooper and Penny were hooking up then, and dancing around each other. The dildo that Penny accidentally hit me with had met an untimely demise earlier in the day. And a guy with the greenest eyes I'd ever seen and a smile like a crescent moon couldn't stop looking at me.

"I'm scared," I admit.

"Because it matters." He leans forward, squeezing my shoulder. "It's always scary when it matters."

I muster a smile. "Yeah."

"I think you're good together, for the record. I know how much you mean to Penny, and Sebastian deserves to be with someone like you. You're whip-smart and funny, and he's never let himself have someone in his life like this."

I tuck my hair behind my ears. "Thanks, Coop. I like you and Penny together, too."

By the way he smiles, he's thinking about her. I send another thank you to the universe for giving Penny this. She deserves it, completely and wholeheartedly. She's changed so much since last year, and it's all for the better.

He settles back, downing the rest of his beer. "Just don't break his heart."

39

SEBASTIAN

I TILT MY HEAD to the side with my eyes closed, listening as my bedroom door opens, shuts, and locks. When we got home from the bowling alley, Mia told me to go upstairs and wait in my room with my eyes closed. I've been patient—I lost our bet fair and square, after all, even if she hid her bowling prowess from me to secure victory—but the anticipation feels palpable, dragging across my skin. I haven't touched myself yet, but my cock is half-hard already. I want to touch her, to taste her, to spank her for playing me for a fool... but it's her night. Her win. I can already sense the electricity between us, that live golden wire dancing in the quiet of the room.

I hear her footsteps across the floor, and then I sense her. With my eyes closed, I focus on her warm presence and her jasmine scent. She must lean in, because something tickles my cheek; her hair, I'd be willing to bet. It's a struggle to keep my hands to myself as my cock twitches in my jeans.

"You can open your eyes now," she murmurs.

I take my hands away from my eyes, blinking a few times. When I shut them, the overhead light in my room was on, but now it's off, with only the glow of my desk lamp illuminating the space. Mia stands before me in a black silk robe—and those gorgeous suede boots. Her hair hangs long and loose over her shoulders. She's wearing the same jewelry as before, her little gold hoops and a matching gold chain, and she must have freshened up her makeup as well, because her lips shine with gloss.

My mouth goes dry instantly. No one—absolutely no one—comes close to her beauty. I know every guy thinks they've landed the most gorgeous girl in the world, but me? I actually have her. "Angel."

She lets the robe fall off her shoulders, revealing a set of lacy black straps. I reach forward, but she shakes her head. Her lips press together like she's holding back a smile. "Just sit back and relax."

"You're torturing me," I say.

She presses her finger to my lips. "I haven't even started, babe."

She takes a step back, running her delicate hand through her hair, shaking it out over her shoulders. The robe slips down a couple more inches, showing off her toned arms. "Siri," she says. "Play 'My Heart Has Teeth.'"

I settle against the headboard, lacing my fingers together behind my head. I've never heard of the song she just turned on, but the beat that fills the room is dark and fucking sexy. She moves her hips to the music, toying with the tie on the robe.

If I'm not careful, I'm going to come in my pants before she even touches me.

The beat of the song feels like a handprint against my

heart. I fist my fingers in my jeans, forcing myself to keep from pulling out my cock and giving it a stroke. A wicked smile plays on her lips as she unties the robe. She lets it fall slowly, moving all the while. When it slips away from her front, I can't help it, I groan aloud.

She's wearing a bodysuit made of black lace and mesh. The neckline plunges down between her breasts, and delicate swirls of lace just barely cover her nipples. Ribbed mesh covers her stomach, leading down to a scrap of fabric that shows off the groomed triangle of hair between her legs. Garters extend from the bodysuit to sheer thigh-high socks that come an inch above the suede boots I bought her.

She's always sexy, no matter what she's wearing, but right now, it takes all of my willpower not to pull her into my lap and lick right over the thin lace covering those pretty pink nipples. I clench my ass to fight the wave of arousal that goes through me when she drags her finger from her collarbone, thrown in sharp relief against her outfit, all the way down to the rib leading straight to her cunt.

She gathers her hair in her hands and lets it fall as she bites her lip. Her eyelashes flutter.

"Fucking hell," I say, my voice low and rough. I can't help it; I squeeze my cock through my jeans.

She lets go of her lip slowly. I can't take my eyes off the slick lip gloss, imagining that it's spit and my seed coating them instead.

"Not until I give you permission," she purrs.

The song kicks up a notch. I can barely pay attention to the lyrics, not when I have a literal angel dancing for me, but what I do catch sounds so perfectly Mia that I smile. She turns in a slow circle, showing off the way the fabric just barely covers the sweet curve of her ass. There's a heart-shaped cutout right at her lower back, and the garters extend straight down the backs of her thighs, teasing lines that make my cock jump. I want to slap her bottom until it turns pink, maybe fuck her there, too, but it's her show. I'll beg her for whatever she wants to give me, whether that's fucking her or letting her tease me all night. If she wants to drag me along until a single touch will make me blow my load, I'll let her. She's my dark angel, and by the curve of her smile as she looks over her shoulder at me? She knows it.

She slides her hands down her sides, over her ass, and gives herself a little smack before turning around. As the song launches into the chorus again, she dips into a crouch, then rises slowly, her hips gyrating all the while. She slips one strap down, and then the next, pulling the bodysuit down far enough to free her tits. She palms them, letting her head fall back. Letting me hear the evidence of her pleasure in the way she moans.

I'm so stiff in my pants that I'm afraid to move. She gives me another smile, smug because she knows exactly what she's doing to me, and saunters over.

She crawls onto the bed, her hair spilling over her shoulders, her eyes dark and shining. When she straddles my lap, I nearly buck my hips. She leans down, leaving her lips half an inch from mine, and says, "Keep watching. Hands to yourself, but take off your shirt."

I do as she says, hoping for a kiss, but she doesn't indulge me. She runs her nails down my chest, tracing over the lines of my tattoo. She rocks back and forth against my crotch. My balls draw up tight, aching without contact; it'd only take a stroke or two to send me over the edge.

"Fucking love your body," she says, as breathless as I am. She squeezes my bicep. "You're so strong."

Even though she's in control, I see how difficult it is to maintain it; I know she wants to kiss me just as badly. There's nothing sexier than seeing her like this, just as needy as me, wanting so much even as she struggles to keep up the game.

"Sweetheart," I beg. "Just one kiss."

She reaches between us and strokes my cock over my jeans as the song fades. Her lips brush against mine, feather-light. The gloss on her lips is strawberry-flavored, an unexpectedly sweet taste that I want more of. When I try to deepen the kiss, she pulls away, pushing me against the headboard.

She rises to her feet carefully, balancing over me on the bed. I can't help myself; I reach up and run my hand down her long leg, the soft suede of her boot. I've had dreams about these boots, but none of them have come close to this. Electricity zings down my spine, settling low. It's so hard not to pull her down and roll us over, to kiss her until I steal the breath right from her lungs, to claim her until there's no doubt in either of our minds that she's mine and I'm hers.

Her smile turns downright feline. She lifts her leg, planting the heel of her boot right against my tattoo, and grinds down.

At the bloom of pain, I come right in my fucking pants.

"Holy fucking shit." My head thuds against the wall as I groan through the orgasm, the delicious rush of it jolting like lightning.

She gasps, as if the sight of me coming is enough to send her wobbling over the edge too, and drops into my lap. Her hands wind through my hair, tugging firmly, as she kisses me, licking into my mouth. I wrap my arms around her, digging my fingers into that maddening lace, and kiss her to calm my racing heart. My chest aches from her heel.

I've never felt so fucking wanted. I've never come harder in my life. She knew just what to do to bring it to the next level, to take command even as she's giving me everything she has.

She pulls back after a long moment. "Wanna ride your face."

I groan. "You're gonna kill me."

She laughs as she kisses me again. "That was so hot."

Her laughter is music to my ears. I join in, and for a moment, we just laugh together, hopped up on adrenaline. There's something about Mia that makes it so easy to go from serious to goofy, inside the bedroom and out. I brush her hair back, pressing a kiss to her jaw and biting down gently. "Oh yeah?"

"Been dreaming about that," she murmurs. "Seeing you lose control got me so close to the edge, baby."

"Keep the boots on," I say as I drag my hands down her back. I trace along the heart-shaped cutout, pleased when that makes her shiver. "Can't get enough of you in them."

"Aren't I supposed to be giving the orders right now?" she teases. Still, she wriggles out of the bodysuit the rest of the way. As sexy as she looks in all that dark lace, my heart races at the sight of her bare, her face flushed, her nipples pebbled in the cool dark of the room. I scoot down, settling on my back, my cock stirring again already as she sits right on my face.

I could die happily right here and now, with Mia's soft, strong thighs on either side of my head and her cunt pressed against my mouth. No hesitation, no shyness. She knows what she wants, and I want nothing more than to deliver. I settle my hands on her thighs, breathing against her delicate skin, and relish in her shivering.

"So pretty," I murmur right against her skin. She cries out from the vibrations of my voice. "You taste like heaven, Mia Angel."

"I was going for devil," she says, ending the sentence on a gasp as I nudge her clit. I turn my head into her thigh to give it a kiss. I grab her ass, urging her to give me all of her weight.

"Never," I say breathlessly. "You'll always be an angel to me. You might try to be a devil to everyone else, but you're my angel."

Her eyes widen. "Sebastian."

I smile against her. I dig my fingers into her firm ass, licking and sucking wherever I can reach. A constant stream of whines and whimpers escape her mouth, but I don't let up, not when she's so close to the edge. She moves against me, just a little at first but then gaining steam, her hands sinking into my hair and tugging sharply.

"Spank me," she says with a whimper. "Please, I need—"

I slap her bottom hard enough she gasps. "I'm so close."

I hit her again, on the other side, fucking her with my tongue as I do. Her body tenses, and then she's coming, crying out my name loudly enough I hope Cooper and Penny are too busy with each other to notice. I keep licking at her, dragging my fingers over the crease of her bottom, until she whines, twisting out of my grip. She flops next to me.

For a long moment, neither of us say anything. We just lie there in comfortable silence, listening to each other breathe. My chest continues to ache, and I bite my lip as I smile. I hope the skin bruises. I want the reminder of her on my skin for days to come.

Eventually, I wriggle out of my ruined jeans, turning so I can cuddle against her warmth. She meets my eyes, her hand stroking through my hair again, gentle this time.

I throw my arm over her and bury my face against her tits. I press a kiss to her flushed skin, right in the middle of her sternum.

"Was I good enough for you?" I tease. "Kept up my end of the bet?"

"No complaints here." She strokes her thumb over my tattoo. I shiver. "You're okay, right? That wasn't too much?"

"You're kidding, right? That was the hottest fucking thing in the world. Patting myself on the back for replacing those boots."

"I've always wanted to try it."

I kiss her on the lips, licking off the remainder of the gloss. "You can always try anything with me."

40

MIA

PROFESSOR SANTORO FLIPS through the article in her lap as she taps her foot against the floor. She scans the room, a classroom filled to the brim with lab assistants, the graduate students, and the other professors in her department. The moment she walked onto campus this morning—earlier than expected, which sent Alice into a tizzy—everyone dropped what they were doing and flocked to her for an impromptu discussion of her latest article draft.

During these discussions, I know when to hold my tongue and listen, but I did manage to sneak in a couple good comments, plus one question that set off a round of arguing, so all in all, I'd consider the morning a success.

Moments like this are both humbling and inspiring. I know that I'm not the most knowledgeable person in the room, and perhaps not the smartest, but if there's anything I am, it's stubborn and a hard worker. One day, I want to be at the head of the table like Professor Santoro, doing research that matters.

"I think this is a good place to end the discussion," she says. She takes off her reading glasses, twisting them between her thumb and forefinger as she nods. "Good contributions, everyone. Thank you for the feedback. Mia, can I talk to you for a moment?"

I sit up straighter. As far as I know, I'm still giving a presentation at the symposium—but I haven't started it yet. Our reworked program is nearly in good shape, thanks to Alice's feedback, which was smart even if it lacked in delivery, but I have simulations to run and data to process, not to mention condensing the whole subject into something I can give a talk on, and defend—because if there's one thing scientists love to do, it's ask questions. If there isn't debate when you bring forth ideas, you've fucked something up.

I swallow, adjusting my ponytail as I try to ignore the look Alice gives me before leaving the room along with everyone else. At least I'm presentable this morning; Sebastian tried to keep me in bed way past when I had to start getting ready for work, but I showered and got dressed in record time. I don't blame him for wanting to stay in bed, though. He has that interview with the reporter from *The Sportsman* today, and I have the sense he would rather perform a root canal on himself with a pair of tweezers than talk to her.

Professor Santoro gives me a smile, tilting her head to the side. "How have things been?"

"Good." I force myself to stop playing with the ponytail. I could tell her about Alice, but there's no point in making it into a bigger deal than it is, so I just say, "I've been working on everything I'm assigned. Alice has been giving me good feedback to work with."

"But you're not finished with it yet?"

"No." I meet her gaze. "I just need a few more days."

She nods. "A couple more days, then I want to see it up and running, Mia. If we need to work out any kinks, I would prefer to do it with enough time to process and synthesize it. You've been putting in the hours, right? I know I need to check the timesheets you left in the mailbox."

"Of course." I rub my thumb over my knuckles. "I've been coming in early every day. Staying late, too, when I need to."

Technically speaking, I had been doing that, but ever since things changed with Sebastian, I've spent more time with him than in the lab. Yesterday, I went to his practice—something I literally thought I'd never do for a partner—and enjoyed myself. It brought back memories of playing softball in high school, and seeing him run around like a badass in his practice gear wasn't a hardship, either. Neither was dancing with him in the kitchen in the middle of another sleepless night while curry simmered on the stove.

Still, I've been so caught up in him lately that my focus isn't as sharp as it should be. I made myself a promise that I'd never let a relationship get in the way of my ambition, and regardless of how I feel for him, I can't compromise with myself. Not on this.

The mere thought of that sends a little tendril of panic through me, because Sebastian does deserve a girlfriend who is there for him. Not just for a random weekday practice or to vanquish bad memories, but for all the shit that matters in his own life and career, and staring that in the face is terrifying.

I just need to recommit. I can't let this opportunity slip through my fingers. Failure isn't an option under any circumstances, but especially not now, with Professor Santoro counting on me and a semester at the University of Geneva on the line. If I have a shot at making my parents understand what I want to do, I need to succeed at it.

"I know it's a lot," she says. "But I want to push you. If you're going to keep doing this, you need to get comfortable working under time constraints. We'd love all the time and budget in the world to get our work done, but that's not how it works if you want to work on these large projects. Keeping up with the little milestones leads to the big breakthroughs in science, every time."

"Absolutely."

She gives me a long, considering look. She must approve of what she sees because she nods. "Good. And how are things with your family?"

"They're fine."

"Did you mention the symposium to them?"

"Not yet."

She purses her lips. "I'll need to know who to expect, Mia."

"Don't expect any of them." Admitting it hurts, but it's the truth. My plan all along has been to come clean after I have the study abroad lined up; they'll see how serious I am when I have the acceptance in hand. But I need the symposium to secure my spot, and I don't want to risk messing it up by involving my family. "Maybe my... I have a boyfriend, and maybe he'll come. But it's not a good time to talk to my parents."

"A boyfriend?" she asks.

"It's recent."

"I met my husband while I was in graduate school," she says. She smiles slightly, clearly remembering something. "It's hard to maintain relationships in this field. Very hard. I think it worked because he was in academia too—for biology, of course, but he understood the demands."

"Did you ever..." I trail off, because while I've gotten candid with her about my family, and she's shared some information about hers, we haven't spoken about personal things beyond that. I knew about her husband; he works in the biology department here at McKee, but I don't know much more. "Did you need to do things long-distance?"

"My first position as a professor was at Stony Brook, on Long Island," she says. "And Sam was all the way in California, at Stanford."

"No way."

"It was hard, but we made compromises." She fiddles with her wedding ring, a simple gold band with a floral engraving. "The thing was to choose which compromises to make. We had non-negotiable things, and others that were more flexible. Eventually we wanted to get on the same coast, and we made that happen. Is your boyfriend a student here?"

"Yeah. He's on the baseball team."

"Ah," she says. "So he's busy right now."

"Giving an interview as we speak," I say wryly. "I don't know if the name Sebastian Callahan means anything to you, he studies history, but—"

"Jacob Miller's son," she says.

I blink. "Yeah. How did you know?"

"Sam is from Cincinnati. He's a huge Reds fan."

"He'll want him to be on the team eventually, then."

"I don't pay much attention to the specifics. But his name is recognizable, yes." She laughs slightly. "I won't lie to you, Mia.

It's hard to be in two places when you're trying to have one relationship. There will be choices to make, and you might not always like the answer. Sam and I nearly didn't make it, although we're stronger now, having gone through the hardship."

I dig my fingertips into my palm. "I can't give this up. It's... it's all I've ever wanted. Ever since the first time I looked at the stars through a telescope."

Something cracked open in my heart that night as I stood on the beach with Nonno, staring up at the nighttime sky. I felt so connected to the world around me, to that endless, diamond-studded black, my mind crowded with so many questions I could barely think. All science starts with a question, and I had enough for several lifetimes. I know, in the deepest, most vulnerable, most guarded part of my soul, that I was given this passion for a reason.

"Nor do I think you should. A mind like yours doesn't come around very often. It's been years since I've had such a promising student."

My breath sticks in my throat. "Thank you."

She sighs, gathering up the papers scattered around her and sticking them back into a manila folder. "Let's schedule a time to go over the readings I gave you before the conference, then get to work."

After she lets me go, I settle into my workstation, redo my ponytail, and put on my blue light glasses.

I debate it for a moment, but I turn off my phone and shove it into my bag. The world won't end if I focus and catch up with Sebastian later. He knows that I'm working just as hard as he is, after all. Proving myself to Professor Santoro, to Nonno, to my parents, when I work up the courage to come clean to them—it's more important than anything else.

I pull up the program and the notes Alice gave me, then dive in.

I can't imagine my parents watching me work, but I like to think that Nonno bears witness to it, wherever the mystery of the universe called him to, and that he's proud of me.

41

SEBASTIAN

"I NEED YOU TO HOLD STILL," the wardrobe assistant, a tall, laser-focused woman named Kat, says. "Just—still, okay? Let me adjust the pants."

I chew the inside of my mouth as I try to convince myself I'm a statue. Easier said than done. Being at the baseball field brings out a desire to move; ever since we arrived an hour ago, I've wanted to take a couple laps around the diamond. I'd sprint from home plate to the warning track in center field, over and over, if it meant avoiding the camera setup I see out of the corner of my eye. One time, around the anniversary of the accident, I was feeling so fucking pissed about it that I mouthed off to my coach, and he made me do sprints from one end of the outfield to the other until I puked. I hated him for it, but the activity helped clear out the thoughts racing through my mind.

I wonder if those are the kinds of stories that Zoe Anders is hoping to get out of me with this interview. If she wants to talk about stats or my game, that's great, but the rest of it? It's hard to think to myself, much less say aloud to another person. And that's without bringing a camera into the mix.

Before I headed out today, Richard called me to check in, and he reminded me of the one thing I need to hold close, above all: this is about my father's legacy as much as it is about my future. His people have been keeping an eye on all the articles and social media posts and remembrances that have cropped up, especially in the past few months. This interview is an opportunity to put my own words into the world.

"That's better," Kat says, taking a step back to confirm. "And you'll hold the bat over your shoulder in the first shots, that's perfect."

Her assistant hands me a baseball bat. The weight of it surprises me; it's a little longer and heavier than the one I usually use. Like most ball players, I'm particular about my equipment. A bat that doesn't feel right in my hands will just lead to strikeouts.

"This isn't my bat," I say.

"Oh, I know," Kat says. "We wanted the contrast of the black against the rest of your outfit."

I glance at Zoe, who glances up from her tablet. "Does that work, Sebastian?"

Zoe Anders looks as put together as she did during our video call; she's wearing a pair of tailored cream linen pants, a hot pink blouse that flows in all the right places, and—even though we're standing right next to home plate—expensive, cherry-colored loafers. Apparently, *The Sportsman* pays their people well. She's wearing a necklace as well, chunky, gold, and impossible to ignore. I'm going to have to work to look her in the eyes when we talk.

I want to get Mia a piece of jewelry. I know I've given her

gifts before, but it would mean something different now that we're dating. She'd never be caught wearing the monstrosity around Zoe's neck, but I saw a delicate gold chain with a star pendant the other day, and it reminded me of her.

When I get home later, I'll order it. I like the thought of her wearing a necklace I gave her. It'll look pretty with those gold hoops she loves.

"Sebastian?"

"Huh?"

"I said, we'd prefer you to use that bat for these photographs, but if you want your own equipment when we photograph you in the McKee uniform, we can do that."

"Oh," I say. "Um, sorry. Sure, whatever."

"You good?" she says. "There's a lot to get through today, but let me know if you need a breather."

I try for a smile as I swing the bat over my shoulder. "I'm fine."

"Good." She tilts her head to the side, considering me. "I think he looks great, Kat, but let's get Eddie's opinion."

After a few more minutes of fussing, the photographer, Eddie, officially approves, so we start the shoot. I feel so fucking awkward standing at home plate with the bat over my shoulder that I almost burst out laughing, but I manage to rein it in. It's mid-morning now, with sunshine drenching everything. I wish I had sunglasses on, but that wouldn't go with the 'look.'

The look, by the way, is just how I normally dress. Sneakers, jeans, a t-shirt. Maybe a little nicer than usual, but nothing too fancy. Thank God Cooper decided to visit his teammate Evan instead of tagging along; he'd be losing it trying to hold back laughter. Probably less successfully, too. Part of me does wish that Mia was here. Even if she was in the background, feeling her presence would be enough to take the edge off my nerves. When there's a lull in the photographing, I send her a selfie, but she doesn't reply right away.

Eventually, we move to the dugout, and they take a couple more pictures there before Kat sends me off to change into my uniform. Even though it's what I wear to every home game, the deep purple of the jersey with 'McKee' written in white script over the front, she takes her time fussing with it before the next set of photographs.

"One more set," Eddie promises. "Elbows on your knees, hands over the bat holding it straight down... Perfect."

When we're finally done, I desperately want to crawl into a hole, but we haven't even gotten to the hard part yet. I follow Zoe to the training center, where Coach Martin meets us. *The Sportsman* and the university had to coordinate to make the interview happen on campus, but Zoe fought for it, to get a full sense of where I train and play.

I respect her; she seems good at her job. I'm just dreading the conversation entirely.

"It's so nice to meet you in person," she says, reaching her hand out to shake Coach Martin's. "Your comments about Sebastian were very insightful."

"Seb's a hard worker," he says. "One of the best players I've ever had the privilege of coaching."

"How could he be anything else, with Jacob's genes?" she quips.

My heart stutter-steps when I hear my father's name come out of her mouth. I follow them down the hallway, past the staff offices. There's a room we use when we break into position-specific meetings, and Coach takes us there.

"This will be perfect," she says. "Thank you so much."

"Take your time." Coach squeezes my shoulder. "Make us proud, kid."

I muster another smile. This morning has already been filled with a ton of smiling, but sure, I'll keep doing it. I'll smile all day, if it means Zoe won't pry too deeply into the details of my life.

"Want to take a seat?" she says. She sets her phone on top of the table, along with a notebook and a pen. As I sit, she starts an audio recording. "Thank you again for offering to work with me on this interview. I'm sure it's been a busy time for you."

Did the interview start already? I settle in the chair across from her, trying to stop myself from gripping the arms too tightly. I feel like I have one of Mia's masks on my face, the pleasantness working overtime to hide my true feelings.

I tug at my collar. "This late stretch in the season is always intense."

"Doesn't seem like you're going to make the playoffs for America East," she says, a perfect note of sympathy in her voice.

"It's a great group of teams," I say. "Super strong, all at once. We knew we had to keep the pressure on to have a shot, and it just hasn't been coming together, particularly at the plate."

"Does that weigh on you? Your batting average is lower than in previous seasons at McKee."

"Yeah, definitely." I yank my collar again. "My fielding is strong, of course, but I've always prided myself on my swing."

"Lefty, same as your father."

"Yeah."

"Did you try it both ways?"

"I started swinging a bat before I even had the concept of

righties versus lefties," I say. "I think my dad just set me up the way he did it, and it worked out."

"Your swing is very similar to his. I've spoken to a lot of your former coaches, and of course Coach Martin, and they've all said that you emulate your father on the field. Your leg kick is even the same."

"Like I said, he taught me."

"When did you start? How young?"

"Three or so."

"So it's what you've always known." She taps her pen against the edge of the table. "Was there ever a thought in your mind that you'd consider a different sport?"

"I played a couple other sports when I was younger," I say. "Everyone does, it's good for building up skills across the board. But I never thought I'd play football long term, or soccer, or any of that. I've loved baseball since the beginning."

She picks up her pen and poises it against her notebook. "Why?"

42

SEBASTIAN

THE CONVERSATION HAS been flowing better than I'd hoped, but that simple question trips me up.

Why? Why baseball?

Lately, the usual answers haven't led to that same sense of calm and focus. I could talk about the beauty of it, or how fast my heart beats when I run onto the field, or the perfect moment when my bat connects with the ball and I know I've bested the pitcher. There's the smell of the field when it's freshly mowed, and dirtying up my uniform when I slide into home, and all the handshakes and fist bumps and inside jokes with my teammates. There's harmony in baseball. Poetry, recited without speaking a word.

If James is a general and Cooper is a warrior, I'm an assassin, waiting for the perfect moment to strike.

"Sebastian?" she prompts.

"I think at first I loved it because my father did," I say. "And then I loved it because it still connected me to him."

"And now?"

I give a half-shrug. "Both of those things are still true."

"Tell me a little more about your dad. I remember watching him play."

"I do too." I run my hand through my hair. "He was great. Baseball means a rough schedule, but he made the most of the time we had together. Even if he just got home from a road trip, or only had an hour before he had to head to the stadium, he was there, ready to spend time with me."

"And your mother?"

"The best damn cook ever." I pause as Zoe laughs. "I didn't have any siblings, and not much family we spoke to, so it was just the two of us when my dad was on the road. It's a good thing she loved baseball as much as him, because she was the one taking me to all the practices and games."

I can almost see her, for a moment. Jeans and sandals, sunglasses perched atop a reddened nose, a mystery novel tucked underneath her arm. She'd steal my dad's shirts, old practice gear, and tie them in the front. She took so many videos of me playing to send to Dad, she might've been a documentarian.

I wonder where those videos went. Maybe Sandra has them somewhere, along with the rest of the things I haven't managed to look through.

"And that obviously continued after the accident," she says, crossing one leg over the other. "Before we go into your adoption, though, the accident—do you have anything you personally want to say about it?"

The back of my neck prickles. "What do you mean?"

"Well," she starts, flipping through her notebook. "When I did some digging, I did find... some belief that your father may have been driving under the influence at the time of the accident."

"Bullshit," I say.

"You were there," she says, her voice soft. "You were in the backseat of the car. Was anything off that night, Sebastian? What do you think led to that accident?"

I stand, the chair skidding back several inches. "I'll talk about my family, but not that. Not if you're going to recite lies."

She takes a deep breath. "Okay. I'm sorry. Just sit down."

"He wasn't drunk," I say sharply. "I know they said that, and that he was fighting with my mother, and whatever other shit they tried to pull when the accident went public. They hated my father since the moment she met him; they would have said anything to discredit him. You interviewed them for this? I haven't spoken to them since the funeral."

"I was just exploring all the angles," she says.

I stare at her for a moment longer, but eventually, I sit back down. "Don't print that. They mean nothing to me. They're not my fucking family."

"You have a family," she says, seemingly unruffled by the intensity in my voice. "The Callahans. Your father's best friend and his wife, and their children."

I need to rein it in. I take a deep breath, trying to loosen my shoulders. I still remember what my mother's father whispered to her mother at the funeral; I overheard them talking over her fucking body at the viewing. *A horrible thing, but at least if she had to go, so did the scumbag.* All because they thought my mother could have done better, and my father sullied her by knocking her up and convincing her to run away with him.

"Yeah," I say.

"Richard mentioned it was a pact that he made with Jacob

when they were young. A promise to take care of each other's families if anything like this happened."

"What about it?"

"Given that, would you truly consider them your family? How has it been, growing up with the Callahans?"

I can still remember the moment Richard and Sandra told me that they'd be taking care of me from now on. It was before the funeral, which they organized. They were in Cincinnati before the hospital discharged me, handling everything because my dad didn't have any family to do it and my mother's family was threatening to give her a separate funeral. Sandra, who by that point was my mother's best friend, fought tooth and nail for her to be buried with her husband.

Up until then, I saw them a couple times a year; James, Cooper, and Izzy were like cousins I hung out with on holidays. With my dad based in Ohio and Richard in New York, it was the best they could do. That morning, though, after days of working out the details, they sat me in a chair in the hallway outside the church with the social worker who had been handling my case. Richard had on a suit, and Sandra a navy-blue dress. He looked at his wife, waiting for her final nod, before he leaned in and said, "Son, you're coming home with us."

Sandra had hugged me then, and I remember letting myself think it was my mother instead. Just once. I was eleven, but plenty old enough to understand there wouldn't be any going back.

I trace over the fake leather of the chair's arm, unable to tear my gaze away from Zoe's phone. That stupid blinking red light is sending my heart rate into overdrive.

"It's strange to think about, sometimes," I say. "It's been a decade of a different life than the one I was born into. In some ways, it's incredibly similar—and I thank Richard and Sandra for keeping things as normal as possible and keeping me in baseball. But it's not what it could have been, and I'll never not wonder how things would be different. I'll never not miss my mother and father and wish they were in my life."

"Of course," Zoe says softly. "I lost my father a few years ago, and it hasn't been the same. Nothing completely heals that wound."

"No." I blink away sudden, stinging tears. "But my life is great. I love my family—and they are my family—more than anything. James is the best big brother anyone could ask for, and Izzy's the best little sister, and Cooper's my best friend. Richard and Sandra are parents to me, absolutely. They've supported my baseball career every step of the way, keeping in line with my father's wishes."

"So it truly was your father's dream for you to play baseball."

"Yeah. He'd be so excited about the draft." I laugh slightly. "I've seen a lot of things people have been writing, and honestly, I don't think he'd care about whether I go in the top ten or the last slot of the last round. He'd just want me to make it."

"And this is your future? Your lifelong passion, just like your dad?"

I look at her for a long moment.

Yes. Always.

No other option.

So why is it so hard to say aloud?

That light keeps blinking, impossible to ignore. Taunting me. I rub my chest, right over the tattoo I got with James and

Cooper a couple summers ago in OBX. The bruise Mia gave me with her heel is still there, a comforting tenderness when I press down. I wish I could check my phone to see if she texted back, but I don't want to be rude.

I take a deep breath. I can finish this. It's not that bad.

Zoe notes my hesitation; I can see it in the way she uncrosses her legs and leans in. "I'm wondering about the last name 'Callahan' on your jersey. Is it just for practicality? Are you going to switch to 'Miller' once you're playing baseball professionally?"

"I'm not sure."

"Have you thought about what your father would think?"

"He's dead," I snap. "I don't know what he would think."

"Do you think you have the talent to match or surpass his records?" She flips to another page in her notebook. "What about the fact he didn't play long enough to make the Hall of Fame? Do you think he should be in it regardless since he holds the National League home run title?"

My chest feels tight, my heart aching. I can feel the beginnings of a headache around my temples. I cast around for something to say. Anything to get her off this line of questioning, and to calm myself the hell down. "I have a girlfriend."

She picks up her pen. "A girlfriend?"

"Her name is Mia." I work my hand through my hair again, tugging on the ends. "She's studying astronomy and physics— she's a genius. She wants to work for NASA one day."

"Is she a student here at McKee?"

"Yeah."

"You lit up, just now," she says. "She must mean a lot to you."

"She's one of the best people I've ever known. Absolutely the smartest. I'm just a jock, but she's special. I'm grateful that she gives me the time of day, much less wants to be with me."

"Adorable," she says. "Will I see her at tomorrow night's game?"

"Yeah," I say, even though I haven't spoken to Mia about attending my games. I haven't wanted to push, since she's so busy with her lab work, but it would be nice to see her in the stands at least once before... before the end of the season. "She'll be there."

She smiles, fiddling with that ostentatious necklace. "I can't wait to meet her."

I NEVER THOUGHT I would be the sort of girl who liked holding hands, but it turns out that I do like it—a lot. Sebastian takes my hand as we walk to Vesuvio's, and his is so warm and big that when he holds mine, it sends a shiver straight down to the base of my spine. I wonder how long it'll last; if I'll always feel this when our skin touches, or if eventually, it'll fade.

I hope it doesn't. I hope there's a future for us, and that whenever my hand brushes his, I'll feel something slotting into place in my heart.

"Ready?" he says, squeezing my fingers tightly, like he can tell what I'm thinking. "No training wheels this time, gorgeous."

I nod, letting him lead me into the restaurant. When he suggested Vesuvio's for dinner tonight, my first instinct was to deflect, but he had a tough day with the interview, so I broke out the dress I initially bought to wear on our date at this restaurant and let Penny add waves to my hair. By the way

Sebastian looked at me when I walked down the stairs, you'd think he was taking me to prom. I half-expected him to pull out a corsage.

Instead of my prom, I went to a robotics competition. My mother was furious—she bought a dress for me and everything, and somehow procured me a date, who I think was the son of one of her friends—but I didn't give in. I detested St. Catherine Academy and had no desire to spend a whole night dancing with a stranger and the rest of my tiny grade, a couple dozen girls who hated me and thought I was strange at best, or a bitch at worst.

The hostess takes us to a table by the window, and before I can pull out the chair, Sebastian does it for me.

I bite back a smile as I open the menu. "You've been dying for the chance to do that, haven't you?"

His hand encircles my wrist, squeezing lightly. "You know me pretty well by now, you know," he says.

"I've learned most of it against my will."

He smiles, and I can't help it; I smile back. "I'll take it."

"You're so dorky sometimes."

"And yet you like it."

I give him an exaggerated sigh. "I suppose I do."

Dork or not, he looks hot as fuck tonight, his light hair slightly damp and curled at the ends, his jawline sharp enough to cut. His father's old necklace glints in the hollow of his throat, framed on either side by his floral-patterned shirt, unbuttoned at the top. He's tanner than when I first started to stay with him; the practices and afternoon games are treating him well. I realize after a moment that I'm gazing at him instead of the menu.

"You're staring," he says slyly. "The concept of a dinner date can't be that foreign to you."

"I might as well be on Mars."

"Come on."

"I'm serious! I've never sat down at a fancy table like this, across from someone I liked." I take a sip of water. "How about you?"

"I dated a bit in high school. Up until now in college, not so much." He sets down his menu. "You look stunning, by the way."

I glance down at my dress, automatically adjusting it. "I bought this back when you first asked me. Well, the second time you asked me."

His smile softens. "I'm glad you kept it."

When the server comes around, we order a bottle of wine to split, a burrata appetizer, and our entrees; we both opt for fish, although he picks the salmon and I pick the grouper. It's nice, sitting with him, enjoying a glass of perfectly chilled white wine. I can use the break after the hours I spent focusing on work earlier. By the way he sighs, settling more comfortably into his chair, I think he's thinking the same thing. He didn't just have the interview, after all; he also had an afternoon game. At least they won today, and he went 2-for-3, with a home run. I made sure to check as soon as it ended.

"How did it go?" I ask. "I'm sorry I wasn't around; Professor Santoro came home from her trip early and Alice was all stressed about impressing her."

The conversation I had with Professor Santoro returns to the front of my mind. It was nice to tell her about Sebastian, but the way she spoke about the future hurt. She's lucky that her husband is also in science, so at least they have that in common.

"It's okay," he says. He scrubs his hand over his face. "But it wasn't good."

"Oh," I say. "I'm sorry."

"And the stupid photographs from that practice are all over Twitter, apparently. Which—it's not negative, you know? I'm sure some of the comments are, even though I'm not even doing anything, but most of them aren't. I just hate that they're out there in the first place."

I nudge my foot against his underneath the table. "Why wasn't the interview good?"

"She just—she asked a bunch of invasive questions." He pauses as the server brings around the appetizer. "She wanted to know about my parents, my dad especially, and I get it, I haven't said that much about him publicly. But she spoke to my mom's family too, and they had nothing good to say about him, so defending him... I hated having to do that."

"I'm glad you didn't end up with your mother's family after your parents passed." He told me a little more about them, and they sound horrible. If I ever meet them, they should run in the opposite direction, because I'll protect Sebastian with everything I have.

He snorts. "Who knows what I'd be like right now."

I spear a forkful of food and hold it out to him. "Try it. Good food always puts you in a good mood."

To my relief, he smiles. "I want to do something with burrata. Maybe this weekend? I've been wanting to play around with eggplant."

I burst out laughing. "Babe."

"What?" he says. "That was completely serious. Grilled with some nice olive oil drizzled on top, warm burrata, herbs, maybe walnuts for texture? I could make a vinaigrette with a flavored molasses, do the sweet and sour thing."

"Eating at a fancy restaurant and you're rewriting the menu in your head," I tease.

"Richard knows the owner of this place," he says. "I asked him if I could work here, back in freshman year, but he wanted me to focus on baseball."

I glance around. I've never worked in a restaurant; when I was in high school, I worked at a local coffee shop, and that has continued at McKee. Part of me wants to make it into the study abroad program just to get a break from The Purple Kettle. "What, as a server? Having a job in college kind of sucks. I hate making lattes over and over."

"Oh, I know it wouldn't have been easy. But I wanted to be in the kitchen. Even as a dishwasher, you know? Just to experience it and learn more about food."

"You definitely know a lot about food. Everything you make is delicious."

He shrugs. "Yeah, I try when I can, here and there. But the restaurant world is its own kind of beast."

"Maybe you should go on one of those cooking competition shows. They'd love that, a pro-bound baseball player who can make perfect filet mignon."

He shakes his head. "No way. I can barely stand the thought of the twenty people who tune in when they televise my games."

I take a sip of wine, considering him. "I hate to break it to you, but way more than twenty people watch MLB games."

He drags his hand over his face exaggeratedly. "Don't remind me."

I reach over and poke him. "Might want to prepare yourself, whatever you need to do."

"Wear racehorse blinders, something casual like that. Won't be weird at all on ESPN." He mimics blinders with his hands, sending me into a fit of giggling. "I mean, it's fine. Today was a trip. I felt like I was naked the whole time, and everyone was staring."

"To be fair, it's hard not to stare when you're naked."

That comes out of my mouth at the exact moment the server sets down our entrées.

My face erupts into heat as Sebastian's mouth drops open. "Wow. You know what, thank you. I feel so much less embarrassed now."

I find his foot underneath the table and stomp on it. "You're terrible."

"Is that why you came into the shower with me again the other day?" He leans back, propping his elbow on the back of his chair, a shit-eating grin on his face. "I had no idea I was so irresistible to you."

"I hate you."

"Come on, sweetheart." He drags the tip of his shoe up my bare leg. I can't keep from swallowing visibly, and I know he can tell by the way his gaze zeroes in on my throat. "We both know that couldn't be further from the truth."

"If you insist." I know my blush gives me away, but it's too fun to keep up the ruse. He clears his throat, taking a sip of water.

"I know you're busy with work right now," he says, "but there's a game tomorrow night. Not many left in the season. I was wondering if... you wanted to come. To see me play."

I smile, hiding it behind my hand as I chew. "You want me in the stands?"

"Yeah. If you want to check it out. I know my first attempts at giving you tickets were total fails, but I figure that now—"

My heart beats a little faster as his words sink in. "I was already planning on going, actually."

"Wait, really?"

"This is probably a surprise, so don't say anything, but Izzy is coming up." I take a sip of wine, liking how his eyes light up at the mention of his little sister. "We're going to go together. Cooper and Penny too, probably."

He stands suddenly, sending the chair backwards.

"Seb?"

He takes my face in his hands and presses a kiss to my lips. "Thank you. I'll leave a jersey out for you."

I blink as he steps back. "You're that excited?"

"Excited? I feel like I could go out and hit a fucking grand slam."

Part of me feels guilty that I didn't try to go to any of his games until now, but I shove that down. Things were different before. What matters is now. "I'll be there."

He strokes his knuckles over my cheek before heading back to his seat. "I'll make it worth your while."

44

MIA

THE SECOND SEBASTIAN parks the car, I slip into his lap.

It's a tight squeeze until he gets the seat back; he grunts with surprise, his arms coming around me automatically. The whole drive back from Vesuvio's, I couldn't pay attention to a fucking thing but his hands, strong and capable and so good at touching in all the right places. We should probably go inside, but the kiss I press to his lips tastes sweeter this way. I can still catch the wine on his tongue, and the caramel from our shared dessert. My belly does a happy flop as my tongue tangles with his. We didn't finish the whole bottle of wine, so I'm only the barest hint of tipsy, but part of me still feels drunk. Drunk on him and the way it feels to be around him.

I'm realizing, in a slow, inexorable way, that there's no one in the world like him. No one who makes my heart race the way he does. I'm free-falling, a meteor burning up in the atmosphere.

He nips at my lower lip as he strokes those perfect hands

down my back. When they settle on my ass, squeezing, I moan into his mouth.

"I'm super horny," I say breathlessly.

"I can tell." The note of amusement in his voice would usually piss me off, but right now, it just makes me want to spread my legs. He rubs his fingertips over my already-damp panties, eliciting another strangled noise from my throat. "What's got you so wound up, angel?"

"Don't tease." I wind my hands through his hair and tug sharply. "You know what."

He traces little patterns into my back over my dress. "You're extra pretty when you're needy."

"Sebastian—"

He plays with the zipper. "You're the one who climbed into my lap."

I reach for his waistband, but he stops me with one of those strong hands. I huff out a breath. "What?"

"We should go inside."

I lean in again and bite his jaw. "Or you could fuck me in the backseat."

"Tempting," he says. "But I'm fucking your ass, angel, and I want you in my bed for that."

My mind short-circuits at his words. Not just at what he's suggesting, although I very much want that, but at the confident tone. He's no stranger to confidence, but he's never used it to sound quite so sexy before. "Oh."

"Is that acceptable?"

He's definitely having fun with this. I pull back, school my face into my sternest expression, and cross my arms. "You seem certain I'll say yes."

His gaze settles on my tits for a long moment. I smirk, but then he cups my jaw, pressing his thumb against my lips.

"I know what you need right now," he says. I lick his thumb, satisfied when that makes his gaze darken. "You need to be overwhelmed, and you need to feel me deep, and I figured the best way to make that happen would be to stuff a toy up your pretty cunt while I bury my cock in that perky fucking bottom I can't stop staring at."

He emphasizes that last bit with a slap against my ass, hard enough I feel the sting. I gasp, rocking down against his lap as I screw my eyes shut. I can't look at him right now; it'd be like staring directly into the sun.

He tilts my face up. "Open those beautiful golden eyes for me."

I listen, in part because no one has ever called my eyes golden before, and shiver. His eyes are verdant, yet he's the one complimenting mine. My stomach somersaults again as blush rises to my cheeks.

"Is that what you want, Mia Angel? Did I get it right?"

"Yes," I say. "Fuck, yes, I want it. I need it."

He rewards me with another kiss, long and lingering. I indulge it, but before he can work on getting us out of the car, I reach around for the handle and swing the door open. I slide out, barely managing to avoid the steering wheel, and steady myself for half a second before taking off running.

"Mia!"

I hope he hears my laughter. I race up the porch stairs, unlock the door in record time, and slam it shut.

I'm halfway to the second floor when Sebastian bursts in. I freeze on the stairs like a rabbit being stared down by a fox. He looks like he's torn between growling at me and laughing, so I just give him a little wave before bolting up the rest of the stairs.

I hear him thunder after me. He catches up right as I'm opening his bedroom door, shutting it firmly and pressing me against it. I moan at the feel of his body against mine, the weight and solidity of it. He's right, I need this. I need *him*. I've never been with anyone who can take me out of my own head the way he can, and right now, it's all I'm craving. I want to think about nothing but him and how well we fit together. No past, no future—just now, right here, his touch sparking a fire in my body. I wriggle onto my tiptoes and kiss him. I earned this, after the work I put in today.

"What the hell was that?" he says against my lips.

I pull him even closer. "I felt like racing."

"Racing," he repeats. "You totally cheated."

"But you caught me anyway." I loop my arms around his neck, dragging him into another firm kiss. "I like that you caught me."

Something softens in his gaze. He fumbles for the doorknob without moving his body away from mine and walks us into his bedroom. He swoops in and picks me up before I can escape, depositing me on the bed and spreading out alongside me.

I curl into his side, finding his lips and the hem of his shirt all at once. We don't bother to take our time undressing; in about thirty seconds, our clothes litter the floor. I reach between us and give his cock a slow twist, relishing in his shudder.

"I liked catching you," he murmurs as he cups my face with both hands. He kisses my temple, my cheeks, and finally my mouth, his tongue teasing the seam until I open up. "I liked that you let me."

"Fuck me," I whisper. I swipe my thumb against the head of his cock to make him hiss. "Just like you said. Give it all to me."

He rolls away long enough to root around in his nightstand drawer for lube, a condom, and Cleo, which pretty much lives in his bedroom now. When I pull him back into my arms, we make out for a few minutes, kissing until we run out of breath before diving in again. It's comfortable, as natural as breathing, our bodies slotting together as though someone carved them from the same piece of wood. I can't remember ever being this comfortable in bed with another person, or as trusting.

"Elbows and knees," he whispers eventually, emphasizing the order with a little bite against the underside of my breast. "Spread yourself open for me, sweetheart."

When I'm in position, he presses a kiss to the top of my spine, stroking his fingers between my legs a few times, getting them wet. Then his hand, wet with lubricant and my slick, traces down my ass. I turn my head to the side, breathing against the pillow. I'm at his mercy, but I feel nothing but anticipation, wanting more of his touch. He slaps my bottom a few times with his dry hand, dragging out more moans. Sebastian's a nice guy, and I love that about him, but right now, he's tapping into that intense, commanding side he works with on the baseball field—and the kitchen—and it's sexy as hell.

"We're alone in the house," he says, emphasizing that with another spank. "I want to hear you. Give me everything you have."

I let myself get louder as he rubs his wet fingertips against my asshole. When he pushes in with one finger, slowly but firmly, I gasp, fisting my hands in the sheets.

"Fuck," I whine.

"Relax for me," he says. "Like last time, my good girl."

The memory hits me like a train. Way back in March, we showered together and made out against the counter with my hand pressed to the fogged-up mirror. When we were both shivering, he brought me to bed, and my wet hair soaked into my pillow as he rimmed me, then fucked my ass. The vulnerability of that moment brought me right to the brink of tears.

I don't know if this will bring me back there, but part of me hopes it does. If I'm going to cry in front of anyone, I want it to be Sebastian.

He stretches me carefully, murmuring praise all the while, his other hand rubbing my hip soothingly. His fingers feel so fucking big, spreading me in a way that's both strange and wonderful. My clit is throbbing, begging for attention, and the insides of my thighs are sticky with my own slick. I try to rub my clit to take the edge off, but he pulls my hand away.

"I've got you," he whispers, rubbing it for me.

My belly clenches at the feeling of his rough fingertips on that sensitive little nub, becoming a tight rubber band. Just when I'm on the verge of begging him to move faster, he pulls out his fingers. When he replaces them with the tip of his cock, sheathed in a condom and wet with lube, I choke out a moan, pressing against him wantonly. I don't care how it looks, and I don't care how needy it makes me. I just need him.

"Fucking perfect," he says. "You're being so good for me. God, Mia, I can't handle how beautiful you are."

He presses his chest against my back, his arm coming around to hold me in place. He kisses my shoulder blade as he presses in one inch, then two, then three. By the time he's in all the way, I'm shaking, whimpers slipping from my mouth in a near-constant stream. He's fucking thick, splitting me open in this extra-intimate way. He keeps working my clit as he lets me adjust to the feeling, continuing to whisper in my ear about how beautiful he thinks I am.

Tears prick my eyes. Maybe it's the sensations, or his words, which sound so soft and genuine. Maybe it's the vulnerability of the moment, but whatever it is, I take in a deep breath that ends in a sob.

"Talk to me," he says. "You good?"

"Yeah," I whisper. "Really good. Keep going."

"Such a good girl," he says, just as quiet. "You take my cock so well no matter where I put it."

He rolls us onto our sides, pressing my leg up to my chest to deepen the angle, and gives an experimental thrust. I cry out, overwhelmed by the new position, the slow drag of him inside me. "Sebastian—"

He reaches for the vibrator and turns it on, pressing it against one of my stiff nipples. "So fucking perfect, angel. You're everything. Fucking everything."

"God." I pant, twisting in his arms as the vibrator tortures my sensitive skin. It sends a spark of sensation right to my core, making me clench around him even more tightly, if his groan is any indication. He drags the vibrator over my other breast, then down my front. He gets it wet with my slick, thrusting his hips shallowly all the while, and pushes it into my cunt in one go.

I let out a sob that's half a scream. He keeps the vibrator inside me as he thrusts; the sensations combine to overwhelm me until I come, unbidden, my body shuddering through it. Another orgasm starts to build almost immediately, dragging me back to the peak. At my urging, he keeps going, working up a deep, urgent rhythm. I feel him tense, then relax, as he comes, his name on my lips, and that sends me over the edge again, chanting his name.

I reach back as he pulls out the vibrator. He holds my hand tightly, entwining our fingers. "Holy shit."

I laugh, my breath catching on another sob. "Yeah."

He pulls out. I flop onto my back, wiping at my eyes.

"You're crying." He wipes away a tear with his thumb. "Are you okay? Was I too rough?"

I shake my head, not trusting myself to speak. The air smells like sex, and he's just sweaty enough that I want to lick him, and something in my chest feels better now. It's like I had a crack in my heart, and I didn't realize he was fixing it until it already happened.

"Mia."

"It was perfect." I look at him, biting down on my wobbling lip. "So much, and so perfect."

He pulls me into his arms, hugging me tightly enough I can feel his heartbeat. For several long, warm, comfortable minutes, neither of us say a word. My body might be sated, but my mind keeps going, my imagination spinning in an ever-expanding orbit. It runs over my research, my readings, the questions I've been mulling over, some for a day, others for months.

"Sebastian."

"Mm?"

"I want to be alive long enough to see high-definition images of exoplanets." I meet his steady gaze. "I want to investigate the universe and see the details, not just the big picture. The individual planets, hiding in the light of their suns. I want to see the skies that spit diamonds. The seas of mist and long-abandoned mountains. The craters the size of our moon, the amethyst forests, the red oceans. Some people think it's impossible, but I don't believe that. There has to be a way to engineer it."

"That would be incredible." His eyes search mine. "Is this what you want to do in the future?"

"I want—"

I cut myself off as an idea crash-lands into my mind. A fragment of thought, but still, large enough to hold on to, teased out by Alice's feedback. The last snag in our program, turned on its side and made irrelevant.

"Wait," I say, scrambling off the bed. "I have an idea."

45

MIA

"STOP FIDGETING WITH IT," Izzy says, slapping my hand away from the front-tie of the jersey. "It's great."

"I feel weird," I grumble.

"Well, feel hot. Because you look hot." She tilts her McKee baseball cap to me. "So hot, he's not going to be able to pay attention to the game."

"Let's hope that doesn't happen," Cooper says dryly. He holds out a McKee cap. "Want it or not?"

I snatch the hat from him and squish it on my head. I can't remember the last time I wore a baseball cap—probably when I was still playing softball, honestly. That was the last time I went to a game, too, although McKee's main baseball field is way bigger than anything I played on. Penny gives me a smile, looping her arm through mine as we walk through the gates.

It's a hot June night, so I'm only wearing a bra underneath the jersey, plus jean shorts and sandals. Sebastian managed to hand it to me, neatly folded with a note on top, before I ran out the door this morning.

The note is in my bag now, hidden in my planner. I stared at it at least twenty times throughout the day, even though I didn't have time for daydreaming. I couldn't wait to share the breakthrough I had with Professor Santoro, and she rewarded me with the go-ahead to make the changes to the program, but that means extra crunch time work before the symposium.

Angel—

Aren't you glad we became friends?

Love,

S

P.S. Thank you.

Love. *Love.* What kind of love is it? Did he think about it before he wrote it? Did he mean it in the casual way people use the word, or did he agonize over it? And when did the word 'angel' become so deeply entrenched in how he thinks of me that he put it in writing? Part of me wants to cling to the note so tightly he'd never be able to pry it from my fingers, and part of me wants to pretend I never saw it.

Still, I put on the jersey when I left the lab to meet everyone at the ballpark. It's a McKee home jersey, purple with white lettering over the front, his last name in block letters on the back over the number '17.' It smells clean, but it's clearly used, and I'd never admit it, but I sniffed it a couple times to see if I could catch a bit of his scent.

"What are you thinking about?" Penny asks.

"Huh?"

"You seem kind of distracted." She tugs me to the left. "We're sitting on the third base side."

I follow her through the crowd to our seats. There are more people here than I thought there would be, honestly. With most of the McKee student population still gone for summer break, the town of Moorbridge has stepped up. A couple kids run past, gloves in hand. A group of older men laugh together as they take their seats. A family with matching 'Perrin' jerseys—he must be on the team—pass around signs to hold up. Pop music pipes through the speaker system, cutting through everyone's chatter.

Sebastian deserves this kind of atmosphere when he plays, and I'm glad he's getting it, even if this season has been tough. I should have been here sooner. If I managed to make it to Cooper's hockey games—supporting Penny, but still—I should have been here for Seb since the season started. Even just as his friend.

I gaze at the field. The floodlights are on, illuminating the perfectly mowed grass. Beyond the fence, there's practically a forest, the summer-bright leaves on the trees rustling in the wind. McKee has nice facilities everywhere, but this ballpark, with its archways leading to the upper deck seats, brick accents, and purple-and-white color scheme, feels extra special.

Both teams are on the field, warming up. Sebastian is playing catch with a guy I think I recognize as Hunter Kirby. Something warm and golden slips through me at the sight of him in his element. Anyone paying attention to Sebastian would know instantly that baseball has always been in his life.

I wonder if he's actually as nervous as he sounded

yesterday about the prospect of playing on a bigger stage. The interview definitely rattled him.

"This is nice," I say as we settle into our seats. We're in the front row of the lower deck along third base, which gives us a good view of the whole field. Sebastian will be in the outfield not too far from us, and I already know I'll be looking straight at him every half-inning.

Penny glances over. "Yeah. We went to a game a couple weeks ago that was completely sold out, standing room only."

"When?"

"You guys weren't talking then." She shrugs. "You know it doesn't matter now."

"Right." I duck my head as I blush.

"I can't believe you didn't pregame with me," Izzy says on my other side. She elbows me so I look up, then holds out a water bottle. "I had to make do."

"Is that vodka?" Cooper asks.

"Tequila," Izzy says.

He raises both eyebrows at his sister. "You brought an entire water bottle full of tequila to your brother's game?"

"Oh, please. Like we don't drink at all your games."

"You're not old enough to drink."

"You're so funny sometimes, Coop," she says sweetly. "Do you want a sip or not?"

"Fine," he says, snatching the bottle from her. He grimaces as he takes a gulp.

When it comes to me, I take a sip, ignoring the gasoline-like taste. It's cheap as hell, but whatever. It'll make cheering more fun, and I intend to get as loud as I can for Seb.

After a couple minutes, I'm starting to feel warm from the

booze, and all four of us are talking over each other. I burst out laughing as Izzy needles Cooper into yet another overprotective reaction. She's so good at it, it should be criminal.

"What's so funny?" someone calls.

Sebastian is leaning over the railing a few feet from us, glove tucked under his arm as he runs his hand through his hair. My mouth goes dry at the sight of him in his uniform. The deep purple plays nicely against his light hair. The white pants are tight in all the right places, and his arms look especially muscular with the short sleeves of the uniform top. The eye black on his cheeks and the belt at his waist tie everything together perfectly. Even the elbow guard he's wearing is making me feel some sort of way, which is ridiculous. And yet right now? I don't give a damn.

I hurry over to him, looping my fingers through the mesh screen separating us. I know it's for safety, but I wish I could kiss him right now.

"Looking good, gorgeous," he says. "I'm glad you're here."

"I am too." I glance over my shoulder at Penny and his siblings. They're hanging back, giving us some space, but Izzy waves excitedly at her brother. Sebastian waves back. "I'm sorry I didn't come to any of the earlier ones."

He shrugs. "Just happy to see you now."

"Callahan!" someone calls.

"Be there in a second!" he answers. He looks back at us. "Enjoy the game, yeah? I'll come find you after."

"Good luck."

He blows me a kiss as he jogs backwards. "Gonna have to keep from staring at you in between pitches, Mia Angel!"

"Ugh," Izzy says. "That is so cute I'm going to throw up."

"Please don't," Cooper says, alarm in his tone. "I can't do a repeat of the last time you barfed on me."

BY THE TIME the fourth inning rolls around, McKee is leading by two runs. Sebastian hit a double his first at-bat, sending his teammate on third base home for the first run of the game. I didn't realize he batted cleanup until now. No wonder he's been so stressed about having trouble at the plate.

It's fun to see him hit—he does have a nice swing, the way everyone seemingly can't stop talking about—but the outfield is a whole different game entirely. He's incredibly fast out there, and accurate with his throws. In the second inning, when a Binghamton player got greedy on a base hit and tried to slide into second, Sebastian's lightning-quick throw sent him straight back to the dugout.

When the Binghamton pitcher strikes out the McKee player at the plate, ending the inning, I head to the bathroom with Penny. As I'm washing my hands, two girls come in, giggling and falling over each other.

"God," one of them says as she tries to lock the stall. "He's *so* hot, I just want to lick him."

"I know!" the other says. "Why won't this fucking—there we go. And he's a Callahan. Well, kind of. Close enough, right?"

"If I can't have the dad, I'll take him."

Both burst into laughter. Penny raises her eyebrows at me.

"Richard?" she mouths. "Oh my God."

I stride to one of the stalls and bang my fist on it. I don't know what I'm more pissed about—them talking about

Sebastian as if he's a sex toy, or insinuating that he's only partly a member of his own family. "You're talking about Sebastian while his girlfriend is standing right here. Just so you know."

"He has a girlfriend?" one of them says.

"Nooo," says the other. "This is so tragic."

"Stop talking about my fucking man." I pause. "And his dad. That's extra weird."

Penny gives me a high-five. "Look at you. Mastering commitment."

"Mastering something," I say, an edge to my voice. "Annoyance, maybe."

"Let's go," Penny says. "We should get popcorn. Or caramel corn? We need to soak up the booze."

"He's a Callahan, by the way," I call as we leave the bathroom. "Not kind of. Idiots."

We're barely around the corner when someone says, "You're Sebastian's girlfriend?"

A woman, maybe in her early thirties, with dark blonde hair and smooth red lipstick, holds out her hand. She's wearing a navy pantsuit with a silk top, and a truly atrocious necklace hangs around her neck. "Zoe Anders, *The Sportsman*."

"Oh," I say, taking her hand reluctantly. I hope I don't smell like tequila. Was she lurking outside the bathroom waiting for me? "You're the reporter Sebastian spoke with yesterday."

"Yes," she says. "And you're Mia di Angelo? His girlfriend?"

"She is," Penny says warily. "What are you doing here?"

"I can't write an article about the future of baseball without seeing him play some games, right?" she says. "Who are you, a friend of Mia's?"

"My best friend Penny," I say. "Um—it was nice to meet you. I hope you're enjoying the game."

"I was wondering if I could get your thoughts on Sebastian," she says before we can escape. "And I'd love to have a picture of you for the article. You mean a lot to him, you know. He was singing your praises yesterday."

"I don't..."

"It'll just take a few minutes and it'll be a big help. You want to help him, don't you? This article will solidify his draft capital no matter how McKee's season ends."

I glance at Penny, who is worrying her lip. "I'll be back in a couple minutes."

"You sure?"

"Yeah. It's fine. Send a search-and-rescue if I'm not back by the seventh inning stretch." I smile, hoping I sound casual, but Penny frowns before she heads back to the seats.

"You're a doll," Zoe says. "Wearing his jersey and everything, it's adorable. I dated a baseball player in college."

"Are you still with him?"

"Nope," she says breezily. She pulls her phone out of her pocket. "Let me just text my photographer, one second."

46

MIA

BY THE TIME I finally manage to extricate myself from Zoe, it's the sixth inning. On the way back to the seats, I realize that Sebastian's about to come up to bat, so I pause where I am, behind the rows in front of home plate, to watch him step into the batter's box.

Like most baseball players, he takes a moment to settle into his stance. He widens his feet, rotates his waist a few times, and taps the bat on the toes of his cleats before settling it in place over his shoulder. He takes the first pitch, an outside ball, and readjusts for the next one. Another ball.

"Throw a strike!" a guy wearing a Binghamton shirt yells at the pitcher.

I cup my hands around my mouth and shout, "Go Seb!"

He gets another ball. The pitcher isn't giving him anything to hit. There's already a runner on second base, so maybe he's being cautious, trying to get past Sebastian to an easier batter later in the lineup.

The guy looks back at me. I shrug. "Girlfriend duties."

"Your boyfriend sucks," he says.

I give him my best bitch look. "You want to go there?"

"There you are," Penny says, grabbing me by the elbow and dragging me in the direction of our seats. The pitcher throws a fourth ball, and Seb tosses away his shin guard before jogging to first base. "I was getting worried. You left your phone at your seat, and I just saw that Giana called a bunch of times."

The noise of the game fades away for a moment. "What?"

"I'm sure everything is fine."

"Maybe." I speed up the pace. Giana wouldn't call more than once unless there was an emergency. "Or maybe it's not."

Penny hurries down the steps after me. When I get to the seats, Izzy holds out my phone right away.

"She started texting," she says. "But we didn't see any of them, don't worry."

I don't bother listening to her messages; I just call her and press the phone to my ear. Sebastian's team is back on the field for the top of the seventh. I turn away, walking back up the stairs to a quieter spot, as Giana picks up.

"Oh, good. I've been calling for the past fifteen minutes, you know."

"What's the matter?" I duck into a little corridor between the lower seats and the stairs to the upper deck. "Is everyone okay?"

"Everyone's fine. Didn't you read my messages?"

"I'm at Sebastian's game. I just saw that you've been calling, I didn't stop to check the messages."

"Oh, you're at the game right now."

"What do you mean?"

"Remember my friend April, the one you were going to go

to the conference with? You never got in touch with her, by the way."

"What about her?" I say, just barely refraining from snapping.

"She sent me this picture on Instagram? Or a tweet? Wait, I think it was a tweet. Anyway, it's of you in a baseball jersey, which is adorable, by the way—"

"Giana," I interrupt. "What about that made you call me five times in a row?"

"It's just strange," she says. "The caption is talking about how you're trying to work for NASA."

"*What?*"

"Mia di Angelo, Sebastian's girlfriend, is as talented in the lab as he is on the field. She's double majoring in astronomy and physics, and aiming to work for NASA one day," Giana recites.

I drag my hand over my face. I didn't mention that to Zoe when we talked just now, so Sebastian must have said something during the interview. Fuck. I can't even be mad at him, because he doesn't know that I've been hiding things from my family, but this could upset the delicate balance I've been maintaining. If Giana already started yapping about it to everyone else, I'm toast. There's no way it's not getting back to Mom and Dad.

"Giana," I start.

"This is what's true, right?" she says. "It's what you're trying to do? You never planned on becoming a teacher."

"No," I admit.

"I figured something was up when you wouldn't tell me anything about this student teaching you were supposedly doing," she says. "Or when you didn't get in touch with April."

I don't say anything. I'm not sure what to say. I bite my lip, watching as a couple walks by, hand-in-hand.

"That's it?" she says eventually. "No explanation? No apology?"

"I didn't mean to lie," I say. I swallow the hurt rolling through me. "It's just... you know how impossible it is to do anything Mom doesn't agree with."

"So you thought you'd lie to your entire family about something this important? All because you didn't want to upset Mom?"

"I didn't want to disappoint anyone!" I tear the baseball cap off my head and run my hand through my undoubtedly messy hair. "I thought I'd... I'd go to school and figure it out, and then, once I had something I could show as proof that I'm cut out for this field, I'd explain everything."

"And how is that going?"

"I'm working for a professor this summer," I snap. "And it's hopefully going to get me into a top study abroad program. So I'd say pretty well."

"I can't even believe you're the one getting defensive right now." She laughs shortly. "You do realize that our parents help pay for that private university, right? I know you got a scholarship, but it's not like they contribute nothing. All so you could go to an accelerated teaching program."

Shit. I forgot that one of my fake selling points for McKee was the ability to fast-track and get the teaching masters you need for certification all in one program, rather than go to a separate graduate school after undergrad. To be honest, I barely thought about it then, and now, I've been too busy dreaming about dissertations and NASA projects and coordinating with engineers to give it a thought.

"Do you even hear yourself? You sound just like Mom. She said enough negative things about law school that you gave up and did exactly what she wanted."

"This is not about me and my choices." Her voice is as hard as granite. "This is about me realizing that my sister is an ungrateful liar."

Tears burn in my eyes, but I'm not going to cry. Not here, and not because of my sister. "Did you tell anyone yet?"

"No. I wanted to hear about it from you first." She sighs deeply. "But you have to tell them, Mia. Soon. Tell them at the barbecue."

"Are you insane?"

"You never come home otherwise." I hear the hurt in her voice, and it makes my heart ache, even as I want to rail against her and how unfair she's being. "Were you planning on ditching the barbecue, too? Lying about something coming up with your fake job?"

"No," I say, fighting to keep my voice unaffected. "No, I'll be there."

"Tell Mom and Dad the truth. I'll keep your secret until the barbecue, but only until then. I have to go."

"Wait, Gi—"

She hangs up before I can finish.

47

SEBASTIAN

IT WAS REALLY FUCKING HARD to concentrate on the game when I knew to look for Mia in the stands.

I managed to settle in after a few innings, but it took all of my self-control. It was worth it, because I made a nice defensive play early in the game and went 3-for-4, and most importantly, we won the game and therefore the series, but it was torture, too. A very specific brand of self-inflicted torture, since I'm the one who gave her the jersey to wear. The rush of possessiveness that went through me whenever I even glanced in the direction of the stands should be illegal.

The second Coach Martin releases us, I head into the stands. Most of the guys are going to go straight to the locker room for a shower and change of clothes, but I can't wait that long to see her. If she's not in my arms in the next minute, I might lose my mind.

I spot my brother first. He pulls me into a hug, pounding on my back. "Nice game, man. Fantastic from start to finish."

"Thanks," I say as I step back, giving him an exhausted grin. "Fucking glad we pulled out another series win."

Penny and Izzy join us. I give them each a hug, looking around for Mia. "Where's Mia?"

"Something came up with her sister," Penny says. "She was talking to her on the phone."

I frown. "What kind of something?"

"I'm not sure." She gestures to one of the staircases. "She went that way. Will you go find her? I have a feeling she'll want to talk to you right now, not me."

"Yeah, of course." I take off my cap and stuff it into my back pocket. "We'll see you at the house later, okay?"

After I say goodbye to them, I head in the direction that Penny pointed out. A couple of people in the departing crowd stop me, wanting to say hello. I sign a baseball for a kid and shake the hand of a guy who claims to have played in the minor leagues with my father before I manage to spot her. She's tucked away in a little alcove next to a supply closet, arms crossed, worrying her lower lip.

I know the way she looks when she's trying not to cry, and this is exactly it. Shit. "Mia?"

She looks up at the sound of my voice. "Hey."

"Penny mentioned that something happened. Are you okay?" I reach out, but she shrugs away.

"Did you tell Zoe Anders about what I want to do in the future?"

"What?"

"She posted something about me wanting to work for NASA."

"Oh." I have no idea why that would be upsetting, so I tread carefully. "Yeah, I spoke about you. What's the matter?"

"Damnit, Seb," she snaps. "Why did you have to do that?"

I stare, swiping at my still-sweaty forehead. "Because I'm proud of you? What, is it a secret?"

She just looks at me, teeth digging into her lip, that ever-present fire blazing in her eyes.

"Wait," I say. "It actually is a secret?"

"My family doesn't—didn't know about it, Seb." The frustration comes through in her voice like a crack of thunder. "I told them I was studying to become a teacher. Graduate school, NASA, all of it—they don't know. Except now, thanks to you and Zoe, my sister knows fucking everything."

"I'm not following. Why did you tell them that?"

"It's complicated," she says shortly. She wipes carefully at her eyes. "My family isn't like yours. I couldn't just…"

"Do the thing you're good at? The thing you're passionate about?"

"Don't say it like it's easy."

"It sounds pretty easy to me."

She shakes her head. "I'm sorry I missed some of your game. First Zoe wanted to talk to me, and then Giana called, and now it's over."

"It's okay."

"But the season is almost over." Tears sparkle in her golden-brown eyes. "You deserve better."

I pull her into a hug. "Mia. Come on. You were here, and I appreciate that. Thank you."

She's frozen for a moment, but then she wraps her arms around me in return. "I don't want to think about it right now," she whispers. "I'm sorry for snapping at you. It's not like I told you about it."

"And I'm sorry I talked to the reporter about you without

asking." I pull back far enough I can meet her gaze. I brush her hair away from her face and press a kiss to her forehead. I have a million questions, but if she doesn't want to talk about it right now, I won't push. "She wouldn't stop asking me about my dad, and you were—you were what I wanted to talk about instead."

She smiles slightly. "Really?"

"Oh, definitely. I'll take any chance to brag about my genius girlfriend."

Her smile widens. I take that as a win, looping my hand through hers. "You know, you still haven't shown me your softball pitch."

We start walking in the direction of the exit.

"Why do I feel like there's a challenge coming?" she says.

I pull her closer, messing with her hair. She shrieks, trying to stomp on my feet.

"Not a challenge," I say. "An adventure."

"IF IT'S TERRIBLE, you're not allowed to laugh," Mia warns me. "I'm serious, Seb."

I mimic zipping my lips shut. "I promise. Throw the ball."

Technically speaking, we're not allowed on the practice field if we haven't booked time, but I decided to take a risk and bring Mia here, along with my gear and a bucket of softballs. This field is behind the ballpark, so there's enough light bleeding over to see, but it's completely deserted except for us. I figure that if she's mad, whatever the details of the situation, it couldn't hurt to work them out with a little ballgame. I'll return the softball equipment to its proper place as soon as we're done.

Mia makes a face as she looks down at the neon yellow

softball. "Reiterating again that I haven't thrown a softball in years."

"I think I'll manage to hit it anyway," I say. I rest my bat over my shoulder, adjusting my helmet. The metal is lighter than the wood of my baseball bat. It's going to make the most delicious ring when I crush the ball with it. "Go on. Don't be scared."

She glares at me. "Rude."

"Unless you *are* scared, in which case I guess you're not up for my adventure."

"Rude!" she says again. She winds up and throws the pitch.

I swing—and completely miss it. It nearly knocks me off balance. I can hear Mia's laughter clear across the diamond.

"Oh, you're right," she says. "I feel loads better now."

I shake my head, picking up the bat. "Again."

She throws it again. Too low for me to hit; it rolls right past home plate. I shake my head at her. "Come on, di Angelo. You can do better than that."

She grabs another softball, getting herself into position. I can't make out all her features in the low light, but judging by her body language, she's ready to go. She winds up and releases, and this time, I make contact with a satisfying smack. The ball sails over her head and into the night. I do an exaggerated bat flip, which makes her dissolve into laughter again.

"And the crowd goes wild!" she calls.

I jog to the pitcher's mound, holding the bat out to her. "Your turn."

"Oh, God," she says. "I was not good at hitting."

"Try it," I say, wiggling it in front of her. "It feels good to hit things sometimes."

"You're lucky I heard that in context," she teases, taking the bat from me. She grabs the helmet off my head and puts it on hers. "Same rules apply. You can't laugh if I suck."

"I'll be cheering." I pick up a softball. It feels gigantic in my hand, a grapefruit instead of an orange. Weird. Izzy played softball for a brief period before she settled into volleyball, and I remember how strange it felt to practice with her. "Because you're gonna crush it."

She rolls her eyes. "The only reason I played softball was because I had a crush on a girl on the team. And then I kept playing it after she left because it looked good on my college applications. The schools liked seeing that I wasn't just a nerd."

"Did you get with the girl?"

She grins. "Obviously."

"So confident," I say, deepening my voice so I sound like an announcer, "but can di Angelo back it up at the plate?"

She sprints to home plate with the bat held over her head like a sword. "Yes she can!"

"Hell yes she can!" I toss the softball into the air and catch it. "Righty hitter, nice."

She drags the end of the bat through home plate before settling into position. "I forgot how weird this feels."

"Stick your butt out more."

"Is that a genuine suggestion, or are you just acting piggish?"

I toss the ball again. "Totally legit. Power comes from the lower half."

She puts her hands on her hips, cocking them to one side.

I hold up my hands. "Hey, I'm just trying to help. If it happens to show off assets I appreciate, I'm not in control of that."

She adjusts her stance, widening her feet slightly, and holds the bat over her shoulder.

"Elbow up—good girl." I settle onto the mound, digging my toes into the clay. I have no idea how to throw a softball pitch, but I figure a nice easy underhand should be simple enough for her to hit. "Ready?"

She nods, so I wind back and toss the ball. She swings and hits it softly, but too late; she barely makes contact, and it rolls foul.

"Try and get on it faster," I say as I pick up another ball. "Ready?"

This time, she hits it with some power. I jump out of the way as it rockets right up the middle of the diamond. She does a little dance at home plate. "Do it again!"

I toss her a third, which she hits right where the shortstop would be, and a fourth that goes all the way to the outfield. At the last one, she takes off running, losing the helmet halfway to first. I cheer, whooping, as she rounds second, then third. On her way home, I run over to meet her. We collide at the plate, landing in a heap of laughter and dirt. She's on top of me, and her hair is in my face, and her eyes are as bright as the stars overhead. I loop my arms over her back, hugging her close, urging her to give me all her weight.

"And the crowd goes wild," I murmur.

Her heartbeat races against mine. She kisses me deeply, our teeth practically gnashing together, her hands tugging on my hair. The warm weight of her sends heat to all the right places, and my mouth goes dry when she pulls off the jersey. She has on a purple bra, the same color as the jersey, showing off the two perfect handfuls of her tits. Her gold chain swings gently.

"Angel," I say hoarsely.

Her smile is small and tilted to one side, and it means more to me than anything in the world. My Mia is brave. It takes guts to go after what you want instead of what's expected of you, and it sounds like she made that choice long ago, when it would have been easier to give in to the pressure and expectations. I don't know the full story yet, but I will someday soon, and when I do, that's what I'll tell her. She's brave. She's not letting anyone dictate her future but her, and that's the most admirable thing I've ever known.

"Maybe outdoor sex can be our thing," she says teasingly. She traces down my chest, playing with the buttons of my uniform. "What do you think?"

My mind is racing a million miles a minute, but I don't indulge the thoughts. Not now, when I have Mia sitting on top of me, looking good enough to eat. Not when letting them in would mean acknowledging what I can't push away any longer.

I have a future, but not in baseball.

Even though I loved tonight's game—even though I love playing every game—my father's legacy belongs to him. My life can't be an imitation of his just because it was what he wanted for me before he died. I have to make my own future, even if it means giving up the sport I've revolved my life around for as long as I can remember.

And that's fucking terrifying.

So instead, I pull Mia into another breathtaking, overwhelming kiss. "Come here, gorgeous."

48

MIA

SOMEWHERE IN BETWEEN stealing home and carrying me to the dugout bridal-style, Sebastian got pensive. I'm not sure what happened, but he won't stop kissing me, even to talk for a moment, and he's holding me so tightly I wonder if I'm going to be sore in the morning.

I love it, but I'm worried, too.

This dugout isn't anything like the one in the main ballpark; it's just a long bench with a step and a railing. It's not at all comfortable, but that's not the point right now, not when each kiss is like a drop of water after wandering parched in a desert. Not when there's something hanging in the air between us, as delicate yet unbreakable as a string of silk. It's wrapped around his heart and mine, shining in the quiet night. If we didn't have the floodlights from the stadium bleeding over the sky, I'd barely be able to see him.

It's a good night for planet hunting, as Nonno would say.

I gasp, arching my back, as Sebastian bites my nipple. He drags his hand down my side, curving over my hip bone before settling it on my bare thigh. The moment we got to the dugout, he made a makeshift blanket out of the jerseys, and I undressed the rest of the way without ceremony. He hefted me back into his arms, holding us chest-to-chest, and we made out against the cinderblock wall until I begged him for more contact. I got what I asked for, but he's still too quiet. Normally I'm overwhelmed by the praise, teasing and laughter. This feels different. Serious. The pleasure is there—my clit is throbbing; I want his touch so fucking bad, and I know he's hard—but he's not himself.

I reach up and stroke my fingers through his hair. I feel him shiver as he kisses between my breasts. "Sweetheart," I murmur.

"Mia," he answers, my name slipping from his lips like a prayer.

"Are you okay?"

His eyes are bright even in the dark. "Are you? Are you too cold?"

I sit up a little. "I'm fine. You're just... being quiet, I guess."

He pulls me into his lap, wrapping his big arms around me. I throw my arms around his neck, happy for the contact. I bury my face against the hollow of his throat, feeling the press of his dad's necklace, as I breathe in his sweat.

It's sweet that he wears that necklace all the time. I like my hoops because Nana gave them to me from her personal jewelry box, and I like my chain because Nonno got it for me to match the earrings. He hasn't spoken about it much, but I know the necklace holds the same level of significance to him.

"Sorry," he says. "I'm just thinking about how much I admire you."

Of all the things I was expecting to hear, it wasn't that. "Seriously?"

"You're incredible," he says. "Your ambition is... it's everything. It's fucking sexy, Mia."

I shake my head, laughing slightly. "Sebastian."

"What? It's just the truth." His hand skitters down my spine. "I'm a lucky man."

I swallow, trying to dislodge the sudden lump in my throat. "Thank you."

"And maybe I'm just thinking about that tonight." He brushes his hand over my cheek. "About you, and about me, and about us."

I hold his gaze for a long time. I used to think about moments like this and cringe, but I want to stay in this one forever. I'd hate it from anyone but him. He's steady and serious, and I can tell that no part of him is bullshitting me. He doesn't have to; he's not trying to flatter me into bed. He already has me. He's just being himself, and that makes it even more special. I've been told a lot of things about my laser focus on my future, but no one has ever called it *sexy*.

"Can you do it while you're inside me?"

He bursts into startled laughter. "I love you."

My heart starts to beat so fast I'm afraid it's going to run away. "So that's what the note meant."

"What—oh, the note on the jersey." He grips the back of my neck, kneading his thumb against the top of my spine. "Yeah, Mia Angel. I love you."

"When I first moved in with you, I gave myself a mission." I'm not sure why I'm telling him this now, but my thoughts are scrambled, and this is a thread I can hold on to. "Project GOSMC. Get Over Sebastian Miller-Callahan."

He keeps holding me. He doesn't push me away. "And how did that go?"

"It was a total and complete failure." I trace my finger down his cheek. "Most of science is."

"Most of baseball is too. You go up to the plate and strike out more often than you hit the damn thing."

I smile.

"My project didn't just fail," I whisper. "The objectives changed entirely. And now we're here."

The rest of the confession is on the tip of my tongue. I've never said it in a romantic way before, and if I'm being honest with myself, I thought I never would. But if there's anyone who deserves to hear it, it's Sebastian.

Before I can work up the courage, Sebastian pushes me against the makeshift blanket, caging my body with his. He kisses me, his hand slipping between our bodies to rub over my clit, rekindling the pleasure that had been consuming me. I gasp into his mouth as he presses in a finger, then another, curling them inside me to catch all the extra-sensitive places. His dick is still hard, pressed against my thigh, and it doesn't take long at all before I'm arching my back, wanting more than his fingers. More than his teasing. His tongue tangles with mine as he works my clit.

I break away with a moan. "Please," I beg.

He doesn't wait a moment longer. My nails drag down his arms as he pushes into me, slowly but without stopping. He groans when he's in all the way, his hair falling over his eyes as he presses his forehead to mine. We just breathe for a moment, but then I wrap my legs and arms around him, and he takes that as the signal to give me everything he has.

Each thrust is exquisite torture. I squeeze around him tightly, smiling when that makes him grunt. He buries his face in my shoulder, his teeth scraping over my skin. I gasp, wobbling on the edge already. He's never fucked me this deep before, or so completely. I'm trembling. My nails dig into his back hard enough I'm sure it hurts. The pleasure builds in my lower belly, dragging through a want in me so deep, I know it's going to consume me.

"Come for me," he murmurs. "Just like this. You can do it, gorgeous girl."

I come with a cry that he cuts off with a kiss, my entire body clenching and releasing until I'm nothing but a puddle of goo. My scalp tingles, my toes curl, and the whole time Sebastian keeps me safe and hidden, so I can fall apart just for him. Only for him. Starbursts dance in my vision as my breath catches on a sob. He hugs me so close I feel fused to him, and still he moves in me, bringing himself to the same peak.

I don't trust myself to speak without bursting into tears, but I dig my heels into his back and kiss him as fiercely as I ever have, and I know he understands my silent plea. To come in me, to claim me, to leave a mark in me so deep that nothing can take it away.

I feel the moment he lets go, his body going slack. I stroke through his hair as we catch our breath together.

I used to study the stars and imagine planets with knife-sharp mountains. Boiling oceans. Metal rain. Now, I think of something different. Rolling hills. A gem of a lake. A rainforest, thick with life, as green as the eyes of the man looking down at me like I'm the very center of the universe. Part of me always wished I could escape to one of those worlds, but I don't want that anymore. I belong right here, with him, and that is more beautiful than anything I could ever dream up while gazing into a telescope.

It's strange. It's terrifying. It's beautiful.

"I love you," I whisper.

49

SEBASTIAN

AS IT TURNS OUT, the world doesn't automatically change after you decide something life-altering about yourself. In the days since I decided to quit baseball, I've gone to practice, made pierogi from scratch, watched three more movies with Mia (*This Means War*, *Contact*, and *Clueless*), played a double-header in Connecticut, gone to Lark's with Hunter, Rafael, Cooper, and Evan, and researched—however briefly—cooking programs in Europe. I also tried to make soufflé, but that was the biggest failure since my infamous creme brûlée debacle. I need to brush up on my baking skills. Maybe I should bring a dessert to Mia's family's barbecue tomorrow.

On second thought, poisoning my hopefully future in-laws would not be a smart move.

I also need to figure out how the fuck to talk about leaving baseball. There have been some good opportunities, but whenever I'm alone with someone and the words are on the tip of my tongue, I always find an excuse to keep my mouth shut. I want to tell Mia first, get her thoughts before I approach my family, but she's been so busy working on her presentation for the symposium, I haven't wanted to press. When she texted me earlier, asking me to rescue her from the lab, I nearly whooped aloud.

Now, she stares at the rows of brightly packaged junk food with her arms crossed tightly over her chest. "What happened to the importance of eating real meals? You went on a rant yesterday about why everyone should be buying organic eggs."

I adjust my baseball cap. On the way to the lab, I made a plan. A nighttime adventure, complete with truth or dare. If she gives me a truth, I'll give her one too. The right one, the only one I've been able to think about ever since I made the decision.

It's the right one, but I need her support if I'm going to make it happen.

I nudge her hip with mine. "Balance is the key to a happy life."

"You sound like a fortune cookie."

"Thank you."

She rolls her eyes. "This is your big plan? Stock up on snacks?"

"It's not the whole plan. Where we're going, we'll need sustenance."

"Which is where?"

"It's a secret, obviously."

She narrows her eyes at me. "You're being unusually cryptic."

"For example, I'm weak for Doritos." I throw a bag of them into the basket. It took a little effort to find a store that was open this late, but we managed it in the form of a 24-hour drugstore just outside downtown Moorbridge. We're the only ones here besides the woman behind the counter, who is busy playing TikToks on her phone at full volume, and a guy making a cup of coffee the next aisle over. "I'm also partial to Raisinets."

Her nose wrinkles cutely. I'd kiss her, but considering the mood I found her in, it's probably best to give her time to decompress first. It's corny to say, but she goes to another planet when she works. I still don't know why she's been lying to her folks about what she's studying, but I'm hoping she lets me in on that tonight, since I'm meeting them tomorrow. My family is complicated, but Mia's seems to be on a completely different level.

"Raisinets?" she says. "What are you, a hundred years old?"

"I've been told I have an old soul."

She gives me a little shove, reaching out to throw a box of Junior Mints into the basket. "If you're going to buy candy, at least go for something good."

"What about the Doritos? How are we feeling?"

"The Doritos are acceptable." She walks to the refrigerated section. "The soda pick is what will make you or break you, Seb. You're already on thin ice with the Raisinets, so choose wisely."

"Oh, it's Dr. Pepper. No contest."

Her mouth drops open. "Can I revoke our relationship on the basis of irreconcilable differences?"

I reach around her to add a bottle of Dr. Pepper to the basket. "No take backs. That's not how it works."

She tucks a bottle of Coke underneath her arm. "Maybe I wouldn't have given in if I knew there was no way out."

I back her against the refrigerator door. She shivers, but keeps that smirk on her face. From the first fucking moment, I could sense that Mia is the kind of person who would rather die than back down once she's made up her mind about something. The trick is to surprise her, to get under her skin in a way she can't ignore. She might be toying with me, but she has her own weaknesses. Poking her—so she'll poke me back, and we can tussle—makes me feel alive in a way I never have before.

So I kiss her.

And like every other time, there's a split-second of surprise. I hope that never goes away, it's too fucking cute. I feel her frown against my own lips, and then her smile as she winds her arms around me. The cold Coke digs in between my shoulder blades. "Brat," I murmur. "You said you love me. I heard it."

"Excuse me," someone says.

We jump apart. The guy who had been making the coffee steps between us, reaching in for a water. Mia widens her eyes. They're sparkling, thanks to the light overhead. Her smile takes my fucking breath away.

When the guy leaves, I say, "I catalog your smiles, you know."

"What?"

I didn't mean for that to slip out, but fuck it. We're rolling with it. "Whether it's a real smile or one you're putting on. If it's a smile to try and shut me up, or an invitation, or genuine happiness."

Her smile widens. "What am I doing right now?"

"Oh, it's genuine."

"You sound confident."

"You always smile for real after I kiss you."

She pokes me hard in the ribs. "Weirdo."

"I don't hear a denial in there."

She flounces past me, tossing her hair over her shoulder. I

follow her to the counter, but I don't see the woman from before.

"Where do you think she went?"

She shrugs as she looks around. "Ooh, an intercom."

"I dare you to say something into it."

She snorts. "Seriously?"

"Or you can tell me what's going on with your family."

She turns in another circle, but apparently decides the coast is clear, because she presses the button on the control, pulls the microphone over to her, and says, "Number seventeen, Sebastian Callahan, also known as Big Daddy, stepping up to bat."

Her ridiculous nickname nearly makes me fall over with laughter. "*Mia*."

"Standing at six-foot-two, a hundred sixty pounds, his bat is the biggest part of all—"

"Miss," the woman drawls as she walks back to the counter. "Don't touch the intercom."

———————

"WAS THAT THE BIG ADVENTURE?" Mia asks when we're back in my Jeep. "A junk food raid, plus getting kicked out of"—she cranes her neck to peer at the neon sign—"24-Hour Drug?"

I turn on the car and check my mirrors before pulling out of the parking space. "No way. A late-night adventure always has multiple parts. We haven't even started the game, officially."

"What game?"

"Truth or dare, of course."

She turns to me. I keep my eyes on the road, but relish in

the way her hand clasps over my thigh. "You didn't give me a choice!"

"Sure, I did. You could have given me the truth, but you chose the dare."

"You're lucky I love you." She rubs her thumb over my jeans, an unconscious little motion. "Where are we going?"

"Depends if you choose truth or dare next."

"I don't get to ask you first?"

"Nope."

She pouts. "That's not fair."

Once I'm stopped at a red light, I glance at her. "You're the one who agreed to the adventure when I broke you out of the lab."

She shrugs. Her bra strap—highlighter yellow, and distracting as fuck—slides down her arm. I look ahead again, swallowing down the part of me that wants to pull over and see how far back the seats of the Jeep go. We haven't had a chance yet to take that experiment all the way.

"I'm asking anyway," she declares.

"Oh?"

"You're not the boss of me."

"Nah, just the Big Daddy."

"Sebastian!"

I swipe my hand through my hair as I smirk. "What? You set it up too perfectly."

Her laughter sounds like the first song you blast on a long drive—anticipated, and extra sweet. "Truth or dare?"

"Fine." I drum my fingers on the wheel as I make a right turn. We're almost to campus, and from this entrance, it's only a little further to get to the building I have in mind. "Um... truth."

"How have you been sleeping? I haven't heard you get up."

I can't help it; I glance over. "Going right in, are you?"

"I've been worried."

"No nightmares since that one a little while ago. Although not much sleep, either. I've been watching *MasterChef* on mute while you're asleep."

"I guess I'll take it."

I grimace. "Could be worse. Truth or dare?"

"Truth."

"What's going on with your family?"

She sighs. "What's the dare?"

"I know how to get to the top of the library bell tower."

"Wh—oh."

"Feeling brave tonight?"

Her eyes glitter in the light from the streetlamp overhead. "Fine. Bring it on."

Typical Mia. I have the feeling she'd still have chosen the dare if it was between swallowing a sword and answering that question. But that's fine, I can be patient. This is about taking her on an adventure, after all. I can't be picky about how she plays my own game.

The Bassett-Kennedy Library is one of the tallest buildings on campus. It's shaped like a 'C,' with two wings extending out from the center, but in the middle, an old, now unused bell tower rises like the spire of a church. Even though it's frowned upon, a couple of fraternities have hazing that involves sneaking to the top of the tower. To the repeated exasperation of the university administration, the bell still clangs if you hit it. In the early 2000s, the president tried taking it away, but too many wealthy alumni complained, so it's stayed exactly where it is, delicious catnip for college kids.

Pretty much every fraternity on campus wanted me and Cooper to join, but that life didn't appeal to either of us, so our first semester, we snuck up ourselves and had a drink. You can see half of campus from here; the old brick buildings, the gentle hills, the carefully arranged trees.

I pull into the nearest parking lot. "You sure?"

She's already pushing open the passenger door, the snacks and drinks shoved into her ever-present NASA tote bag. "They still have security on campus during the summer, you know."

I shove my keys and wallet into my jeans pocket. "Go around the back."

We could swipe into the building, which has all-hours access, and go up the staircase to the roof. The lock on the rooftop door to the tower isn't that hard to pick, and the security camera never works. But there's a service ladder that goes all the way up the side of the building, and this is a dare, after all.

Time to see just how stubborn my girl is.

She stares at the ladder like it's a wall of fire. "You've got to be kidding me."

"You chickening out?"

She practically bares her teeth at me. "No."

I take a step in her direction, forcing her to angle her head up to meet my eyes. I take her chin in my hand. "I won't push you if it's too much."

There's pure steel in her eyes. "You want to keep those fingers?"

I let go of her and spread my arms out. "After you, angel."

She climbs onto the ladder. Her butt wiggles cutely as she adjusts her weight. "If I fall, save my Junior Mints."

"Absolutely not."

She sticks her tongue out at me. "Rude."

"Just don't look at the ground. You'll be fine."

I stand at the bottom and watch as she climbs. When she's up a few rungs, I pull myself up too.

"Oh, wow," I hear her say when she gets to the top. "This is incredible."

"Wait until you get into the tower." I join her on the roof, wiping my hands on my jeans. "We just need to get the door open."

"Oh," she says. "I can pick the lock."

I grin. "I was gonna do it."

"Nah." She fishes a hairpin out of her bag. Her smile looks like mine feels—bright and unfettered and more than a little giddy. "Truth or dare?"

50

MIA

"YOU'RE GOING to have to pick truth eventually, you know," Sebastian says.

I flop down next to him. In the past hour or so, I've prank-called Penny, balanced on my head—a party trick I haven't broken out in a while—pointed out, correctly and without using my phone, every visible constellation in the sky, and posed like Rose in *Titanic* on the ledge of the tower. I think the last one freaked out Sebastian more than me, because he yanked me back into his arms.

Why was I ever afraid of heights? I can't remember. It felt so fucking good to stand up there with my arms spread wide, no railing, my heart about to beat right out of my chest. I turned in his arms when he grabbed me and kissed him until I couldn't breathe, couldn't think, couldn't focus on anything but the taste of soda and chocolate on his tongue. I'm still breathing fast as I turn my head into his side. His masculine scent calms my racing heart.

I have no idea how he knew I needed this when I texted him to pick me up, but I'm grateful.

"Or you could keep giving me ridiculous dares." I sit up on my elbows. He brushes a dead leaf out of my hair. "You haven't dared me to strip yet."

He rakes his fingers down my bare arm. "I'll take it into consideration."

"It's my turn. Maybe I should dare you to strip."

He snorts. "You're on a sugar high."

"I forgot how magical Coke tastes. My nonno used to keep quarters in his pockets so he could get us one to split if we came across a vending machine."

"He doesn't do it anymore?"

I swallow; it feels like I just ate a shard of glass. It's been years since his death, but it doesn't take much to bring the feelings back. That chasm in my heart is all too happy to open, releasing dozens of memories. Good ones, like the quarters and slightly-warm sodas at the Shore, and bad ones, like the moment Dad picked me up from school—a rarity—and turned to me with heaviness in his expression to tell me the news.

"He passed away when I was fifteen. Heart attack."

"I'm sorry, Mia."

I sit up properly. "It's fine. It's been a long time now."

"Doesn't mean the feelings go away," he says softly. "What was he like?"

"What?"

"Tell me about him. You know more about my family than I do about yours."

"There's not much to tell."

He raises an eyebrow. "Not much, or don't want to?"

I rip up the leaf he rescued from my hair. "Both, I guess."

"We could play a new game."

"Oh yeah?"

"A truth for a truth."

"Tired of the dares?"

"I want to know everything there is to know about you, Mia." His voice is quiet, even though there's no one around to overhear us. "I want to understand you. The other night, at the ballgame..."

The pieces of leaf fall to the floor. "Sebastian—"

"You can choose what to tell me. And when, and how. But I want to know all of it eventually. Everything about you, the big things and the small things, too. I didn't know until tonight that you like Coke and Junior Mints. I want to know that shit as much as I want to know about your family. Tell me your past and what you want for your future, and I'll tell you mine."

He reaches out, entwining our fingers. He's gazing at me like I'm the aurora borealis. A beautiful force of nature, a ribbon of light that he'd be content to stare at forever. I love him. I can trust him. If there's anyone I want to talk about Nonno with, it's him.

"My nonno was the one who got me interested in space. He never went to college, he didn't even finish high school, but he was always interested in the world—history, philosophy, science. He had this telescope, and I still remember the first time we looked at the stars together. He made me want to explore them, and he's the one who encouraged me to keep pushing. I kept it up after he died. Got myself into McKee with a big scholarship."

"I didn't realize."

I shrug one shoulder. "It was here or MIT, and McKee offered me more money."

"And yet you tell me you're not a genius."

"I'm really not. I'm just curious, and stubborn, I guess."

"I'm sure he was proud of you."

My breath catches in my throat.

Some part of me knows that Sebastian brought me here because he knew there wouldn't be distractions. No work to bury my head in, or other people to talk to instead. The resentment I expect to feel doesn't come; I want to give him more. We left things on a precarious note after the Binghamton game, even though the night ended up being so perfect.

"He's the only one in my family who tried to understand me, and he's been gone for years. It's like I said, my family thinks I'm here to get my teaching degree. They think—they think that I'm going to teach science for a few years before marrying some guy and settling down and having a bunch of kids, same as all the women in my family. There's no other option. That's it."

Sebastian rubs my knee comfortingly.

I bite the inside of my cheek. "They don't know that I'm trying to get into this study abroad program in Switzerland, or that I want to get my PhD, or that I want to work for fucking NASA."

"But you're—"

"And I can't even hate them for it, because they're good people, and they love me, and I know they want the best for me. They just have this idea of what's best that's not *my* idea of what's best. Whenever I talk to my mom I want to scream at her, because she loves me so much but in all the wrong ways."

The words tumble from me in a rush, akin to forcing poison out of a wound. I haven't said all of this aloud to anyone other than Penny, and that was after several drinks.

"That would be a waste." He reaches forward and tucks my hair behind my ears, one and then the other. He brushes his lips against mine. It's the softest kiss we've ever shared, and yet I wish it would go on forever. "Not that there's anything wrong with being a teacher, but that would be a fucking waste. Your mind is incredible, Mia. It's meant to help discover the future. You're the smartest person I've ever met."

I laugh a little wetly. "Come on."

"I'm serious."

I sniffle. "I thought if I could just... prove somehow that I'm meant to do this, then when I came clean, it would be okay. That's why I've been working so hard to get into this study abroad program—the director of it is going to be at the symposium. But Giana got so angry when she found out. I know I have to tell them, but I'm afraid they're not going to understand. Or even try to understand."

"Mia."

I feel the burn of tears in my eyes, but I blink carefully, so they don't spill over my cheeks. "Give me a truth."

"I think we should—"

"Give me a truth, please." Every time I imagine the look on my mother's face during this horrible, inevitable conversation, I want to cry. "I want one of yours."

Something cracks in his expression.

"Please," I whisper. "Don't make me be vulnerable alone."

He pulls me into a hug. I hug him back, relishing in the smell of his cologne, feeling the warmth of his body in the now chilly nighttime air. He hooks his chin over my shoulder and says into the night, quiet enough I have to work to listen, "I'm quitting baseball."

"What?" I try to pull away, but he holds me in place.

Whatever I thought he might say—maybe something about his parents, or about his past with the Callahans—wanting to quit baseball never crossed my mind. *I've* thought about it for him a few times, but I wouldn't have suggested it. "But it's your life."

"It was my father's life." He keeps whispering, as if he's afraid of the very air around us overhearing him. "I know I have the talent, but it's not what I want to do with my future. I can't do it just because it's what my father imagined for me."

I keep my voice as soft as his. "What do you want to do instead?"

"When I graduate, I'll have access to my inheritance." I feel him swallow against my shoulder. "I was thinking that I'd travel. Just... experience all the places I haven't yet. Learn to cook for real, work my way up through the ranks in the restaurant world. I could leave McKee after next semester; I have the credits. Cooking makes me happier than anything else. It's art to me. It's... it's a kind of poetry. Everything you've said about space, I feel about food. I want to be in a kitchen, not on the baseball field. Not anymore."

Giving up baseball—a career that will one day lead to millions of dollars and maybe even a place in history—to wash dishes in a restaurant until they decide he's ready to prep the vegetables.

I manage to wriggle out of his arms so I can meet his gaze.

He's biting his lip, his eyes wide with nervousness.

That's when it hits me. No one else knows about this. I'd be willing to bet that was the first time he ever said those words aloud. The interview with Zoe Anders, the expectations from not just the baseball community, but his family and his late parents, the draft in July—it's all pressing in, and he knows that pretty much anyone he talks to will tell him to stay the course.

To forget about cooking, or travel, or anything else he might want to do, just because he's genetically blessed the same way his father was.

I knew the moment I began to apply to college programs that I couldn't go through with becoming a teacher. I couldn't let myself do that just for the sake of my family. When it all comes crashing down, it will be hell, but it'll be worth it, because I'll have the degree that I need for my future. Even if Sebastian could play baseball professionally, he shouldn't have to.

"You should do it."

He blinks. He's probably had this conversation in his head a million times—I know I did—and I'm sure that whoever he pretends to talk to doesn't react the way I just did. I understand his worry. His family is full of athletes. James already plays his sport professionally, and Cooper is trending in that direction too. This would be a huge step in a completely different direction, and I know better than anyone how difficult that can be to reconcile.

"You're sure?" he says.

"Yeah," I say. "You're incredible at cooking, and you have the passion for it. This is a good plan, Seb. I want to see you in that chef's jacket."

I hear the relief in his laughter loud and clear. "You're amazing."

"I'm just telling you the truth."

"It was you, you know." He presses another kiss to my lips. "You're so focused and committed, and I realized that I wanted to feel that way too. Just not for baseball. For the thing that's mine and mine alone. Thank you, Mia."

My heart dances at his words. I know how he feels, and I'm

proud of him for taking the leap. There's nothing easy about it, but if it's what's in his heart, then it's what he needs to do.

"Maybe you should go on that cooking competition show, then," I say slyly, poking him in the ribs.

He snorts. "Let's see about telling my family first."

51

SEBASTIAN

"IT'S THE ONE AT THE END of the cul-de-sac," Mia says. "With the blue shutters."

"It's a nice house," I say as I wedge the car in between a driveway and an SUV. The whole street is crammed with cars, even though it's barely noon. "There are a lot of people here already."

Mia has a grim look on her face. "I told you it would be busy."

I squeeze her hand, glancing at Cooper and Penny, who are both unbuckling in the backseat. "It's not too late to bail. We could get lunch somewhere, or just go to James and Bex's place early."

She shakes her head before I even get the whole sentence out. "I told Giana I would be here. I want to keep that promise, at least."

"We've got your back," Penny says. "I'm not above telling off Momma di Angelo if things get weird."

"It's her specialty," Cooper drawls.

Mia slides out of the passenger side of the car, slinging her purse over her shoulder. "Thanks, guys."

"If you want to leave early, just say something about Philly cheesesteaks," Penny says. She smooths down the front of her sundress, balancing on the curb.

At Cooper's look, she adds, "What? Your brother lives in Philly. I thought that made complete sense."

"I love you," Cooper says, sounding both fond and exasperated.

I hold out my hand, glad when Mia takes it, and let her lead us in the direction of her parents' house. I still can't get over the outfit she's wearing; when she came downstairs earlier, I nearly did a double take. She's in a light pink dress with a matching cardigan and sandals with white bows on top. I don't know where she unearthed it, but she's carrying a matching pink purse, and there's even a pink clip in her hair. When I stared at her, raising my eyebrows, she just gave me the finger. She looks a lot like Izzy in this getup, but I know better than to tell her that.

When we get to the door, she stops, smoothing my hair back. "Maybe you should have worn the blue shirt."

"I'm sure this is fine," I say. I'm in jeans and an Eagles t-shirt, because I intend to respect the rules of the land I'm about to enter, and in addition to the cookies I made for the dessert table, I have a bunch of James Callahan signed jerseys and hats for Mia's relatives. Her dad is a huge football fan, so Cooper and I are prepared for a touch football game. We don't have a lot of extended family, so this is foreign to me, but I know when to turn on the charm. By the end of the day, Mia's family will love me, and hopefully, that will help ease any tension. I might not be a baseball player for much longer, but they don't have to know that right now, and I intend to milk that all-American image for all its worth.

Mia sighs, taking a step back. "I guess you look acceptable."

"That's her favorite compliment," I say, grinning at our friends.

She rolls her eyes as she gives Cooper and Penny a once-over. "And I guess you look fine too."

"Hey," Penny says. "Who spent an hour in the bathroom with you before we left?"

"True," Mia concedes. "Okay, let's—"

The front door swings open, revealing a woman who looks like a version of Mia a couple years into the future: the same dark hair and eyes, the olive complexion, the heart-shaped face. She's wearing a spring green dress and an apron dusted with flour.

"Mi-Mi. Are you going to make your friends stand on the porch all day?"

Mia smiles. It's a mask of a smile, one I recognize from the days she tried to brush me off. She steps forward to hug the woman. "Hi, Giana."

"Giana," Penny says, accepting a hug from Giana next. "It's nice to see you again."

She gives me and Cooper flour-and-rosemary scented hugs too. "Let me guess," she says, gesturing to me. "You're Sebastian."

"Guilty," I say. "And you're Mia's sister? It's so nice to meet you."

She waves us into the house. "Oh, you're so handsome. Auntie Carmela especially is going to *flip*. Too bad you're not Italian, but no one's perfect."

MIA WASN'T KIDDING when she said she had a big family. In the past half hour—because it took that long for her to go around introducing us to everyone—I've met her Nana, her parents, her older brother Anthony and his wife Michelle, plus their two children, Giana's husband Peter and his family, her extended family on both sides, and what must be half the neighborhood.

I shake hands with everyone, but more often than not I'm drawn into a hug, and I definitely have lipstick on my cheek. Giana wasn't kidding about Aunt Carmela. (Mia's mother's side, but not actually Mia's aunt—she's a cousin of a cousin.) We don't get a moment alone until Giana finally thrusts sodas into our hands and tells us to make ourselves comfortable by the pool, but won't you come help in the kitchen, Mi-Mi?

Mia grimaces as her sister walks back to the house, stopping on the way to fuss with the buffet. "I can probably take the long way into the house."

"I'll come with you," Penny offers.

I look around the backyard. It's a big, sloping lawn that backs up to trees, currently littered with plastic chairs and tables decorated with vases of flowers. A couple of the little kids are splashing around in the pool, Mia's father and uncles hold court at the grill, and laughter floats out of the kitchen, mixing with the rock music in the background. When we first arrived, Mia's mother took one look at me, kissed both my cheeks, and told me that she had to run inside to finish arranging the cheese platter.

"This is nice," I say, gesturing with my soda can at the sunny lawn. I enjoyed meeting everyone, but I'm wary, knowing they've placed such strict expectations on her. If things were so bad that she didn't even want to be honest with them about what she wanted to major in, I need to keep up my guard, and protect her if necessary.

"Yeah," Cooper says. "Thanks for inviting us, Mia. Whatever your dad is cooking smells great."

She snorts. "Chaotic, definitely. Nice, I don't know."

"No, it is." I watch as two kids race past with water guns. "I liked meeting everyone."

She licks her thumb and wipes at my cheek. "Of course they all love you."

"Isn't that what you want?"

She wraps her arms around herself, worrying her lower lip. She looks beautiful, even if it's not how she normally dresses. "Sure."

I set down the soda on the nearest table and pull her into my arms. "Hey. What's the matter? Do you want to leave?"

She stays frozen in my arms, refusing to thaw and hug me back. I press my lips to her forehead, anyway, rocking us slightly. Cooper meets my eyes over her head, a frown on his face.

Her mother's voice wafts over the lawn. "Maria, come see your poor mother! Bring the dessert your boyfriend was nice enough to make. Didn't I teach you a thing about cooking?"

"I'm fine," she says, pulling away. "I'm fine. Go talk to Dad, okay? Anthony is a Mets fan, if you want to talk baseball."

"Are you sure?"

She nods. "Yeah. Go enjoy yourself. Keep making a good impression."

I kiss her cheek. "Okay. I love you."

Her smile is fleeting. "I know."

52

SEBASTIAN

"HOLY CRAP," Anthony says, shaking his head. "You're James Callahan's *brothers*."

"Yep." I shift my weight as I take another sip of beer. Fortunately for me and Cooper, the first thing Anthony did when we walked over to the grill was take the sodas out of our hands and give us beers instead. Mia's dad is in a deep conversation with a couple of the older guys, but Anthony welcomed us right in; I think he was happy to point his kids in the direction of the pool. "You see him play in person yet?"

"Haven't had time," he says, shaking his head slightly. "Kids, man. They fuck with your whole life. Hey, Rick, come here. Mia's boyfriend is James Callahan's brother."

The guy who must be Rick—one of Mia's cousins—ambles over. "The Eagles QB?"

"Yeah. Both of them. Sebastian and—what's your name again, man?"

"Cooper," Cooper says, a note of dryness in his tone.

Anthony either doesn't notice or doesn't care because he just claps Cooper on the shoulder. "Cooper, right. The hockey player. And Sebastian here plays baseball. Isn't that insane?"

"Your dad was Jake Miller," Rick says, snapping his fingers and pointing at me. "I remember reading something about the Callahans adopting you."

"Yep," I say, because I'm not sure what else to say about it at this point. It's always weird when someone points out a fact of your life like they expect it to be news to you, too. "We brought along some jerseys he signed. Figured it could be a good—"

"This guy," Anthony says, pounding me on the back. "This guy knows what's up. You any good at football, or is it just baseball for you? We're going to play touch in a bit."

"Little Mia finally did something right," Rick says. "The bar was pretty low for you, though, man—at least you're not a chick."

He laughs, and Anthony laughs with him.

"What do you mean?" I say, fighting to keep my voice neutral as the back of my neck prickles. Cooper gives me a warning look, but I ignore him.

"She went through this phase a while back where she kept saying she was into girls," Anthony says. "That she was queer, or whatever. I don't know the specifics of that shit. Obviously she isn't, if she's with you."

Anger moves through me with the force of a wave. If this is the sort of shit Mia gets when she comes home, it's no wonder she doesn't want to be here. "It wasn't a phase."

"Huh?"

"It wasn't a phase," I say, my voice slipping lower. "She's bisexual. So yeah, she could be with a girl right now, or a person who identifies some other way. But she's not. She's with me, and I'm fucking grateful for it."

"Jesus," Rick says. "We were just joking around."

"Cut it out." I take a step closer, grateful that my bulk backs up my words. "It's not funny. She's your family, you should respect her, no matter who she's dating."

To his credit, Anthony looks chastised. "We're just surprised," he says. "She barely talks to us, and suddenly she's here with you. Is it serious? You're with my little sister?"

"Yes," I say shortly. "She's—"

"Sebastian," Mia's father says. "You grill at all, son?"

I pause, looking over my shoulder. "Pretty good at it, sir."

"He's being modest," Cooper says. "He's fantastic."

"Come help me with this sausage," he says. "Anthony, get some more burgers from the fridge, we're nearly out already."

I wonder if he heard us, and if so, what he thinks. I know Mia's parents are aware she's bisexual, but knowing it is different from accepting it, and I wouldn't want to make things worse for her. Regardless, it can't hurt to talk to him and keep up my good impression. We might end up being family one day, after all. I really hope so.

"Of course, sir." I turn back to Mia's brother and cousin. "She's my girlfriend. It's serious. Watch your mouths around me."

I stare at them for a beat longer before walking over to the grill. Mia's father—also named Anthony, although most people seem to be calling him Tony—is a big man, broad-shouldered and barrel-chested. I wonder if he played football in his day. He pokes at the sausage with a pair of tongs, glancing at me and grunting before concentrating on the grill again. I stand up a little straighter. Mia's idiot brother was one thing. Tony di Angelo is a different beast entirely.

"So. You're dating Mia, huh?" he says eventually. "She's never brought home anyone."

"Yes, sir," I say.

He glances at me again. "Baseball player, you said?"

"Yes, sir." I swallow, glancing at Cooper. He's talking to a couple of Mia's uncles; one of them laughs heartily at something he just said. "I'm on the McKee baseball team right now."

"Going pro, like your old man?"

"Thinking about it," I say, because there's no way I'm going to get into the whole situation with a stranger, especially not with my brother four feet away.

"I've heard you mentioned often enough lately," he says. "On the radio and everything. You're more than thinking about it. That's good. Good for Mia to be with someone like you, someone who can take care of her."

"Of course."

He turns the sausages over with a careful hand. The smoke billows, and he covers the grill. "Is that what you're doing? Taking care of her?"

"I'm trying my best."

He nods, apparently needing a moment to consider that. "If you're going to be with her, you make sure it's serious. I know how much time athletes spend on the road. Baseball especially."

The thought of cheating on her is so ridiculous I almost laugh, but I school my face into a neutral expression. "It is serious, sir. I love her. I'd never hurt her like that, I wouldn't even think about it."

He grunts again. "Mia's always been a special girl."

I nearly sigh with relief. Finally, someone who recognizes that. "Yes, she's amazing. She's the smartest person I've ever met, I swear she runs—"

"She's always resisted what's best for her," he interrupts. His brown eyes, the same shade as hers, sear into me like a brand. "Things have never been easy where she's concerned. A good kid like you, keeping her in line—she needs that. I'm glad she finally has it, so don't fuck it up."

For a moment, I just stare at him. If I thought Mia's brother and asshole cousin got me pissed off, it's nothing compared to this. By his tone, he's completely serious.

He thinks she needs to be controlled.

He thinks that's part of my duties as her boyfriend.

I stuff my hands into my pockets, so I don't clench them and clear my throat. Part of me wants to rush inside, grab Mia, and leave right fucking now, but I can't. Her family is important to her, even if they clearly don't know a thing about her or what's truly best for her. If I have to get through this with a smile on my face, I will, but I can't let it slide completely.

"Respectfully, sir," I say, "it's not my job to keep her in line. I love her, I support her, but I'm not her keeper."

He slaps me on the back, startling me, and bursts into laughter as he points at me with the tongs. "I like you, kid. Fire in your belly."

I blink. Whatever I had been expecting, it wasn't that. "I just—"

"I'm sure she'd try to bite your head off. She's as crazy as her mother sometimes." He shakes his head, gesturing with the tongs. "I love that woman, but she's goddamn stubborn. Mia's sister, she takes after my side of the family. A softer touch, you know? Mia, though? Mia's all Pancheri."

"Hey," someone half-shouts. I think he's one of Mia's uncles on her mother's side; he has graying hair at his temples and more crow's feet than I can count. "What did you say about us Pancheris?"

"Enough for him to understand the situation with Miss Mia Pancheri," Tony calls with another bark of laughter. "Come here, you old bastard, meet her little boyfriend. He's Jake Miller's kid."

"The Reds player?"

I swallow down my sigh and raise my hand in a wave. If I'm anything, it's not little or a kid, but I have a feeling that no matter what I say, it'll get twisted, so the best thing to do is ride the current. I don't understand all the dynamics at play in this family, clearly. "Yep. How's it going, sir?"

53

MIA

WALKING INTO THE KITCHEN sparks a kaleidoscope of memories.

Working on homework at the kitchen table while Mom prepped dinner, Food Network playing on the television.

Shrieking at my brother when he pulled on my hair on the way to grab something from the fridge.

Stealing bites of antipasti before taking it to the dining room during dinner parties.

Laughing with my sister over crushes, ice cream bowls in hand.

Stomping upstairs to change when I tried to alter my Catholic school uniform too boldly and got a scold from Nana.

Hugging my dad goodbye as he gave me the keys to the car.

Sitting quietly with Nonno as he drank espresso and read the paper, a box of pastries open on the counter between us.

Some of the memories are jewel-bright, but others are dark and sharp enough to cut. Kitchens have a special place in all kinds of families—they certainly hold a lot of significance for Sebastian, who developed a passion for food alongside his mother—and mine has always been the center, the proverbial hearth. For all my family's faults, the food is always impeccable. I'm sure my mother was at the Italian butcher yesterday, buying sausages and mozzarella, bread and rice balls, olives and marinated mushrooms. She's been on a firstname basis with the guy who owns the store since before I was born.

Right now, the kitchen is complete chaos. Platters cover the breakfast table, with stacks of plastic cups and plates crammed in between. All five burners on the stove are going and the oven is on, making the room at least twice as warm as the rest of the house. My mother holds court at the counter, putting together a gigantic salad, and my aunts and older cousins hover around, chatting loudly as they cook.

"Wow," Penny says, flattening herself against the wall as Aunt Carmela passes by with a platter of hot dogs. "How many more people are coming over?"

"Girls, there you are!" Mom wipes her hands on a dishcloth before hurrying around to hug us, never mind the fact we already said hello when I introduced her to Sebastian earlier. I couldn't tell if she was more surprised about the fact I came home with a date in tow, or my stupid pink dress. The last family gathering I attended, I wore jeans and a Metallica t-shirt, and she told me I looked disgraceful, so I figured I'd borrow a dress from Izzy's closet this time.

"We could use some more sets of hands in here, the neighbors are still arriving," Nana says.

"Don't forget about Rick's friend, Paul," my cousin Raquel says. "Step back, I need to open the oven. I think the stuffed shells should be done."

"Paul and his girlfriend," Aunt Dottie says, making a face. "Have you seen the way she dresses?"

Mom cups my cheek, studying me with those sharp eyes that miss nothing. I've tried to get a lot of things by her over the years, but she has an uncanny ability to sniff out bullshit. "Are you eating enough?"

I'm not sure when she went from telling me not to eat too much to worrying I eat too little, but I just shrug. "I'm fine."

"You look tired." She turns my head from side to side, then fusses with my sweater. "Tell us more about Sebastian, honey. He seems like such a good young man. Very polite."

"Um—"

"And thank goodness he's a young man," she interrupts, voice low, as she continues to fuss with my outfit. "It makes the whole thing so much easier."

I resist the urge to jerk away. Penny throws me a look, eyes wide, but I ignore her.

This afternoon is going to be torturous.

"That boy is so handsome," Aunt Carmela says as she walks back into the kitchen. "And an athlete, too?"

"No wonder he has so many muscles," Raquel says as she waggles her eyebrows, sending half the kitchen into a fit of laughter. Even Nana, sitting on a counter stool as she very carefully arranges a plate of antipasti, chuckles.

"He plays baseball," Giana says. She's at the sink, scrubbing a gigantic pot. "Right, Mia?"

"He doesn't just play it," Penny says, bumping her hip against mine subtly. "It's going to be his career."

I'm glad she's here, even if part of me wishes I just came to the party myself—no Penny and Cooper, no Sebastian. If Giana goes through with her threat to tell Mom the truth about how I've been spending my time at college, the fallout will be nuclear. I tried to talk to her when we first arrived, but she brushed me off.

"Yep," I say. As far as I know, Sebastian hasn't told anyone else about his decision, and it's his news to share, not mine. "The draft is soon."

Mom clasps her hands. "He's perfect. I'm so glad you finally came to your senses and found yourself a nice boy, Maria."

The rest of my aunts and cousins voice their approval. I'm not usually the one who earns this kind of reaction—I've always gotten the exasperated looks, the reprimands—and it feels weird. I'm not doing anything to earn it; it's not like I'm dating Sebastian because he plays baseball. I force myself to keep smiling.

"A professional baseball player," Aunt Carmela says. "You'll be set."

"You might not even need to teach at all," Mom teases. "Come help take all of this outside."

I follow her into the yard with the salad bowl in hand. When I look at the grill, I relax slightly. Sebastian's talking to my father and one of my uncles. Giana is closer to both of our parents than I am, but still, it means a lot to me that he's taking the time to get to know Dad.

The reactions to Sebastian haven't surprised me in the slightest. He's charming and handsome, golden through and through. Who wouldn't love him? I thought part of me would find satisfaction in that, but instead, I feel like I'm balancing on a ledge, and one false move will send me plummeting.

When we're back in the kitchen, Mom smooths back my hair the way she did when I was little.

"This is wonderful, Maria," she says, her voice low enough my aunts and cousins can't listen in. "I hope you realize what it means to be with a man with that kind of career. You need to be prepared to support him. If you're going to keep him, you need to make sure he's happy and taken care of."

For a moment, I just stare. She's spoken to Sebastian exactly once and is already thinking about ways I could fuck things up.

"Right," I say. "He's—well, we're happy."

"Your aunt is right," she says. "It's not every day that someone has the opportunity to be with someone so successful. He'll have attention no matter where he goes, so it'll be up to you to keep it."

I glance around. Penny is chatting with my grandmother, my aunts are arguing over how to serve the stuffed shells even though someone makes them for every single party, a couple of my cousins run inside for more sodas. No one is looking at us except Giana, soapy up to the elbows, her brows drawn together.

"I trust him," I say.

Mom waves her hand impatiently. "It's not about trust. It's about making sacrifices. Goodness knows you've never once understood that concept when it comes to our family, but maybe with him—"

"Seriously?" I interrupt. "It's not like I'm some terrible—"

"Not that this is about us," she says, a little louder. "This isn't about that. This is about recognizing that you could have it all, Maria. He's a good man, he's going to want a girlfriend and eventually a wife who is there for him. Maybe instead of tying yourself to a school district after graduation, you could tutor and travel with him."

"Well, it doesn't matter because I'm not getting my teaching degree anyway."

The words leave my mouth before I can think better of them. I wince; I was loud enough that everyone in the room heard.

"Wait, what?" someone says into the silence.

My mother grabs me by the elbow and drags me into the living room.

Not the hall by the staircase or the den or even my room, but the formal living room in the front of the house with the pristine couches we only sit on during holidays. It's my mother's favorite place for a lecture, and I feel like a seventeen-year-old again, caught doing any number of stupid things.

I wrench my elbow away from her. "Mom, stop. I'm not a little kid."

"You'd call that mature? Talking nonsense in front of half the family? Your friend?"

"It's not nonsense." I smooth down the skirt of my horrible dress, wishing I could rip the thing in two. "I've been meaning to talk to you about it."

"Are you even still in school?"

"Yes. God." I take a deep breath. "I'm just... I'm majoring in astronomy and physics. I want to get my PhD. Do research, maybe even work for NASA. Not teach and be a housewife."

She stares at me like I really did just rip the dress off. "And when do you expect to have time for marriage? For children? What about Sebastian?"

"This isn't about him."

"So you declared a new major and conveniently forgot to mention it to me or your father?"

"It's not new."

"What?"

"It's not new," I snap, unable to keep my voice steady. "It's what I've always wanted to do, but you didn't listen."

Giana appears in the doorway, her arms crossed tightly over her chest. Mom looks at her, then back at me with such disappointment in her expression, my knees nearly buckle.

"Your father and I have worked so hard to make sure you could attend that fancy private university," she says. She takes a step closer. Even with the carpet muffling the sound of her heel, I sense the intention in it. "So you could get an accelerated teaching degree, like we agreed."

"I never agreed." I cross my arms, resisting the urge to take a step back. "You just decided it for me and expected me to go along with it. Nonno is the only one who understood me, he encouraged me—"

"My father was many things, but a realist was not one of them," she interjects. "Jesus, Mia, come on. Stop dreaming."

"It's not just a dream." I feel the beginning of a sob building in my throat and swallow it down. "It's what I'm meant to do."

"And what about what Sebastian is meant to do? What about what he deserves? A wife who will support him and his career. Who will take care of his children. You can't do that if you're working around the clock."

"It doesn't matter!" I throw my hands up. "I told you this ages ago. I don't know if I even want to get married and have kids anyway."

She's silent for a moment. Then she says, in a voice that cracks like ice, "I can't believe I raised such a selfish daughter."

A tear rolls down my cheek. I wipe it away roughly. "Nice to know things haven't changed."

"What?"

I laugh wetly. "The last time I told you that, you said I would be welcome to leave the family if I decided not to get married or give you grandchildren."

There's genuine confusion on her face, warring with the anger. "I never said that."

"You did. You threatened to fucking disown me if I didn't make myself someone's good little wife."

"Do *not* curse at me."

I can't believe she doesn't even remember. I've thought of that night a million times now, but it didn't even matter enough to her for it to stay in her memory. What was a crushing blow to me was nothing to her.

Nothing.

My stomach rolls. Giana says something, but I can't hear her over the buzzing in my ears. Why did I ever think there'd be a way forward? That my family would truly see me for me?

I push past Giana, past my aunts and cousins and Penny and everyone else listening in, and throw open the screen door. It slams shut behind me.

"Sebastian!" I call.

He looks up, along with half of the people in the backyard. I know it's rude to leave, but right now, I don't care how it looks. I just need to make it to the car without crying. "I need to leave."

54

SEBASTIAN

MIA HASN'T SAID a word the entire ride to Philadelphia.

I tried, when we first got in the car, but she gave me a glare so cutting that I stopped mid-sentence. A couple tears spilled over her cheeks, but she didn't let me wipe them away. Or kiss her. Or hold her hand. Anything that could bring her comfort, she ignored. When I asked if she still wanted to visit James and Bex, she nodded and turned her body so her head rested against the passenger door window.

It was awkward, with her brother and father, but something must have happened with her mother. Something big enough to turn my normally fiery Mia into a lifeless version of herself. It's been agonizing to drive instead of barraging her with questions. I turned on a rock playlist to try to get her out of her funk, but not even Pink Floyd helped. The other day while we were cleaning the house, she scream-sang the lyrics to "Young Lust" while using a duster as a microphone. I laughed so hard I nearly fell down the stairs. Today? She didn't even tap her foot to the beat.

Once we get to James and Bex's place, I hope I can find a moment alone with her to talk. I'm sure the first thing she'll want to do is get out of that dress. I'm half-surprised she didn't change right there in the passenger seat, our backseat companions and other drivers be damned.

"Almost there," I say as I turn the car onto James and Bex's street. "Maybe we'll get lucky with the parking."

"This is such a pretty neighborhood," Penny murmurs from the backseat. I glance into the rearview mirror and see that she's holding hands with my brother. They've had their phones out a lot during the drive, and I'd bet my car that they were texting about what happened at the barbecue. "I'm excited to see their house again, too. Mia, there's like five different levels."

"And a rooftop patio," Cooper says. "Maybe we can use the fire pit later."

Mia slowly unglues herself from the door. She runs a hand through her hair. "That would be nice."

Her voice is flat. There's no emotion in it, good or bad. She reaches for the pink purse at her feet, pulls out a makeup bag, and flips down the sun visor to use the mirror.

I glance over quickly as she starts to touch up her makeup. "Are you still sure you're okay to visit? We can always go back to Moorbridge."

She shakes her head. "No, it's okay. Your family is tame in comparison to mine."

"Do you want to talk about what happened?"

"No," she snaps. Her face falls as soon as the word leaves her mouth, blush coloring her cheeks. "I'm sorry, I just—no, thank you."

"It's okay." I find a spot not too far away from the townhouse and pull in. "If you need some space, take some space."

For whatever reason, that makes her bite her lip so hard I'm afraid she's going to draw blood. I try to hold her hand as we walk down the sidewalk, but she sidesteps, balancing along the curb instead.

I know I shouldn't let it hurt me. Mia is a black cat sometimes, always ready to bring out the claws. If I give her space, she'll come to me. If there's anything I *don't* want to do right now, it's fight with her, and with the mood she's in, I'm not sure how she'd react to a push.

At the door, Cooper steps forward and rings the doorbell. I remember the bright yellow door from the listing James showed us, back when he was considering whether to make the investment. It's a beautiful house, fit for a superstar quarterback, but he didn't want to live in it alone. His engagement to Bex last summer helped seal the deal, and as far as I know, they've been happy since. He made sure that wherever he lived, there would be room for a nice photography studio. Beckett Callahan Photography has taken off in the past year, just like James' football career with the Eagles.

It's adorable that she uses our last name even though they're not officially married yet. I think she's found a home with the family, the same way I did. The way I want for Mia, if I'm being honest with myself. She deserves better than the family the universe gave her.

Bex opens the door, her arms already out to pull the closest of us into a hug. "You guys! You're early!"

"Hey, Bex," Cooper says. He kisses her on the cheek. "How are you?"

"Better now," she says, pulling Penny into a hug next. "Mia, it's so nice to see you again. We're so excited for you all to—Kiwi, stay right here."

A sweet, gangly puppy with a white-and-brown speckled coat pokes its head out of the doorway. Bex blocks the entryway with her body, leaving the dog to bark plaintively. "Babe, the dog is trying—"

"I'm here, I'm here." James scoops up the puppy, flashing us all a smile. "Sorry, we're still trying to get him to understand the concept of doors."

"When did you get a dog?" Cooper demands.

The puppy—Kiwi—squirms, trying to lick James' face. When we're all safely inside, he shuts the door and sets him down. He promptly runs in a circle around us, sniffing excitedly at our feet and our overnight bags.

Penny drops to her knees, coaxing the dog into her arms. He licks her across the face, but she doesn't flinch. "His name is Kiwi? I'm dead, that's too cute. Mia, come pet him."

Mia looks wary for half a second, but then Kiwi plops right in front of her and rolls onto his belly, and she can't resist. I think I catch a flash of a smile as she bends down, thank God. To be fair, there isn't much that an adorable dog can't fix, and this one has cuteness in spades. I have no idea what kind of dog he is, but his wiggly energy and bright eyes are infectious.

"I can't believe you didn't tell us," Cooper says. "I think you broke the bro code by not texting us pictures the moment you got him."

"Seconded," I tell James. "I'm personally offended you didn't introduce him to his uncles immediately."

"How many pictures of my cat daughter do I send you on a weekly basis?" Cooper says. "At least ten."

"More like twenty," says Penny. She gasps. "Wait. I just realized he has a fruit name too. This is amazing."

"It's recent," Bex says, a note of dryness in her tone. "Wait until you hear why we have him."

"Jumping right into it, princess?" James teases.

Bex reaches up and kisses his cheek. "Drinks first. Can I get you guys anything? I have a cheese plate ready to go."

"I'll get everything," James says. "Show them the living room, honey."

He leads the way upstairs, continuing, "She's working on this beautiful gallery wall—you have to see it. We're collecting some pieces, but of course her work is the star."

Bex is positively pink by the time we make it to the living room. She tucks her hair, a little shorter than the last time I saw her, behind her ears. She's not at all dressed up; she's wearing leggings and an oversized Outer Banks sweatshirt, but she looks pretty as always, her diamond-and-sapphire engagement ring shining on her finger. The way my brother gazes at her before he disappears into the kitchen is how I hope people notice me looking at Mia.

We settle onto the comfortable couches in the living room. I don't know if they hired someone to do their interior decorating or if they picked everything out themselves, but the whole room is airy, done up in whites and blues. It faces the street, with huge windows to let in light, and across the far wall, the beginnings of the gallery wall are taking shape. I recognize Bex's work immediately; the photograph of her mother's old diner, the beach at Kitty Hawk in the morning, a close-up of what has to be James' hands, holding a football.

I pat the seat next to me, but Mia holds up her bag.

"Hey, Bex?" she says. "Do you have somewhere I can change? I'd love to get out of this dress."

"Oh, of course," Bex says. "If you go upstairs, there's a guest bedroom to the left. We figured you and Sebastian could have that one, and Penny, you and Cooper could have the one on the right side of the hall."

Mia smiles at her. "Thanks. Your house is beautiful, by the way. I can't wait to see the rest of it."

"And I can't wait to get to know you," Bex says. "I remember you from The Purple Kettle. You always seemed really cool."

"Yeah, it's so funny that you worked there too," Mia says.

"She is the coolest, can confirm," Penny says. "How's the studio going, by the way? Your Instagram totally exploded over the past couple months."

"I think that's mostly because everyone realized who I'm engaged to," Bex says. She pulls Kiwi into her lap, petting him between the ears. "Although—"

I hurry after Mia. I saw her fond eye roll at Penny's words, but also the way her face fell.

I catch up to her on the next floor, reaching for her hand. "Sweetheart."

She opens the door to the guest room, easing away from me. I walk in after her and shut the door behind us. She sets her bag on the bed, which has a cheery yellow throw blanket folded over the end and matching throw pillows at the head, and pulls the dress right over her head.

"What happened? Did your mom find out about your major?"

She rips the clip out of her hair and reaches down for the shoes. "I saw you talking to Dad."

"Yeah. He's... well, honestly, I didn't love the way he was talking about you. Or your brother, he was rude."

She snorts. "Fantastic."

"I tried to shut it down, but they seemed pretty determined to ignore me."

She yanks a t-shirt over her head, then pulls up a pair of cutoff jean shorts. "Don't worry about it. It's... it's the way they are."

I grimace, but I know I shouldn't get into it. Not now, and not here. If I had my way, she'd never have to talk to any of them ever again. "I totally get if you need a minute to—"

"Sebastian?" she interrupts sharply. "I'm good. I'm fine. Give me five seconds alone."

55

SEBASTIAN

"IS EVERYTHING OKAY?" Penny asks when I sit back down, thanking James for the cocktail he just gave me. Judging by the copper mug, it's a Moscow mule.

I hide my grimace with a sip. It's a little heavy on the ginger beer, but that's forgivable. "I'm honestly not sure."

"Should I go up?"

"She said she wanted to be alone."

"She seems stressed out," Bex says. She scoots a little closer to James on the loveseat, wrapping her arm around his.

"Her family is full of assholes," Cooper says darkly. "It explains so much."

"Hey," I snap.

"Not about her," he says. "Jesus. About why she's kept her distance. The thing with her brother and that idiot cousin of hers? I'm impressed you handled it so well."

"Believe me, I wanted to punch them," I say. "I just figured it wouldn't be a good look for my first meeting with my future in-laws."

Bex clasps her hands together. "It's that serious?"

"I sure as hell hope so," I say, scrubbing my hand through my hair. "I love her."

"I'm going to tear up," she says. She actually sniffles. "That is the sweetest thing I've ever heard."

"I won't get into it, but things didn't go well with her mom," Penny says. She swirls her drink around, biting her lip. "The whole thing was just—hi, Mia."

Mia, the makeup wiped away from her face entirely, her hair in a messy bun, sits next to me. I hold out my arm. She gives me a look, something that I can't quite catch flickering in her expression, and curls against my side. Kiwi, realizing there's someone new in the room to terrorize, takes a running leap into her lap. She startles, but hugs him tightly.

"He's the cutest," she says into the silence. "Why did you get him?"

If she cares that we're all staring at her with concern, she doesn't show it. I wish she wouldn't put that armor in place right now, but I get it, too. I'm sure she wants James and Bex to like her as much as I wanted her family to like me. Well, at least until I met them.

Whenever I think about her father, I have to take a deep breath to calm myself. If he thinks I'm going to clip Mia's wings just because we're involved with each other, he's delusional. What the hell was it like for her, growing up in that house? No wonder the death of her grandfather hit her so hard. If he was the only one who cared to listen to what she wanted, and she lost that at fifteen, she had years of their bullshit to endure before she made her way to McKee.

"What do you mean?" James says.

"Bex said she'd tell us why you have the dog." She keeps petting him, moving her wrist away when he tries to gnaw on it. I wonder if she would want to get a dog one day. If we move in together for real after graduation, maybe we can go to a shelter and adopt one. "I'm dying to know."

"Oh," Bex says, looking at James again. "It's... I mean..."

He gives her a little squeeze. "Go ahead, princess."

She smiles widely, showing off all her dimples. "I'm pregnant."

It takes half a second to sink in, but then I jump to my feet to pull her into a hug. Cooper does the same, his entire face lighting up in a smile.

"Holy shit," he says. "Congratulations!"

"This is amazing!" I add, rocking her for a moment before embracing James in a tight hug.

"A baby," Cooper says. "You're having a baby."

Bex wipes away the tears shining in her eyes. "Yeah. You're going to be uncles, both of you."

Cooper gives me a look that's positively boyish. "We are going to crush the uncle gig."

I high-five him. "Absolutely crush it."

"Congratulations!" Penny says, stepping forward to hug them both as well. "How far along are you? You look fantastic."

"Yeah, you look great," Mia says. Kiwi barks, wagging his tail as he runs in a circle around us. "To be clear, I didn't realize that would be the reason."

Bex laughs. "No, no, it's okay. We wanted to tell you all tonight. I'm fifteen weeks, so officially into the second trimester, thank God."

"The first was a little rough," James says with a wince.

"I could eat about three things without getting sick," she says. "And everything made me cry. Actually, everything still makes me cry. The other day I saw a TikTok about a duckling who thought a cat was her mom and cried so hard James thought something was wrong."

He gives me and Cooper a wild-eyed look, making both of us laugh. "Please don't scare me like that again."

"And then he got me Kiwi, since I was so anxious that I would be a terrible mother." She laughs slightly. "Because obviously the answer was to give the pregnant woman more responsibility."

"Clearly," Penny says, a dry note in her voice.

"And it's working out perfectly," James says. "He adores you, and you take such good care of him."

"Wait," I say. "When are you due?"

Bex winces. "December."

"We're going to make it work," James says, a soothing note in his tone.

"We wanted to have our first baby in the offseason," she says. "December is *not* the offseason."

"It was meant to be," he says. "We just need to roll with the punches."

It's clear that they've had this conversation before. Bex draws her brows together, frowning as she looks at James. Cooper and I share another glance. I know they'll be fine, but December is when the NFL is in high gear before the playoffs, so I don't blame Bex for being stressed out. Depending upon when she goes into labor, James might need to leave mid-game to meet her at the hospital.

I didn't choose to quit baseball because of Mia and what I

hope we have in the future, but I can't deny that I like the thought of making things easier on the both of us. I couldn't imagine playing a whole baseball season, road trips included, while Mia is pregnant or home alone with a baby. She'll have her own career, too, and the last thing I'd want is to make her feel like she needs to sacrifice anything for me.

"We'll help out as much as we can," Cooper says. "Did you tell Mom and Dad yet? What about Izzy?"

"Izzy knows, actually," Bex says. "I got lunch with her a couple weeks ago and she could tell immediately."

"That's so weird and yet exactly what I would expect from her," Mia says with a snort.

"I know, right?" she says. "Anyway, the plan had been to tell everyone once we were sure everything was going well."

"And she's doing great," James says. "She's healthy, the little chickpea is healthy. We're going to tell Mom and Dad soon—we just wanted to tell you guys first."

"Mom is going to flip out," Cooper says. "I can't wait to hear what she has to say."

He's right about that. Sandra has been excited about the prospect of grandchildren ever since James and Bex got engaged, although she wouldn't have pushed them, or any of us, about it. They better get ready for the presents she's going to lavish on them.

"You're going to make great parents," I say. "I can't wait."

Bex pulls me into another hug, her eyes shining. "Thank you," she whispers against my ear. "I haven't forgotten how much you wanted me to be part of this family."

I squeeze her back. "You deserve this."

I remember that snowy day at her mother's old diner just as

vividly as her. I told her that I hoped she'd become my sister-in-law one day, and I meant every word. Not just for my brother's sake, but for hers. She deserved a family and a future that she was excited about. Same as Mia... and me.

Life is simply too fleeting for anything else.

"ARE YOU GETTING MARRIED before the baby?" Penny asks. "If that's too nosy, just tell me."

Bex laughs slightly as she peers into the stove, checking on the roast chicken that she has going. "We are, yeah. James insisted. I wouldn't have cared, but he wants to make sure we square away everything before the baby comes."

I have to keep myself from staring too openly at her beautiful kitchen. I might not know what to do with them, but I recognize high-end when I see it, and this kitchen has it in spades. The cabinets are a deep blue, and the countertops are sparkling white, and the appliances are all spotless stainless steel. A colorful tile pattern behind the massive range gives the space another pop of color, and a set of copper pans hangs on the wall like an art display.

I wonder if Sebastian has cooked in here yet. He offered to help her, but she insisted that he stay in the living room and catch up with James. Penny and I ended up in the kitchen with her instead, and it's been nice, chatting with her. Our schedules didn't overlap much at The Purple Kettle, but she seemed fun at Cooper's birthday party. Now that I'm getting to know her a bit more, I can see why Penny speaks so highly of her. She's funny and gorgeous and fits in with the Callahans just as well as Penny does.

I take another sip of my drink, trying to keep the scowl off my face. This is so different from my family's kitchen, I could laugh. I'm so exhausted, it feels like today happened in another lifetime. Compared to that chaos, this is neat and perfect. A roast chicken with potatoes and salad. Moscow mules and a cheese plate straight out of Whole Foods.

Penny swings her feet as she finishes up her Moscow mule. "That makes sense."

"We're planning something small, probably for August," she says. "After training camp but before the season starts would be ideal. He's going to ask Richard and Sandra if we can have it at the house."

"I'm sure they'll say yes," Penny says. "You're going to make a beautiful bride."

She snorts as she pulls lettuce out of the fridge. "I'll be something."

"You'll look perfect. Right, Mia?"

I nod, trying for what I hope is a natural-enough smile. I wish I had Kiwi to distract myself with, but he stayed in the living room. "You'll be stunning."

She smiles at us. "You're both so sweet."

"I'm not sure what kind of wedding I'll want," Penny says. "Part of me wants to have it in Arizona. Cooper loved it there as much as me."

"Have you talked about it?" Bex asks. She throws the

lettuce mix into the bowl, then washes the rest of the salad ingredients.

"Let me help," Penny says, watching as she pulls out an avocado and sunflower seeds as well.

"Same," I say. "I know enough to chop vegetables, at least."

"Sebastian would be so proud," Penny teases. She bumps her hip against mine as she passes me a knife and the cucumbers. "And yeah, we kind of did, but we're not going to get engaged anytime soon. The tattoos are enough for us right now."

"Yes!" Bex says. "Wait, show me. I know I saw the picture, but I'm sure it's even prettier in person."

I appreciate that Penny is trying to keep things light, but honestly, it's just making me feel worse. I don't particularly want to hear about her perfect relationship with Sebastian's brother right now. Not when I have Bex's pregnancy to contend with. It's not about me and I know that, but that doesn't mean it doesn't hurt to hear about how much her future mother-in-law will love having a grandbaby when earlier, I told my own mother not to expect that from me.

I watch as Bex exclaims over Penny's tattoo—her definitive commitment to Cooper, even if it's not an engagement ring yet —and nearly cut myself with the knife. I hiss, snatching away my hand and gnawing on the inside of my cheek instead.

I've been ignoring the future, but right now, it's staring me in the face.

Does Sebastian expect me to be here a couple years from now? I don't know.

Does he deserve it? Definitely.

"What about kids?" Bex asks. "Down the line sometime, maybe?"

"For sure," Penny says. "Cooper is into the idea of it. Although pregnancy sounds super weird. You were really throwing up all the time?"

"Yeah," Bex says. "There were a couple of days where I couldn't keep down anything but crackers. James called the doctor three times, he was so freaked out. But then it got better, and now I feel good. The second trimester is apparently a lot easier."

"My brother's wife said that as well," I say. I remember way too much about her first pregnancy, even though I told everyone repeatedly that I didn't care to learn the details. I love my nephews, but I didn't need to hear the whole thirty-two-hour labor story.

Thirty. Two. Hours. *Twins*. Even the thought makes me want to shudder. Something tells me that Bex won't appreciate it if I tell her that story.

"Aw, that means you're already an aunt," Bex says.

I scrape the celery into the salad bowl. "Yeah. I have two nephews, but I think my sister is going to start trying with her husband soon."

"Imagine getting pregnant on purpose," Bex says, laughing. "God, I wish I could have a glass of wine right now. Can I open a bottle for you two?"

JAMES AND BEX'S house is incredible—while the chicken finished in the oven, Bex took us on a tour, and judging by the way she spoke about it, she had a lot of fun working with the interior designer—but the rooftop patio is something else. Strategically placed plants give it privacy, but there's still a stunning view of the city. In one corner, there's a set of comfortable outdoor chairs and a fire pit, and in another, an area to do yoga and lift weights out in the fresh air. Bex set the roomy table in the center earlier, and it looks beautiful laden with food and a centerpiece of bright, summery flowers. There must be a speaker system, because James turns on a playlist while Bex lights the candles.

"This is so pretty," Penny says as we pass around the food. "Thank you again for having us."

The food smells so good, my mouth starts watering the moment it's on my plate. The crisp salad we helped Bex make, complete with a nice lemon-avocado dressing that I know Sebastian will want the recipe for, juicy roast chicken, and potatoes cooked right in the pan. Sebastian told me all about the wonders of chicken fat the other day, and I swear I've never seen him so excited. I felt like I was talking to a nicer, American version of Gordon Ramsay.

"Yeah, Bex, I'm impressed," Sebastian says. "What's in the salad dressing? I love the idea of using avocado for creaminess."

Penny gives me a little smile. "You called it," she whispers.

I lift one shoulder in a shrug. "He's so predictable sometimes."

For a few minutes, Bex and Sebastian chat about cooking, and the rest of us just enjoy the meal. I nurse my glass of wine as I look out at the city lights, coming into focus now that night is falling.

"Hey, everyone," Sebastian says. "I have an announcement."

I snap my head up. "Babe?"

"And I'd wait, because I'm excited about the baby and I'm also a little afraid that Bex has a secretly intense pregnant side," he continues, "but it's time-sensitive, and I... I want to tell you all now, here, while we're together in person."

Oh my God.

"Sebastian," I say, digging my elbow into his side. "Are you sure..."

"It's okay," Bex says. "We don't mind."

"Not at all," James says, although there's a frown on his face. Hopefully it's one of concern, not annoyance. "We're all family here. What's up? Is everything okay?"

Once the words leave his mouth, he can't take them back. Right now, his decision to quit baseball only exists to the two of us. Once his family gets involved, it'll change the equation. However they react, whatever they think of his plan—that's going to stick in his mind forever. I put my wineglass down, irrationally afraid I'm going to crack it from holding it too tightly.

Maybe I shouldn't have encouraged it. Maybe he should stick with baseball. Maybe there's some part of him, even if he doesn't recognize it, that's doing this for me, and I'm ruining his life.

My mother is right. He deserves everything, and baseball can give him that. He's giving up a steady path, however high-pressure it is, for one that's a lot less certain. He might think he wants this now, but what about five years down the line? What about when I tell him I'm not sure about marriage and kids? What if this decision ends up being a compromise to be with me, when he can do way better anyway?

"It's about baseball," he says. He looks around the table, his gaze lingering on me. I try to smile, but my face is frozen. "I'm quitting. I'm going to withdraw from the draft."

For a moment, no one says anything at all.

"Holy shit," Cooper says, finally, into the silence. "You're serious?"

"Yeah." Sebastian reaches over, taking my hand and squeezing it tightly. "I realized... I can't do it just because my father wanted it for me, or because it's always been the expectation. I still love it, and I don't regret focusing on it for so long, but I don't want it to be my career."

"What are you going to do instead?" James says. He doesn't sound disappointed or upset, just contemplative.

"I'm going to graduate after next semester," he says. "I have the credits to do it. I want to figure out if the food industry is a good fit for me. I think... I want to be a chef. If I graduate early, I can take some of my inheritance from my parents and travel around, maybe follow Mia to Europe for her study abroad program if she'll have me. I could even do a cooking program if it makes sense."

I rip my hand away from his and stand, sending my chair flying backwards. Kiwi startles, darting out from underneath the table.

"Mia?" he asks, his smile fading.

"I'm sorry," I say. Everyone is staring, and I'm making a fucking scene, just like at the barbecue, but I feel like I'm about to crack into a million pieces, and the last place that can happen is here. "I just—I can't be here."

I practically run to the patio door and crash down the stairs. I hear Sebastian following, but I don't stop until I'm at the door of the room we're supposed to stay in tonight. I yank it open, and he follows me inside before I shut it.

"What the hell was that about?" he asks.

I whirl on him. "You're making a huge mistake."

"What?" The pain on his face cuts me like a knife. "But you said—"

"You really want to give all of this up? You're not going to have a life like this"—I gesture around the impeccably decorated room of this beautiful house—"if you're a cook at some restaurant."

I hate his wounded expression, but I can't stop. I'm burning up in the atmosphere, and by the time I crash-land, there won't be anything left. My heart is beating so fast I can hear it in my ears. "You know that I'm not going to compromise on my future because it's all I've *ever* told you, so you're compromising on yours instead. You're taking an easier path for me, and I'm not even worth it."

"Mia, slow down," he says. "What the hell are you talking about?"

"I don't want kids," I snap. "I've never wanted them. I don't even know if I want to get married, Sebastian."

"Fine," he says. "So we don't get married or have kids."

"Stop doing this!" Tears spill over my cheeks. "I know you. You want those things. Don't try to lie, I know it."

He takes a step closer, reaching out like he wants to brush away my tears, but thinks better than to actually try it. "Where the fuck is this coming from? Your family? I don't give a shit about what they think, Mia. You need to stop letting them in."

That stops me in my tracks. "They're my family."

"You need to cut them off. They're ruining you."

"They're my family!" My voice echoes in the little room, too loud and grating. "Don't talk shit about my family."

"Some family they are," he says, bitter laughter in his voice. "Your brother thinks your sexuality is a joke, your father wants me to control you like you're a doll, and whatever the *fuck* happened with your mother is sending you into a spiral so deep I barely recognize you right now. Cut them out. If they don't want to help you pay for the rest of college, we'll figure it out."

"You might've been fine throwing your mother's family away, but I can't do that." I take a step back, putting more distance between us. Anger courses through me, as swift and pointed as a snake bite. "And the fact you think that it's that easy is sad, Sebastian. Not everyone is lucky enough to have two perfect families. Some of us have to stick with the one the universe gave us, no matter how much it hurts."

He freezes. "I didn't throw them away. They threw *me* away. They tossed my mother aside like garbage because she didn't do what they wanted her to do with her life. You, of all people, should understand that."

My lip wobbles. I take in a shuddering breath. "That's not the same thing."

"Isn't it?"

"*No*. You aren't even trying to—"

"You can't let them hurt you forever when you deserve so much more," he interrupts. "Jesus, Mia, come on."

A sob works its way out of my throat, too sudden for me to stop it. "But I don't. I don't. You don't know that now, but you will. I was selfish, I let myself have you anyway, but it was always going to lead to this."

"Are you listening to yourself right now? Why are you hurting both of us for no fucking reason?"

He tries to pull me into his arms, his eyes searching mine, but I shrug away. If I let him give me comfort, I'll be tempted to give in, and I can't. I should have listened to myself when I broke things off the first time. I shouldn't have let him pull me in to begin with. That afternoon in the library, that morning in his bedroom, that starry night at the baseball field—none of it should have happened in the first place. "Don't."

Something cracks behind his eyes. "Angel, come on."

"Marriage, kids, someone who fits in with your life—you deserve that, Sebastian. Go back upstairs to your perfect family." I wipe away the tears roughly. "It would have led here no matter what. I can't be your angel."

He kisses me. I can't help it; I kiss him back. One last time. One more kiss, fleeting in its flawlessness, setting me ablaze even as I fall into the cold embrace of space. He pulls away slowly, his touch a lingering bruise.

"You're part of that family," he whispers.

My heart cracks right down the middle. "You don't understand."

"You know I don't give a shit about how my life looks as long as I have you, right?" His voice cracks; he's holding back tears too.

I shut my eyes, willing myself to think of the future. Better to have it crumble now, instead of after I take his name. One fatal slash across the gut instead of a million tiny cuts that would never heal.

I push him in the direction of the door. "I need to be alone. Please."

"We're not finished with this conversation," he says as he reaches for the doorknob.

I shut the door in his face.

Then I slide to the floor. One sob, then another. I wipe my face and tear a piece of paper from my notebook.

When I'm finished, I pull my phone from my pocket and tiptoe down the stairs.

The Uber pulls to the curb right as I open the front door.

57

SEBASTIAN

I DON'T WANT to go back to dinner. No part of me wants to sit down and answer my brothers' questions about my future right now. But I'm the one who started this conversation, and Mia clearly wants to be left alone, so it's my only option. Maybe by the time the meal is over, I'll bring her a plate and we can talk. *Actually* talk, not fling words around like poison darts. I'm as guilty of it as her, but I meant it when I told her this conversation wasn't over. We have to figure this out, even if our words are cutting each other deep.

A future without her is no future at all.

I linger on the stairs, taking a few deep breaths to calm myself. Stubborn tears linger, so I press the heels of my hands to my eyes. My feelings are a fucking jumbled mess right now, anger and sadness warring with a tsunami of worry. Who cares about whether we get married or have kids? I care more about my future with her than I do about any hypothetical children I might have.

Maybe I should try talking to her again.

I shake my head, even though I'm alone, and drag my hands down my face. That would just make things worse. She's listening to all the wrong things, all the dumb shit that came out of my mouth instead of what's important. And the way she accepted my kiss, then pushed me out of the room?

I play with Dad's medallion, running it over my mind. I never thought I'd ever want to take back a kiss from Mia di Angelo, but right now, I wish it never happened.

The moment I get back to the patio, Penny jerks her head up. Something in my expression must give her pause, because she opens her mouth, but doesn't say anything. I settle into my chair, but the food doesn't seem appealing anymore. My stomach pinches in on itself. All the effort that Bex put into making this nice meal, while pregnant, and I made a mess of it. I should have kept my mouth shut about baseball for the time being.

Does Mia really think it's a bad idea, or was she just panicking? When I first told her about it, she seemed so supportive. I just have to believe that those are her true feelings about it.

I rub my chest. Regardless of her intention, she succeeded. She has to know that I'm not aspiring to become some line cook at a random restaurant. I'm dreaming of The French Laundry, not Outback Steakhouse. I want to learn from those who have mastered their respective cuisines, all over the world. I want to wear the white chef's jacket with pride, and have status in a kitchen when I've earned it. Eventually, I might want a restaurant of my own, or perhaps a whole group of restaurants. My competitive spirit and drive to succeed didn't disappear—I just decided to change its focus to something that's wholly mine.

I know Mia. If she didn't think it was a good idea to begin with, she'd have told me. She's just upset, especially since I pushed her too hard on her family. Pushed her to the point that she snapped at me about mine.

Fucking hell. I should have known better. She's told me a dozen times how much her family means to her, even with all the bullshit.

"Are you okay?" Cooper nudges his shoe against mine. "What happened?"

"I don't want to talk about it."

"Should I go downstairs?" Penny asks.

I shake my head. "Give her some space."

"For what it's worth," Cooper says, "I think it's a good plan."

My shoulders nearly sag with relief. "Really?"

"Yeah, definitely. Right, James?"

"Cooper and I were just talking," James says. "If it's not what you want, don't do it. Don't tie yourself to it just because you feel you have to. Having played football professionally for a season now, I know that if it's not what I wanted to do, I'd be toast."

"And you're incredible at cooking," Cooper says. "We know how much you love it. You'll be a success no matter what you do with it."

I duck my head as my cheeks heat up. "Thanks, guys."

"You're our brother," James says. He presses his fist to his heart; to the tattoo he shares with me and Cooper. "We're always going to support you."

My heart sprints in my chest, the good emotions warring

with the bad. "Even if I'm not... an athlete anymore? Not like you guys are?"

"To be clear, I'll still be challenging you at the gym every chance I get," Cooper says. "And I'll definitely be sad if you leave me a semester early."

James shakes his head fondly at our brother. "Seb, you're not our family because you play a sport. You're our family because we love you."

Bex sniffles, clearly on the verge of tears again. "This is so sweet."

He squeezes her hand. "It's just the truth. Remember the fight you got into the first week at Albright?"

"That was a good fight," Cooper reminisces. "Definitely worth the lecture from Mom and Dad."

"I jumped into the fray for you then," James says, "and I'd do it now and always."

It's quiet for a second, while I figure out how to talk again. I don't know why I was so worried about their reactions. I guess it's impossible to calm the anxiety when it comes to moments like this, even if they've accepted me as their brother since day one. "Thank you."

"Wait," Cooper says. "Do Mom and Dad know your plan?"

"Not yet," I say. "I wanted to tell you two first."

"Poor Richard," Penny says, although she doesn't sound all that sorry. "Learning he's going to be a grandfather and this all at once."

"We'll back you up," Cooper says. "Whenever you want to tell them, we'll support you."

James nods. "I guess it does need to be soon, since the draft is in a few weeks. What do you have to do to withdraw, write to the commissioner's office?"

Penny gets up, pressing her phone to her ear. "Hey. Are you okay? Do you want me to bring you down a plate?"

Mia.

I get up too, circling around the table to her. She shoots me a look as she runs a hand through her hair. Her eyes widen as she takes in whatever Mia is saying.

My heart leaps painfully.

"Oh," she says. "I mean—shit, are you serious?"

"What?" I demand. "Is she okay?"

"Sure. I'll call ahead and tell Dad you'll be there." She pauses. "Right. Are you sure this is what you—"

I don't waste any more time listening in. I run to the bedroom and skid to a halt in front of it, throwing it open without bothering to knock.

It's empty. Mia's bags are gone.

And on the bed is a note.

S—

Thank you for everything. Please know that I do believe in you. You're going to make a wonderful chef.

I'm sorry for this. It was so easy to love you.

Goodbye,
M

P.S. We were always friends.

58

MIA

I SHUT MY COMPUTER and slide down until I'm horizontal on Penny's bed.

Part of me wants to scream. Screaming sounds like an acceptable course of action, given the fact Alice won't stop blowing up my phone about the presentation, Professor Santoro keeps piling on the requests, Giana hasn't gotten the hint that I don't want to rehash the barbecue with her, and I haven't seen my boyfriend in over a week.

Ex-boyfriend.

He's not mine anymore. I made sure of that when I wrote him that note.

That doesn't mean it doesn't hurt. Somehow, I thought that the heartbreak wouldn't be as deep if I was the one initiating it, but that was a lie. I've thrown myself into work since the moment I got back to Moorbridge, because the moment I take a breather, I can't think of anything or anyone but Sebastian. I might be staying at Penny's dad's house, but there are reminders of him everywhere. When I found the note he left on the jersey in my bag the other day, I shut myself in the bathroom in the lab and tried to breathe through the tears—until Alice banged on the door.

Whenever I do let my mind wander, it runs over all the memories, big and small, and I miss him so much I feel like I just took a rusted knife to my throat. I hurt him. I know he's ambitious, I know he's going to succeed at whatever he ends up doing. There's probably going to be a Sebastian Callahan restaurant empire one day. And what we said about each other's families...

It's better for him if I'm not involved in his life. He'll find someone else eventually, a woman with a family he loves and is happy to be part of. A woman who fits into his life so perfectly, he'll laugh when he thinks about how he thought I could ever be that person.

I just have to scream through it until the feelings fade.

By the time he got back to New York, I had already moved all my things from his house to Penny's father's place. Mr. Ryder and his fiancée, Nikki Rodriguez—also Penny's boss at the ice rink in town—have been generous about letting me stay here. It's what I should have done in the first place, sucked it up and spent a few nights here, then moved into the new dorm room McKee offered me. If I had stayed firm, I wouldn't have gotten involved with Sebastian again.

I wouldn't have fallen in love.

I wouldn't have had to steal back my heart.

I grab a pillow and press it over my face. I do scream, my voice hitching on a sob by the end. My phone chimes again. It's practically Russian roulette whenever I look at it. Will it be Giana? Alice? Izzy? Sebastian?

There's a knock on the door. "Mia? Can I come in?"

I throw the pillow aside and sit up. "It's your room."

"Well, just in case you were naked or something," Penny says as she pushes open the door. She frowns as she takes me in. I've been too busy to do much but eat and take quick showers. My hair hangs limp, I have chipped nails, and I've been wearing the same sweatshirt for days. "Is everything okay?"

"The presentation is a disaster."

She sits on the end of the bed. "No way. It looks amazing."

"Alice chewed me out for mislabeling a diagram."

"She can go to hell."

I snort. "She's right, though. I'm working on it nonstop, and I keep messing shit up. The symposium is next week, and I've barely practiced."

"Work on it more later," she says. "I have pizza on the way."

At the mere mention of food, my stomach growls. I'm not sure when I last ate. Maybe the protein bar at the lab earlier?

Sebastian wouldn't let it stand. He'd already be in the kitchen, whipping up something amazing.

Something I told him not to pursue.

I flop against the bed again, my breath hitching.

"I thought maybe we could do each other's nails," Penny says. I hear the concern in her voice and bite my cheek to keep the tears at bay. "And pick out another movie to watch. Dad and Nikki are going out to dinner, so we can use the big TV in the living room."

"Fine."

"I won't even suggest any rom-coms this time."

"It's whatever, Pen. Put on whatever you want."

She frowns at me. "Sebastian came back from his road trip today. Last of the season."

"Please don't—"

"He wants to come talk to you."

I shut my eyes. The day after I left, he visited the house, asking to speak with me. Penny deflected, which I'm grateful for, even though I'm sure it wasn't comfortable for her. I need to work on being extra nice to her right now, because she's the one caught in the middle between me and the Callahans. I'm sure Cooper is positively thrilled with me.

"I can't."

Penny's voice is hesitant. "That's fine, I'll tell him to leave the things on the porch."

"What things?"

"A pair of shoes and your jacket. I guess you left them at the house."

"You should give him back his jersey."

"I don't think he'll miss it."

I lean over the side of the bed and rummage in my bag until I find it. My heart squeezes at the sight of it. The one and only time I wore it, he took it off so tenderly. "Take it. Give it to him or throw it out, I don't care. I don't want to see it again."

Her face falls. Her kindness and her father's kindness are helping keep my dream alive right now. I need to remember that.

"Please," I add, holding it out.

She takes it. "Okay. But for the record, I still think you should talk."

"Noted."

"You were friends too, you know."

I laugh hollowly. "Believe me, I do."

"So maybe even if it doesn't work out romantically, you could just—"

"It already didn't work out," I interrupt. "He thinks I should cut my family out of my life."

"He was just frustrated," she says. "We all saw what they were like at that barbecue. You don't think they're perfect either."

"We're just—we're not compatible," I say, even though we've had this conversation over and over. I know she's trying to help, but I'm getting tired of explaining myself. "It would have fallen apart no matter what."

"You didn't get what you wanted," she says, a little edge to her voice. "He's still quitting baseball."

"That is what I wanted."

I didn't want him to stick with baseball, not even for a moment, after our conversation in the bell tower. Now that I've had time to think, I know that he's not quitting because of me. I might've helped him along, somehow, but he's not doing it for anyone but himself. Still, that doesn't change the fact that eventually, he'd need to compromise for me, whether about marriage or kids or something else, or I'd end up compromising for him. It would ruin us, and the only variable would be how long it would take.

Penny flicks her braid over her shoulder. "Isn't it? You wanted him to be miserable because your mother got you scared."

"I need you to stop being Cooper's girlfriend for a second and be my friend instead."

The moment the words leave my mouth, I wish I could take them back. Her face falls, something shuttering in her eyes. "Wow. Okay."

"Pen—"

"I wasn't saying that as his girlfriend. I said it as your friend *and* Sebastian's."

"I didn't mean..." I trail off as my phone rings. I glance at it with a grimace before picking up. "Alice?"

"You said you'd be at the lab half an hour ago," she says. "Where are you?"

I completely lost track of time, but there's no way I'm going to tell her that. "I'm close. Be there in a few, sorry."

"Mia," Penny says as I slide off the bed and start cramming shit into my bag.

"Sorry. I have to go to the lab."

"We should keep talking about this."

"What do you want me to say? You fit in with them, Penny. You're going to have a beautiful wedding with Cooper one day, and beautiful children, and your dad is even Cooper's coach. It's like you were made to be a Callahan."

"And Sebastian isn't asking you to do any of those things."

I shove my feet into sandals and toss my phone into my bag. I look like shit, but there's nothing I can do about that right now. Alice will just have to ignore it. She doesn't look fantastic herself; she must be at least a few weeks behind on her next dye appointment.

Maybe I should cut my hair before the symposium.

The fact that a haircut sounds like such a good idea to me right now is more depressing than the stained McKee sweatshirt I'm wearing.

"I like to think I know him pretty well," she says as I open the door. "Just like I know you. And for the record, I don't think he ever does anything he doesn't truly want to do. If marriage and kids were deal breakers for him, he'd have said that."

I just give her a tight smile. "Raincheck on the pizza?"

I wonder if there's a pair of scissors at the lab.

59

SEBASTIAN

WE DIDN'T MAKE the playoffs.

Even if we win our last three games of the season, the one remaining series against Norfolk State University, it won't be enough. We're finishing at the bottom of America East. And while I'm sad for my teammates, especially the seniors, I don't feel anything but relief.

There's a definitive end date. One last hurrah.

Mia won't be there, but I'm starting to get used to that.

When she left James' house, leaving behind a note that made me wish I never wrote her any of mine to begin with, I hoped, at first, that she'd come around, and we'd talk. But that hasn't happened. She doesn't want to see me or talk to me, even for a moment. I have to resist the urge to keep asking Penny how she is. I know she feels bad, but she was Mia's friend before she became mine.

She didn't come home with us this weekend, but James and Bex are here, like they promised they would be for this announcement. Cooper, too, and Izzy. Even though I'd rather do anything else in the world than tell Richard and Sandra I'm quitting the sport they worked hard to keep me in all these years, it has to be now. I already started my letter to Commissioner Scofield, asking to be released from the draft pool, and I have to tell Zoe about it too. She sent me her draft of the article the other day, but I haven't read it.

I keep telling myself that I don't want to see how she wrote about my parents' passing, and that's part of it, but really, I'm dreading reading about what I said about Mia. I meant every word and I still do, but that just makes it worse.

Cooper clasps my shoulder as he sits across from me. We're in the den, the room in the house with the comfiest couches and all the board games. I love this room; whenever I'm in it, I think of Monopoly on Christmas and late-night Mario Kart battles. Birthday cake and karaoke. Arguments and laughter, all jumbled together. This is the private family room, away from the magazine-ready space in the front of the house, and I have a decade of memories here.

When I told James and Cooper my plan, there was a split-second where I wanted to take it back. Not because I doubted myself and this path, but because I didn't want to sever the bond between us. The Callahan boys, each an athlete, same as Richard. But their reaction bolstered me for this moment. I might be Jacob and Danielle Miller's son, but I'm a Callahan. Not because of baseball, but because they're the family who chose me, and I chose them back.

"How are you doing?" he asks.

I know he doesn't just mean baseball. I shake my head. "Don't know."

"She still might come around."

"I don't think so." I fiddle with the medallion, looking down at it instead of into my brother's eyes. "I had a chance, and I blew it."

"She's scared. That might not last forever."

"I love her."

"I know," he says softly.

"I thought... she loved me too. I thought we were forever." I laugh. It's a lonely, hollow sound. "I thought she'd be by my side for this."

"We are," James says, sitting down next to me on the couch. "We've got your back."

"If Dad gives you a hard time, for even a moment," Izzy says, plopping down on my other side, "I'll show him the research. I have a slideshow handy if necessary. I even photoshopped you into a chef's jacket."

I'm honestly not sure if she's joking. I shake my head again, pulling her into a sideways hug and kissing the top of her head. "Thank you."

"And we're talking about Mia after this," she says. "She might be ignoring all my calls, but she'll come around eventually. I can be very persuasive."

"She called me the other day," Bex says. "To apologize for leaving so suddenly."

I blink. "You didn't tell me that."

She shrugs. "I think Penny gave her my number. She seems sweet, Seb. I'm sorry it's not working out the way you wanted."

"Yes," Sandra says, walking into the living room with Richard. "Oh, sweetie, come here."

Kiwi—who has apparently decided that Richard is his god —trots after them.

She pulls me into a hug, smelling of peppermint, and kisses my cheek for good measure. "What did you need to discuss with us? Is it about Mia?"

"No." I take a deep breath. "It's... it's about baseball."

"Did some pricks try photographing you again?" Richard demands. Kiwi jumps onto his lap, mouthing at the buttons on his shirt. He scolds him gently, and Kiwi looks at him in outrage for a moment before settling down.

I take another breath. I might need a whole breathing exercise to get through this. "No."

"Is it missing out on the playoffs? It stings, but it happens," Richard says. "You played well, I know you put your heart into it."

"Honey," Sandra says, "why don't you let him talk?"

I sit up straighter. Cooper catches my eye, nodding.

I can do this.

"I'm quitting baseball," I say in a rush. "I'm going to withdraw from the draft."

Sandra's eyes widen. Richard's elbow slips on the arm of the chair.

"I'm going to graduate a semester early," I add, the words pouring out now that I've started. I keep looking at Richard, at those deep blue eyes that each of my siblings inherited, and ignore the jackrabbiting of my heart. "After next semester, I'll have the credits. I'm going to use some of my inheritance to travel, so I can explore different cuisines, and work my way up in the food industry. As a chef."

"A chef," Richard repeats.

"I have the passion," I say, before he gets in another word. "And I have the intensity and instincts. I realized that even though I love baseball—and I do, I'm not saying I don't—I don't want it to be my career. Even if it's what my father wanted for me. Even if I have the talent. Even... even if you were a professional athlete, and so is James, and so will Cooper."

Richard sits back, contemplating that with his brows drawn together. "Does this have anything to do with Mia?"

"No," I say quickly. "I mean, she helped me realize it's what I want. But I'm not doing this for her. I'm not doing it for anyone but myself."

"And you've thought about it," he says. "Really thought about it. Because it's a lot to walk away from, son."

"I know my dad wanted me to play baseball professionally," I say. "And I'm so grateful that you and Mo—that both of you kept me in baseball. But this is what's right for me."

Even if it's a future that doesn't include Mia, it's still the one I want. I'd rather a cramped kitchen than the vast expanse of left field. A chance to make my own name on my own terms, instead of worrying about living up to someone else's reputation.

Sandra looks at her husband, her eyes shining.

"Danielle would be so excited," she says. "She loved cooking so much."

"She did," he says. There's a faraway look in his eyes. "Remember the time Jake surprised her with that gigantic turkey for Thanksgiving?"

She laughs. "She was so worried it wouldn't thaw in time."

"Best damn turkey I ever had." He swipes at his eyes. "Oh, Sebastian. There's so much of them in you."

Tears sting my eyes, but I don't bother wiping them away. James rubs my back comfortingly.

"Thank you," I say, my voice breaking. "So it's... it's okay?"

"I don't recall you asking for permission," Richard says, just a touch of dryness in his tone. "But of course it's okay."

"I just know how much my dad wanted this for me."

"What he wanted was for you to be happy," Sandra says. "And that's what we want for you too."

"They'd be so proud of you." I meet him halfway as he pulls me into a hug. His embrace is tight, reassuring, and I allow myself a moment to just breathe, my face squished against his neck. "Jake would be so goddamn proud of you. You've become such a wonderful young man."

In my old game, I'd bargain away every single one of Richard's hugs for my father's embrace instead, if only for a moment. But right now, I don't want that. I want to stay right here, in the present, with this father of mine.

Mia was right. I am lucky to have had not one good family, but two.

"What about you?" I whisper. "I was worried that I wouldn't be... as much of a Callahan as the rest of you, I guess. I didn't want to lose this family."

"You're my son," he says. He pulls back, so we can look each other in the eye, his voice as serious as I've ever heard it. "You're my son regardless of what you do with your life."

"You don't need baseball to have our love," Sandra says. A tear slips down her cheek as she smiles. "You're Jake and Danielle's, but you're ours too."

The words on the tip of my tongue aren't "Richard and Sandra." I've wanted to say them, over the years, but I always held back. Always found an excuse to keep that distance.

No longer.

They're my family. I'm a Callahan.

I'm my father and mother's son, but I am Richard and Sandra's as well.

I look at my family—*my* family—and feel so much love I can almost forget there's someone missing. Mia slipped through my fingers like a damned daydream, but this is forever. "Thank you, Mom and Dad."

LATER THAT EVENING, I have the letter to the commissioner drafted and ready to go. Richard helped me with some of the wording, and after, we called Zoe and gave her permission to break the news once my season wraps. Izzy promised to post it on my Instagram, too.

I would feel lighter than air, except for the fact that I want nothing more than to talk to Mia.

I pull up her contact in my phone for what has to be the hundredth time in a week. If I called, would she pick up? If I texted, would she reply?

I'm sure she's still at the lab. The symposium is so close. While I'm playing my last-ever game, she'll be giving her presentation. Right now, she's probably poring over data, adjusting slides, and practicing what she's going to say. For half a second, she feels so close I swear I could reach out and touch her. Her hair is probably in a precarious bun, her glasses perched atop her nose. If she messes something up, she'll make a face at herself and glance down at her notes before starting again, from the top.

Before everything happened, I promised I'd listen to her practice it as many times as she needed.

Instead, I'm in my family's backyard, gazing at the stars.

I'm sure there are so many others hiding in the nighttime sky, the same as those billions of exoplanets, but the stars I can see scatter across the black like glitter against velvet. Maybe she's looking at them too, like that night in Albany when she told me to find the moon.

"Pretty, right?"

Izzy nudges my hip as I turn. Earlier, she was wearing shorts and a t-shirt, but now she's in leggings and a worn, oversized sweater. Her dark hair, hanging loose around her shoulders, shines from the glow of the patio light. "I brought you a hot chocolate."

"Oh, thanks." I take the mug she's holding out. Hot chocolate is an odd choice on a warm night in late June, but I take a sip anyway. "What are you up to?"

"Well, at first I was going to do work," she says. "There's a wedding this weekend in the Hamptons that Katherine is convinced is going to be a disaster, so she's having me go over all the details again. But then I thought I should be social, so I went to go hang out with Mom and Bex, only they were talking about how painful childbirth is, and I can't deal with that energy until I'm at least twenty-five, so I thought I would make hot chocolate, and I figured you needed it too. If there was ever a time for hot chocolate, it's now. You're literally looking up at the stars like a lovesick puppy."

I just blink. The best way to make sense of Izzy's mini speeches is to start at the top and work your way through. "Who is Katherine again?"

"Katherine Abney. My boss."

"Right. And why hot chocolate?"

"It's the most comforting drink." She takes a sip, as if to punctuate her words.

"It's almost the Fourth of July."

"So?" She clinks our mugs together. Mine says 'McKee Royals' on it, and tiny hearts cover hers. "You drink beer in the winter, and beer is best cold."

I guess she has a point. Most of the time she does, even if it's not the one I would have expected. "Do I really look like a lovesick puppy?"

She holds up her hand and puts her thumb and forefinger about half an inch apart. "Just a little. It's mostly cute, though."

"As long as I look cute," I say dryly.

"Penny kind of explained what happened," she says. She runs her hand, decorated with thin stacks of rings, through her hair. "She hasn't said anything to you?"

"She doesn't want to see me."

She makes a quiet noise. "I guess words wouldn't help anyway."

"What do you mean?"

"Mia's a scientist, Seb." She tilts her head to the side as she looks at the sky. "Scientists need evidence to believe things. You can't just say something and expect her to believe it without question, you know? You know how you feel, but unless you give her something concrete that she can't push away, she's not going to let it sink in."

I'm quiet for a moment, considering her words.

I told Mia once that what I deserve is what I want, and I still believe that. Part of her has always felt that she's not enough for me, and I'd be better off with some hypothetical woman who can give me more than her. More career support, or kids, or whatever she thinks I'm expecting, without question or compromise, from my partner.

That's bullshit. She's more than enough for me—she's

everything and more—but Izzy's right. Kids or no kids, marriage or no marriage, her family be damned, she's it for me. She needs evidence, otherwise she'll just keep pretending she doesn't hear what I'm telling her.

"Izzy," I say. "Has anyone ever told you how smart you are?"

I'M NOT USED to having hair this short.

I mess with it over the sink, making a face. Maybe I should tie it back. It's at my shoulders now, six inches shorter than before and harder to tuck behind my ears. I don't want it to fall into my face while I'm onstage.

Right about now, Sebastian is getting ready for his last-ever game.

And I'm across campus, about to enter the symposium's auditorium.

Hair aside, I look okay. Skinny-fit black slacks, loafers, a light blue silk button-down shirt, and a black blazer. My hoops and gold chain are extra pieces of armor. I'm about to walk into a room crowded with scientists, most of them men, and being taken seriously means dressing the part. I fiddle with an earring, taking a deep breath.

Even if we were still dating, I wouldn't have gone to today's game. He wouldn't have let me miss this moment, and truthfully, I wouldn't have offered. If anything, he'd be in the audience, and it'd be yet another thing he gave up for me.

Every time it hurts so much, someone might as well be driving a rusty stake through my ribs, that's what I have to remember.

Our stars don't align.

We're not even in the same galaxy.

"Mia?" Alice says as she opens the door. "Where the hell— oh, there you are. Good. You're late."

I finish adjusting my jacket before looking at her. She opted for a dress and flats today, and clearly at some point between when I last saw her and now, she went to the hairdresser. "Hi, Alice."

"I still can't believe Beatrice wants you to give such a big presentation." She doesn't bother hiding the envy in her voice. "Someone who's an actual expert should be talking about this."

"It's always been the plan."

"And you're just an undergrad. This is my dissertation. You barely know what you're talking about."

"Good luck defending it," I mutter as I brush past her.

She steps in front of the door to prevent me from leaving. "Excuse me?"

I could pretend that what I said was genuine. But she's spent weeks doing nothing but denigrating me just because she's insecure, and I've held my tongue for the sake of professionalism. She can think whatever she wants, but I earned the right to give this presentation. I'm jittery with nerves and lost in an ocean of heartbreak, and she doesn't get to walk all over me. Not anymore. Not today.

I've hidden my claws until now, but she picked the wrong day to mess with me.

"I said, good luck defending it. Especially since I rewrote most of your code."

She flushes. "Don't be ridiculous."

"You know it's the truth." I take a step closer. "Alice, you're smart, but not when it comes to the technical details. I tried to help you, but you didn't want to work together."

"It's not like I asked Beatrice to bring you into the lab."

"Look at the audience out there," I say. "It's almost all men. We could have been supporting each other this whole time as two women in a field that is still dominated by men, and instead, you acted like I was some idiot you had to put up with. I made the program better. Professor Santoro's next paper will be better for it. Your dissertation will be better for it. I deserve to give this presentation."

She flushes deeply, opening her mouth and closing it before finding her voice for a reply. "If you fuck it up, it's going to come straight back to me."

I reach around her for the door handle. "Good thing I've got this."

Once I'm in the hallway, I don't linger; I don't want to get into an even bigger argument with her. I duck into a classroom and check the time.

I have ten minutes before I need to be in the auditorium.

Robert Meier will no doubt be in the front row, questions ready. There are videos online of how he approaches these events, and he always has a notebook open on his lap, full of observations and queries. Sometimes, he'll interrupt the presentation to ask them, pressing for more information, more analysis. If I manage to make it into his program next spring, I'm going to be challenged like never before.

The thought of it makes me nervous and excited all at once.

Aside from Penny, who insisted upon coming to the symposium, even though I told her I wouldn't mind if she would rather go to Sebastian's game, there won't be a friendly face to look at. I haven't spoken to my family since the barbecue. I know I have to suck it up soon and reach out, because the longer this lingers, the worse I'll feel, but a part of me is still holding out hope that Giana will be the first to apologize. If I'm being even more honest with myself, I hope my parents will be willing to hear me explain my plan in depth, instead of ignoring it and disapproving from the sidelines.

My phone buzzes with a series of texts.

> **BEX**
>
> Good luck today, Mia!
>
> **JAMES**
>
> Good luck Mia!
>
> **COOPER**
>
> You're going to crush it :)
>
> **PENNY**
>
> I can't wait <3 You're going to be amazing!
>
> **IZZY**
>
> Go get 'em, space genius <333

I bite my lip as I stare down at my phone, but the last text—the one I truly want—doesn't come.

Instead, Izzy texts me again, privately this time.

> Thought you might want to see this before it goes public
>
> I made Penny promise to take a picture of you onstage <333

I click on the image she sent me. It's a screenshot of a letter. Sebastian's letter to Major League Baseball.

To Commissioner Scofield and Those it May Concern:

With the MLB Draft Day approaching, I want to thank the 30 major league teams for their interest, both in me as a player and as a person. Baseball has been a major part of my life since the very beginning, and I know how much it meant to my father, Reds legend Jacob Miller. Some of my earliest memories include playing catch with him and listening to Marty Brennaman shout, "This one belongs to the Reds!" after victories. It has been an honor and a privilege to follow in his footsteps, and I will always love the sport.

In considering my future, however, I have realized that I need to follow a different path. As such, I am withdrawing my name from consideration for the MLB Draft, now and in the future. I am grateful for all that baseball has given me, but it's time for me to pursue my own passions.

In addition, I will be graduating McKee University a semester early, making this season my last. The past three seasons have been some of the most challenging and exciting of my life, and I thank Coach Martin, the staff, and my teammates for helping me grow into the man I am today.

I would like to thank my family for their support, as well as Mia di Angelo for showing me that I need to define my own future. I don't know what it holds, but I am excited to find out, and I know my parents would be proud of me.

Sincerely,
Sebastian Callahan

Tears blur my vision by the time I finish the letter. It's so him, I feel like I could reach through the phone screen and touch him. I've missed being able to hug him whenever I want, which is something I thought I'd never say about someone. I wipe my eyes, careful not to mess up my mascara.

He thanked me. Despite everything—despite leaving him and loving him and leaving him again—he thanked me.

I wish I could be at the game, even just as his friend. I'm sure it means so much to him, one last time spent doing the thing he learned to love from his father. While I'm glad his family is there to cheer him on, I wish I was there too. But just like he's defining his own future, I need to define mine.

Our stars don't align. I'm being devoured by a black hole that wants to squeeze me into nothingness, but this heartbreak, however deeply it cuts me, is nothing compared to the future heartbreak we'd have inflicted on each other. That night at James and Bex's was just a taste.

I have to make him a memory, starting now.

I enter the auditorium from the back. Professor Santoro is starting the symposium with a welcome speech and presentation of her own, and then I'm up first. She's already at the podium, talking into the microphone, her silver-threaded hair glinting under the stage lights.

"One of the best parts of being a professor is discovering a student you know has what it takes to go the distance," she says. "Someone you know is going to surpass you one day, because frankly, she's smarter than you." This earns her a couple of chuckles. She pauses to smile, looking out at the audience—and then over her shoulder at me, waiting in the wings.

"This has happened to me a few precious times in my career, and from the moment I met Mia di Angelo, I knew she was something special," she continues. "She has the passion, the smarts, and above all, the curiosity that someone needs to do great things in this field. I've been so proud to have her as an undergraduate researcher this summer, and I can't wait for you all to meet her."

I realize a beat too late that that's my cue and hurry onto the stage, aiming for the podium. My first slide is up on the projector behind me, ready to go. My footsteps sound so loud against the wood stage that I can't focus on anything else.

She smiles as we pass each other, squeezing my arm. "Chin up. Speak clearly. You've got this."

This isn't the first presentation I've given, and it won't be the last. This is just the beginning. I give her a nod as I settle in at the podium.

I look at the crowd and nearly knock over the microphone.

My family is sitting in the first row.

Giana. Mom, Dad, and Nana. Penny is at the end of the row next to my sister, beaming.

I meet my mother's gaze, and she gives me a slight nod.

I steel my spine and begin.

61

SEBASTIAN

I LACE UP MY CLEATS, making a double knot and tucking in the loops. Socks, belt, buttoned-up jersey. Dad's necklace tucked underneath my collar, my baseball cap, my sunglasses. The pieces of my uniform come together the same way as they always do, one last time. I paint two thick stripes of eye black on my cheeks, then help Rafael with his.

The usual cheer in the locker room is subdued. We split the two previous games in this series, and it would be great to go out with one final win, not just for me but for the team, but it doesn't feel nearly as exciting as it should. No matter how well we play, it won't lead to a spot in the playoffs. This is the end of my baseball career. My last time jogging out to left field. My last time stepping into the batter's box. My last time walking off the field at the end with my teammates by my side, win or lose.

I'm at peace with it. The letter went to the Commissioner's Office this morning, and by the end of the game, Zoe Anders will have broken the story. She still wants to do a video interview, but I'm going to decline. I said all I needed to say in that letter. I don't owe anyone more of an explanation.

And who knows, maybe one day, baseball fans across America will recognize me for my food instead.

It's a perfectly warm, perfectly cloudless late June day in New York, the kind of baseball weather they depict in the movies. My family is behind home plate, ready to watch me play. Even if I go o-for-4 or commit an error, I won't care. I'll have given it my all, one more time.

I just wish that Mia was here.

I check the time. She's probably doing last-minute preparations for her presentation. I hope she's not too nervous; I'm sure she's going to crush it. I saw how hard she worked on this project, day after day, night after night. By the end, before everything went sideways, she'd be up in the middle of the night with me, working at the kitchen table, bathed in the blue glow of the computer, while I cooked.

Today is an ending for me, but a beginning for her. I just hope her family came through on their promise and actually showed up.

"Ready?" Hunter says quietly. He's the only one who knows the truth of today besides Coach Martin.

I adjust my cap. "I feel good. No regrets."

"Then that's all that matters." He claps me on the back. "I'm going to miss you next season."

"You'll have to keep me updated."

"You still think you'll go to Europe? Even without, you know?"

I nod. "I'll start there and see where I end up."

"You should start a food Instagram or something."

I snort. "The spotlight still isn't for me."

"Sebastian," Coach calls from the other end of the locker room. "If you want to talk to the guys, now's the time."

I push past my teammates, most of them staring with interest thanks to the announcement, and stand next to Coach Martin by the door. When I told him my decision a couple days ago, he was quiet for a long time—longer, even, than Dad—before embracing me and telling me that he wished me luck. Now, he claps my back as he smiles at me. He wanted to make sure I had a chance to address the team on my own terms before Zoe posts the letter.

I take a deep breath. The royal purple and dark wood of the locker room has always been a warm, safe cave to me. The Reds locker room felt like that too; in my haziest memories, I can remember the excitement of being let loose in the room. My father would swing me over his shoulders if I got too nosy about the other lockers, tickling me until we both dissolved into laughter.

I take off my cap, run my hand through my hair, and clear my throat.

"Last game of the season," I say.

The guys nod, murmuring to each other. My heart squeezes with love. I'm going to miss everyone, even the guys who are a pain in the ass, like Ozzy. By walking away, I'm giving up the practices and training sessions, the road trips and home games. The slammed locker doors and broken bats, but also the celebrations, all of us chanting and making up handshakes.

"It's also my last game." My gaze lingers on Hunter and Rafael. Hunter smiles at me, and Rafael gives me a thumbs up. "I'm withdrawing from the draft, and I'm going to graduate after next semester, so this is officially my last baseball game ever."

The guys break into conversation, talking over each other.

Coach raises his hand, and the noise dies down slowly. "Let him finish."

"I want to thank everyone," I say. "Thank you for being the best teammates a guy could ask for. Thank you, Coach, for all your guidance. I've loved playing with you all, and I'm sorry it's over, but this is what's right for me."

"Tell them all what you're doing next," Hunter calls out.

I shake my head, smiling. "Maybe after the game. Let's go and do this fucking thing, yeah? Let's end the season strong. We might've missed the playoffs, but we can set the tone for next season right here and now. I'm hanging up my glove, but I'm still a Royal."

"Bring it in," Rafael shouts. "Royals on three, Seb leading!"

We gather in the center of the room, putting our hands together. I miss this already, but in the way you miss an old friend. The memories are bittersweet. You wonder what might have been while still being grateful for what you had.

Across the circle, Ozzy gives me a nod. "I'll miss seeing you in the majors, Callahan."

I nod back. "Good luck, man. I'll be waiting to hear your name on draft day."

I lead the countdown for my team one last time.

62

MIA

I'VE NEVER BEEN SO grateful to finish a presentation.

When I'm finally finished answering all the questions the audience had, I walk off the stage with legs so rubbery, I'm not sure I'll be able to make it to the hallway. I handled everything they threw at me—especially Robert Meier, who I swear asked more questions than anyone else combined—but honestly, the debate itself was nothing compared to knowing my family was watching it all unfold.

I tried my best not to look at them, but it was hard. I was aware of their presence in an impossible-to-ignore way. There wasn't a literal spotlight on me, but it felt like it.

I'm barely out of the auditorium when they burst through the doors, all of them, talking over each other like a flock of seagulls. Dad has a bouquet of sherbet-colored zinnias in his arms, tied together with a black ribbon. Penny finds me first, tackling me in a hug so tight I can't breathe, but I just squeeze her back. I wish I could hide here all day, face buried in her hair. Anything to avoid whatever's going to happen when my family catches up to me.

"Wow," she whispers. "You're a fucking genius."

I half-laugh, half-sob. The adrenaline coursing through me eases, leaving me bone tired. "How... how are they here? What's going on?"

"Mia," I hear my mother say. "What did you do to your hair?"

"It's much better this way," Nana says. "I hated it long."

"Nana!" Giana scolds.

"She looks more grown up," Nana says decisively. "That's a good thing."

I laugh again, wetly, and pull away from Penny. "Did you do this?"

"No," she says. "It was—"

She breaks off, her eyes widening, as Robert Meier walks over to us.

"He's terrifying," she whispers.

"Miss di Angelo," he says, holding out his hand. "It was a pleasure to finally meet the student Beatrice speaks of so highly."

I shake it. "It's nice to meet you as well, sir."

He's a tall, thin man with eyes like chips of ice, carefully combed hair, and a slight accent. Despite the warm June weather outside, he's wearing slacks and a pullover sweater. I hope he didn't hear what Penny just said. He's not scary, just intense.

I glance around; my family is standing off to the side, mercifully quiet—and very obviously listening in.

"I understand that you have some interest in my international undergraduate program," he says.

"Yes, sir."

"I'm looking to take on ten students next year," he says. "Only those that I feel are both serious and passionate about research, and it's clear that you have both in spades. You have a mind for the details, and that's harder to find than you'd assume."

Professor Santoro walks over, a cup of coffee in hand and a small smile on her face. "I see you've met each other."

"Yes," he says. "I was just telling Miss di Angelo that she has a spot in my program, assuming she's willing to accept."

I think my heart stops beating for a moment. "Are you serious?"

"This wouldn't be a typical study abroad program, but I think you know that already. The research we'll be doing is already in your area of interest, so perhaps it could even be the start of what will one day grow into your dissertation." He raises one thin eyebrow. "You are going into a PhD program after your undergraduate degree is out of the way, yes?"

I nod. "Definitely."

"Good," he says. "Please don't let me keep you from your family. I'll be in touch about the program details soon."

"I'd love to introduce you to Alice Farley," Professor Santoro says, although she's smiling at me. "She's one of my graduate students, you'll hear her present later."

I stare at the two of them as they walk in the direction of the refreshments. Penny tries to pull me into another hug, but Giana beats her to it.

"Mi-Mi," she says. "I'm so sorry I was rude to you."

"Oh," I say. "It's—"

"It was bad," she says. She takes my face in her hands,

looking at me with tears in her big brown eyes. "I didn't mean what I said about you."

My head spins in circles. The high from the presentation, Robert Meier, and now this... it's a perfect moment.

Almost perfect.

"Gi-Gi," I say, "not that I'm not happy to see you, but why are you here? Why are all of you here?"

She cups my cheek for a second before stepping back. "Sebastian."

The sound of his name on her lips sends an ache through my heart. "What?"

"He called us," Mom says, coming over to pull me into a hug. "How many times, honey?"

"At least a dozen," Dad grumbles, kissing the top of my head. "He drove down to talk to us, too."

"Twice," Nana says, a touch of dryness in her tone. "He's a nice boy, but very insistent."

"Anthony couldn't get away, but he would have been here if he could," Mom says. "He went out with Sebastian the other day."

"I don't understand," I say. "What did he tell you all?"

"He told us that we had to come see you," Giana says. "He said we needed to see you at work to understand just how brilliant you are. And he was right. You're incredible. I barely recognized you up on that stage."

"He told us the truth," Mom adds, her voice full of emotion. I don't know if I've ever heard her sound so affected. "He showed us the work you've been doing and how much it means to you. And sweetheart, I'm sorry I didn't listen before now. I'm sorry I didn't take your ambitions seriously."

I feel like I fell through a trapdoor straight into

Wonderland. That would be more believable than what's happening right now. I try to reply, but the words crowd my throat, a jumbled mess I can't sort through.

Sebastian convinced them to come see me. Despite his personal feelings about them, he brought them back into my life. He realized how much I needed them here, and he made that happen, even after I hurt him.

Longing washes over me like the tide.

I pushed him away, and he's still reaching out.

Mom smooths my hair back. A tear rolls down my cheek, and she brushes it away. Her wedding ring is a cool weight against my cheek. "You really do look so grown up."

"We're proud of you," Dad says. He gives me the bouquet of flowers in his arms. "Maria, a secret genius. Who knew?"

"She's always been a little different," Nana says.

If that's the best I'll ever get from her, that's fine by me. I can't stop looking at my parents. There's pride in my father's eyes. Love in the way my mother can't stop fussing with my hair, my blazer jacket. It doesn't erase years of arguments and misunderstandings and pain, but I'm hopeful that it could be the start of something good. They've always meant the world to me, even when things were tough. I'll never be the kind of person who will give up on them entirely, and the thought of a fresh start, without lies, means more than I could ever express in words. I throw my arms around them both.

And yet, however much I love that my family is here, there's someone missing. Someone I wanted to see in the crowd, even above my parents.

He called us family.

I was too scared to let myself have it, but that's what we are. Family.

"I have to see him," I whisper as I pull away.

Mom gets what I mean immediately. "I was hoping you'd say that. Men like him don't come around that often, you know."

I take a deep breath, steadying myself. As long as we're being honest, there's one more thing I need to get out in the open.

"Mom," I say, "this doesn't change me. Not my sexuality, or how I feel about marriage and kids. And I need you to listen to that. Really listen, this time."

Her gaze doesn't waver from mine. "I'm listening."

"I don't know for sure what the future is going to look like. But I know how I feel about this now, and I don't see it changing anytime soon. I need—I need to know I'm enough for you. Not because of a future husband or children. Just... for me."

My mother—my wonderful, stubborn, difficult to please mother—lets out a breath that sounds suspiciously tearful. I freeze, my heart practically stopping mid-beat, but then she nods, pressing her palm to her heart.

"You are enough for me, Maria. Just as you are." She takes a tissue out of her purse and dabs at her eyes carefully. "You have been ever since the moment I first held you in my arms."

She pauses, squeezing my arm with her long, wine-red nails. I don't doubt the love in the gesture, and another tear slips down my cheek. I'm going to be a wreck by the time I make it to the ballpark. "But tell me you're going to that boy."

I look at Penny. "Are they still playing?"

She checks her phone quickly. "Cooper's been texting me updates. It's the eighth inning."

"We'll get you there by the ninth," Dad promises.

63

MIA

TODAY'S TICKET isn't under a special name or moniker. Just *Mia di Angelo*, written in Sebastian's sprawling handwriting across the top. Billy tips his baseball cap to me as he scans it and sends me through the gates, Penny at my heels.

We run up the steps to the main level. It's crowded, even for the last game in a season that isn't going anywhere, and I can't tell which team is at bat. I find the scoreboard, blazing neon from the outfield like a beacon.

It's the top of the ninth inning. McKee is winning, 5–3.

I take off running.

It's not a conscious decision. It's not even a thought. It's a feeling, singing through me, propelling me forward. I nearly collide with a couple, but twist away in time, and sidestep an old guy. I think he shouts a curse at me, but I don't care. Penny calls my name, but I don't look back.

Once I'm past the netting protecting the space behind

home plate and the foul lines, I hop the fence, kicking up dirt. It's hot out here without shade; the sky a deep, cloudless blue. Distantly, I hear the shouts of people realizing what's happening, but I don't give anyone a chance to catch up to me. I just step out of my shoes and sprint barefoot across the grass.

Julio stares as I run by.

Rafael whistles.

An umpire shouts for me to get off the field, but I don't turn my head, and I definitely don't listen.

I don't pay attention to anyone except the man standing in left field, looking at me.

My man. My love. My future.

When I'm close enough, I launch myself at him, sending him staggering backwards as he catches me. His glove falls to the ground, along with his baseball cap. I pull his sunglasses off and cup his face with both hands, kissing him with as much force as I can muster. He tastes like lip balm and sweat, my favorite combination, and his skin is warm from standing out here in the sun. He's frozen for a moment, just long enough to send a wave of panic through me, but then he fists his hand in my hair and kisses me back, and something clicks into place in my soul.

I never want to go another day without one of his kisses. Never.

"I'm sorry," I breathe out against his lips. "I'm sorry for all of it."

"Don't be sorry," he whispers.

"I am. I left you. I let myself stay scared." I smudge my thumb over his eye black as I cradle his jaw, pressing another kiss to his lips. "But I love you, Sebastian Callahan. I love you

and I'm never letting you go again. Come on an adventure to
Europe with me."

His green eyes are shining. He tucks my hair behind my
ear, a blindingly beautiful smile on his lips. "You got into the
program?"

I nod, too choked up to speak. He pulls me into another
hug, spinning me around. "Hell fucking yeah, di Angelo! I'm so
proud of you!"

"I want you to be there," I say through wet laughter. "Start
your career in Switzerland with me. Please."

"Callahan!" someone shouts. "Come on, man!"

"My girlfriend just got into a fucking awesome study
abroad program! Give me a second!" he calls.

He takes both of my hands in his, squeezing tightly.
"Absolutely. We can start planning it right away. You know
why?"

I smile. I feel so warm, I might catch fire. "Why?"

"Because I love you too." He leans in for another kiss, his
lips lingering on mine. "Feels like I've loved you forever, you
know."

"I know that now." I wipe at my eyes with the heel of my
hand. My smile is wobbling, but I don't care. "I know you
mean it."

"More than anything in the world, angel." He leans in a bit,
tugging on the ends of my hair. "You know that everyone in the
stadium is staring at us, right?"

"Absolutely." I bite my lip as I smile. "I'm probably going to
be banned for life, so it's a good thing this is your last game."

He bursts into laughter. "There's my girl."

He scoops up his hat and glove, then picks me up. I loop my

arms around his neck as he starts walking across the field. It's ridiculous, I can't stop blushing, but at the same time, I don't care enough to twist out of his grip. I want everyone to know I'm his.

"The game isn't over, you know." I crane my neck for a glimpse of the scoreboard. "Only two outs."

"They'll have to start carrying on without me sometime." He hefts me even closer. "I want to hear all about the symposium. And the haircut. Looks good, by the way."

"I can't believe you convinced my family to come."

"They love you." He stops for a moment, looking down at me with serious eyes. "I'm sorry I ever suggested you cut them out of your life. I know how much they mean to you, and I wanted them to have a chance to see just how amazing you are. They all showed up?"

"Anthony couldn't get away, but yeah. Even Nana."

He brushes my forehead with a kiss. "Lovely woman."

"Well, let's not get carried away."

"Not to interrupt the love fest," Rafael hollers, "but are we finishing the game or what?"

Sebastian ignores him, walking us all the way to the dugout. He chucks his glove at a kid on the bench. "Position's going to be yours next season, right? Why not have a go at it now."

He walks right into the locker room with me still in his arms.

When we're at his locker, he finally sets me down. I settle on the bench, peering in at the space that's been his ever since he started college. It's neat and organized, just like him, and the brass '17' hammered above gleams in the low light.

"We only have a few minutes before the guys come in," he

murmurs. He kneels in front of me, swiping a hand through his sweaty hair. I tuck his father's necklace back underneath his collar for him. "I just wanted to see you alone for a moment, before the game ends and my family comes to find us."

"Mine too," I say, playing with the ends of his hair. It's longer than when we first started living together, curled at the ends from the humidity. Sweat runs down the side of his face. I wipe it away with my fingertips carefully. "They drove me here."

"We should all get dinner together, then."

"Oh, God."

"I'm serious. It'll be nice."

"My dad would love to meet James."

"James is great with his fans. Very enthusiastic, as long as none of them act weird around Bex." He sighs. "He's going to be a nightmare when she's too pregnant to hide it. I can hear him complaining about it already."

"Sebastian?"

"Yes, love?"

I shove at his shoulder until he laughs. "I hate you."

"No, never." He pecks me on the lips. "Not even a little bit."

My lips twitch into a smile. I hate to bring the playful mood down, but I have to make sure we're truly on the same page with this. Words are nice, and talking to my family is wonderful, but for this to last forever, I can't let any uncertainties linger. "I know you said you're sure, but are you really sure? About kids, and all of that?"

He puts his hand on my knees, squeezing. "You're my True North, Mia Angel."

My breath catches in my throat. "Sebastian."

"I read about it the other day, and I kept thinking about it, you know? I don't know a better way to describe what I feel for you." He strokes his knuckles down my cheek. "No matter where I go, or what I do, I want you by my side as my partner—my equal partner, because I wouldn't expect or want anything different. I don't care about the rest of it—if we get married, if we have kids, if we stay in one place or if we travel the world. Whatever happens, I want to do it with you. Switzerland is just the beginning. And I know those are only words, so I got you a little something to prove it."

My eyes narrow. "What?"

"It's not that. It never has to be that, and I mean it." He reaches around me, into the locker, and pulls out a little black velvet box. "But I'd love it if you wore this sometimes."

He hands me the box.

Nestled inside, there's a gold necklace with a diamond-studded, star-shaped pendant.

"Oh, wow." I pull it out, admiring the way it glitters. As much as I love my gold chain, I know already that once this goes around my neck, it's not coming off. The pendant is small, not at all flashy, and absolutely perfect. "Another gift?"

He shrugs. "And definitely not the last."

"I love it." I kiss his cheek tenderly. "Thank you."

"Can I help you put it on?"

"Please."

He takes it from my outstretched hand carefully. I turn to the side, and he brushes my hair over one shoulder to clasp it around my neck. After he adjusts it, I swing around and kiss him on the lips properly.

We're still kissing a few minutes later, when his teammates thunder into the locker room.

"Are we interrupting anything?" Hunter asks.

I untangle myself from Sebastian. "He's here to celebrate with you all one more time."

64

SEBASTIAN

"CAN I TAKE OUT the gazpacho now?" Izzy asks. "We ate our way through the cheese platter."

I grab the oven mitts from the kitchen island. "Let me just take the roast out. It needs to rest so the juices recirculate."

She wrinkles her nose. "Juices?"

I set the platter on the stove. The roast pork loin looks and smells perfect, a deep golden-brown crusted with fragrant garlic and rosemary. Drippings cover the crispy potatoes cooking around it. Paired with a peppery arugula salad studded with peaches and slivered almonds, it'll be a perfect plate of food. "It was a cheese plate."

"That thing was a platter. *Seven* different kinds of cheese?"

"I wanted to give everyone variety." I check the temperature on the meat, and once I'm satisfied, glance at my sister. "How are they liking the drink?"

Izzy holds up her half-empty glass. "I could use a refill if you're going to make another pitcher. What's in it again? Bourbon?"

"Mia's favorite, yeah. It's blackberry bourbon lemonade with a brown sugar syrup."

"Well, it's fucking delicious."

"Honey," Mom calls. "Do you want help serving the gazpacho?"

She gives me a kiss on the cheek as she walks into the kitchen. I'm a sweaty mess, since I've been in the kitchen all day, but she looks lovely in her pink sundress, a new pair of earrings courtesy of Dad glimmering in her ears. "It smells amazing in here."

"Thanks." I consider the spread of food in front of me. The salad is ready to go, I'll move the roast and potatoes to a platter as soon as they're done, and the little cups of cold zucchini soup with crème fraîche and cilantro are perfect. The strawberry icebox cake is in the freezer, ready for later. "Yeah, why don't you take out the soup, and I'll make another pitcher of the cocktail while the roast rests. We'll bring out that and the salad together."

"Yessir," Izzy says. She grabs two bowls of soup and brings them outside.

I shake my head fondly as I stare after her.

"I think she's talking to someone," Mom says.

I nearly slip as I turn to the freezer for more ice. "A guy?"

"She's been giggling at her phone all afternoon."

"I guess that's fine," I say, although my mind immediately starts running over the possibilities. She hasn't mentioned anyone, but she could have met practically any guy in the world during her internship this summer. New York City is huge, after all.

Mom laughs. "James pouted when I told him the same thing."

"She's our little sister. It's a very serious business."

She gives my forearm a squeeze. "Why don't you go run upstairs and change? I'll handle the cocktails."

"You sure?"

"I'd love to. Match the rest of us, it's beautiful out on the patio."

"Is Mia having fun?"

"She's drinking a delicious cocktail courtesy of her boyfriend and talking to her best friend. I'd say she's happy."

I give Mom another kiss on the cheek. "Okay. See you in a moment."

I hurry to my room—the room Mia and I are sharing this weekend, her first overnight at my parents' place—and change into a short-sleeve button-down patterned with palm leaves. I swipe a comb through my hair and wash my face, too. By the time I make it back downstairs, Mom is ready to go with the pitcher.

"Why don't you serve the roast outside?" she says. "That way you can sit and enjoy yourself. You've been working hard all day."

I move the roast and potatoes to a serving platter. "I had fun with this one."

"I had a spoonful of the gazpacho. It's perfect, honey. You have such a talent for this." She peers outside at the patio, where our family is sitting. Sunflowers decorate the middle of the table, which is done up in blues and whites; Izzy spent an hour making it perfect this morning. Dad sits at the head of the table with Kiwi in his lap, deep in conversation with James,

Cooper, and Penny. Bex, Izzy, and Mia are laughing together over something on Izzy's phone.

Mom watches as I admire Mia. "She's wonderful."

I look over. "Isn't she?"

"It makes me happy to see you so happy," she says. "And it's clear that she makes you very happy."

I keep my gaze on Mia as I walk outside. Her shoulder-length hair set in waves. She's wearing her star pendant and her gold hoops, plus a white sundress that shows off her tan. Later, we'll probably go swimming in the pool, and that'll set off my desire for her in a whole new way. Right now, though, I'm content to just sit next to her with my hand on her knee, squeezing lightly. She keeps talking to Bex, but gives me a quick kiss mid-sentence.

Being here with my family means the world to me, but having the opportunity to cook for them is even better. Weeks ago, the draft came and went, and it was a blissfully ordinary day for me. I worked my new job at Vesuvio's, cooked dinner with Mia, and ended the night watching a movie with her, Cooper, and Penny. Dad called, and we reminisced about baseball for a while before we talked about cooking programs. I haven't decided yet what I'm going to do next year in Europe, but the more research I do and the more I work at Vesuvio's, the more certain I am that I'm meant to be in the food industry.

"Who are you texting?" I ask Izzy as I take a sip of my drink. She has her head buried in her phone, but at my question, she looks up quickly.

"No one," she says.

I raise an eyebrow. "Oh?"

She snorts. "Believe me, it's best kept a secret."

I turn to Mia, but if she knows, she's not telling. She eats a spoonful of the gazpacho, squeezing my thigh underneath the table. I kiss her again, just because I can.

"Why a secret?" I ask.

Izzy glances at the other end of the table, then leans over. "Cooper would totally flip."

Before I have a chance to reply to that, Dad clears his throat.

"We should toast," he says. "Does everyone have a drink?"

I raise my glass. He looks at all of us, making eye contact with me last. I sit a little straighter.

"It makes me so happy to see everyone around this table," he says. "My beautiful wife, my children and their partners, Bex's little one on the way. When Sandra and I bought this house, we hoped we would get here one day, and being able to witness it—it's a joy. A complete and total joy."

Sandra gives him a smile. "It's everything."

"And Sebastian—thank you for this meal. It looks incredible."

I flush. "Thanks, Dad."

"Can I add something?" Mia asks.

"Of course," he says.

She turns to me with love in her eyes and pride in her smile.

"I just wanted to say thank you," she says. "To you, Sebastian, of course, but to all of you as well. Thank you for welcoming me into this family. I never pictured this for myself, but I'm grateful I'm here."

Dad raises his glass. "Cheers."

As we follow suit, I glance at the sky. It's early evening, so the stars haven't come out yet, but I catch a sliver of the moon. Fireflies wink across the lawn.

Tonight, when it's dark, we'll take Mia's old telescope to the beach. I'll bring a blanket, so we can stay there all night.

And I'll listen to my angel talk about the universe while I hold her in my arms.

65

MIA

EPILOGUE

January 15th

I FIDDLE with my star necklace as I wait at the Starbucks counter. Early in the morning, even John F. Kennedy airport is quiet, hushed.

It doesn't match my energy at all. I'm practically humming with excitement, even though we have a long flight ahead.

I've never been on an airplane before. I've never seen the world from the sky in any capacity.

This is a beginning, and I have Sebastian by my side.

The barista slides our coffees over. Iced with oat milk for me, a whole milk latte for him. "Thanks."

"You're not going to drink both of those, right?" She leans across the counter, readjusting her apron. If I had to guess, I'd say she's just a couple years older than me. She knotted her sleek black hair into a bun, and freckles dot her face like splattered paint. They remind me of Penny. I miss her already

—but at least she and Cooper are coming to visit over spring break. "Who are you traveling with?"

"My boyfriend." I take a sip of my coffee. I don't need the caffeine jolt, with such a long flight ahead, but the taste is comforting. I hope I'll be able to find a good coffee place near the university. Honestly, it could be mediocre, and I'll just be glad I'm not the one making it. "He's getting breakfast tacos for us."

"That's nice."

"What's your name?"

"Aadhya. What about you?"

"That's pretty." I take another sip of coffee. "I'm Mia."

"Also pretty." She grabs a rag and wipes down the countertop. "Where are you going?"

"Switzerland. I'm doing a study abroad program. Astrophysics."

"Is he doing it too?"

"That would be a disaster," Sebastian drawls as he walks over to us. He gives me a kiss, languid and casual and yet possessive too, and cuffs me lightly under the chin as he steps back. "I stopped paying attention in science class after ninth grade."

He's in gray sweatpants and a McKee sweatshirt, his backpack slung over his shoulder, and he's wearing a new necklace around his throat. My Christmas present to him, which I gave him after our Monopoly win against his siblings on Christmas Eve. A gold compass to match the star he gave me last summer.

"And I'll repeat, yet again, that cooking is science," I say.

"Nah," he says, giving me a grin as he plucks his latte out of my hand. "Cooking is art. Baking is science."

"You make such a cute couple," Aadhya says.

"We're something," I say dryly at the same time Sebastian says, "Thank you."

I roll my eyes. The grin doesn't leave his face. I'd elbow him in the stomach, but I don't want to risk anything happening to my precious coffee in the ensuing battle.

"Sometimes she has trouble expressing the depth of her feelings for me," he says. He clasps his hand over his heart dramatically. "Her favorite way to ask for sex is to say I look acceptable in whatever I'm wearing."

I can't help it; I stomp on his foot. "Sebastian!"

His laughter peals through the air like bells. "Love you, angel."

I try to step on his toes again, but he's too quick. "You're lucky I love you," I grumble.

"Oh, believe me, I know." He reaches for my hand. "Come on, let's eat before it gets cold."

"Good luck," Aadhya says. "I hope you have a good flight."

"Thanks," I say. "I hope you fight off the zombie horde of under-caffeinated travelers successfully."

Her laughter follows us as we walk down the long hallway to our gate. Early morning sun streams in through the large windows, lighting a trail for us to follow, step after step.

"I'm proud of you," he says.

"For what?"

"For everything." He stops in his tracks, even though we're nowhere near the gate, and tilts my face up. He looks serious enough my breath catches in my throat. "But right now? For trusting me to go on this journey with you."

I rise onto my toes and kiss him. He smells of mint and tastes of espresso, and for a moment I let myself lean into it. I love these kisses of ours, unhurried and deep. I keep thinking I'm going to get used to them, but I haven't yet, and I hope I never do.

Eventually, I step back, and he holds out his hand. "Ready?"

I take it, squeezing our fingers together without reservation. Without fear. Without anything but love coursing through me, connecting us like planets orbiting the same sun.

Our stars align.

I smile—my true smile, the one I only use with a very small list of people that is headlined by him—and know he sees everything he'll ever need to know in that smile. He's mine and I'm his, and this adventure is just the beginning of a long, purposeful, passionate future. A future that belongs to us, together, and no one else.

"I'm ready."

ACKNOWLEDGMENTS

If *First Down* was a leap of faith and *Breakaway* was a fever dream of inspiration, *Stealing Home* was like mining—pulling out the story bit by bit, scrabbling at the rock with my fingertips. I am so proud to have shared this story with you, but I definitely didn't do it alone!

To Anna, Moira, and my parents: thank you for always being willing to hear about the Callahans! Cat, Shelby, and Kristen, thank you so much for your insightful beta feedback—the book would not have come this far without you. Thank you Brittany, Stephanie, and Bruce for being the best long-distance colleagues/friends ever.

Thank you Gabby for illustrating the cover of my dreams, and Sarah for shaping it into something beautifully consistent with the series. Emma and Sierra, thank you for your detailed, insightful editorial feedback. Jen, thank you for coming into my life at the exact right time.

A big thank you to my assistant, Ally—without your support and fierce dedication, this book would not exist! And thank you to my wonderful agent, Claire, who has advocated tirelessly for my work and supported me from the moment I said I wanted to try my hand at indie publishing.

MIT astrophysicist Sara Seager's moving memoir, *The Smallest Lights in the Universe*, provided essential background for me as I developed Mia's character. If you're interested in space and the search for life on other planets, I highly recommend it.

Last but not least, thank you to my amazing, passionate readers. It has been an honor and a privilege to share my work with you, and your support means the world to me and helps me keep going, especially on the tough days. Much love, and many books to come!